Killer Holidays
A John Seraph
Anthology

C. G. Eberle

Published by
Melange Books, LLC
White Bear Lake, MN 55110
www.melange-books.com

Killer Holidays ~ Copyright © 2015 by C. G. Eberle

ISBN: 978-1-68046-038-4

Cover Art by Lynsee Lauritsen

This book is dedicated in loving memory to
Herbert H. Hellman
(October 7th, 1939 – November 2nd, 2013)

Loving husband, father, grandfather, good friend to many, kazoo player extraordinaire, and the perfect holiday host, making sure all guests had a full plate or glass. Although I did not know Herb as long as my brother, it was my honor to call him more than friend and family. He's now at peace and probably asking all his departed friends and family if he can get them anything to eat or drink ... always the host ... always thinking of others rather than himself, his memory will be cherished. We miss you, Herb.

Contents

Halloween:
All Hallow's Evil

Before *Family Ties*

Thanks Washington, Thanks Gaston, and to those who still believe in trick-or-treating, bobbing for apples, carving jack-o'-lanterns, visiting haunted attractions & believing in ghosts, telling scary stories, and watching scary movies. To those who are enjoying their first Halloween or their fiftieth, keep the youthful spirit alive.

Friday, October 31st

My name's John Seraph and sometimes my life feels like a schizophrenic, bucking bronco. I'm a student at Buffalo State College in Buffalo, NY, where I'm earning my B.A. in English Education, but I sometimes wonder if that's what destiny has in store for me. For the past month the campus was being terrorized and a professor marked for death. Amazingly, I somehow saved Professor Crosby and stopped the Headless Rider, who'd been 'haunting' the college grounds. You may have heard some bits and pieces from the news, or from some witnesses who were there. Now let me tell you what actually happened, the true story.

* * * *

The day was Halloween and the college hosted a Safe-Hands

1

Halloween Fair, which was a safe alternative to trick-or-treating in the streets. Kids could go through the different levels of the school's student union where they could trick or treat, get their faces painted, visit the 'haunted maze', pig out at a pizza party held in the cafeteria, and take part in the scavenger hunt held in the Barnes & Noble bookstore. Student volunteers staffed the fair and we earned extra credit for certain classes. I can't speak for the others, but I always feel pretty good doing something for kids.

It seemed everyone on campus was looking forward to the fair, which had been a major change, because for the past four weeks most folks were on edge due to a number of attacks that had taken place all over the school's grounds. I'm good at hiding my emotions when I have to, but I admit I was feeling pretty anxious myself, too.

After my second class I left school early because volunteers who lived off campus were given a pass to cut their afternoon classes to prepare for the fair.

My two bedroom apartment is in the Irish neighborhood of South Buffalo, and technically part of the Queen City, but the area feels like its own modest suburb. Normally, I check my mail box and answering machine, then settle in for the night, unless I'm doing something. As soon as I arrived home I ran inside the back door of my building and into my place, tossed my school bag on my love seat then I headed into my small kitchen, two steps off the dining area.

I tossed a turkey dinner into the microwave, brought out a couple cans Diet Mountain Dew, then changed for the fair. A minute later I emerged from my bedroom partially dressed. I'd finish dressing after I ate. No way I was going to take a chance with gravy and cranberry sauce staining my rental. I usually watched the news as I ate dinner, but since it was earlier than normal I was forced to watch Jerry Springer, not quite the same thing. Before you ask, I live alone, don't have any roommates, and I'm not especially close to my family, but that's a story for another day.

After dinner, I finished dressing, except for my cape and mask. I'd put them on once I returned to school since it was impossible to drive with the mask on my face. I arrived at five-to-five and parked in the small student lot behind the library, just like every other time I was on campus then I walked over to the student union.

The sun began to vanish and the sky became a gold and scarlet tapestry on sapphire. Temperatures started to drop a few weeks before and it had been cool all day. According to the weatherman clouds were supposed to roll in later, but there wasn't any sign of them.

The decorators did an amazing job in the student union. Orange and black streamers hung from the brick walls, Halloween and the same festive colored balloons were arranged as bouquets in the furnished areas, which were tied down to sand filled party favors. Halloween Mylar balloons were placed throughout the cafeteria and the sitting areas, as well as the bookstore. Paper images of witches, ghosts, jack-o'-lanterns, vampires, and haunted houses were taped to the pillars and doors, but most amazing of all was the haunted maze.

The students and staff set it up in the nearly abandoned recreation center, the job took us nearly a week to finish, but it was worth the sore muscles. Years ago the rec-center had been a video arcade until it closed down. Nowadays it was normally an unused, empty space. Five sections made up the maze: there was a cave with a puppet-like dragon that moved and roared over a skeleton chained in the cave, a haunted barn that had a scarecrow running around, a pyramid tomb with a mummy, a castle and vampire, and a forest with a werewolf. Kids would walk through the entrance, follow a winding path, with its twists and turns, past the smoke machines, pulsating strobe lights, sound effects, and inside volunteers were dressed up as maniacs and monsters, all with one goal in mind, scare the bejeezus out of visitors.

I stopped in the foyer of the union and put on the final touches of my costume, black gloves, and a black cravat, with gold trim, a black cloak/cape, and finally my Phantom mask. It covered half my face and was a special two-piece mask. The outer layer was the classic white Phantom of the Opera mask. Attached by Velcro to the underside was a scared face matching the white mask perfectly, so one can wear it before or after being un-masked. The only thing missing was Christine Daaé on my arm.

Inside the student union I reported to the activities coordinator, Cassie Laqueta. She was dressed as a green skinned witch and looked hot. Because this was a children's event the female volunteers couldn't dress slutty. "John, you look fabulous," Cassie said once she realized who I was.

"Thanks, Cas." I bowed the way I imagined the Phantom would on screen or in the novel.

"Makes me wish I dressed to match you." I took her complement, but was thankful Cassie's full-out lesbian girlfriend didn't hear her.

"Where do you need me?" I asked while scanning over the decorations and some of our fellow costumed students, who were taking care of a few last minute touches.

"We need a doorman for the maze," she said after double checking her clipboard.

"I'm on it." I spun on my heels to go downstairs but before I left Cassie gave me a wolf whistle. I felt a touch of flattery and a twinge of embarrassment, grateful my mask hid my face which I suspected was blushing.

* * * *

The doors opened at six o'clock and for the next two hours I lead kids and their escorts into the maze, and from the screams inside I knew the volunteers were doing their jobs well. After the kids found their way out, I gave each child a pre-made baggie of candy, stickers, and small toys. When I ran low on treats, I restocked with supplies hidden behind the black draperies that lined the doorway.

At eight o'clock a girl in a female vampire costume took over for me, so I headed up to the cafeteria to get some apple cider and mini-donuts. Everything looked like it was going well. I saw at least forty kids running around, eating, having fun, and laughing. We'd attracted children of all ages, from babies and toddlers enjoying their first Halloweens up to middle-schoolers, most in a costume of some kind.

Cassie and some volunteers were talking, and since everyone was in costume, I didn't know who was who. The group came over to me.

"Looks like the fair's a hit Cas."

"Yeah John, all the parents are happy with the fair. Some asked me if the school will do anything in December for Christmas."

"Not a bad idea, but I don't do elves." I took a sip of cider then asked, "So what's the topic of conversation?"

"The Rider," a male student dressed as a gray-headed alien said. The temperature and good feelings plummeted like a sky diver with a malfunctioning parachute.

"John," Cassie started, "we all know what happened when you were with the Honor's Club."

"What you do mean, Cas?" My gut told me what she meant, but I wanted it straight. I was never one for beating about the bush.

"John, everyone knows how you saved that guy in your honor's class from being expelled and arrested."

My first semester at Buffalo State two major things happened: First, I cleared our club treasurer of being an embezzler when I served as club secretary. Second, the student body talked about my family and their infamous history all the time. "What's your point, Cassie?"

"We were all wondering, I mean is it possible... do you think you can find out who the Rider is?"

Before I could say anything, Cassie and the others explained how scared everyone on campus had become. I knew this, and to be honest, I'd become a bit uneasy myself.

Beginning in the last week of September and continuing in October, three students had been chased down by a motorcyclist, a.k.a. 'The Rider'. The Rider heaved jack o' lantern bombs when he was close enough to them. I know how it sounds, but it's true. Even crazier, all the victims claimed the Rider was headless. Now I love a good ghost story as much as anyone, but my first thought when I heard the stories was that this had to be an asinine stunt. The bombs weren't powerful and didn't hurt anyone, they just scared the targets more than anything. But people were becoming more afraid that the Rider would eventually kill someone, because each explosion was a bigger one than the last. Scariest of all was that no one knew who the next target would be or when the Rider would strike again. Thanks to the criminal and security reports published in the college's newspaper most of the details were made public.

"Cas," I started, "I'm no detective, besides aren't campus security and the police looking into this?"

"Yeah, but campus security is equal to mall cops and the police only show up after the fact," someone dressed as a pirate said. "We need someone who's hands-on, someone who gives a damn, and who can find this lunatic."

"John, this is Roger Toni. Roger and I, have chemistry together. It was his idea we talk to you," Cassie said.

I shook Roger's hand. "See, we know how smart you are, John."

Through his makeup and costume I saw how nervous Roger was, just like everyone else, but I wasn't positive. You ever try to read the face of an alien, a ghost, or a faceless phantom? If I had to put it into words, these people were holding out for a hero.

I said, "I wouldn't know where to begin."

Now, I admit I'm good at figuring things out, but I'm not a police officer or a private investigator. If anything my family's the complete opposite of law enforcement. Thanks to my family's lawyer I learned a few things private citizens can do without having to deal with the limitations police officers have to face. I thought back to the Honor's Club and how I started there. After a moment or two, I agreed.

"I'll want to talk to the Rider's victims. Do you guys know if any of them are here?"

"Yes, I am," the phantom said, as he took off his red and black faceless mask. "The name's Greg Crane."

"Nice to meet you, Greg." I turned back to Cassie. "Ah, listen I need to talk to Greg. Can someone watch the maze for a few minutes?"

"Take all the time you need John," Cassie replied. Through her green makeup she seemed relieved.

Two minutes later Greg and I were upstairs in one of the lounge areas. The third level of the student union is home to private offices, meeting rooms used by student organizations, a formal dining room, and study areas. Nobody was around so we were able to talk in private. "So, what happened to you Greg?"

After he plopped down in one of the oversized, leather lounge chairs, Greg told me his story, as I stood over him with arms crossed.

"Last week I was walking with a couple buddies after our night class. We were behind Upton Hall and everything was fine. Then we heard a motorcycle racing down Iroquois Drive. At first I thought it was on the thruway, you know how close we are to the Scajaquada Expressway."

"Right," I said.

"Well, the motorcycle was on the campus, it came past Moore Hall then we saw him, the Rider." He began shaking his head in disbelief.

As I listened I realized Greg was still scared. It was in his eyes and I could hear it in his voice. I paid attention to his physical reactions because I learned a few things from some of my old man's employees on how to tell if someone's lying.

"He was carrying a jack o' lantern in his right hand. It glowed and was smoking. He sped up, the Rider jumped the curb, and aimed at us and man we hauled ass. Then I realized he was chasing after me and I ran out of the way, but the motorcycle was right on top of me. I panicked, somehow I got cornered, then the Rider threw his bomb at me. It blew up then the Rider took off."

"Were you hurt?" I asked.

"Nah, but my ears were ringing. My buddies found me after the Rider took off, and saw I was only in shock." Greg paused for a moment then said, "Now that I think about it, the bomb seemed more like a huge firecracker, like an M-80, you know?"

I nodded. I was fascinated by Greg's story, but then again I've always loved a good ghost story. I felt my wheels begin to spin and I began to wonder about the people, and motives behind these attacks.

"Greg have you had trouble with anyone recently?"

He sat there, looked out one of the huge vertical windows that runs from the ceiling to the floor, and overlooks the courtyard between the student union and the library. "No, there isn't anyone."

"Have you had weird phone calls or noticed if anyone's been following you around?"

He shook his head. "No, John, nothing like that."

"Okay." I struggled with what to do next and asked the first thing that came to my mind. "Did you or your friends call campus security?"

"Yeah, my pal Charlie did. They showed up almost right away, but by then the Rider had vanished."

I bit my inside cheek to keep from laughing or smirking. I didn't want Greg thinking I was making light of the situation. "I got to ask, what did the Rider look like?"

"You mean did I see a head?"

I nodded slowly.

He looked me square in the eye. "John, I swear he was headless."

"Okay," I slowly said, not believing this part of his story.

"I don't think the Rider's a ghost or anything like that. It just had to be someone in a Halloween costume."

"At least we got that straight. I didn't want to think I walked into a Saturday morning cartoon."

"I know how you feel," Greg said then laughed at the thought. "But rumors are spreading around."

"Yeah, I've heard a couple of them myself." As I spoke I recalled some of the stories going around; one said the Rider was a ghost of a Buff State student who died in the 1950's in a motorcycle accident. Another claimed it was the spirit of an escaped patient from the Buffalo Psychiatric Center, which has been around since 1870 and sits literally around the block from the campus. A third claimed it was a specter of a murdered victim who was killed at the 1901 Pan-American Expo, which was held on the three hundred and fifty acres surrounding the university and the asylum.

"You said security showed up. I assume they took a report and called the police."

"Yeah they did, as a matter of fact..." Greg stood up and reached inside his black, monk's robes. "I brought this just in case you agreed to help." He pulled out a crinkled up copy of the report security took and handed it to me.

Greg had stapled his copy of the report the Buffalo Police Department took to the report from campus security, then I skimmed both reports.

"Security notified them because of the explosive device and I think the cops contacted the ATF, makes sense," I continued to read, in part it said, "...samples taken from the device matched previous designs, and showed signs of a sparkler bomb with the container being a sugar pie pumpkin."

I dabble in the kitchen pretty well and knew sugar pie pumpkins were a smaller variety, used mainly in cooking, unlike their bigger cousins folks used as jack o' lanterns. I could see someone hollowing out a pumpkin and placing a small device in it, but the main question was why. My gut told me the why would lead me to the who.

"Greg, do you know any of the Rider's other victims?"

It took him a moment then Greg looked like he got slapped in the back of his head.

"Son-of-a-bitch! Yeah, I never put it together, John. Josiah Washington and Amanda Bones."

"How do you know them?" There had to be a common denominator. Once I realized that, I knew I might be able figure this whole thing out.

"We're all taking the same biology class, and something happened last month."

"What went down?"

"We were taking a test and a student, Abraham Laurence, uh, he was caught cheating."

I didn't see the connection. "Why would Laurence care about the three of you?"

"Amanda and I saw him getting answers from Josiah's test and we agreed to appear at the misconduct hearing."

"Did the hearing take place?" I felt my face tighten up at my right eyebrow and at the left corner of my mouth. It happens whenever I get really curious about something.

He shook his head. "No, we're going to meet with the committee next week."

My right hand instantly rose under my mouth and chin. "This could be a way of trying to scare all of you from testifying." Just then a dire thought tore through my mind, "Greg who's your professor?"

"Professor Van Crosby. Why?"

"He'll be at the hearing too, right?"

"Of course." Greg looked baffled, then, his confusion became a mask of fright when I made my point. "You're onto something John, I can see it. What is it?"

I stared out the window across the empty concrete courtyard, to arrange my thoughts. My gut told me I was onto something. "Greg, I'm thinking Crosby could be next."

We ran back downstairs where we found Cassie handing some gift baggies to a group of kids who had just came out of the maze. She was telling them and their parents how to get to the bookstore for the scavenger hunt. I didn't want to say anything in front of the kids so I waited till they headed up. We found some privacy in one of the lounge areas near the maze. We were next to a couple pay phones and a pair of big, brown lounge chairs alongside a brick wall. Cassie and Greg sat down, while I stood and over them and I kept an eye on the maze.

"Cassie, Greg told me there's a connection between him and the Rider's other targets."

"What? What is it?" She was clearly stunned. We told her Greg's story, and my theory Crosby could be the next target.

"Cassie, do you know if Crosby is here tonight? You're running the show," I said.

"Some professors are already here, but I haven't seen Crosby," Cassie said. "They're making sure their students are working, but I don't know if he'll be here." All of a sudden we heard a group of kids scream bloody murder from inside the maze. The sudden shock made us all jump up a bit and with the mood of the evening I felt an abrupt case of heart failure for a moment.

"Crosby's going be here later," Greg told us after we recovered. "He's got a late class on Fridays. It's going on now and he should be wrapping up in about five, ten minutes."

"How do you know he'll be here?" Cassie asked him.

"Professor Crosby announced in all his classes he'd make the rounds to confirm his students are working the fair."

"Really," I said then glanced at Cassie, in a way that said 'I really should talk to Crosby.'

Cassie gave me her permission, "Go ahead, John, it's alright."

* * * *

The air chilled me as soon as I stepped outside. I must have looked like a sight, the Phantom of the Opera rushing in between the buildings and courtyards. Then something hit me, if security saw me they might mistake me for the Rider. I breathed heavily because I rushed to the sciences building, without actually running. I didn't want to take the chance of missing Crosby, or passing by him on my way there. I saw my breath and figured the temperature must have dropped by ten degrees since this afternoon.

The sciences building only had a couple of late classes, but I cursed at myself for not asking Greg what classroom Crosby would be in. So I played the odds and waited in the main lobby. To my left were classrooms and the main lecture halls, to the right were the elevators and a staircase. I figured if I stayed were I was, I'd get my man.

I didn't have a long wait, in less than five minutes the last classes filed downstairs and I got some bizarre looks. Glad my mask hid my smirk and slight embarrassment. I stopped a couple of girls before they left the building. "Excuse me. Is this Professor Crosby's class?"

"Ah, yes," a cute brunette said, as she looked over my costume.

"I'm working at the kids' fair," I explained. "But I need to see Professor Crosby, is he still here?"

"Oh yeah, he'll be down in a minute. He's headed over to the fair. A bunch of us are going there, too," a redhead with a curly ponytail told me.

"Thank you."

"Are you going back to the party?" the brunette asked me.

"Once I'm done with the Professor."

"Nice." She seemed happy I was going back. "I'll look for you over there, handsome. Name's Tiffany. Great costume you have there. I always loved the Phantom of the Opera."

"Come on, Tiff," her girlfriend said.

I grinned. "I look forward to seeing you later." I tried to come off sounding like Cary Grant in *North by Northwest*. Usually with girls, I sound more like Jerry Lewis in *The Nutty Professor*.

The girls left for the student union, and a minute later an older man came down in the second elevator. The classic tell-tale tweed jacket, with leather elbow patches told me I had my man. "Professor Crosby?"

"Yes?" The spectacle-wearing, gray, curly haired man looked at me oddly, just like everyone else.

"My name's John Seraph and I think you could be in danger, Professor." I knew I had his undivided attention. I told Crosby why I was there, and what happened, then I explained my theory. "After Greg realized there was a common thread, it's logical to assume you could be next."

"Mr. Seraph I appreciate your concern in this matter, but I think I'll

11

be all right. No one's been hurt," Crosby continued to dismiss my assumptions.

"So far," I added. "Professor, maybe you didn't get the whole picture, but I read the reports from campus security and the police. The Rider's been using sparkler bombs, packed inside small pumpkins…"

"It sounds like you have an over developed sense of drama," he added interrupting me.

"Maybe, but each pumpkin bomb has been stronger than the last. I'm thinking the next one might kill." My point made the impact I wanted and Crosby realized how serious I was. The look on his face took on a terrifying comprehension. The realization finally set in.

"So what do you think I should do, call campus security?"

"No, let's get you over to the student union, as planned." I had an idea but I kept it to myself. I didn't think Crosby would appreciate it. "You'll be safe over there. I don't think anything will happen inside the building."

"What about on the way there?" The man had a point. There were two courtyards between the sciences building and the student union. I smiled at my sudden flash of brilliance.

"Come with me." We walked the length of the building, exited, then went next door into Perry Hall. We repeated the process; cut through Perry and, crossed an outdoor walkway over to Cassety Hall. From Cassety we reached the student union safely.

As we walked with caution, I asked Crosby about the cheating incident. "Greg told me what happened, and if you can't say anything I understand."

"What do you want to know, Mr. Seraph?"

"Greg said Abe Laurence was caught cheating off Josiah Washington's test?"

"Yes, Mr. Laurence denied it of course, but Mr. Crane and Ms. Bones claimed they saw him. As soon as that happened I confiscated Laurence's test. Then Catherine Tassel called them liars, and swore he'd never cheat."

"Who's Catherine Tassel?" I asked. "It seems like a big limb to go out on, considering the situation."

"No not really. See Ms. Tassel and Mr. Laurence are involved."

"Oh, okay."

"And she wasn't the only one."

"What?"

"Yes, Jacob Irving and Rob Brunt also claimed Laurence had no reason to cheat. The problem is that they are friends of Mr. Laurence's as well."

"So that means they're all pretty partial. What happened next?" I tried to get all the players straight in my head and wished I had a pen and paper with me.

"Mr. Laurence became hostile, and swore his innocence. I told him there was zero tolerance for cheating and that I was notifying the department chair. This meant an automatic disciplinary hearing, especially since Mr. Laurence denied the allegations. He plead for another chance, but I told him he made his bed, now he had to lay in it.

"He erupted at me, called me a fascist, among other things and how his life would be ruined. I'll spare you the language he used. Then he stormed out of the classroom. That was the last I saw of him."

"What happened after that?" I asked as we crossed from Perry to Cassety. Even though we were going building-to-building I kept an eye and ear open for a motorcycle. It may have been a little paranoid, but I didn't want to be caught with my pants down.

"I notified Professor Winston, head of the department. He officially notified Mr. Laurence by phone, the date of the meeting, and that he has the right to defend himself. We intend to speak to Mr. Washington, Ms. Bones, and Mr. Crane as well, but we hadn't heard back from Mr. Laurence since he left. Now that I think about it, no one I've talked to has seen him either. Let me ask you something Mr. Seraph."

"What?"

"Do you really believe there's a link between this incident and the Rider?"

"I'm playing the odds, Professor. I think someone's trying to scare the others but you might be another matter. Tell me, how bad will this screw Laurence up?"

"Severely. From what I understand he's been looking to transfer to the University of Buffalo for pre-med. With this on his record I doubt they'd take him."

"So there are plenty of motives to go around."

"Exactly."

Crosby looked uncomfortable as we made our way into the student union. "I need to confirm my students are here. Where will you be?" He brought out his student rosters from his briefcase.

"I'm working the haunted maze down in the rec-center. If I'm not there, find Cassie Laqueta. She's in charge and dressed as a witch. She'll know where I'm at. If the worst case scenario happens, keep your head, don't panic, and call campus security."

"Alright," Crosby said nervously.

I tried to reassure the man. "Professor, don't worry. Nothing's happened indoors." Once he realized I was right, Crosby smiled then went into the book store to take his headcount.

* * * *

I went back down to the maze, bobbing and weaving around and through the kids who ran around like jackrabbits in springtime, and out distancing their parents. I found Cassie manning the door. "So how'd it go?" she asked.

"Found Crosby. At first he didn't believe me, but I made him realize he could be in real trouble. I thought I had one suspect, now I've got four."

"Ouch, so what are you going to do?" she asked as a couple of kids dressed as a clown and a ninja turtle came out of the maze with their parents in tow. The roar of the dragon roaring and screams followed them out. Cassie handed them some goodie bags and they all went upstairs.

"I don't know. Crosby's here making sure his students are working. At first I thought the Rider could be Abe Laurence, but now I've got three other suspects, Catherine Tassel, Jacob Irving, and Rob Brunt."

"John, they're all here too," Cassie announced. She looked uneasy, which was an understatement.

"What?"

"The guys are working the pizza party in the food court. Jacob is dressed as Dracula and Rob's Frankenstein's monster. Cat's in the bookstore helping out with the scavenger hunt. She's dressed in a devil

14

costume. Go, I'll be fine down here."

Ninety seconds later I was two floors up in the cafeteria looking for two monsters.

* * * *

The food court smelled of tomato paste, garlic, and real Buffalo wings. Just from the aroma I could tell the pizzeria used the real deal, Frank's Hot Sauce, and butter. The spicy aroma made my mouth water.

There are two sections to the food court with one half being a semi typical lunch line with trays, cups, plastic utensils, etc. You can normally get breakfast, lunch, or dinner off the grill; eggs, chopped steak, hoagies, typical meals you might find at a good three a.m. diner. The second half has a mall food court feel with plenty of booths and tables and there are three vendors, The Train Grill, 2mato, and a franchise of Spot Coffee.

I found Irving, Brunt, and other students all in costume handing out pizza, wings, and chicken fingers on paper plates, along with celery, carrot sticks and blue cheese, while everyone helped themselves to soft drinks from one of the two fountain dispensers. I headed straight for the pair after I caught sight of their costumes and I could imagine, with some minor modifications, making either appear headless.

Once the kids they served rushed back to their table, I approached them. "Jacob Irving, Rob Brunt?"

"Yeah," Irving said after he put some more pizza on the serving tables.

"My name's John Seraph and I have a couple questions for you guys about Abe Laurence." I saw their confusion in spite of their impressive disguises. "I wanted to ask about the incident in Professor Crosby's class last month. Is there someplace a little more quiet we can talk? It won't take long."

Irving said, "Ah, yeah over this way." He led us toward the lunch line half of the food court since it wasn't being used and the kids weren't allowed into that section. For the fair it was a staging area for the pizza, wings, and fingers.

"What about it?" Brunt asked and I could see neither was too comfortable with me.

"I heard Laurence was pretty upset over the matter."

"That's right. Crosby could've given him another chance, but no! The asshole reported Abe," Brunt went on. "The man's an arrogant prick who could have let it slide, but he doesn't give a shit!" For a second I wished I had a pitchfork or burning torch for Frankenstein's monster.

I didn't want to antagonize them, so I steered the conversation in another direction, to learn about their friend. "Tell me, how positive are you he didn't cheat?"

Brunt answered me first. "Abe's a smart guy, maybe smarter than some of the professors here, so he wouldn't need to cheat."

"Why you bringing this up, anyway man?" Irving asked. I finally realized he was wearing porcelain fangs and not the usual, cheap, dime-store vampire teeth.

"I was asked to look into … some odd incidents that started up around the same time."

"What are you talking about?" Irving asked.

"I'm trying to find out who the Rider is."

"And you think Abe's the Rider?" Brunt asked.

"I didn't say that, but I'd like to talk to him. The problem is he hasn't been on campus since the day of the test, so I have to talk to those who were there. Also, the timing doesn't jive for me."

Brunt frowned at me and I felt some hostility from him. "How so?"

"Well, the test takes place, Laurence is accused, he vanishes, and almost right away the Rider's attacks begin," I said.

"What are you trying to prove?" Irving asked me.

"Nothing. I'm just trying to help some people, because the next bomb the Rider throws could kill someone."

"Do you think Abe could be involved?" Brunt asked.

I shook my head. "I don't know, but it wouldn't take the wildest of imaginations."

"Listen asshole," Irving exploded, "Abe's a stand-up guy, he'd never …"

I interrupted him and snapped back with, "Hurl bombs at the three people who could testify against him. I know he wants to be a doctor, but after what happened, the man's got a motive." Irving made a threatening move, but Brunt grabbed his friend's shoulders to prevent a scene and attracting unwelcome attention from the kids nearby. "And being the friends you are, I have to wonder how far you'd go to help a friend in need. Tell me, where were you two during the attack on Greg Crane?"

Irving broke away from his bolt-necked buddy and came right at me. He raised his right fist, about to swing it at me, but I side-stepped him, bent my left knee, while extending my right leg, and threw an underhand right of my own, right into his balls. He gasped, let out a squeal of a shooting pain, and dropped to his knees in a heartbeat. Irving groaned out like a lovesick cow, sucking in oxygen. I knew all too well the agony he felt.

I leaned over to Irving, but kept an eye on Brunt. "You really oughta be more careful bubba. You rush around like that and you can get hurt easy." I looked up at Brunt and added, "Better get your buddy an ice pack. He's going to need it." I didn't like doing that, but my old man taught me, when you know there's going to be violence, strike first and strike hard enough to make sure your enemy doesn't get up. I got out of there before things went from bad to worse. I was angry with myself that I didn't get what I wanted from those two.

* * * *

With my cape fluttering behind me I went down to the main floor and walked over to the bookstore. Inside were adults standing around, trying to keep an eye on their kids, and some sat back in the coffee shop, which extended its hours due to the fair. Costumed kids darted in between the rows of books, as they hunted for hidden items for the scavenger hunt.

I looked for Catherine Tassel and almost bumped into a little girl, who had her face painted up like a lion. A number of kids who attended couldn't afford a full-on, expensive outfit, so face painting was a viable alternative and it wouldn't surprise me if a number of parents were grateful for the option, especially if they couldn't afford a pricy Halloween costume. She didn't see me as she turned a corner and blasted right past me. "Sorry, Mister," was all I heard as she continued. I just laughed because being around kids always makes me feel better.

I found Tassel, as promised in a red devil costume, complete with pointed tail, pitchfork decorated with stripes of red cellophane as a fire, a short cape and a black domino mask. I approached her carefully, because

I've learned when a strange man, approaches a younger woman, it could look uncertain. "Catherine Tassel?" I asked.

"Yes," she said as she looked me over. I admit she came across like the kind of girl you want to bring home to mom and I wondered what nuzzling her ears and neck was like. I composed myself and told those old instincts of mine I was there to work, not pick up girls.

"I'm John Seraph. I've a couple of questions about Abe Laurence. Do you have a moment?"

"Uh, sure, hang on a second." She ran over to her supervisor and told her she'd be right back. Tassel took me to the employee break room, near the storage and warehouse area so we had some privacy.

"Before you start, have you seen Abe?" From her tone the lady sounded worried but I wasn't positive.

"Ah, no, to be honest, I've never met him."

"Then what are you doing here?"

"I talked to some students about the Rider, and I discovered the timing between the attacks starting and your boyfriend's self-exodus is close."

"You think there's a link between Abe and the Rider? Do you think he could have hurt Abe?"

She brought up something I didn't consider before; could Laurence have been the Rider's first victim? Could something have gone disastrously wrong?

I began to imagine Laurence being chased down, a bomb thrown and somehow he got killed by accident, then the Rider disposed of the body. For the lady's sake, I hoped not.

"I doubt it. It seems the Rider is only scaring folks." I didn't want to scare Tassel. She appeared calm but she could've been on edge for all I knew. There was no way I'd add to her anxieties.

"What can I tell you Mr. Seraph?"

"Have you seen or talked to your boyfriend, since the incident in Professor Crosby's class?" I took off my Phantom mask because I was sweaty underneath it and needed some fresh air.

"You mean the cheating?" I nodded. "No, after Abe stormed out of the classroom, he took off. I went after him, and tried to calm Abe down but it didn't do any good. He rushed out of the building, and almost

18

knocked me over. I got back to class to finish my test and I figured we'd catch up later. I have no idea where he went to after leaving the building."

"Then what happened?"

"I tried calling Abe, but I only spoke to his mother. His parents live in Arcade, and they haven't heard from him either."

"Did they file a report with the police?"

"Yes, and they checked out their properties."

"They have more than one?"

She nodded. "Yes, a house in Arcade and the family's farmhouse in East Aurora."

"Ms. Tassel, don't take this the wrong way, but what reason would your boyfriend have for cheating, if he did it?"

She shook her head. "I can't think of one. Abe did well in class, he's one of the smartest students around, and he still had a chance at the hearing coming up."

"You know about that?" My arms crossed one another over my chest automatically. I didn't realize it until after I stopped speaking.

"I know when there are accusations students have the right to defend themselves. Besides, the department chair called Abe and told him the date of the hearing."

"What I don't understand, and maybe you can explain it to me since I don't know Abe, he has the hearing to appear at, but he can still attend his other classes. Do you know why he hasn't shown up for them?"

She shook her head again. "I honestly don't know." She paused, took a deep breath, and removed her mask. I looked into the lady's green eyes, from which she'd wiped a few tears. "Abe's had his heart set on becoming a doctor and to do that he'd have to go to U.B."

"There still may be a chance he can do that," I offered.

"Anything's possible, but I'll feel better when I reach Abe and tell him everything's alright."

* * * *

Back at the maze I found Cassie talking to Greg and Tiffany, which was a surprise. "John, what happened?" Cassie asked.

"I don't think I made any friends upstairs. I told you I'd see you

19

again, Tiffany. Where's your girlfriend?"

"Jenny's in the bookstore. After talking to you I got curious about everything and found Greg here. We share a chemistry class."

Greg asked, "So now what, John?"

I hated to admit it, but I didn't have any real answers. I had the crimes, the suspects, and the motives, but two major elements were missing: means and opportunity. Someone had the skills to make sparkler bombs, which anyone could learn about online, and sugar pie pumpkins are available everywhere throughout the fall.

"John?" Greg asked again.

"Sorry guys, I got lost in thought. Here's what I know. All of the Rider's targets are connected to Laurence's cheating, and Crosby reported him to the Department Head. Since then Laurence hasn't been seen for almost five weeks.

"Laurence's friends swore he wouldn't cheat, but we have witnesses with no grievances, insisting he's guilty. Since then the Rider has chased down said witnesses, hurling the pumpkin bombs, and each explosion has gotten more powerful than the last."

"John, we know all that," Greg said.

"Sorry, Greg. It's just when I say things out loud, it helps me get the facts straight in my head and figure things out. See, we've got four suspects, plenty of motive and the means aren't complicated."

"John? What's missing?"

I looked at Cassie. "Laurence for a start, no one's seen him. I'd like to talk to him. Also, opportunity is missing, Cass."

Tiffany then asked, "Are you positive Laurence and the Rider are connected?"

I shook my head. "No, but I don't like the timing, and to be honest, I'm playing the odds. Greg, you said the Rider came down Iroquois Drive?"

"Yeah, he came out of nowhere, and vanished right after the blast."

A sensation I hadn't felt in a while ran up fast and slapped me in the back of my head. I call it my tuning fork. Another term I use is my 'built-in-bullshit detector'. It's as if I'm being told, "Hey stupid wake up and pay attention!" "Greg you didn't say that before."

"Funny, I didn't think about it. I mean, I heard his bike, when I was with my friends, then he just vanished."

"Do you remember if the Rider threw the bomb and took off, or waited until it exploded then rode out?"

Greg thought about it for a moment or two, "I can't be positive, I mean I was dazed."

"Take your best guess. Right now it's all we've got."

He went slowly and recalled as best he could. "The bomb went off. I fell backwards, heard the motorcycle roar briefly, then nothing. It seemed like he vanished, as if he was a real ghost." Greg sounded as if he was in a stupor. I guessed he wasn't over the attack.

"John? What are you driving at?" Tiffany asked.

"I'm not positive and remember, I'm just taking a guess here, but I think the Rider is hiding his bike on campus."

"What? That'd be a hell of a risk for him," Cassie uttered.

"I agree, but I bet there are some small places someone could hide a motorcycle. I'm beginning to wonder if Laurence, or his buddies, are bike riders."

"Yeah, they are," Tiffany said.

We all turned to her just as a small group of kids charged downstairs and entered the maze. We stopped talking until they were all inside the labyrinth. Once in the clear, I asked Tiffany, "How do you know?"

"I know Catherine a little bit from a class we share. She, Laurence, and the others are all members of the Buffalo Soldiers, a motorcycle club."

"A motorcycle gang," Cassie said.

Tiffany shook her head. "No, no they're just a club of motorcycle enthusiasts."

I said, "Yeah I've heard of them. There's something like fifty members and they've taken part in those charity rides Ruben Brown from the Buffalo Bills puts on. So they all ride, hmmm."

Before anyone could say another word, Professor Crosby came downstairs. "Good to see you all, and Mr. Crane, you're the last one." Crosby then made a check mark in his roster book. "Nice to see everyone's here and it seems, Mr. Seraph made an impression on Misters Brunt and Irving."

"Not quite, but if Irving didn't back off I would've made a real impression on him he'd never forget." My fist clenched up tight, which I hid it under my cape. I didn't want anyone to see any anger.

"Have you made any progress?" Crosby put his roster away in his briefcase.

"Some, but I don't have anything nailed to the wall, yet. Basically, Irving and Brunt blame you for Laurence getting busted. So, I can see them having some hatred toward Greg and the others, if they're willing to testify. Tassel isn't happy with you but she said if this is true, Laurence did it himself. I don't know about Laurence, since nobody's talked to, let alone seen him." I got quiet then asked, "Have Laurence's friends been showing up to class regularly?"

Crosby nodded. "Yes, they may not like me, but I doubt they'll do anything to endanger their G.P.A.s."

"Professor, who knows you're here tonight?"

"Everyone," he answered. "I told all my classes I'd be here to make sure they were working the fair, so I'd credit the right people."

"I told you that before, John," Greg said.

"Right, I forgot." Then I had a thought and muttered, "This could be bad."

"What's wrong, John?" Cassie asked.

"Don't you get it?" Tiffany said. "If the Rider's one of Professor Crosby's students he'll know where and when to strike." The girl was quick, I liked that.

"Tiffany's right. You might have a bull's eye painted on your head Professor, so …"

"Mr. Seraph, what do you think I should do? You seem to have a head for this sort of thing: it's peculiar."

"What is?" I asked.

"With your family's background, it seems you're the other side of the coin." My family's reputation spread throughout Buffalo and the Western New York region like a creeping fungus, and I hated the fact that their actions kept boomeranging on me. I was forced to repeatedly prove I wasn't one of them. *Da chi mi fido, mi guardi Dio, da chi non mi fido guardero io*, that's Italian for "A man's worst enemies are often those of his own house." For now I had someone to protect and a headless motorcyclist to catch.

Halloween: All Hallow's Evil

* * * *

When I escorted Crosby to the student union, I got an idea of how to draw out the Rider, but kept it to myself. I once heard a fisherman say "Live bait works best." Essentially, it was a last ditch plan formed out of desperation. If ever there was a Hail Mary pass, this was it.

I was convinced that the Rider was on campus somewhere, waiting for Crosby, but I didn't know if he wanted to scare Crosby or kill him. Either way, I wasn't taking any chances.

I told Crosby to call campus security and ask for an escort to his car. He parked directly behind the library, and right across from Iroquois Drive and where I parked, so I knew the layout of the area well.

It was almost nine-thirty when I left the student union and before the security escort showed up. I walked the path between the library and Bacon Hall, then hid myself in between the bushes and shadows by the first doorway, alongside the library. I had a clear line of sight from the student union to the teacher's parking lot.

I let my senses take over. I didn't hear anything, except for the traffic along the Scajaquada Expressway and Elmwood Avenue. After what seemed an extreme amount of time, I finally heard a pair of footsteps coming from the direction of the union. Then I caught sight of Crosby and one of the guards walking in my direction as their footsteps echoed off the cement and in between the buildings. The clouds had finally rolled in and hid the moon and stars, which only added to my anxiety.

A minute after Crosby and the guard walked between the library and Cleveland Hall, I heard a volatile, dangerous roar that seemed to come from the opposite side of the library. The bait was taken and I wished I had my revolver with me. I knew it would stop a motorcycle in a New York minute. The only thing I had with me was my SAP gloves. They're black leather gloves, with eight ounces of steel sewn inside the knuckles. Police have been known to use them when they need a little extra punch. The only reason I wore them was because they fit my costume perfectly, and my rental didn't include gloves.

I readied myself because the shit was about to hit the fan. It sounded as if the motorcycle flew along Iroquois Drive, just the way Greg had described.

If Greg was right about the Rider stopping, throwing his bomb, waiting to see it blow up, then vanishing, I'd have one chance to catch him. So I couldn't blow it. I remembered the looks Cassie, Greg, and the other students gave me, and I made a blood vow to myself, I wouldn't let them down.

Crosby and his escort stepped into the parking lot and their footsteps still echoed, even though they were now on blacktop. The approaching motorcycle quickly drowned the sounds coming from the Scajaquada Expressway and Elmwood Avenue. As soon as the single headlight sliced open the dark, I moved. At first I couldn't believe what I saw, but right in front of me was the Headless Rider. He was all in black with a top-coat and flowing cape. I saw what looked like black pants and black boots that reached up to his knees.

The Rider flew into the parking lot, and slid in front of Crosby and the guard, with a jack o'lantern in his left hand, as sparks and smoke erupted from the top.

My legs pumped as hard as I could make them go. I crossed over the footpath in less than three seconds and I aimed myself right for the Rider. I'm not positive if he heard me or not but I suspected he may have, because before he could throw the bomb, the Rider's torso turned toward me, just as I leapt upon him, and tackled him to the blacktop, separating the Rider from his bomb.

We hit the ground, tumbling like lovers, and the Rider fought with me but I grabbed his arms and swung my left fist into him. He groaned out loud. I looked down and finally got a good look at the Rider's motorcycle. In that moment I knew who the Rider was. As the Rider threw his fists, he kicked at me with his left leg. His right leg was pinned under the motorcycle and after I struggled with him, I knew this was just another Halloween costume and not a ghost.

"Watch him!" I ordered Crosby and the guard as I rose to my feet and straddled the Rider, who tried to pull himself out from under his motorcycle. As he scrambled to get free, I swung my fist just under the neck. I figured the wearer's head was just about where the neck was.

Once he stopped moving I turned my attention to the bomb. "Watch him!" I yelled again to the guard then ran to the smoking and sparking pumpkin.

Now, I admit I didn't think about it at the time, but running up, grabbing the bomb, and throwing it into the garbage dumpster may not have been my brightest move, but it was the only thing I could think of. As soon as I threw the lid down, I got the hell out of there as fast as my feet could carry me. I ran back towards Crosby, the guard, and the Rider, still pinned to the ground by both men. In less than a minute the bomb detonated, blasting the cover straight up off the dumpster, and bounced the container into the one next to it. The sound was a metallic, echoing thunder that was louder than I imagined. My only exposure to this sort of thing was from television and movies and for a minute there I had a solid ringing tone that echoed in my head.

Once my hearing cleared I heard, "That was incredibly risky, Mr. Seraph," Crosby said.

"It was the only thing I could think of. I don't know what the bomb was packed with, but I figured the trash dumpster would shield the blast. As to our friend here…" I gestured towards the Headless Rider, who was now seated on the ground, and being held down by the security guard. "Did you call your office?"

"Yeah, my boss is calling the Buffalo cops. He'll be here in a minute," the security officer answered. "So this is the Headless Horseman, huh?"

"Not quite, but close enough," I replied. "And I don't think we can use the word man in that term." The second I finished speaking I grabbed at the Rider and tore at the costume. The officer and Crosby were staggered at my reaction and for a moment didn't do anything to stop me. My gut told me who was behind everything and somehow I knew I was right.

As soon as the costume was ripped apart, I said, "Good evening, it's nice to see you again, Ms. Tassel."

The beautiful, young brunette looked up at me with a burning hatred and tears in her eyes. She glanced over at Crosby, and the expression on her face told me she wanted him dead. Guess it was a good thing I got the bomb in the trash before anyone could be injured or killed.

* * * *

Two hours later I was in the student union talking to Professor

25

Crosby, Cassie, Greg, and the others who asked for my help. Tiffany was also there, and she sat right next to me in one of the oversized, leather lounge chairs.

While Crosby and I talked with campus security and the Buffalo police department, the fair ended. We had to fill out incident reports for both parties which took us the rest of the night. We were told we'd be contacted by detectives and the D.A.'s office later on.

When we got back to the student union our friends were still there, with leftover donuts and cider. I was grateful because I needed the sugar boost they gave me.

Crosby and I told everyone what happened after he left for the parking lot. "Campus security had control of the situation, Catherine had been handcuffed, then she was put in the back of one of their cruisers," I explained.

Crosby took over, "When asked, Ms. Tassel admitted to everything. I suppose she didn't see much point in denying the charges."

Cassie broke in. "John, before you told us you had four suspects, did you have an idea who it was, when you waited for the Rider?"

"Sort of." With everyone's eyes on me, I began to feel like Hercule Poirot in *Murder on the Orient Express* giving the full explanation. "I didn't have anything tangible, only guesswork, and a theory. I admit I made a mistake. I assumed Laurence was the Rider, but that was impossible. I'll explain about that in a minute." I paused to sip my cider then continued. "There was something Catherine said that struck me, but I guess I didn't think about it hard enough. It didn't register with me until I saw her in the Rider's outfit."

"What was that?" Greg asked.

"Catherine mentioned that neither she, nor Laurence's parents had seen or spoken to Abe after he left school. When we talked about the upcoming hearing, she said and I quote, '...the department chair called Abe and told him the date of the hearing', unquote. If she hadn't been in touch with Laurence, how did she learn about the phone call?"

"Makes sense," one of the students who dressed as Raggedy Andy said. "How'd she know about the phone call, and besides, there's more, right?"

"Yeah." I took a bigger sip of cider. Not as good as it could've been, say warmed up and with cinnamon, but at least I wasn't thirsty. "First the call. On the day of the test, Catherine went to the Laurence farmhouse in East Aurora and played the answering machine for messages. It was a habit they'd gotten into at each other's places, to make sure the other got their messages. Second, even though Laurence's friends had the means, motive, and opportunity, I knew for certain Catherine was the Rider once I saw her motorcycle."

"John? How could you be positive?" Tiffany asked.

"I recognized the Rider's bike as a Harley Davidson, Superlow motorcycle. That told me the Rider had to be a woman, without a doubt. The Superlow model is designed for women and … my family had dealings with motorcycles a ways back." I didn't tell everyone those 'dealings' were my old man's employees hijacking a large shipment of motorcycles just before I cut my family ties.

"Alright, I can understand why Cat did this but she didn't think the attacks would get Abe back into school, did she?" Cassie asked.

"No, see, Abe won't be coming back to school, ever." I continued.

"What do you mean John?" Tiffany asked me.

"After the police arrived, Catherine told us she wanted to hurt the witnesses, but she wanted Professor Crosby dead. That last bomb would've killed him. Catherine loaded the pumpkin with nails and screws, which she didn't do with any of the other bombs."

"Because of the cheating and the upcoming hearing?" Andy's date, a girl dressed as Raggedy Ann asked.

"In a roundabout way," I said. The professor and I stared at one another uneasily. I let out a lengthy sigh because Crosby and I knew the grisly truth and it was time to share with the rest of the class.

"When we were filling out the reports for Campus Security and the police, Catherine told us the whole story. When she went out to the Laurence's place in East Aurora, she'd found Abe in the barn—he'd hung himself that day." I knew the news would be a terrible shock to everyone but they had to be told the truth, no matter how ugly it was. After the huge numbers of "Oh my Gods" and gasps everyone composed themselves I continued.

"Catherine found his body and a suicide note. In it Laurence said he had barely understood the material in Professor Crosby's class and that your class wasn't the only class he had trouble in. He may have been smart as his friends suggested, but he needed help and a lot of it to pass."

"He never told me he was having difficulties," Crosby said.

"According to his note, Laurence realized he'd never become a doctor. There'd been five generations of MDs in his family, including both of his parents. Laurence admitted he cheated on the test, then after his blow-up in class, he killed himself. The pressure he felt must have been great. Catherine found him and something in her mind might have unhinged."

"What makes you say that?" Cassie asked. "Are you saying Cat's insane?"

"No, nothing like that, but I do think she needs help, though. After she found Laurence's body and his note, she cut him down then buried him on the family property. There are a couple of acres, so there was plenty of room."

"She never said anything to his parents," a fella dressed as an alien said. "Shit, that's cold."

"I don't know about that, but like I said Catherine can use some professional help."

Greg said, "Alright, I get Cat wanted payback, but where'd she hide the Rider's equipment?"

"Actually we weren't that far from it. You know how Caudell Hall is next door to the student union, and behind Caudell is its annex? Sandwiched in between the annex and the small, staff parking lot, is a shelter for recycling dumpsters and the groundskeepers' equipment. Catherine hid her costume, motorcycle, and bomb supplies in that shelter. Being along Iroquois Drive, it's easy to see why you thought the Rider vanished like a ghost."

"Wasn't that risky since any of the maintenance people could have gone in there?" Cassie asked.

"Not really. One of the security guards told me that shed is mainly used to house some of the lawn mowing equipment. The groundskeepers usually stop cutting the grass around here in the first couple weeks of September. Once Crosby was dead, the attacks would've stopped, and the Rider would have vanished, becoming a legend. In a sense, Laurence's ghost was haunting the campus." I finished my cider. "And that, ladies and gentlemen, is that."

The janitorial staff came upon us so we left the union and headed to our cars. They locked up the student union behind us and to be honest, I was glad I was headed home.

"John, I really have to thank you." Greg said.

"I believe Mr. Crane speaks for us all, Mr. Seraph," Professor Crosby added. "You have my gratitude."

"I'm just glad I could help. To be honest after the second bombing, I was on edge too."

* * * *

We left Crosby at his car, and crossed Iroquois Drive where most of us had parked. Cassie got into her coupe, Greg, the alien fella, and Raggedy Ann and Andy piled into Greg's mini-van, leaving just Tiffany and me. "That was really impressive tonight."

"Thanks." I peeled off my cape and mask, and the cool breeze that picked up felt good. She came closer to me.

"You know, the Phantom of the Opera is one of my favorite movies and plays?"

"Ah, no, but glad to hear it." I was unsure where she was headed with this.

"And I've always wanted to do this." Unexpectedly, Tiffany reached out and kissed me.

A moment later after our lips parted, all I could say was "Wow!"

"Here's my phone number. Call me." She palmed me a slip of paper, and headed to her car, I just stood there in a daze, grateful the insanity was over, hoping nothing like this would ever happen again, but my gut told me this wouldn't be my last time.

THE END

'Twas the Fight before Christmas
by John Seraph

'Twas the fight before Christmas, when all through the house, Not a creature was stirring, since Charlie was dead as a louse; He was laid out by the chimney without any care, But no one minded Charlie was no longer there. The suspects were all nestled in the living room, As visions of prison time added to their gloom.

Detective Bishop arrived, wearing her new winter's cap. She came in from the cold, not in the mood for any crap—when from upstairs there arose a roar, I sprang down below and kicked in the door. Bishop rushed towards me in such a flash—

She ran into me and we almost crashed. The chandelier's light fell like the snow,

Shining on the object I carried below. When, what to Bishop's wondering eyes should appear, but the bloody fireplace poker I brought near. With my movements and speed, so lively and quick, I thought in a moment the killer would get sick.

More rapid than eagles, their denies came, and I whistled, and shouted, and called the suspects by name: "Now! Murray, now! Harry, now! Mary and Steve,

"On! Larry, on! Fran, on! Tony and Eve. "One of you killed Charlie, and had plenty of gaul! Justice will be served! And the guilty will fall!"

Bishop looked at me and asked, "Why did he die? Plus none of his

I answered her, "Charlie cheated, and lied, and fooled around."

"It's not a surprise someone wanted him buried underground." And then in a twinkling, I heard on the floor, the sound of running footsteps headed to the door.

I ran after the suspect, after turning around, then I leapt on him, in a single bound.

We crashed near the chimney, landing from head to foot, and our clothes all got covered in ashes and soot.

The suspect looked like a turtle on its back, and he acted like drug addict hooked on crack: His eyes—very shifty! His face, how weary. His cheeks were like radishes, his nose like a raspberry; He looked nervous and ill at ease, and began to beg on his knees.

Then I saw through gritted teeth, Murray's face turned red, and glowed like a wreath. Down past his broad face and little round belly, was a bright, red stain that looked like raspberry jelly: He was chubby and plump, and looked like an elf, but I knew Murray was guilty in spite of myself.

I showed Bishop the bloodstain, with a nod of my head, And Murray admitted he made Charlie dead. He spoke not a word as Bishop went to work, Then Murray was handcuffed and taken away with a jerk. I laid out a smile under my nose, and I watched as Murray's anger rose.

I leapt back inside with a brief whistle, as he flew away in a squad car, quick like a thistle: But I yelled to him, as he drove out of sight— "Merry Christmas Murray, God I love being right!"

John Seraph (a.k.a. Giovanni Angelo)
Merry Christmas & Happy New Year!

Christmas:
The Fight before Christmas

Before *Family Ties*

Here's to all those who keep Christmas alive throughout the whole year.

Saturday, December 26th

Just like everyone else, the holidays are hectic for me, especially when you throw in a murder. Between shopping, getting my Christmas cards out on time, decorating my two-bedroom apartment, and preparing things for any seasonal guests who might drop by, it can get overwhelming especially when you top it all off with my college classes, working at my college's library, and dealing with my family issues, that make the Mansons look like the Waltons.

My name's John Seraph. I was to be the heir apparent to the Arm, my old man's criminal organization here in Buffalo, New York. Everything changed when I walked away from my family and didn't look back. I moved away from all of that and into the Irish neighborhood of South Buffalo, and began attending Buffalo State College. While there I picked up a part time job at the Butler Library, manning the front desk.

Two weeks ago the fall semester ended and everyone's work hours were cut; I was down to one day a week, hence the need for a second job. I found some seasonal work at Bookmarks, an independent, local bookstore here in South Buffalo. I won't get rich but I won't starve and can still pay my bills.

32

Christmas: The Fight before Christmas

Bookmarks borders the South Buffalo and West Seneca neighborhoods, on Seneca Street. It's in a converted two-story, storybook, Tudor style house that almost looks like it came out of one of Grimm's fairy tales.

I got the job just after Thanksgiving and usually I'm straightening up the store, cashing out customers, or stocking shelves. For the most part everything was fine, that is until Charlie Thorndike was beaten to death with a fireplace poker.

* * * *

Christmas Eve was two days ago and I started work at eleven a.m. The store was open from ten-thirty until six and everyone was scheduled to work, so owners Murray and Fran Fordon hosted a day-long Christmas party on the second floor. They brought in platters of fruit and cheese, cookies, and sub platters of ham, turkey, and roast beef half subs. There were plenty of Christmas candies, soda, and coffee, and candy canes of course. The Fordons laid everything out upstairs and the staff worked in shifts, with at least four or five employees on the floor at any given time while the others ate and kicked back upstairs.

Work was steady but not excessively busy. A flow of locals from the South Buffalo, Lackawanna, and West Seneca neighborhoods, who were looking to buy locally kept everyone from falling asleep at the counter. Plus, we had Santa Claus there as well. All right, it wasn't the real Santa—Murray dressed as the big guy. I guess the real Santa was too busy.

The first week of December we set up a display; it was a nice, cozy little scene near the gas fireplace, in a corner of the middle of the first floor. It was complete with a fully decorated Christmas tree, gift wrapped packages, and Santa's throne. Murray talked to children who visited, we served hot chocolate to them and their folks, and handed out candy canes, then at one o'clock Santa read aloud *A Visit from Saint Nicholas*. We had about fifteen children there, and although I was in the holiday mood around the kids, I flat out refused to wear an elf hat or reindeer antlers like most of the rest of the staff. I do have a certain amount of dignity and pride.

Things finally slowed up around two-thirty when the customers lessened, and eventually they dried up altogether. It'd been gray and cloudy, and the weatherman said the Buffalo area would be hit by a snow storm, it was a matter of when, not if. The city was expected to get a couple inches. Some folks further south of the city were looking at totals in feet. The good news was that this was going to be a fast moving system, which meant it'd blow through Buffalo in less than twelve hours, but a lot of snow was going to fall, and bring with it some thunder and lighting.

The weather that morning and into the early afternoon was cold but clear and we had a steady flow of customers, then after three o'clock the skies opened up, the snows fell and things quieted down.

I manned one of the three cash registers, while the others either worked a swing shift or partied upstairs. At a quarter-to-four, I finally noticed everyone had vanished and I was alone. Being alone wasn't bad, after all, I was used to alone. There weren't any customers, which suited me fine, besides since I had to keep an eye on the store, I didn't have to pretend to have a good time with everyone else upstairs. To be honest, I'd rather have been hitting the heavy bag and banging away at the weights at the Steel Mill Gym. It may not have helped my attitude, but I'd have gotten a decent workout and blown off a ton of steam.

Finally, Fran came downstairs and was surprised to see me alone. "John, are you here by yourself?" she asked while juggling a drink and plastic plate of goodies and part of a sub.

"Yeah, been this way for a while now." I checked my watch. "There hasn't been a customer for almost forty minutes." My only company was the stereo, set to a station that had been playing the sounds of season twenty-four/ seven since Black Friday.

Fran laid her stuff down on the hand crafted, wood counter. "You can take a break and get something to eat. I'll watch the registers," she offered, sounding motherly, which really didn't seem to fit her at all. Fran may have been fifty-something, but her body and general outlook seemed to be more in the early thirty-something range. She always seemed upbeat, and her red, wavy, medium hairstyle and dressing youthfully helped. Today it was a green and red festive sweater, a blue and silver scarf, form-fitting jeans, and brown boots. She accented her face with snowflake earrings.

I didn't want to appear rude. "Ah, no thanks. I'm not hungry. Besides it's only a couple more hours till we close, besides I don't think we'll have to many more customers thanks to the weather."

Fran walked to the front windows and looked over Seneca Street. The snow flew in slantways and although the streets were passable, I wouldn't call them safe. In the past forty minutes I saw about four dozen cars on Seneca, driving cautiously. That's amazingly light traffic for Seneca, which is one of the main arteries of Buffalo and West Seneca.

"I see what you mean. Maybe we should close early," Fran considered out loud. She let out an audible "Hmmm" as the winds and snows shifted and now seemed to be coming straight down.

I secretly hoped she and Murray would tell everyone to leave since I was anxious to go home and shut out the world. Like a lot of people, I get the Christmas Blues and this year had been tough for me on more than one level. Emotionally as well as financially. I wasn't able to afford gifts for anyone, and I knew everyone would understand, but that didn't make me feel any better. On top of that, I was alone for Christmas since my old man took my family, grandkids and all, to Disneyworld for the holidays, and most of my friends were out of town as well. The end result: I was in a really bad mood. I quickly reached the point whenever someone said Merry Christmas to me that they almost wound up on a free ambulance ride to Mount Mercy Hospital.

"By the way, thank you for the necklace." The staff went in together and got Fran a silver locket and a black and mother-of-pearl left handed men's watch for Murray. "Murray loves his watch too."

"You're both welcome. I'm glad you guys like your gifts, but you need to really thank the girls. We all gave Eve and Marry our money and let them shop, since they know you and Murray best. Besides, you think they'd trust a bunch of guys to shop?"

"No, not really." Fran laughed softly, "I've seen most of you all in action. Frankly the idea of you guys selecting gifts like these is hard to imagine. It would be easier to believe the Loch Ness Monster was Jack the Ripper before I'd think a couple of the guys upstairs could make these choices. You, I'm not so sure about, maybe."

We both laughed at that and I had to agree with Fran. Even though I'd been at the store since Thanksgiving, I knew there were one or two of my coworkers I wouldn't trust to go on a beer run.\

Before either of us could say another word Marry Fikner, Jonah Tobias, and Steve Gay came downstairs carrying drinks and plates. They're all nice enough but I never gave them, or really any of my other co-workers much thought when I was at home. "Hey John, aren't you gonna get something to eat?" Marry asked as she juggled her plate nearly losing her sub and cookies.

"Nice save." I laughed at Marry's quick recovery. "Umm, I really wasn't planning on it." I hated to admit it but the food looked good, I was just being pigheaded, which seems to be my nature. When you're raised Catholic you either become obedient or obstinate.

The bookstore seemed darker and almost gloomy despite the music, décor, and party upstairs, but I knew it was just my shitty attitude that made it seem that way.

Fran then said, "Seriously, John, you can take a break. We'll watch things down here." I admit I was getting hungry and seeing the subs had my stomach growling with anger. I hopped off the stool a quarter of foot, stretched my legs, nodded towards Fran, and headed on up.

The second floor was divided into three sections, the front room which overlooked Seneca, the middle that was party central, and the rear room that overlooks the backyard.

The party was in full swing with Murray and the rest of the staff enjoying themselves. In the middle room, was an eight-foot long wooden table. I knew it was the type used by convents. The Fordon's bought it from an antique store in West Seneca, and they had spread on the table platters and trays of food. At one end were plastic plates, napkins, and forks. On a side table, next to an outlet was a coffee maker with cups, spoons, milk, sugar, and napkins. The odor made me gag. Along the outer beige walls was a wood television table, with a large ice cooler on it, filled with cans of all kinds of sodas.

I finally realized I was hungrier than I first thought and made up a good sized plate. In the front room I saw Harry Lex dancing to a Christmas song with Eve Naman. I wasn't positive if they were dating, but they looked as if they stepped out of one of those early sixties movies like *Where The Boys Are* or *Gidget*. To be honest, they seemed to fit perfectly, with her five foot, two inch, curvy and slender, blonde body fitting into his six foot three inch football player's frame, which was topped off by thick black hair. The front room was decorated with the small pre-lit Christmas tree I set up a few days earlier when Fran, Eve, Tony, and I decorated the upstairs.

Standing around in the center room, eating and drinking, Steve, who came back upstairs, was talking with co-owner Murray, and Larry Rocknerry. From the snippets of conversation I picked up, I guessed they were talking about the Buffalo Sabers and how their season looked so far and whether or not they'd make the playoffs in six months. Once I realized what they were discussing, I dropped out of ear shot.

Then I heard fellow part-timers Charlie Thorndike and Tony Caroline in the rear room, where we stored extra stock and supplies.

"I told ya man, there's no way I can do it now. You're just gonna have to wait till after the first," Tony said as I put a portion of turkey sub on my plate next to some cheese slices, grapes, and strawberries. I didn't know what they were discussing, but they wanted privacy. Charlie closed the door between the middle and rear rooms.

I grabbed a Diet Pepsi and headed into the front to sit and relax. I listened to the Christmas music and watched Harry and Eve, who smiled at me. "Nice to see you're finally joining us Johnny," Eve said.

"Well, someone had to stand watch, while you all were getting loaded up and partying hard," I joked. "So when's the beer keg come out?"

Harry answered back, "We're bringing it out when the strippers get here." He laughed, I laughed, Eve just swatted at his chest.

"Smart ass," she said to him.

"My ass don't think, babe," Harry said back as they continued dancing to Barbara Mandrell's *It Must Have Been the Mistletoe.* My good feelings passed and the melancholy returned. Like I said, I tend to get the holiday blues, but this year it felt worse. Being alone, and I mean romantically, at Christmas sucks. Seeing couples around February is one thing, but for some reason at Christmas time it seems worse.

"Care to take over for Harry?" Eve asked.

"Ah, no thanks, I'm not up for it today. Besides I doubt I could keep up with you," I joked. "Actually my knee's acting up," which was the truth. When I was in high school I got into a car accident where I totaled my car and nearly crushed my left knee. Every so often when the weather gets nasty my knee feels like a bag of broken glass.

I continued eating and outside the window the snow was still coming down and I wondered how deep my car was buried. I cringed at the thought of unburying my car. As I nibbled on some of the Christmas cookies, Charlie flew out of the back room and thundered down the staircase. Everyone turned to watch him storm off, then Tony came out tending to his right fist. He was rubbing it and his face was beat red. Murray came up to him and asked, "Tony are you all right? What was that all about?"

Tony ran his left hand over his bald head after shaking his right fist and then extended his fingers back and forth. I was familiar with the reaction and had a feeling something had gotten ugly inside the back room. "It's nothing. Charlie's just got no holiday spirit and really a lousy attitude," he said over the Christmas music and just as swiftly the good mood vanished like the Ghost of Christmas Future.

Harry, Eve, and I just looked at one another, and I broke the unnerving silence by whispering, "What the hell's going on? The way Tony is seeing to his hand I think he decked Charlie."

They sat down in the love seat next to me and I set my plate on the end table, as Tony cracked open a Pepsi and talked to the others. Harry spoke softly, "I think it may have something to do with poker."

"They play?" I asked as I took another sip of my pop.

"Yeah we've had a semi-regular game going for a while. This was before you were hired. It's kinda a closed game, no offense, John. See the way it goes is, when you're here long enough and we're a hundred percent sure you won't blow the whistle, we'll invite you to sit in the game."

"No problem, I've got some family who have something similar going on."

"I dropped out of the game a few months ago, partly I needed the money for Christmas."

I felt my 'tuning fork' go off. "Partly?" I asked.

Harry looked uneasy, then double checked that no one was listening. "Ah, yeah," he paused and looked at Eve who put her hand on his. For me this confirmed it, they were involved.

"Go ahead and tell John, it's got to come out sometime," Eve said. "I think we can trust him."

"The other reason I stopped playing, I think Charlie was cheating."

This grabbed my attention, "Really?"

Harry nodded. "Yeah, I think I saw him dealing seconds and switching cards."

"Hand mucking, huh?"

He gave a slight nod. "That's right big man."

"What's hand mucking?" Eve asked.

I answered her. "Mucking's when a player will hide a good card, like an ace or a king, through some sleight of hand. They'll take it out of the game, so they can put it back later on to give himself better odds." Then I asked Harry, "If this was the case why didn't you tell the others?"

He shook his head. "I wasn't absolutely sure Charlie did it. At the time I could of have sworn he dealt from the bottom of the deck, but if I was wrong I'd be accusing him falsely. So, I figured the best thing was to quit playing till at least until the holidays past, then decide what to do."

"Makes sense," I said. Then I put the whole thing out of my mind and I tried to focus on the season and Christmas and blow past my holiday blues.

* * * *

It was just past five and the party took on a more joyous mood and everybody seemed relaxed, especially after Fran and Murray closed up earlier than planned. They figured since the customers stopped coming in, and it being Christmas Eve, it was best to close up the store early. With weather conditions the way they were, nobody was in a hurry to leave and we all figured it was best to wait for the plows to hit the streets, before trying to make it home. So, after locking up and counting down the cash registers, Fran and Murray rejoined everyone.

The merrymaking had gone from the upstairs, to the downstairs, and back again as the staff had split into groups of twos and threes in the front and middle rooms and downstairs. In his office Murray changed from the Santa suit into a bright yellow dress shirt, red suspenders, and black slacks, which was roughly his normal attire. Frankly, I thought his outfits made Murray look like an employee of Willy Wonka. Murray did keep his Santa coat out because he got cold easily and either he wore it or took it off when he got too warm.

When I asked him about the change he told me, "Santa's clothes get awfully warm after a while. No wonder he lives in the North Pole." We were at the central table with Fran and Steve who laughed at the joke. I have to admit I felt better and my mood shifted, but without warning we heard a ruckus from downstairs.

"Get your damn hands off me!" I bolted downstairs with Fran and Murray right behind me.

Marry shoved Charlie back, hard. Charlie just laughed because he didn't go back that far. "Aw, come on, babe," he said with a smirk over his chiseled face. He had an air of arrogance I never noticed in him before. He had Marry backed up against the counter, that is until he saw us coming downstairs. As the Fordons reached the foot of the staircase, I clenched my oversized fists. It's a physical trait I inherited from my grandfather Marcus' 'the Hammer' Angelo, and believe me he didn't earn his nickname in shop class.

"Marry, everything all right?" Fran asked as she came up and placed a comforting hand on her shoulder.

"Ah, yeah, Fran, I could use a drink." They headed upstairs leaving Murray and me with Charlie. Both of the ladies looked back in disgust at Charlie.

"Now what was that all about?" Murray sternly asked Charlie, who just let out a light laugh and a smirk opened up on his face.

"Oh it was nothing, boss. Just a difference of opinion between Marry and me."

And I can fire whole coconuts out of my butt, asshole.

I noticed a sliver flask on the counter and quickly realized it was Charlie's because of the engraving, C.T. on it, then I smelled cheap whisky on his breath. "You've been drinking again," Murray said, "I warned you about that."

Charlie then showed off a combination of bravado and stupidity from the booze by stepping right into Murray's face. "You know, if I were you I'd stop worrying about the help and take care of my home life instead."

Murray just stood there and blinked for a moment, I didn't know what Charlie meant, but I didn't like what he said, or him for that matter.

I hadn't worked with him that much and seeing Charlie like this made me glad I wasn't around this piece of cheese that much. Charlie took his fluttering eyes off the boss, who just stood there, almost frozen, then he focused on me. He swayed a bit as he talked, "And if I were you, Johnny-boy, I'd go upstairs and forget all this. It's none of your business."

I stared Charlie down in his blue eyes and I admit I wanted to duke the son-of-a- bitch, but punching out a drunk is way too easy. "I don't like guys who force themselves on women, so I'd be happy to show you who's the biggest bull in the barn. Anytime you're up for a game of squeeze-the-skuz, let me know, skippy."

"I'm telling ya, man," he started then began poking me in the chest, "You don't want to deal with me. I'm more than you can handle."

If Charlie was sober and knew the truth about my past there's no way he'd have thought that let alone said it. I quickly snatched his fore and middle fingers, and twisted them counter clockwise, hard. "Ahhhh," was the only thing Charlie could say as he collapsed to his knees, as his eyes teared up.

"I don't know what your problem is, and to be honest, I don't care. I've dealt with a lot worse than you, hell, compared to some of my family you're nothing more than a pimple on a flea's ass. You bother anyone else and you and I are going to take a ride on the merry-go-round and I can promise you it'll be a trip you'll never forget, bubba."

I released him and headed upstairs. As I pulled myself up on the wooden railing, I heard Murray say, "Charlie, you best drink some coffee and sober up. Then maybe re-think your future here."

Tending to his fingers Charlie defiantly said, "You better think about your family, old man!"

Upstairs, everyone was in the front room sitting around eating, drinking, and talking. Marry looked better, things seemed to calm down, then I learned how bad Charlie really was.

The others told me Charlie had a number of short comings on top of cheating at cards. Evidently, he cheated on his girlfriend, loaned money to some of the players when they ran short, but with an interest rate, and periodically demanded his money sooner than agreed upon, which was happening with Tony earlier. Charlie was also suspected of ferreting out secrets and blackmailing individuals.

Finally, I asked, "If this was all going on why is he still working here?"

Fran answered, "We don't have any real proof of the more serious issues, without actual evidence Murray and I would be opening ourselves to a lawsuit."

"Right." As I drank some more Diet Pepsi I seriously considered asking my old man to send out a couple of his boys and have them persuade Charlie not come around anymore. The problem with that is a mob boss will be happy to do you a favor, but believe me, you're going to pay for it one way or another. Besides that'd be like hunting for flies with handguns.

About an hour passed and the party broke into smaller groups either in the front room, middle room, or downstairs, where Charlie had stayed alone after the dust up. The weather seemed to finally let up and Harry and Eve wanted to head on out. They started to head downstairs and Fran said she'd let them out in a moment because she was showing Marry a holiday recipe for homemade Turduckin. Murray, Larry, and Tony were playing cards, without gambling, in the front room and invited me to sit in. As I took a chair, I asked Murray why he put his Santa coat back on.

"I got cold again and knew this would help and warm me up." Then, Larry dealt the cards on the small, wood table we set up and we heard Eve shriek out loud and Harry yelled, "Oh my God! Help!"

Everyone rose from the table and followed Marry and Fran who were the first down the staircase. By the time I made it down behind the women, Marry let out an audible gasp and Fran cried out loud too. Laid out in front of the fireplace was Charlie, dead. It looked like he took a single blow to his right temple from the fireplace poker that was on the floor next to his body. It looked like someone rammed the hook into Charlie's skull once and that's all she wrote. Blood pooled onto the red brick tile in front of the fireplace, and surrounded the tip of the poker. I knew the police would make the official determination, but Stevie Wonder could see what happened. All I could think was *Figlio di puttana.* That's Italian for son-of-a-bitch.

I came off the staircase and cut in front of the women; everyone else was frozen. I was careful as I approached the body and over looked the whole scene. I put my left fore and middle fingers on Charlie's wrist, there was no pulse. He was dead.

"John, is he…" Larry began to ask.

"As a doornail," I answered back. "We need to call the police."

Everyone was anxiously quiet. The situation was unsettling and frightening for everyone, including me. I don't care how many times you've been around a dead body, it's never fun, trust me. Eve and Harry looked at one another, as did Fran and Murray. Most of the others just stared at the body or me, and Marry closed her eyes tightly as if she were trying to block out the whole scene. Then I dropped a bombshell on the group. "I think we have another problem people."

"What's that, John?" Fran asked.

"What time did you lock the door and close up?"

"Around four-thirty, give'r take," Murray said.

"And neither of you opened the doors to let anyone in nor out, right?"

"That's right," Fran said as she nodded and took a step closer to me. "What are you getting at?"

"Just this," and I hated the idea but it was the only one that made sense. "This wound looks really fresh, we know Charlie was alive an hour ago when he was harassing Marry. The floor by the front door is dry, no footprints either coming or going, leading to or away from the body, nor towards the rear of the building." Everyone looked in the directions I pointed out. "No one but Fran or Murray has keys and you just said no one entered or left, so I'm afraid that leaves us with only one option."

"Oh my God, John, are you serious?" Fran asked. She was quick and knew already where I was headed.

"Yeah Fran, the killer's right here."

I convinced Fran and Murray to bring everyone back upstairs, while I called the police on my cell. After the nine-one-one operator picked up I explained the situation.

"I'm at work and there's real trouble here. I'm fine but a co-worker took a fireplace poker to the skull." I told her what I suspected since

43

nobody entered or left the building. She took my information and did her best to make sure I'd stay calm.

"Don't worry. I'm not the problem you all have to worry about."

"Your theory seems to make sense but there's another problem."

"What's that?"

"There's a driving ban's in effect for the city, streets are blocked off pretty good. I know the plows are out clearing the major routes, now where is your store?"

I gave her the store's address. "We're on Seneca, past Cazenovia Park, just before the Harlem/Seneca intersection."

"Alright." I knew she was taking my information down. "We'll call dispatch now. We may have to have call in a snow plow to clear a path, but Seneca being a main evacuation route, they may have already cleared it."

"Right," then she asked for my help.

"Can you to keep everyone there? We'll get officers there as fast as we can, but between the weather, the roads, and the number of traffic accidents it might take some time."

"Okay." I tried to let myself feel good that the Marines were on their way, but being locked in a building with a killer isn't the most comforting feeling in the world. This is what happens in slasher movies. I wished I had my revolver.

"What I also need is for you to keep everyone away from the crime scene and keep them calm. Situations like this can affect folks kind of oddly, if they're not used to them. A lot of folks will be on edge easily."

"The store's owners have everyone upstairs now."

"Officers will get there as soon as they can."

"Good, because I don't know how long I'll be able to keep everyone from leaving."

After I hung up I took another look around at the scene and it seemed unreal. Charlie was dead, with fresh blood soaked into his spiked, blonde hair, a portion of his face and his shirt collar. The fireplace poker had been dropped alongside the body and the hook looked like it had blood, muscle, and I wasn't positive, but there may have been some brain matter on it too. Whoever did this really swung for the fences.

Robbery didn't seem to be a motive because Charlie still had his rings and watch on. He carried a wallet with a chain attached to it, and the chain was still connected to a belt loop of his black jeans, and it looked like his flask was sticking out from the inside of his black, leather vest.

I stepped around Charlie's legs to double check the rear door, which leads to the deck and the backyard. The door was locked tight, same for all the windows, and when I looked outside, all I saw were mounds of fresh fallen snow. It looked like the storm was finally let up and I could see the backyard was a clean, even field of shimmering snow with no footprints. *Damn.* This probably meant I was right.

I headed upstairs and the atmosphere had changed. Instead of the Yuletide feeling that was with us earlier, the ambiance took on the feel of an Agatha Christie novel. As I reached the head of the stairs, everyone suddenly stopped talking, and I was reminded of all those scenes where the detective confronts all the suspects, then reveals the truth. I thought, *Hercule Poirot and Nick Charles I'm not.*

"I called the police and they're coming. The operator asked that everyone stays up here until the first officers arrive, they'll be here soon, but the weather's a factor. There's been a number of accidents on the roads, and there's a driving ban in effect for the city right now. I guess a lot of folks don't have their winter driving skills yet."

"So we have to sit up here and just wait for them?" Marry asked.

"I'm afraid so," I said as I took a seat in between the front and middle rooms. My co-workers were all in the front room sitting on folding chairs, the loveseat, and in a pair of older high-back chairs that were near the front windows overlooking Seneca. As I sat there, I snitched a few cherry thumbprints cookies and one of my favorite Christmas candies known as stained-glass windows.

"John, I don't want to stay here with that..." Marry couldn't get the words out.

"Believe me, Marry, I understand how you feel, maybe better than you might think," I said in between bites. "Babysitting a dead body isn't any fun, but I told nine-one-one the whole story and how I suspect there's a killer among us. Officers are coming and they're trying to get a snowplow from the street's department to clear a path, but right now there's no telling how long we've got to wait." I changed my tune. "So anyone have anything to ask or say?" Then I ate one of my cookies.

"Are you saying we can't leave?" Harry asked sounding rather excited. "Or what, you want a confession, John?"

"No, Harry, but let me put it this way. I think it's best if everyone sticks around for a couple reasons. First, the police are going to talk to you all, sooner or later, and believe me sooner is better. Second, it won't look too good if you leave before the cops arrive. They may suspect you have something to hide." I let that sink in for a moment as I ate a piece of stained-glass candy and watched their faces for reactions. "So maybe while we're sitting around we should talk."

"Talk about what?" Tony asked as he ran his hand over his bald head again.

My first instinct was to go smart-ass, but I held it back. "Who had a motive to kill Charlie? Since I didn't know him that well, and didn't work with him that much, I never realized what a horse's ass he was until tonight. And from the looks of things, I'm willing to bet he pissed off more than just a couple of you all."

Fran spoke up. "John there's no proof anyone did anything downstairs."

"Except for the dead body," I shot back.

Murray said, "John's right folks, if we talk this out, we might be able to get to the truth."

"Okay boss," Steve said. "Where was everyone when Charlie bought the big one?"

"That's going to be a problem Steve," I said. "Murray and I were downstairs just over an hour ago and Charlie was alive. He seemed to be sulking like a five-year old after the scolding we gave him. Everyone was up and down the staircase all day, even after closing. I mean, I'm assuming I wasn't the only one to go downstairs to use the restroom."

"John's right," Larry said. "But are you taking charge?"

"I'm not in charge of anything, Larry. I'm just bouncing ideas around and seeing what sticks to the wall. Besides I know what the police will expect."

"I don't care! I want to go home, now!" Eve screeched out. "It gives me the creeps that we gotta sit around with that body, and what do you mean you know what the police will expect?"

Now it was truth time, I paused and let out a deep breath. "Back on Halloween I was involved with someone running around Buff State hurling small pumpkin bombs, and who tried to kill a professor. I helped stop her and figured out who she was before the cops were called in.

"What happened?" Eve asked.

"Justice was served," was the only thing I said. I noticed some looked even more anxious and uncomfortable than before, if that were possible.

"Also, have any of you heard the name Stefano Angelo?" Some nodded as others shook their heads. "He's the head of the Arm, Buffalo's biggest criminal family and he's my father." I was looking at their faces for a reaction, trying to see anything that would give me a sign of panic.

"Now there's something I'd like to know, besides the reasons mentioned before, does anyone else have a motive for wanting Charlie dead?"

"John," Fran started, "This whole thing's ridiculous. Even if someone here had a motive to kill Charlie, why couldn't someone have come in while we were all up here? Charlie could've let them in and they kill him then sneak away. John we're family here."

BOING!!! I felt my tuning fork go off again, as if someone struck it with a sledgehammer. I was struck with an idea, but it'd be a gamble.

"Well, Fran, all families have baggage. Hell, my family has more baggage than the Buffalo International Airport deals with. It definitely sounds like there were plenty of motives to go around, thanks to Charlie."

I got up to stretch my legs and I ran down the suspects. "Let's see, we've got Harry and Tony who gambled and got cheated, and Steve— did you play cards, too?"

"Uh, yeah," Steve said as he gave me a dirty look. He wasn't the only one as I continued.

"There's Charlie's piss-ant loan sharking, which I'm willing to bet had a couple of the card players on the hook, right guys?"

"Are you saying I killed him?" Tony yelled as he bolted upright and pointed his finger at me.

I smiled at the thought of what I did to the last guy who pointed his fingers at me. I stepped towards Tony and put my hand on his shoulder.

"No big man, I'm not. Easy, take it easy." *Play it cool and keep them all calm bubba.* I gestured towards his chair, which went back a foot, when he bolted up. "I don't think you'd have duked Charlie then killed him with everyone around. It wouldn't have been the smartest thing in the world." He calmed down then sat back down.

"Earlier, Murray, Fran, and I broke up Charlie harassing Marry." I stopped, crouched to look her in the eye. "Marry, I'm not doing this to embarrass you, but it's important to know. How long has this been going on?"

She looked back and forth to Fran and Eve, which I understood in her looking for friendly female support. "Long enough," she said and looked towards the floor, almost ashamed it seemed. "Do I have to go .on?"

"No," I placed my hand on hers. "I'm just sorry I couldn't stop him myself." Marry looked at me in a way that said she knew men stand up to guys like Charlie. "My point is, there are plenty of motives, but let me ask you something, Eve." I turned to face her. "Did Charlie ever harass you?"

Eve shook her head. "No, he knew if he tried anything Harry would have caved in his skull." Then she stopped herself when she realized what she said. "Oh my, I'm sorry I didn't mean that with…"

"It's okay, and I don't think Harry killed Charlie either."

"Why's that? Not that I'm not grateful," Harry said placing his hand on Eve's shoulder.

"I'll get to that in a moment. Fran, did Charlie ever try anything with you?"

"Ah, no," she said. Fran's body language told me she was hiding something. I knew about this sort of thing from dealing with my family and our lawyer Aldrich Kaufman.

"I asked because Charlie said something to Murray earlier about his family and when you said the folks here are a family it struck a bell for me."

"What do you mean, John?" Murray asked as he got up from his chair.

Here's where I played my cards and took a huge gamble.

"Murray, I have to ask you something." I let out a sigh because I prayed I was wrong, because I liked these people.

"What?" he asked.

"Please take off the Santa coat." Everyone paid careful attention to what I was saying.

"What? Why? John, I think you've read too much Agatha Christie," he said, and laughed out loud in his normal cheerful manner.

"You may be right about that, but Murray, please."

"John, there's no reason for me to take off my coat. I'm cold and I've a circulation problem, right honey?"

"That's right, John," Fran said. "Murray's always had poor circulation ever since I've known him." She got up next to her husband, almost looking like they were taking their wedding vows. "Now what are you saying? Just tell us," she ordered.

"Believe me, I'm not happy about this, but if you don't take it off, Murray, I'll tell the police my suspicions the second they walk through the door."

"Wait a minute," Fran yelled as she stepped in between her husband and me. She turned to face him. "You don't have to do anything he says, honey." Then Fran aimed at me. "Do you think Murray killed Charlie?" I stayed quiet as I looked Fran in the eye. I may not have known these people long, but my gut told me the Fordons were good people, as their staff were. I hated to think Murray was guilty, but nothing else made sense.

"Yes, I do, Fran. If I'm wrong I am truly sorry, but there's one thing nobody can overlook, something I know the police are going to look at intently."

Fran said, "And just what's that?"

I let out a deep breath. "Charlie was hit on his right temple."

"So?" she asked.

"Make like you're going to swing at my head with a poker." Fran rose her right hand and aimed at my left temple. "There!"

"What do you mean, John?" Harry asked.

"If a right-handed person gives an overhand swing to someone directly in front of them, the way Fran just did, the blow would naturally come to the left temple. Charlie's wound is on his right temple,

49

indicating the poker was swung by a southpaw. And there's only one left-handed person here."

As I spoke, I turned to look at Murray. His smile faded and he had a melancholy look overtook his face, which suddenly turned ashen and gray.

Then, he surprised everyone by unbuttoning his Santa coat. There were some blood spatters along the left side of his bright yellow shirt that stood out like a mass of flies on a wedding cake.

"He's right, Fran," Murray said as Fran turned back towards him. "Oh God, I'm so sorry." He began crying as he fell to his knees.

"Murray, what happened?" Fran asked as she knelt beside him and began caressing his head.

"Everything John said was right about how Charlie was acting and treating everyone. When I went downstairs to use the bathroom, I spoke to Charlie afterwards. I told him I thought it'd be best if he finds another job, and soon. I decided to let him go next week."

"Then what happened, Murray?" I asked as I looked down on him and Fran. I pulled my seat closer to them and sat down.

"Charlie said he'd ruin us and the store."

"How could he do that?"

Fran looked beyond uncomfortable and fessed up. "Because of me." They looked at one another and both gave a semi-nod, as if they knew it was time for all confessions and sins to come out.

"A couple of years ago Charlie and I had an intense, but extremely brief, affair. I won't say it was a love affair. Our marriage hit a rough patch, to the point we separated for a time, and Charlie was there." She looked ashamed and humiliated. "It was a real kick to be with a younger man, who didn't seem to mind crow's feet, or stretch marks, or a few gray hairs."

"It's okay, we're all adults here and we all know things happen," I said as I looked at Fran. "So did Charlie have photos or something?"

"Worse, he secretly video recorded our sessions and when Murray and I reconciled, Charlie started acting like a horse's ass and threatened to post the videos on You Tube and make sure our regular customers got them," Fran said.

"How could he do that?" Steve asked.

"Our customer e-mail subscriber lists. Charlie said he'd upload and send the videos to them all," Fran admitted.

"And that would've hurt Bookmarks," I added.

"More than that, it would've driven a stake through our hearts," Murray said. "When I talked to him, Charlie was even drunker than before and he told me he'd be staying and began forcing his hand even harder than before, otherwise the world would learn everything."

"So that's what he meant about your family matters?" I asked.

"Yeah."

"Then what happened, Murray?"

"I told him he couldn't do that. Fran and I had put everything we have into the store, that he should be grateful for having a decent job here. He just laughed and said I was a loser. I couldn't keep Fran happy in bed and that I was a clown for entertaining the customers and their kids the way I do. Finally, he said he should post the videos just to watch Fran and me burn and that it'd be worth losing his job to see the regular customers turn on us. That was it, all I felt was pure hatred for him, despite everything else he'd done and I remember my face felt hot and flushed and I couldn't think straight. I glanced around and saw the fireplace poker, grabbed it, and swung as hard as I could at Charlie's head.

"I don't remember much after that and blacked out for a minute or two, It was almost like going into a stupor. I dropped the poker on the floor and knew I'd have to do something but I didn't know what. I thought since Charlie's body was by the fireplace, towards the rear, and because the lights were down, and the restroom's towards the front, nobody here would see it. But I guess that was wishful thinking. The only thing I could think of was to put on my Santa coat to cover the blood stains and think things out."

Then Murray looked right at me and caught me off guard. "I didn't plan this and I understand the police will take me in. To be honest, I'm glad you figured things out. It's a relief, son. Now what?"

Oh boy. "I'll talk to the police when they arrive, I think the worst case scenario you're looking at manslaughter due to provocation. I'll contact my family's lawyer to see if he can help out. Aldrich is the best defense attorney in all of Western New York. I'm sure he can help."

"John," Eve interrupted, "Isn't there any way we can call the police and tell them not to come?"

"Eve, this isn't like canceling a pizza. There's a dead body downstairs and as much as I sympathize with Murray and Fran, the police need to be involved. There's no way around that," I said. Just then I had a thought that seemed totally inconceivable for me.

I thought about Murray and Fran and how they were good people. They didn't deserve to be caught up in this situation because of a drunken pezzo di merda. I have a lot of beliefs, but I think the strongest of them is in justice. A long time ago, I realized that justice and the law are two different things. I once heard a saying, 'Sometimes to uphold justice, you must break the law.' And that's exactly what I did. I made up my mind and couldn't believe I was going to pull off what could be argued as the biggest, boneheaded play of my life.

The others began talking and trying to figure out if there was something we could do to help Murray. Before anyone could do anything that hurt more than help I told everyone to stay calm and I'd handle it. "Murray, come with me. The rest of you stay here. I'll take care of it."

Nothing had changed downstairs since I headed up less than ten minutes before. Charlie was still laying there, dead. His head wound seemed to have stopped gushing blood, or maybe it was my imagination. Murray stayed behind me. "John, what are you doing?"

"You have to trust me." I went to the fireplace and I pulled my handkerchief out from my jeans, careful not to step in Charlie's blood or touch anything I didn't intend to touch. With my handkerchief I took the tongs out by the neck out of the wrought iron holder, then I placed them in Charlie's right hand, closed his fingers around the handle, using my hankie, then laid the tongs alongside the body. I knew what I was doing and what this meant. It wasn't the first time I did the wrong things for the right reasons and something told me it wouldn't be the last time, either.

"John, what the hell are you doing?"

"You're a good man, Murray, and I know you admitted to striking Charlie, but a manslaughter charge in New York can give you one to fifteen years, that's a long time for you and Fran. Now here's what happened. I came down the staircase to use the bathroom, when I saw Charlie, drunk, arguing with you. You told him he'd have to find a new job, and that's when he grabbed the fireplace tongs and swung them at you. You grabbed the poker and swung back in self-defense."

"John, we can't do that!"

"Murray, listen to me, I've seen enough bad people get away with the wrongs they've done, some are really evil men, then there's you. From what everyone said, yes. I agree Charlie needed to be dealt with and I don't think killing him had to be the first club out of the bag. I know that wasn't your intention. It was the heat of the moment."

Murray had a look on his face that was indescribable. "I'm not sure what a plea of self-defense brings, but you have a clean record, right?"

"Yes, I mean, when I was eighteen I got ripped good one night and drove drunk, but that's it. John why are you doing this?"

"Fiat justitia ruat caelum," Murray looked confused then I translated. "That's Latin. It means 'Let justice be done though the heavens fall', you being put in prison for one to fifteen doesn't help Fran or serve justice."

"John …" Murray started to speak, but just then a huge snow plow with a salt spreader drove past the store and the truck was followed by two police cars. All three vehicles had their flashing lights going which looked odd since the plow had a yellow/orange spinning light and the police cars used the standard red and blue flashing lights.

I took Murray's keys from him and unlocked the front door as the police cars turned around, and parked once the plow cleared space in front of the store. "Good evening, officers. My name's John Seraph and we have a dead body for you. Merry Christmas."

Two of the police officers headed upstairs, while I led the other two to Murray and the body. The scene was secured, and upstairs the pair behind me wanted to talk to the others. It was a bit of a risk, kind of like passing notes in class, when I told everyone how things "happened". Everyone got quiet as we came up and I spoke up to make sure everyone heard me. "Officers, this is the rest of the staff, but I don't know what they can tell you, since I was the only one who saw Murray defend himself, like I told you."

As I spoke, I looked right at Fran, who I could tell had been crying since Murray and I went back down alone. I figured, and found out later, I was right, upset couldn't begin to describe how she felt. It took her and some of the others a moment to catch up. "See, I told you Fran, Murray would be okay. It was self-defense."

"Mr. Seraph, we'll take your statement in a moment, please. If you could tell us everyone's names we'll get started," the black officer said, who looked a foot taller than me and a half foot wider.

"Sure, no problem. This lady is Fran Fordon, Murray's wife." It took Fran until that moment to realize what I was doing.

"Ah, yes, officer," she said, composing herself, then offered her hand. "I was upset at the thought of my husband going to prison." The staff just watched the scene play itself out and I saw the light bulbs finally go off.

"Well, ma'am, don't worry. If your husband was justified, I doubt he'll be looking at any real time," the first officer said as he unzipped his jacket and took out his notebook and pen.

I stood behind the police and smiled at Fran as the realization finally hit her. I had a feeling, as I suspected she did, that everything would be all right.

* * * *

All that happened in less than forty-eight hours and things are looking good for Murray and Fran. The police believed my version of what happened and the forensics backed up what Murray and I told them.

Don't get me wrong, I've got a lot of respect for police and the D.A.'s office, but my conscious wouldn't let me sit back and watch a good man go down for one heated lapse in judgment. I'm not condoning what Murray did, but the man doesn't need to be sent to prison for fifteen to twenty. I know someday I may have to answer for it, but Murray and Fran are together, their store is still running, their employees are still working, and even though I covered up the truth, I can live with the results. The way I see it, I couldn't give them a better Christmas gift.

THE END

Thanksgiving:
Fashion Statement

After *Family Ties* & before *Family Plots:*

Here's to the smell of roast turkey, homemade stuffing, watching parades, and kicking back with your family, and just being thankful.

November 25th

I love Thanksgiving and almost everything the holiday brings with it. The holiday bug hits me sometime in mid-October when the leaves change colors and the air gets that first crisp chill of the season. The perfect autumn day would be to ride through the Boston Hills or out to Chestnut Ridge Park and take in the awe inspiring views of God's painted canvas, then stop off at the Myer Brothers Cider Mill. The only thing I'll never understand about the holiday is the insanity of Black Friday.

I'm a smart shopper and I like a good deal when I find one, but shopping at midnight, or even earlier, after a big, holiday meal and spending time with friends and family, when I can be in my warm bed to me is beyond stupid. No one needs a plasma screen or video game system that badly. I've never heard of a Black Friday sale saving a life.

On the other hand, if it wasn't for Black Friday this year I wouldn't have gotten back into my old man's good graces, which happened when I cleared my sister Alidia of murder.

Usually I spend the holidays alone after I cut my family ties, but I'm always invited to their holiday dinners and get-togethers by my neighbors Charles and Dixie Baxter. I've always been appreciative and have taken them up on their offers in the past, but not this year, partly because their daughter Jolene was home from college. Every time she gets around me, Jolene chases me around like it's mating season.

I was also invited to Thanksgiving dinner by Crystal Bell, but I don't think her family wants me around her. Crystal's life was endangered when I led a killer to her doorstep, never mind I saved our lives by setting him on fire, but that's another story.

* * * *

This year, my Thanksgiving consisted of watching the Macy's parade, one of my traditions, finishing two final papers for school, and cooking dinner for one. I made hot turkey sandwiches, microwaveable mashed potatoes, sweet corn, and served with cranberry relish. Things were quiet and uneventful, except for the occasional, annoying phone calls I got from some of my family. I ignored them all and let my answering machine or my voice mail take them. After watching *Miracle on 34th Street* I went to bed, having no idea how insane Friday would be.

Alidia and I have always had a special relationship, which I believe came from me being the oldest sibling and her being the baby. Our bond is the only reason she was able to talk me into meeting for lunch at the Walden Galleria, on the busiest shopping day of the year.

I left my apartment around eleven, even though we planned to meet around one. Traffic and parking would be a nightmare, so I figured the sooner I got to the mall, the better. The sun and blue skies played hide and seek behind the clouds, and with the chilly temperatures, it felt colder than it actually was. At least it wasn't snowing.

Traffic was light in South Buffalo, but as I made my way through West Seneca, into Cheektowaga there was more traffic out, but the roads were passable. Once I pulled into the Galleria parking lot it was bumper to bumper. I knew this was coming when I agreed to meet with Alidia, so I didn't bitch. I knew what I was getting into. I wasn't happy with the traffic or the crowds, but it'd be good to see my baby sister.

As I circled the perimeter of the parking lot, I only saw a sea of rooftops of cars, trucks and SUVs and wondered how anything got accomplished on days like this. With Christmas carols coming over my radio, I tried to remember the lay out of the Galleria, because it'd been awhile since I'd been there. Over the past five or six years there'd been a large number of renovations, additions, and changes, and I thought it best to park as close as I could to one of the stores Alidia shopped at. The only one I was positive about was Lord & Taylor, which is one of the two story anchor stores. I circled around the building, drove past J.C. Penny's, up near the Walden Avenue entrance, and Sears then came around to Lord & Taylor.

I circled the upper parking level and it took me less than ten minutes to find a parking spot. I lucked out and got one near the end of the row and on the outside. A couple of women loaded up their trunk and back seats with what had to be fifteen to twenty shopping bags from various stores. I guess they started very early. I patiently waited with my left turn signal flashing. As soon as they cleared out, I pulled in, just as a mini-van driver made two hairpin turns and tried to beat me to the space. The look on the driver's face told me they were really upset with me. Fair's fair and I was there first.

I'd an hour to kill before meeting Alidia, so I strolled around the upper level to do some window shopping. I thought I might get an idea what to get Crystal or another good friend of mine, Bobbie Bedell.

The Galleria was fully decked out for the holiday season, with Christmas decorations of all kinds, even though the holiday was over a month away. The maintenance staff must have started decorating the first week of November. Oversized, old-fashioned ornaments hung from the ceiling, rows of green and silver garland spread out on the walls, like festive cobwebs, and bands of multi-colored twinkle lights seemed to suspend in mid-air. Below me, on the ground level, centered between the two sides and among the kiosks, were groups of small, pre-lit Christmas trees with twinkle lights. Surrounding the artificial forest were motorized, white wicker reindeer, with clear twinkle lights inside them, and over the p.a. system Christmas carols played throughout the mall. Like it or not, it was official, the Christmas season was here.

Seeing all this always makes me wonder, when did we, as a society, bypass Thanksgiving and pole vault from Halloween to Christmas? When I was a kid everything was closed for Thanksgiving. People stayed home the day after to spend time with their families and friends. It's kind of sad the way the world's gotten into a major rush and makes me wish it was like it was when I was younger.

* * * *

Half an hour later I still hadn't found anything for either of the girls, but to be honest, I only looked at the stores from the outside. I wasn't suicidal enough to go inside with the herds of people pushing and shoving each other. Seeing them all reminded me of a mosh-pit full of slam dancers. My claustrophobia didn't flare up and I finally realized most shoppers were swarming inside the stores, hunting for the so-called best and earliest holiday deals. The pathways in front of the stores was mainly clear, foot traffic moved along freely. People scrambled past one another in a hurry, where I was walking along at a relaxed pace.

As I strolled by Victoria's Secret, I found myself daydreaming about Crystal and Bobbie modeling some of the items featured in the store's window, which is when I felt my cell phone vibrate in my pants' pocket. I pulled it out and Alidia's name showed on caller ID. "Hey Sis," I said.

"John where are you?" From the panic in her voice I knew something was wrong.

"I'm here at the mall, you okay?"

"I'm fine right now, Johnny, but I don't know for how long." I rushed away from the hordes around me and I had to put my index finger to my left ear so I could hear Alidia better.

I reached a small alcove in between one of the major department stores and a corridor that leads to the second level walk way. "Alidia, what's wrong?" I demanded and I recognized the concern in my voice. Once I was clear of shoppers, I could only hear the echoes from footsteps and voices bouncing off the polished tile floors and walls.

"Johnny I need you to call Aldrich, now!" The panic in her voice rose to a new level I never heard before, which started to make me freak out a bit.

"Alidia where are you? What's going on?"

"I'm at Lord & Taylor Johnny, I'm alright, but Johnny…." Freezing up like this was unlike Alidia.

"What's wrong?"

"Johnny, they think I killed someone."

Thanksgiving: Fashion Statement

In less than five minutes I was at the upscale store after charging through holiday shoppers, as if I was at the running of the bulls. I flew past the parents with their children, senior citizens walking slowly, and Salvation Army bell ringers collecting donations. At that moment, I didn't care if I overran everyone in between me and the store. I wasn't thinking clearly and prayed I misheard Alidia, but I knew I didn't.

Alidia told me she was in the manager's office and as I walked in I scanned around for an employee, or anyone who could tell me where I could find her. Finding a virgin in the maternity ward would've been easier, because every salesperson I saw was tied up with holiday shoppers. I gritted my teeth and fought my claustrophobia, because it flared up as soon as I saw the crowd inside.

I approached a young saleswoman, with light brown hair and glasses, and she looked tired. Once she was free from a pair of older women I approached her.

"Excuse me."

After a quick breath she asked, "Yes sir?"

"Sorry to bother you, but this will only take a second."

She looked confused, "Yes sir?"

"I need to speak to your manager, immediately." I leaned in close so only she could hear me, which is when I caught a whiff of a flowery perfume. It distracted me for a moment and I forced myself to refocus. "My name is John Seraph. My sister Alidia Angelo is with your store manager. I need to speak to them now!"

"Ah, yes, Mr. Seraph," she said. "If you'll come with me, I'll take you to Mr. Ravid's office." I followed the saleswoman to the escalator through the mob of shoppers. As we rode down to the first floor, she turned and faced me. "I know a little about what's happened," she said as she extended her hand. "Belle Melodye." We shook hands. "Your sister is a regular customer of ours, and I can't believe she's guilty."

"Belle, what happened?" I asked her as we stepped off the escalator.

"Maybe it's best to let Steven, my manager, tell you the whole story, but it's bad." We reached her manager's office just as Belle finished speaking and I braced myself for the worst, but prayed for the best.

After a couple of knocks at the door, Belle opened it and said, "Steven, Ms. Angelo has a visitor."

C. G. Eberle

I followed Belle in and immediately saw a tall, bald man with dark eyes and a black French Cut surrounding his mouth. He was dressed in dark purple and black, and looked like a scornful teacher, who caught his students cheating on a test.

At the desk, Alidia was slumped in the chair, looking like she'd just come off a solid week of jet-set partying, eating little and sleeping less. Behind her, on the floor were four shopping bags, topped by what I knew was her winter coat. As soon as Alidia saw me she bolted upright like a startled colt, almost knocking over her chair.

"Johnny, thank God! They think I killed a saleswoman!" She grabbed onto my chest so tight I lost my breath for a second there. "Did you call Aldrich or Daddy?"

I would've but our family's consigliore was tied up in meetings all day regarding the old man's business. Translation; there was some sort of major deal being made for or by the Arm. I knew the old man was also incommunicado, that morning he took Mama on a two week Alaskan cruise.

"I tried but I couldn't reach him." I figured it was best to tell a little white lie, and keep Alidia calm. "I'll try again in a little while, now what happened."

"They think I killed a saleswoman!" Alidia said again, this time I noticed her eyes were tearing up.

"Calm down." I put my hands on her shoulders. "Start from the beginning, Alidia," I forced her to sit back down and I crouched, so I could look her in the eye.

"Maybe I'd better explain," the manager said with a raspy voice. "I'm Steven Ravid, store manager, but you already know that." He extended his hand, and as we shook I noticed he had a solid grip and the man liked his jewelry. He was wearing a stainless steel and black bracelet, a rectangular silver and black onyx ring on his right hand and a black, square link steel necklace.

"John Seraph, Alidia's brother. Now what happened?"

"They think I killed a woman!" Alidia yelled again. It was official, she was in full panic mode. It took me a moment to calm her down again, then Ravid told me the story.

"From what I understand your sister got into an argument with one

60

of our saleswomen, Constance Abda, about twenty-five, thirty minutes ago. Their 'discussion' was witnessed by some customers. Then about ten minutes ago one of the ladies ran out of a dressing room area, screaming. She found Connie's body in the women's dressing room area. I was called out to the floor and saw for myself." Ravid shook his head in what seemed disbelief. "I never saw anything like this."

"What do you mean?" I asked.

"The blood, there's so much of it."

"You called the police, I assume?"

"As soon as I got to a phone in the back. I wasn't going to use one of the phones on the floor, at a register, with so many customers here. The police should be here any time now. They asked us to keep the witnesses and your sister here until they showed up." He turned towards Alidia. "It's not that we think you killed Connie Ms. Angelo, but the police told us what to do."

"Right, I understand," she said after she had finally calmed down.

I turned back to Alidia and she was staring off into space. I had a feeling she was beginning to imagine everything that could happen if she were charged, arrested, tried, and found guilty. To a degree, Alidia was a 'mafia princess' like our other sisters, but she was really an innocent compared to them. She was beginning to lose it and I knew I had to find the killer.

Alidia was the baby of the family, she still lived on our parents' estate, and to a degree she lived her life in a bit of a bubble. The old man didn't want anything bad or inappropriate to touch her, which was completely naïve, especially with his employees always around. I crouched back down to look her square in the eye. "Okay, kid, tell me what happened."

"I got here early, about six, shopped, got some breakfast after the restaurants opened up, and went back to the sales."

"Right," I said.

"Finally, I came here and everything was fine. I found some amazing deals, especially this gorgeous Christmas sweater."

I gave Alidia a direct order. "Focus, little sister." She needed this because Alidia gets easily distracted by fashions, Hollywood gossip, and a great many other things.

"I asked this saleswoman, for some help, but she had this really bitchy attitude. I don't know what her problem was, maybe she ate and drank too much yesterday, or she didn't want to work today, or she was just a una brutta."

Belle and Ravid looked confused so I explained. "It's Italian for bitch."

"Usually, Constance's outlook was pretty easy going with customers." Belle said.

"Then what happened?" I asked Alidia.

"A little later I found a beautiful, violet dress and headed to the changing rooms to try it on, and everything was fine. I changed back into my own clothes, and she came into the changing area and gave me an icy stare. I just knew there was trouble and I asked her what her problem was. She said I might fit into the dress better, if I got a bigger size or lost some weight."

"Great customer service you folks got here," I said to the staff.

"What?" Ravid said in disbelief. "That's not like Connie at all."

"Well, it happened," Alidia fired back.

"What then?" I asked.

"She suggested I should shop at Lane Bryant or some other plus-size stores." This was ridiculous, Alidia's five foot even and about one-hundred pounds soaking wet. Connie had an attitude problem of some kind. "I told her I was going to speak to you, the manager," Alidia gestured towards Ravid, and continued. "She laughed at me and said that you'd never believe me, I might as well not even bother. I should just pack up my stuff and get out of her store, as she put it."

I turned to face Ravid, "You ever get complaints about her before?"

He just shook his head, then ran his left hand over his bald head. I figured the man was warm since sweat beads exploded across his brow. I felt the warmth of the small office. "No, I never heard anything like what you're saying, Ms. Angelo. I don't have any idea why Connie would do or say anything like that."

"Then she got into my face and laughed at me. It was like she had her own private joke going on. I admit I lost my cool and I pushed her a little, then she pushed me back. I shoved her back, into the wall, then she bounced off of the stool, seat, whatever you call it, then she hit the wall.

Then those women came into the changing room area and saw us."

"Wonderful," I said. "Where are the witnesses now?"

"Our break room," Ravid said.

"And what did you do about the body?"

"I posted one of our employees there. She's blocking off the area. We're telling customers there's some water damage to the first floor dressing rooms and they have to use the ones upstairs. I just wish this didn't happen today of all days." We all just looked at him, then Ravid realized how that came across. "Sorry, I know how that sounds, I didn't mean it that way."

"Smart." I felt my wheels spin, and I knew the next part wouldn't be easy. "Mr. Ravid, I need to see the body."

"What?" Ravid asked.

Alidia rose from the desk again. "Johnny, what are you doing?"

"What the old man would do, protect you."

"Mr. Seraph, I don't think…"

"I know what you're going to say." I looked Ravid in the eye and played it cool. "Believe me, I understand, but this isn't my first rodeo. I've had some experience in these matters and know how to conduct myself. I worked with the Buffalo Police Department in a homicide investigation last spring, I know the Cheektowaga cops told you to close the area off, but you have to understand, I am going to take a look at the scene."

"I'm not sure about…" Ravid started to say.

I figured it was best to make a deal and give him what he wanted, while I got what I needed. "Tell you what, the last thing I want to do is F-up things, send one of your employees with me to make sure I don't touch anything, all right?"

After a moment of consideration, Ravid caved. "Belle, take Mr. Seraph over to the dressing rooms, but I'm afraid Ms. Angelo will have to remain here."

"Why?" Alidia asked.

"I don't think the police would want you poking around the scene, Ms. Angelo. It's enough your brother is going in there."

"He's right, Alidia, the police might not be crazy about me being there, but they'll really hate it if you go back."

"I'm allowing this 'cause I read about what you did during that missing woman's case. Belle, please show Mr. Seraph the way."

"If you'll follow me, Mr. Seraph," Belle said.

"I'll be back in a few minutes," I told Alidia. I put my hands on her shoulders. "It'll be all right."

Belle led me through the mob of shoppers, past a maze of clothes racks, and the seasonal displays. As we reached the women's changing area, she asked, "Mr. Seraph do you mind if I ask you something personal?"

"Nah, go ahead, and you can make it John."

"Thanks, John. What did you and Steven mean back there, about last spring and a missing woman, that's if you don't mind me asking?"

"No, it's no problem. Ah, a friend of mine asked me to help find his sister. Dana had been missing for a couple of weeks, then after I found Dana, I went after her killers."

"My God, what happened?" Belle was clearly shocked and almost walked right into a middle-aged couple.

"I found everyone involved and it wasn't a happy ending for any of them."

We bobbed and weaved through the crowd and finally reached the changing area. There was another employee standing guard, and like Belle, and most of the staff, another saleswoman who was smartly dressed. She was wearing a blue and black dress and high boots. As soon as she saw me approach she said, "I'm sorry, sir, the dressing rooms are closed, we're having some issues with them. The upstairs rooms are in service."

"That's to say the least," I muttered under my breath.

"It's all right, Diana. Mr. Seraph has Steven's permission to look things over, he knows everything." Belle then leaned in close to Diana, as I walked past the statuesque brunette who reminded me of Lynda Carter. "This is John Seraph, he's Ms. Angelo's brother and an investigator of some kind." I could've corrected Belle but I thought it best not to for the time being.

The ladies talked behind me, blocking the doorway to prevent anyone else from coming in, but they didn't come in any further. From the archway they watched me as I looked over the scene, which I admit was gruesome.

I braced myself, closed my eyes and let out a huff of air. On the white, carpeted floor was the late Constance Abda. She was a platinum blond, with a birth mark on her cheek, and I suspected she was high-maintenance. Abda was dressed in a white blouse with a violet vest, dark slacks, and what looked like tan shoes. They looked comfortable, and having worked retail in the past, I know what good shoes mean.

I tuned out the world and focused on the scene around me. It almost looked like Abda fainted and hit the floor where she lay, except for the amount of blood that soaked into the carpeting around her head. The pool was nearly black near the wound, which really was a deep burgundy, then it eventually became more of a normal blood red as it spread further out. I grabbed my cell phone and took as many pictures as I could as I didn't want to trust anything to memory.

On Abda's cheek there was some kind of deep cut; it looked recent and may have come from a struggle, but my gut told me it didn't come from the fight with Alidia. I got a good close up of it.

On one of the wall-mounted clothing hooks was a mess of hair and blood and I figured whoever killed Abda, rammed her head into the hook. Blood dripped from a metal wall-mounted hanger arm onto a white fabric covered seat. I wanted to move her head and get a good look at her wounds, but I didn't. It was enough that I came this far. I figured I had a couple of minutes, if I was lucky, and began to wonder what was holding up the cops. I took a last photo of the hook and turned to leave.

Although Belle was supposed to make sure I didn't touch anything, both she and Diana had their backs turned towards the changing areas, I supposed they didn't want to stare at the gore, which I could completely understand. Then I asked Belle and Diana about their late co-worker. "Until now, I thought Constance was a total professional," Belle said.

"Me too," Diana said with and nodded. "Except for how much time she got off."

Belle and I looked confused, "What do you mean?" I asked.

"It seemed she got off any day she wanted. To be honest, I'm surprised Constance wasn't written up," Diana answered.

Belle explained. "See, John, the company has a system that allows a certain number of days off, but if you go past them you'll get a warning first. Anymore within a four month period you get a second warning and a write-up."

"I take it Connie got more than the allowed days off," I said.

"Yes, she did," Diana said. "But why did you call her Connie?"

"What do you mean?"

"She always insisted on being called Constance."

"That's right." Belle sounded like she suddenly remembered. As soon as they told me this my tuning-fork went off.

"Hmmmm. Any ideas why she wasn't fired?"

"You'll have to ask Steven," Diana said.

I thought for a moment and switched gears. "Where's your break room?"

"Through the doorway we passed. You make a right and then go straight. Right next to the employee lockers, why?" Belle said.

"I'm thinking I need to speak to those customers."

"I'm not sure about that, John," Belle said.

"I don't want to get you ladies in trouble with your boss or the cops and I appreciate your help, but this is Alidia's life we're talking about here. Just tell Ravid I bolted from you in between the shoppers on the floor."

After a drawn out moment Belle said, "Come with me."

"Thank you." I remembered what she said about believing Alidia was innocent. As we left Diana to stand guard, I saw two uniformed police officers rush towards the manager's office. *Oh shit, here we go.* I knew I had to talk fast.

Belle led me down a small, off-white hallway that was wallpapered on one side with notices, messages, and bulletin boards. To the left were employee restrooms and finally through a swinging door was the break room. Inside, along the left wall were two vending machines, a sink, and a microwave. Opposite all that was a suite of employee lockers, which were small squares and pea soup in color. Between the lockers and machines were a pair of red picnic tables and benches. At the first table, sitting across one another were two women, one older who'd gone completely gray and a younger, redhead, who resembled the first. They were talking and drinking coffee as if everything was normal.

Belle introduced me. "Excuse me, ladies, this is John Seraph. He's aware of, uhm … the incident, and he is looking into the situation," She stopped for a second and for a moment she seemed slightly embarrassed. "I'm sorry I didn't get your names."

I shook their hands as the older woman, Irene Galaway introduced herself and her daughter, Daphne Clairborne.

"If you don't mind, I just have a couple of questions for you."

"Are you with the authorities?" the elder Galaway asked. "I do not see any identification or a badge, young man." Next to her on the bench was a silver fur coat. It was similar to one of the furs my mother owns.

"Well, ma'am, I'm not a police officer."

"Then just what is your interest in this situation, Mr. Seraph?"

"I'm looking to clear the name of a young woman of murder." From Galaway's attitude and the way she seemed to carry herself I got the feeling she had a twelve foot pole rammed up her ass.

"I see."

"I don't think you do. I understand you saw Miss Angelo arguing with the saleswoman."

"Yeah, that's right," Daphne said. Then they told me everything they saw. Alidia shoved Abda backwards who hit the stool, bounced off the wall, then landed on her ass, just as Alidia told me.

"After that, the younger woman stormed from the changing area and Daphne helped the saleslady up. We asked her if she was all right, she said she was quite fine, and the situation wasn't anything to worry about."

"Then what happened," I asked.

"I'd forgotten a scarf I wanted to try with the dress I found out on the floor," Daphne began to say. "We went back to get it—it took us a few minutes to get back because I found an amazing handbag to go with my outfit, then there was this gorgeous gold scarf, a different one from the first, and I wanted to try it out too." Daphne paused for a moment, I could see she was still a bit shaken up. "When we got back to the changing area we found the saleswoman dead. It was horrible."

"Indeed, it was a quite a ghastly sight," her mother added, nodding in agreement.

"So, in five minutes, or less, someone confronted Abda then killed her in a store crammed full of holiday shoppers, and no one saw anything. Great." I had a thought. "Belle, what kind of security cameras do you have here?"

"Pretty good ones, and I think I know where you're heading. There's a camera in the doorway of the changing area, but nothing back in the changing area itself."

"Maybe not, but the cameras will show who went in and out of there. Do you know if they record?"

She shook her head. "You'll have to ask Steven."

"Okay." I took a moment to think of what to do next. "I'm going back to the office. The officers will be here anytime now." Before I left the break room I thanked the women, and then headed for Ravid's office.

Inside, I found a uniformed officer talking to Alidia. He turned to me and said, "I'm sorry sir you can't come in here."

"It's all right, officer, he's my brother, John Seraph. I asked him to be here. I called him a little while ago," Alidia said.

I just stared at the officer as I stood next to Alidia. He looked unsure but let me stay. Of course, it's not like he had any chance in hell of getting me to leave. "I guess it'll be all right, as long as you don't interfere, Mr. Angelo."

"No problem, officer, and the name's Seraph."

Then I realized he was younger than Alidia, so my gut told me we were dealing with a rookie. "Ah… what is Seraph?"

"My last name, Seraph."

"I thought you two were brother and sister."

"That's right, we are." I rolled my eyes and wondered if his parents knew he was playing cops and robbers.

Alidia gave her statement, and he took down everything she said. I just sat there quietly, listening. When they finished, I asked, "Is anyone with the body?"

"Yeah, my partner went with the manager to secure the scene."

Just then, his partner and Ravid came in and he asked the younger unie who I was and what I was doing. I looked up at him and smiled as nicely as I could, as the rookie explained my charming presence.

"Did you call for the M.E. and the detectives?" the rookie asked.

"Yeah." Then the senior officer turned towards me. I kept on smiling. "And your name's John Seraph?" He had a heavy smoker's voice and a hard whiskey drinker's face. I was glad not to be his liver.

"Yes, sir," was my only response.

He paused for a moment put his right hand over his mouth and looked like he was trying to recall something. "Seraph, Seraph … I know the name." I saw the light bulb go off and he shook his index finger at me. "This past spring, you were involved in that fiasco with Senator Addar and his wife." He smiled as he spoke. "Never liked that guy."

"Yeah, that's me." I smiled right back at him with all the beaming pride I could muster. "Actually, Addar was a nice guy, it's his ex who's a real bitch."

"So you two are brother and sister." He looked confused.

"I changed my name a few years back. It's complicated."

"And you were here with your sister?"

"No, we were going to meet for lunch. I was in the mall when Alidia called me. I got here before you guys." Then I switched gears, "Just curious, officer, what took so long?"

"There's a critical multi-car accident blocking traffic along Walden Avenue and the on and off ramps of the 90. It's being cleared up now. We're the first unit to get through."

"What about the Medical Examiner and detectives?"

"They'll be along soon, but we may have to close down a portion of the store," the senior officer told Ravid, who let of a sigh of frustration.

"Are you sure?" He ran his hand over his head again.

"That'll be the detectives' call, but we are dealing with a homicide here."

"If you'll all excuse me, I need to call my district manager and let her know what's happened."

"Sure. Ms. Angelo, Mr. Seraph if you'll come with us," the older, salt-and-pepper haired officer said leading everyone to the break room.

On our way there, Alidia asked, "What did you find out, Johnny?"

"What do you mean, Miss?" the senior officer asked.

Time to fess up. "I took a look around, but didn't touch anything."

"You shouldn't have done that. Why would you poke around?" the younger officer asked. "This is crime scene, not an art exhibit."

"Because Alidia asked me to help her, and she didn't kill that woman."

"What would make you think we'd assume that?" the older officer asked.

"I know how cops think. Two reasons: the argument with the victim that was witnessed, and our father."

"Who's your father?" the rookie asked.

I paused for a moment, then Alidia and I glanced at one another. Having been here before I knew it was best to admit the truth. "Our father is Stefano Angelo."

The older officer said, "Oh shit," and his freckled faced partner looked confused.

In the break room besides Alidia and me, Irene and Daphne were still there. The rookie kept us company, the women were all uneasily quiet. I got Alidia a Diet Pepsi out of the vending machine, then we were joined by Belle, Ravid, and a plainclothes detective.

His name was Casey and it looked like he had more mileage on him than an airport taxi, thanks to crows' feet, bags, wrinkles, a cauliflower ear, and a receding, black hairline. I also got the feeling he was a hardened, tough s.o.b.

"All right, what the hell's going on here?" As Casey took off his classic raincoat, the senior office explained everything and Casey got the general idea of what happened and who the players were. When he looked at Alidia and me, Casey got a peculiar look in his eye. It wasn't fear or respect … I think it was caution. Almost the look of someone who might get if they're forced to cross a crocodile infested river.

"Angelo, huh," Casey said in his own heavy smoker's voice. I picked up the heavy odor of cigar smoke off the man.

"Yeah," was my only response. "Believe me it's not something I'm proud of." Alidia flashed me a semi-dirty look, but this wasn't the time or place to re-hash our complete family history. "I'm here for my sister."

"Understandable. I spoke to the arriving officer outside. He told me you were looking around and spoke to the witnesses here," Casey said more than asked.

"I didn't touch anything—Belle can confirm that."

We looked at her and she said, "That's right officer. John ah…Mr. Seraph only took a look around and some pictures with his phone." Belle seemed to blush a little. I suspect she was slightly embarrassed for using

70

my first name in front of the police.

Casey turned back to me. "Why'd you do a damn, fool thing like that? This sure ain't no Goddamn tourist site."

"I needed something for my Christmas cards this year." Okay I admit my smart-ass side comes out not always at the best times. "I'm trying to help Alidia, besides I know the rules. I took a look around and asked the ladies about what they saw." I nodded towards the mother and daughter.

"Detective," Daphne said, "he didn't try and influence us or anything."

"My daughter is correct about Mr. Seraph's actions. Although I cannot speak towards his motivations, except to say he seems to be watching out for his sister, which is an admirable intention," Irene followed up then took a sip of her coffee.

"Mr. Seraph," Casey started "the police appreciate citizens who are willing to help us, but…."

"I know the speech, Detective. I got it from the Buffalo detectives and the District Attorney sent me an engraved copy. But understand, I couldn't just sit by and do nothing. You want to print me, fine, but you won't find any of my finger prints in the changing area." Everyone got quiet as Casey and I had our discussion.

"What were you doing there?"

"Taking a look for myself, trying to figure things out." I got up and pulled my cell phone out of my shirt pocket. I came over to Casey, by a table near the door and a wall and I sat on the corner. "You saw the scene?"

"Yeah."

"Let me ask you, how tall would you say Abda was? Take a ballpark guess."

He shook his balding head and looked puzzled, "Oh, I don't know. I mean it's hard to judge, with her laying on the floor, and her legs bent at the knees when she collapsed."

"Right," I said. "Belle, how tall would you say Abda was?"

"Oh, maybe five foot ten, maybe a little taller."

"Alidia, stand up." She did what I asked without question. "Now I can tell you, since Alidia was in high school she's been five foot even. I have a very hard time believing someone who's almost a whole foot shorter could reach up, then drive a human head into a clothes hook. Hell, that might be tough even for me and I'm six-two and two-ten."

Casey listened and I could see he began to follow my logic. But being the detective he was, he played devil's advocate. "Makes sense, but she could have stood on that seat under the hook."

I realized everyone got quiet and watched us lob back and forth. "It's safe to assume the killer got blood on them, right?"

"Of course."

"Alidia doesn't have a drop on her." Casey and everyone looked at Alidia's clothes. "Look, Alidia's wearing a tan sweater top that goes past her waist, with beige slacks, and tan boots. Her winter coat is white and light blue, so even if she'd worn it to cover her outfit, her coat would have blood on it somewhere. It'd stand out like a fireworks display."

Casey took a good look at Alidia's coat and clothes. "I'll give you that, but whoever killed Abda could've changed their blood stained clothes with anything else in the store," Casey said.

"What kind of security tags does the store use?" I asked Belle and Ravid while I brought up the pictures on my cell.

"Everything's tagged," Ravid said. "We use two different types, either the Sensormatic, which sets off the alarm system wired into all the doors, if they're not taken off the clothes, or the dye packs. If a shoplifter tries to force the tag off, it'll explode and leak dye paint all over the clothes and themselves. The stuff is almost impossible to wash out of clothes, and the dye will fade from their skin, but it takes three weeks."

"And the only ways to take the tags off the clothes are the detachers, up at the registers, right?" Casey asked.

Belle said, "That's right, Detective. We've two different types of magnetic keys to unlock the tags. There's no way to get around them."

"And they're all anchored at the cash registers, so there's no way to carry the keys around the store?" I asked.

"That's right," Ravid said with a nod.

"So if a customer was caught trying to use one, behind the counters, your staff would be on top of them like the LAPD was on top of Rodney King." Most laughed or smirked, only Casey and Irene didn't crack a smile.

Casey said, "All right, but what's your point?"

"Whoever killed Abda couldn't have been a customer."

"Whoa," Ravid said. "You're saying one of the employees, one of my people is a killer?"

I glanced at Ravid over my shoulder. "Maybe."

"You're just saying this to save your sister," Ravid yelled at me.

I faced him. "What motive would Alidia have to kill Abda? Yeah, she acted like a grouchy bitch, but Alidia could've come to you and filed an official complaint. Or could she?"

"What's that mean?" Ravid asked.

"Alidia told Abda she'd speak to you after the go around. Abda then tells Alidia that you'd never believe her and Alidia might as well not even bother."

"John's right, Detective," Alidia said. "That's what happened. It was as if she thought she was untouchable." The way Alidia said untouchable was different from the way most anyone else would use the word. In the world in which we grew up, it meant someone couldn't be harmed, killed, or even touched without the Boss' permission.

"It sounds like she thought she could get away with anything and you'd have her back." I asked Ravid, "Any ideas why?" He crossed his arms and shook his head.

"It doesn't make any sense. If a customer had a complaint about an employee they could come to me and I'd handle the situation."

I let a 'hmmm' out then turned back to Casey and my cell. "Can I show you this?" I brought up the picture of Abda's right cheek. We saw her on the floor, right arm coming over the head, which was lying on the left side. On the right cheek was the slashing cut I saw, and pointed it out to the detective. "I think the killer was bigger than Abda and is a man."

"Why's that?" Casey asked.

"A couple of reasons. First it'd take real physical strength to drive someone's head into a mounted clothes hook and Alidia doesn't have that kind of power. Second, even though that seat is right by the hook, if someone used it to kill Abda, her body would've fallen at a different angle I'm betting."

"That's possible," Casey said.

"Third, look here Detective." I showed him the picture. "See how the cut on her cheek is broader towards the bottom and it fades as it gets higher."

"Right." I noticed everyone got deathly quiet and paid attention to what I said. "I'm willing to bet that cut, which when viewed close up, almost looks rectangular and was made when someone backhanded or punched her."

I enlarged the picture as big I could then handed my cell to Casey and he took a good look.

"You're right, I've been on enough domestic calls to know this."

"So it's safe to assume that the killer was taller and stronger than both women, that they may have the means to swap clothes, if they got any blood on them, and was possibly a man." Then I remembered something. "Hmmmm, Steve, why do you call her Connie? Belle told me before she insisted on going by Constance."

Everyone watched him, and as best as I can figure, Ravid panicked like a startled colt, he bucked wild and bolted for the door. Before anyone could react, Ravid took five running steps towards Casey and me trying to get past us to reach the door. Without thinking, I stuck my right foot out and the fall and crash he made was beautiful. Ravid crashed hard and landed on his right knee. He yelled out loud and swore.

"Goddamn Sonuvabitch!"

I winced in a moment of sympathy, having cracked up my knee years ago, I knew what he was feeling.

After I tripped Ravid, Casey moved fast for a man his age and weight, which I think surprised everyone as much as my trip did. I was being generous in my description; it was more like Casey belly flopped on Ravid, but the detective did his job. He grabbed Ravid. "Son, when you do things like that it makes me damn suspicious."

* * * *

At seven o'clock Alidia and I were at a packed Pizza Hut on Union Road, near from the Galleria. We had to speak up because of the crowd, but there were so many customers around us, there was no way we'd be overheard.

"So let me get everything straight, because I know Mama and Daddy are going to have a million questions," Alidia said as the deep dish pizza we ordered arrived.

"Okay," I said as I served Alidia a slice of the meat lover's pizza first. Casey allowed me to sit in on the interrogation, which took place at the Cheektowaga Police station, and is also on Union Road and less than a quarter of a mile from Pizza Hut. If there's one thing you can say about Buffalo and its suburbs, nothing is really that far from anything else in the area.

As long as I behaved myself and stayed quiet I was in for two reasons. First, I helped him wrap this situation up quickly and catch Ravid, and second, I told him everything that happened last spring and my catching Dana Tillis' killers. He wanted to hear the whole story, and not just what was in the news.

"Ravid admitted he and Abda were having a secret affair, which is a no-no at Lord & Taylor. I thought something was up, since he was the only one who called her Connie."

"I got that part big brother, but what about the rest," Alidia said as she took a big bite into her slice. Having come out of the oven the pizza was near scalding, Alidia had a Three Stooges type of reaction and chugged half a glass of Diet Pepsi. I couldn't help myself and laughed out loud.

I refilled her glass from a pitcher as I continued. "Okay, Ravid told us Abda had issues. She thought he'd cut her slack with time off, maybe get her a raise, give her the easier jobs, you know that kind of thing."

"He killed her because of all that?" Alidia looked disgusted.

"No, it was the heat of the moment. Abda demanded more and more from him, she wanted to be made assistant manager and get some customers black-balled from the store." I took a bite then washed it down.

"Meaning me?"

"Among others. Turns out Abda was petty, jealous, and vain, and those were her good qualities. She could be a real bitch at times, according to Ravid."

"Tell me about it."

"Abda also demanded Belle and a few of the more attractive part-timers get fired. She wanted their hours, and that's all on top of taking extra long lunches, taking days off, and getting whatever else she could out of the job."

"Just because she wanted all that doesn't mean Ravid could or would cave," Alidia pointed out.

"Right. He made that clear too, but she told him if he didn't give her what she wanted, she'd contact the district manager, and other higher ups in the company. That's when the marinara hit the wall."

"If she told their bosses, wouldn't she also be shooting herself in the foot, so to speak?"

"Right. Abda was playing a dangerous game of chicken with Ravid and it wasn't a game he wanted to play. She laid it all out for him this morning and gave him an ultimatum. He had until the end of the day to make up his mind. Ravid saw Abda and you arguing on the monitors in his office, then he disabled the cameras temporally. He used the stockroom areas to walk from his office to the dressing rooms without being seen by customers or the staff, most of whom were on the floor.

He told her he'd had enough of her shit and she wouldn't take that from him."

"What do you mean?" Alidia asked after another bite of pizza.

"She threatened Ravid and laughed at him, then he snapped. Ravid backhanded her, hard, then rammed her head into that hook. He panicked, ran back to his office and turned the cameras back on."

"Was he trying to frame me?"

"No, it was a case of wrong place, wrong time. But once he realized whose daughter you are, he admitted he thought it looked good and that you might take the fall."

"Wonderful. What do you think will happen?"

"It wasn't premeditated, so he may be looking at involuntary manslaughter, that's for the courts to figure out, but I did tell Ravid one thing."

"What was that, Johnny?"

"It may be in his best interest to admit what he did, and take any kind of deal the D.A. might be willing to give."

"Why?"

"Because if Ravid got a lawyer to provide some sort of wild defense that would get him off, I don't think the old man would like it, considering his baby girl could've been looking at a murder charge."

Alidia laughed out loud at that. "Oh man, you're right."

"And his lawyer really wouldn't be saving him."

Alidia's eyes widened and knew almost certainly I saved his life. "So, now what?" she asked.

"Well, I don't know about you little sister, but I'm planning on finishing dinner 'cause I've some Christmas shopping to get to." I smiled and she laughed again.

THE END

Valentine's Day:
Hearts Afire

After *Family Plots*

Here's to the romantics, may we always stay romantic no matter what.

February 14th

I almost did the un-thinkable, thank God I stopped myself before I pulled the trigger, literally. At Buffalo State College I'm majoring in English Education, to earn my teaching credentials. Eventually, I'd love to teach at the college level. I've been at it for three years now and for the most part it's interesting, and has been rewarding at times, especially when I get to work with kids. Currently, this semester, I'm tutoring grade schoolers at Truman Elementary in Lackawanna, NY. It's a nice situation because Truman isn't far from my apartment in South Buffalo, so I've a short drive, but let me start at the beginning at what made this Valentine's Day my most unforgettable one ever.

My normal, part-time job is manning the checkout desk at the E.H. Butler Library at Buffalo State, but last month I picked up a paid tutoring position through school to work at Truman, and I like the job for a number of reasons. First, it fulfills a course requirement, but mainly helping kids is rewarding and I love working with them. I don't want to sound cliché, but it's true, when you see the spark of understanding ignite in a child's eyes, and then they're able to comprehend, well the feeling in indescribable, besides the extra money never hurts. I tutor on

Tuesday and Thursday, from 2:45 to 3:45, and that's on top of my Monday-Wednesday-Friday four hour shifts at the library.

Today was Valentine's Day and my plans were set when I got up. School in the morning, head to Truman at two o'clock, home for dinner, then settle in for my annual Valentine's tradition, make some popcorn, open a bottle of Diet Pepsi, and watch *My Bloody Valentine,* the original 1981 slasher flick, not the 2009 remake. I do have my standards, but it was a decent remake. Romantic? No, but there have been some major problems with two special ladies in my life, so I didn't make any romantic plans, with either of them, as much as I wanted to.

At 1:30 I lunched at the Butler Library; I opted for a pair of the finest humus wraps and a Diet Pepsi, vintage 2014, a fine year, then drove to Truman Elementary. The ride didn't take long in mid-afternoon traffic, plus the weather finally broke out of a pattern of recent lake effect snows we had since Christmas. Now there was blue skies and sun, but it still felt like the inside of a walk-in freezer, but the sun made it nicer than before.

It was twenty-five after two when I swung into the parking lot, grabbed my assignment folders then I ran inside after being buzzed into the building. School was going to be dismissed in a few minutes, and I could hear the kids clamoring behind the closed doors, like race horses at the starting gates. I rushed past all the red, pink, and white decorations lining the hallways on my way to the library, after I signed the visitors' log, and it was there I had my first surprise of the day.

Mrs. Cavendish, one of the secretaries greeted me, wearing a red sweatshirt, with a massive pink & white heart and naked, fluttering cherubs all over it. "Afternoon, John, care for some Valentine's candy," she offered. On her desk was a plate with candy hearts, chocolate kisses, and marshmallow hearts. I declined with a simple shake of my head as I wrote down my name and arrival time. "Oh, before I forget, we've got something for you here." My curiosity changed to confusion when Mrs. Cavendish brought out a small, heart shaped box of Valentine's candy.

"Are you trying to tell me something? You're a charming woman but I just don't want your husband trying to unload some buckshot in my backside," I joked. I knew the sixty-something year old grandmother didn't have a thing for me.

"Flatterer," she joked back, looking past her glasses at me. "Actually, John, we found this outside the office this morning, with your name on it, and John, it was left anonymously." My tuning fork went off, it usually tells me when something's wrong or I should wake up and pay attention. "Looks like you've got a secret admirer," Cavendish teased. Suddenly I was no longer in a joking mood.

"Ah, thanks, Mrs. Cavendish," I said as I left the office with the candy and my folders. I walked into the main hallway that was properly decorated for the holiday. I noticed there was a small heart shaped card on the box and once I got to the library I read it.

> *Violets are blue and roses are red;*
> *You've entered into more than my head.*
> *You've no idea how you've affected me,*
> *Before long you will finally see.*

I didn't know what this meant, but someone was playing games. It's been my experience someone's playing games things get messy.

Considering I didn't know who I was dealing with, what they wanted, or what the stakes were, I suddenly became on edge.

I put the secret admirer out of mind because I had nine students from the seventh and eighth grades I was to help. Three eighth graders and six seventh graders were either assigned to me by their teachers because their grades were poor or they asked for assistance. I knew even before I began who wanted my help they were the ones who took my lessons seriously.

The lessons were simple; I used copies of reading assignments on various topics I took from teachers' handbooks and study guides. The kids were supposed to read the essays and then complete mini-tests I wrote up at home. These were pretty basic, picking out nouns or verbs, figure out what words were synonyms and antonyms, and finish spelling words. I also assigned weekly homework. I picked up some cheap comic books the kids had to read then write a short essay about the story for extra credit with their English teachers. It isn't always easy, especially since I'm dealing with some kids who don't always take this stuff seriously, but I guess that's normal with students of any age.

Valentine's Day: Hearts Afire

I got set up in the library at one of the larger tables and laid out the day's lessons. While I waited for the kids I stared at the candy box, which I hid under my folders. I needed to focus on the job at hand.

My students came in and the majority weren't too happy to be there, especially since most of their classmates were headed home. I tried to make things light and fun, but educate them as well, which isn't always easy to do on the best of days. My eighth graders Sally, Tom, and Mac sat together, the seventh grade boys Tony, Bob, and Mark went to one table and the girls Amanda, Justine, and Ashley another, which was normal.

"Afternoon everyone," I said, "If I can have last week's homework, thank you." I got eight essays out of nine students, which also was typical. Ashley was my single hold out. She resented being ordered by her teacher, Calliope Nata that to pass English she needed tutoring. I guess there's always one in every group.

"Alright, next if you would hand back the comic books, thank you." My peripheral vision told they were being passed down to Justine. Since she sat closest to me it made sense.

"Thank you, Justine." She smiled back at me with a broad grin and I thought it was good to see her like this. When I signed on-board Calliope told me Justine was a little introverted.

"Alright everyone, here are the comic books I want you to read and do your papers on. This time I want you to tell the story from the point-of-view of an important, inanimate object in the story. It can be Batman's utility belt, Wonder Woman's lasso, Green Lantern's ring, or use your imaginations and have some fun with it. Find something in the story you think works, then go for it. Here's the sign-out sheet." I handed the comics and sheet to Mark, who handed them out. I made the kids sign the sheet, which told me who had what book, which I learned was a good way to keep an eye on any possible cheating.

Next I passed out the day's reading assignment on Mt. Rushmore. We took turns reading out loud and when finished I handed out the mini-tests. "Alright, everybody, you know the drill. You have twenty minutes, do your best, this won't affect your grade, it's only meant to help, and if you have any questions raise your hand and I'll come to you."

The kids got to work and since I had time I checked my email on one of the library's computers. I'd been doing it since my second week, after the librarian, Mrs. Ross told me I could. This became routine, but this time I found a second Valentine's poem waiting for me in my email, and my concern exploded into a near panic.

> *You're always on my mind,*
> *And touched my heart;*
> *Once we're together,*
> *I know we'll never part.*

A reoccurring sickening feeling I've had from time to time overwhelmed me, and I hated it.

I quickly composed myself because I didn't want to freak out in front of the kids. The rest of the hour went by without any problems. "Okay, I'll see you guys Tuesday. You all have a good weekend," I said, then I packed up.

As the others left, Mark, Justine, and Bob hung back. "Mr. Seraph, is everything cool?" Mark asked.

"Ah, yeah, it's just a slight headache." I didn't want them to know I might have a real problem. After I read the second poem I had a terrifying realization my 'secret admirer' was someone from my past who wanted me dead.

I walked the kids to the parking lot doors as they talked about this, that, and whatever. I wasn't able to pay attention because I became totally focused on the past year, which was a bitch. I've had more than my fair share of enemies, which include a Buffalo police officer, who occasionally works for my old man, and a family of Israeli gunrunners. The brother who wants to kill me, the father who wants to employ me, and the daughter who wants to bare my children. Have I got some life or what? La varietà piace, that's Italian for variety is the spice of life. There's a woman locked up in the Buffalo Psychiatric Center who I'm sure is faking and wants me dead, then this past Christmas I pissed off an escaped Nazi commander, who is still wanted for war crimes committed at Dachau.

I waited with the kids at the parking lot door until their rides showed up. There were only a few teachers and staff in the building and although

I wasn't a teacher I felt responsible for the kids, so there's no way I'd leave them alone. Even though the school's lights were on, there was a sudden creepiness to the building. Or maybe it was just me. My silence must have been conspicuous because Tom said something I didn't hear then I came out of my stupor. "I'm sorry, Tom, what was that?"

"I asked has Ms. Nata worked on our grades yet, you know with the extra credit."

"Ah, I don't know. Next time I see her I'll ask." Just then some of the parents came in. Most of the kids all lived in the same neighborhoods so their parents car-pooled in shifts. After they left I went back to the main office to talk to Mrs. Cavendish again.

In the office Mrs. Cavendish was talking with some of the staff, including Calliope Nata. "Hi," I said as I strolled in and tried to sound normal.

"Hi John, so how my kids do?" Calliope asked.

"All right for the most part, but Ashley's still fighting me. She's the only one who's not doing her homework and her tests are only partly done. I'll show you today's tests on Tuesday after I correct them."

"Lord, I know she's difficult but I'll have a word with her tomorrow."

"Also, Tom wanted to know if you factored in their extra credit yet," I said.

"No, I'm waiting until we reach Spring Recess but I'll go over everything with you before that happens. I'll let them know tomorrow, too."

"Good." I put my folders down on the wooden counter, which separates the entryway from the rest of the office, which houses a separate doorway to the Principal's office, a public address system board, and all the normal large office equipment one would expect to find there. I brought up the box of candy and asked, "Did anyone see who left this in front of the office today?"

All I got was a series of heads shaking no or various voices saying the word. "Great," I grumbled out of the side of my mouth.

"Still no idea, John?" Mrs. Cavendish asked.

"No and when the kids were taking their tests I checked my email. There was another anonymous Valentine's poem."

"Oh, baby, I wish I'd get something like that. Sounds like we got a player here," one of the math teachers said. I knew he was ribbing me, I wasn't in the mood.

"Hardly, whose ever sending this stuff to me says they'll see me tonight."

"Geez, John," Calliope said, "Romantic is one thing, but this seems to be on the creepy side. Could it be from a girlfriend?"

"Doubtful. I've been in a holding pattern with someone I've been seeing. Besides, this isn't Crystal's style." Truth was I'd been in a holding pattern with two special ladies since December. "This whole thing has a bad feeling to it, especially after last year."

"That's right," Calliope added.

"What do ya mean?" the math teacher asked.

"John has had some … issues with some nasty characters last year," Calliope answered. When I was interviewed by the principal and Calliope, I told them about my family and the murders. I didn't see the point of denying it when the principal said she recognized me from the news.

I wasn't in the mood to rehash history so I headed out and fell back on my first rule, When in doubt it's time to eat and drink. "I'll see you guys next week, bye."

I felt unnerved and a bit shaky and I hated it. I'd gone up against killers and psychopaths, faced off against crooked cops, and Neo-Nazis. I even fought against my old man and my brothers, who are all 'Made Men' and allegedly untouchable, but this was a first. Someone was coming for me and I didn't have an idea who. I had no clues, plenty of suspects, and felt the sword of Damocles swinging over my skull, and then things got worse.

The parking was cold, nearly empty, and looked like a winter wasteland. As I walked to my car I tried to think of who I was dealing with, then I froze, and it wasn't due to the weather. Under my windshield wiper was a red envelope, my stomach tightened up. The third poem read;

Starlight, Starbright,
John Seraph has righteous might.

Valentine's Day: Hearts Afire

Wish I make, Wish I might
I will see you this very night.

After reading it I went straight home to prepare for war.

On the ride home I tried to plan ahead and there were only two moves I could see; run and hide or stand and fight. Whoever this was I suspected had my address since they had my email and said they'd see me tonight. So I thought it best to be ready and give them a proper South Buffalo greeting, Sicilian style.

My apartment's in the Steeple Bay complex and is less than fifteen minutes from Truman Elementary. I pulled into the small parking lot behind my building and I came in through the back like I normally do.

Inside, I dropped the folders and candy on my dining table, hung up my coat, then went right to my bedroom. I pulled back the mattress and box-spring, reached into the frame and I pulled out my sawed-off shotgun and my .44. I'd just gotten my revolver back from the authorities after a shootout with some Nazis, but this time I brought out the big guns.

In my dining room I loaded both weapons, breaching shells in the Lupara shotgun and .44 caliber Hydra Shok rounds in my Mateba auto-revolver, then I loaded four speed loaders.

As I loaded each bullet I ran down my suspects' list and wished I could speak to my family's lawyer, Aldrich Kaufman. Aldrich has ways of finding out any piece of information that's out there, and he's watched over me for years, like I was his own. In many ways Aldrich has been more of a father than my old man.

Unfortunately, they were both in Miami attending a summit of the current families. They're meeting to discuss cyber crimes, data mining, and the gambling on Native American casinos, on top of how the Russians have begun nosing around the Western New York area, and the old man and his Canadian associates don't like it.

I left the shotgun and its rounds on the dining table, but brought the revolver with me to my love seat along with the candy. I wanted a good look at it under better light. One of the first attempts on my life involved drugs, so I could see someone injecting the chocolates with something nasty as a real possibility.

I looked to see if the package had been resealed but after ten minutes nothing, the cellophane was intact. No scotch tape, no packing tape, no nothing. I was as sure as I could be that there wasn't any tampering, and my gut told me the candy was fine, but my head told me to show caution.

At five o'clock I turned on the news and fought the nervous energy running in my body and resisted the urge to double check my rounds. I knew they were loaded and ready to go, all I could do was sit and wait. Sometimes that's the hardest thing in the world to do.

I could have called some honest cops I know, who I worked with in both murders, but I didn't have anything to give them. No names or proof, just some poems, a box of chocolates, and my instincts, which may be stuck in paranoid mode. Of course, growing up the way I did it's not surprising, but I've learned I'll live longer this way.

At ten after five I heard someone outside my front door, in the hallway, and I went on full alert. I turned the T.V. off, got up, slid my revolver in my belt then grabbed the shotgun. Whoever was in the hallway came closer, their footsteps approached my apartment. From the sound I suspected it wasn't a man, they sounded too light. *A woman* I wondered.

I thumbed back the double hammers on my sawed-off and waited for my visitor to make the first move. *Come on you son of a bitch, I've got a valentine for you.* I slowed my breathing, practically held it, and coming to a dead stop as the footsteps reached my door.

I stood by the table, to the side and aimed dead center. I heard knocks then a girl's voice said, "Hello, Mr. Seraph, are you home?"

Oh my God, Justine? I instantly thumbed the hammers back to the safe position, opened the breach and unloaded it then I laid my street howitzer on the table. I pulled my revolver from my belt and laid it next to the sawed off. I opened the door and she stood there smiling nervously. "Justine, what are you doing here?"

She'd changed from her school clothes into a lavender dress. Her dark hair had been styled to hug her face and complement it. Justine still had on her glasses, but I saw the woman she'd eventually become, and everything came together for me in a New York second.

"Happy Valentine's Day, Mr. Seraph," she said as she smiled through her nerves.

"Oh, my God, Justine, you're my secret admirer honey?" I asked as I brought her inside my apartment and out of the cold hallway.

"Yes sir," she answered as she began to blush.

I pulled out a chair and sat her down, then sat down next to her. "How did you get here?"

"My mom. She's in the car outside."

"How did you find my address?"

"I looked it up in the phone book. I knew you lived in South Buffalo, when I overheard Ms. Nata talking to one of the teachers about you, when you began tutoring us." I laughed out loud at the whole situation, "Mr. Seraph? What's funny? Are you laughing at me?"

I composed myself and looked Justine right in her eyes. "No, kiddo, I'm laughing at something else." I knew what she thought; I was dealing with a school-girl crush, and I wasn't going to make her feel bad about herself.

"Mr. Seraph, am I in trouble?" She glanced at my table, more specifically the guns.

I shook my head. "No, Justine. I was going to start cleaning my guns, you know to take care of them."

"Oh, okay." *Nice save stupid!* She began fidgeting in her chair. "Well Mr. Seraph I was wondering if you would like to have dinner with me and my mom."

There are lines teachers aren't supposed to cross, but I didn't have time to call anyone for advice. I'd been in this situation before, and Justine's mother was there. I saw the hope in her eyes and I couldn't break her heart after she went to all that effort.

"Sure, kiddo. Let me grab my jacket."

We ate at McDonald's and Justine insisted on paying. I guess she needed to feel grown up and I sure wasn't going to stop her. At one point she was in the ladies' room and her mother explained Justine has had a big crush on me since I started tutoring. "See, Mr. Seraph, Justine has talked about you so much and she really wanted to do this so I couldn't deny her."

This may have occurred because her folks divorced and there weren't any other male role models in her life. I've heard of situations like this and I knew I had to be careful if issues like these came up.

"I understand, Ms. Datia, but I've got to tell Ms. Nata. See, with the way things are these days…"

She held up her hand up. "I also understand, Mr. Seraph. See, when Justine talked to me about this idea, I called the school and spoke to Ms. Nata. She told me how you are with the kids and as long as I was here there shouldn't be a problem."

"I got to tell you Justine had me freaked out a bit."

Ms. Datia began laughing and asked, "Why's that?"

"Let's just say there are some people who really don't like me and I've a bit of an overactive imagination," I said. Before either of us could continue Justine came back to the table.

"Well, thank you, Justine. This was a real treat, better than what I planned," which was the truth.

"You're welcome, Mr. Seraph," she answered back with a bright smile, but I had to make things clear. I was just glad her mother was here.

"Justine, when we see each other around school it would be best if you want to show me your feelings we fist bump or give me five—
we can be buddies. I'm a lot older than you, by over thirty years, and I'm sort of seeing someone."

Justine's mother and I watched her for her reaction. I hated moments like these, been through this before and was told how to handle times like these delicately.

"I think Mr. Seraph is saying he'll be your friend no matter what, right?" Ms. Datia asked me.

"That's right, Justine. If you need help with your school work or need to talk to an adult or anything, let me know. I don't run out on my friends."

"Thanks, Mr. Seraph," Justine said. She sounded a little sad, as if she knew I was letting her down and having used the 'F' word I hoped I didn't hurt her. I've been there myself and no matter how easy you're let down this cake tastes like shit.

Back home I put my guns and bullets away and I felt like a horse's ass, which was the perfect phrase to describe me. Granted, it was a better Valentine's Day than I thought it'd be, considering I didn't have to shoot anyone, but I didn't like myself too much. I may have hurt a thirteen year old, lovesick girl, looking for a supportive male role model. Well, I'd be there in the weeks and months to come. I gave Justine my word I'd be there for her and I meant it. I've never broken a promise and I knew eventually she'd believe me in time. Now if I could get things straightened out with the other women in my life, but that'd take Divine intervention or wishing on Aladdin's lamp. Oh well, nothing's perfect especially for me.

THE END

St. Patrick's Day:
Caught Red Handed

Here's to freedom from tyranny, terrorism, and violence in all its forms for all.

March 17ᵗʰ

When I moved away from Newfane to South Buffalo, I knew there'd be major cultural differences. It was an easy adjustment after I realized most of the people here are blue collar, hardworking folks, whose roots go back to the arrival of the Irish, who immigrated in the 1820's and settled in the Old First Ward, which was succeeded by a second wave of Irish immigrants during the 1840's and 1850's, thanks to the Great Potato Famine.

Through all of the hardships these people suffered; starvation, disease, and emigration, prejudice, and poverty, then to live among the squalor of the waterfront, railroads, and factories of the Queen City, all helped give their families and descendants a sense of pride, history, and a strong work ethic that's supported them through good times and bad. All this helped South Buffalo, especially during the four Super Bowl losses and the 1999 Sabers' "No Goal" robbery thanks to Brett Hull.

I mention all of this history because yesterday was the "Old Neighborhood" St. Patrick's Day parade that annually takes place through the Old First Ward and the Valley neighborhoods, and it was here I took a stand for the Irish.

The one thing that hasn't changed and may never will is the hatred between the Irish and the Northern Irish, which is really the fault of the English. Now I admit I don't know the whole history of the Irish/English conflict, but from my understanding there's been enough stupidity and violence that both sides are responsible for. And it's stupidity that brought me into the Irish conflict and making me choose a side.

* * * *

My Saturday started like normal; I got up, made breakfast, and began my homework for my art history class. Frankly, a cavity search by prison guards would a more pleasant than this class has been.

I was working on a report on Neo-Roman Classical artists when Aldrich Kaufman, my family's lawyer called me. "Hey Consigliore, how goes it?" I asked grateful for the interruption.

"Jonathan …" from his tone I knew this wasn't a social call. "Are you taking Miss Bell to the South Buffalo Parade this afternoon?"

"Ah, no Aldrich. We haven't talked this past week." It was the best I could come up with on the moment. Crystal and I had been dealing with some major difficulties of a highly personal nature and I didn't see a way through it all. "Why are you asking?"

"Good, at least you are both safe."

"I said I wasn't taking her, I didn't say Crystal wasn't going. She's headed there with her sister Maria and one of her girlfriends, now what's going on?"

"Oh, God, Jonathan you have to contact her. Tell Ms. Bell they must leave the parade immediately!"

This wasn't the Aldrich I knew, the man never panicked or got excited. "What the hell are you talking about?"

"You are familiar with Hephaestus of course,"

Oh shit, this was going to be bad. Hephaestus is mythical arms dealer who works with my old man from time to time. It's said he can get hold of anything a buyer can afford and he's willing to sell to almost anyone. You name it odds are he can get it. It's only a question of money. Personal firearms, bladed weapons, specialized rifles, both automatics and sniper rifles, and individualized rounds. Bomb making materials, shoulder-mounted missiles, grenades of all kinds, night vision scopes, and aerial drones if one needs support. He has contacts in almost every major military around the world and can get military grade weapons, but the only thing he won't deal in is chemical, radiological, and biological weapons.

The other thing about Hephaestus is his over developed sense of drama. He named himself after the Greek god of fire, metalworking, and crafts, who forged arms and armor for the Gods, including Zeus' thunderbolts. Also no one has ever seen Hephaestus, he always deals with go-between, emails, and delivery boys. Anonymity is the first line of protection in his world.

"What the hell's he got to do with this?"

"Hephaestus contacted me after he learned the details of a deal that went down. Apparently one of his clients named Chulainn, an Irish terrorist, is planning something today during the South Buffalo parade."

"What?!"

"I am afraid so. Hephaestus informed me Chulainn is looking to detonate a bomb at the parade."

"Why the hell would he do that if he's Irish?"

"You do not understand Jonathan, Chulainn is from Ulster, a providence in Northern Ireland. He is almost as secretive as Hephaestus and is responsible for at least a dozen bombings around the world, all in the cause for Northern Ireland and the Red Hand Defenders. And he is one dangerous bastard. Last year the Garda Síochána, the police force of Ireland, thought they had Chulainn cornered in a farmhouse in County Cork. When cornerd, he set off an explosion that blew apart the front of the building, turning it all into wooden shrapnel, and killed four officers."

"Jesus Christ." I needed a minute to get my head together; all I had was just a moment. "How sure are you about this?"

"I am willing to wager my life on Hephaestus' information. He has never lied to me and every time he has done business with your father, both sides have come away satisfied." Okay, so I had the Gospel according to Aldrich.

"So what's Chulainn's plan?"

"I do not know, except he plans to use a bomb of some sort. All we are positive of is Chulainn is a true believer to the Northern Irish cause. His bombings are public, bloody, and he strikes at the heart of his victims. If Chulainn stays true to form he will wait until there is a large crowd to cause maximum damage."

"Oh God, Aldrich, besides the girls there are a lot of innocent folks there." I looked at my clock. "Fottuto! The parade just started!" I moved to my bedroom. "Listen, I need you to call Crystal's phone. She won't pick up for me. I'm going to the parade, but I need a place to start. Any ideas where I should begin?"

"Wherever the biggest assemblage of people would be."

"Christ, Aldrich, I think I got an idea." I put my phone on speaker and pulled my mattress and box spring off the frame.

"Jonathan, what are you doing?"

"Preping for a fight." I pulled out my .44 autorevolver and two speed loaders full of Hydra-Shok rounds. I loaded up and marched back into the living room.

"What was on his Christmas wish list?"

"Seven pounds of C-4 plastic explosive, five containers each, of ball bearings and wood screws, rat poison containing Warfarin, and an electronic pet containment system, one of those 'invisible fences' to keep dogs from leaving one's property."

"Right."

"But here's the oddest item, a cable utility box."

"What?" Okay I was confused.

"I speculate Chulainn is using the box to house a homemade Claymore mine, and from the sounds of things a nasty one."

"Especially with the screws and rat poison."

"That is the one thing I do not understand."

"Rat poisons contain amounts of anticoagulants, the device goes off, with all that shrapnel mixed in good with the rat poison, causes people to bleed out fast. I've heard of terrorists doing that."

"Good Lord. We are dealing with a twisted mind."

"Bubba, that goes without saying. It sounds like Chulainn didn't have time to set things up in advance and was ordering on the fly."

"Perhaps, but being an international terrorist and bomber, does limit one's options and availability to go shopping. Obviously, he could not go to Home Depot and pick up what he needed."

"Especially the C-4. So Chulainn makes the bomb, wires it with parts from the invisible fence, then places it somewhere around here."

"Correct, from what my contacts say Chulainn prefers the triggering device types of explosives."

"So he doesn't even have to be here?"

"True, but also according to my sources Chulainn is always close by, to verify his devices go off."

"So he likes the whole proof of death thing and may even get off on watching his bombs blow."

"I recommend caution, son."

"Just get in touch with Crystal, and I'll try and find her. See if you can get me all the information you can about this Irish bastard, including a physical description. Also, you better call the police and get the bomb squad out there! "

I hung up, stuffed my .44 into my belt and thrown on my suede jacket, which I would've worn anyway because even though it was clear skies, it was cold out. I rushed from my apartment, drove as fast as I could for the Valley and the First Ward.

I cut through South Park, which is home to the Botanical Gardens, South Park Lake, and a nine-hole golf course. Year round folks walk or jog the path surrounding the lake and it's a shortcut to the Valley, because Hopkins Street started/ended at the park and ran the length of South Park Avenue, with only two signal lights.

I circled the lake, made the right onto Hopkins and actually ran both red lights when I saw it was safe. Normally, I don't drive like that, but in this case I didn't give a damn. I wasn't sure of the parade's complete route, but I knew where it started in the Valley, so I headed as far as I could down South Park, until I was stopped by some orange and white, street barricades. I was forced to circle around on Euclid Place and park on Elk Street's left fork, just before it ran into South Park.

By the time I got there the parade was under way and I could see the lead marchers, followed by a green Cadillac. I walked around searching for Crystal and anything that looked out of place. Of course I had no idea what the hell that could have been, but I had one clue, a fake cable box.

I crossed the streets to the Valley Community Center and didn't see Crystal anywhere, but there were plenty of South Buffaloians braving the colder temperatures, and dressed for the occasion. Lining both sides of

South Park were men, women, and children of all ages wearing the green, hell, I was practically the only one there not wearing the color. Trust me. If you want to slip into a group of drunken Irishmen nothing's better than the Irish camouflage I saw. It was a sea of green sweatshirts, jackets, face paints, green afro-wigs, foam fingers, shamrock antennas, Irish flags of various sizes, Kiss Me I'm Irish banners and buttons, and of course green, white, and orange balloons. Parents with new families standing or in strollers and seniors who must have lived in the First Ward all their lives, all showing off their Irish pride.

I walked around where Elk and South Park met up, satisfied Crystal and her friends weren't there I headed over to where the street comes down hill and bends at an angle, where the Valley Community center was and the parade's starting point was. Just then my cell vibrated, it was Crystal. *Figlio di puttana!* I let the call go to voice mail.

I was forced to go along the right side, down Leddy Street and around those remaining parade marchers. I came alongside the community center and looked around the various civic groups marching, the remaining floats, which had riders from Norte Dame Academy and another that looked it was carrying men and women from South Buffalo and preparing to launch orange and green Mardi Gars beads when they moved out. I was also looking at every telephone pole, the side of every building, anywhere where a cable box would fit in. I was also keeping my eyes open for a dog collar that was out of place on floats or cars. I passed by the group of marchers, a couple of bands, and large group of clowns. Nothing, so that told me Chullian may have planted the collar underneath or on something that already left. Not the most pleasant of thoughts.

I began asking folks if they'd seen Crystal and showed her picture I had on my phone, but no takers. Finally, a young nun who I suspected was a novice and hadn't taken her final vows yet came up to me and asked if I was all right.

"Ah, yes, Sister, I am." I lowered my voice because the last thing needed was a full out panic. I walked her over towards the community center because I decided to bring her into my confidence. "Sister? Have you seen this woman?" I showed her Crystal's image.

"No," she said, shaking her head. "Pretty lady, I'm Sister Catherine

Margart."

"Sister, my name's John Seraph, and I need you not to react or panic." I double checked around us to make sure we were clear and couldn't be heard. "I can't go into the whole story now, but I obtained highly reliable information there may be a bomb planted somewhere around the parade route."

"Good Lord," the young brunette replied as she made the sign of the cross and turned white. "Did you call the police?"

"Yes, they're on their way. But have you seen anything out of the ordinary?"

"No, but then again I wouldn't know what to look for."

"Anything that doesn't look like it'd fit for a parade." I took a breath and organized my thoughts; sometimes when I get hyper my thinking gets jumbled, like a bag of marbles. "But then again I'm not sure what would stand out except for Santa Claus, the Easter Bunny, and pilgrims to appear in the parade, but that will be way too obvious Sister. You're a woman of faith. Did anything look odd or feel off or wrong to you?"

"No." She shook her head. Her dark blue habit and gold cross necklace swung with her head's movements.

"My source told me the party responsible is an Irish terrorist, Northern Ireland that is. He's a zealot and his bombings are always public, brutal, and he tries to killas many people as possible."

"Holy Mother, pray for us."

"Yeah, I think we need God and all the saints on our side. There's always a lot of kids at the parade every year."

"You said he'll wait till there's a large crowd to cause maximum number of causalities?"

I nodded, "Yes, according to my source."

"What about at the end of the parade route, at Hamburg and O'Connell streets? The police blocked off the intersection and there's always a decent sized crowd on all four corners, and afterwards a number of parade goers and participants got to McCarthy's. They say it's the unofficial 'City Hall' of the First Ward and the Valley."

"Oh, God, Sister, I'm going up there now. If you're right that's where the bomber is planning on striking. Can you do me a favor?"

"What can I do to help?"

"If you see any cops around here tell them what I told you and my lawyer, Aldrich Kaufman, he knows everything going down and reached out to the police and the bomb squad." She agreed as I started to run back to my car when I heard Sister Catherine wish me luck then my phone vibrated—Crystal again. No sense putting it off. "Hello."

"John, what the hell are you thinking having Aldrich call me…"

I moved with a purpose and interrupted Crystal's rant before she really got going. "Listen, this has nothing to do with us, your decision, or our personal problems. Didn't Aldrich tell what's going down?"

"Yes, he did, but I know how he can embellish things, so I'm inclined to take what he said with more than a grain of salt."

I rushed past a family with three little ones, one being an infant, who was pushed back and forth in her stroller by who I assumed was her father. "Crystal, I didn't call Aldrich, he called me wanting to know if you were going to the parade. Where are you?"

We'd been going through a lot the past two weeks, just as we'd been through a lot this past year. Crystal knew when I was kidding, when I was serious, and when the situation was dangerous. She also knew I still cared, hell, no matter what, I'd always care.

Her voice changed and she sounded scared. "Maria, Emily, and I on Hamburg Street. Emily said this is a great place to watch the parade. Are you saying Aldrich was telling me the truth?"

"Crys, we wouldn't joke around with something like this. You know me better than that." I made sure I was inside my car before I even thought about using the B-word. "The three of you get the hell out of there. We've already called the police, but according to Aldrich, this Chulainn will go for the maximum number of bodies he can get, and I've no idea where his bomb is. But I think it could be near the end of the parade route. Where exactly are you?"

"We're near a pizzeria at the intersection of, uh, let me see, South Park and Hamburg."

I knew exactly where they were. "Okay stay there, I'm headed to the area where I think the bomb is, if I'm right. You all should be safe." It was time to serious up since I had no idea what was going to happen. "Listen, ah Crystal, we'll talk later on and straighten things out, okay?"

"Right, John, you just be careful. Call me when you can, and John?"

"Yeah, kid?"

"I still love you."

"I love you, too."

I meant what I said, I just didn't know if my head and heart could find a middle ground. If they did then perhaps Crystal and I would too, but that was for another time.

I headed to McCarthy's but was forced to circle around the parade route and go from Perry Street to Louisiana Street and down to Republic Street, where I parked alongside the train tracks, across from McCarthy's.

I lucked out and beat the parade but I didn't know by how much. Those floats weren't going to break any land-distance speed records. Outside my car, I double checked my gun and made sure she was snug in my belt, and for some reason I began to feel like Gary Cooper's Will Kane in *High Noon* as I started walking up Hamburg towards O'Connell Street.

As I passed the bar, there were a couple of women standing out in front, watching towards the intersection and the parade. One was a redhead with a ponytail, dressed in a green top, blue jeans and sneakers. The brunette wore a white top, with a green, button down sweater and jeans and sneakers as well. The redhead waved at me and yelled, "Happy Saint Patrick's Day!" I gave a half a wave then crossed towards them.

"Excuse me," I said trying keep up the charm.

"Hi," the red head said.

"Excuse me, ladies, I was wondering have either of you seen a new cable box anywhere around the neighborhood?"

They glanced towards each other and both shook their heads. "Sorry I don't think so," the redhead said.

"Listen, it's kinda important. My name's John Seraph and it's really important I find this cable box."

The brunette extended her hand, "I'm Elizabeth Nyx, this is Shannon Basom. We work here at the bar." I shook their hands. "Can you tell us what's this about?"

"Well, it's complicated, but essentially a new cable was installed around here. I don't have an exact address and I need to check it out. Some of the electrical work may be faulty, someone might get hurt."

98

One of my best talents, folks, being able whip up some South Buffalo Bull on the spot when I need to, thank you Dad and Grandpa.

Elizabeth said, "Wouldn't Time Warner have all that information?"

"Normally, yeah, but the installer is on vacation, and his work orders got lost at the office. The boss has been trying to reach him, but he's out of the country. Right now he's on his way to some fishing trip in a county in Scotland. So the boss sent me out and to find it. All we're positive of is the general four block radius."

Shannon said, "I'm surprised your computers can't tell you."

"Ordinarily they would but we think something wasn't hooked up properly, which may be a contributing factor to the problem."

"I don't recall seeing any new boxes around here," Shannon said. "Liz?"

"No, no I haven't, Mr. Seraph. Ah, tell me, are you going to stay for the parade?"

"I'd like to, but this is a safety issue we're talking about, so I need to find that box, and get it taken care before anyone gets hurt."

"Admirable. Well, if you have the time be sure to stop by the bar. We're running specials on lamb stew, corned beef and cabbage, and Guinness, of course."

"Sounds good. If I find that box fast enough I may make lunch with you guys. Thanks, I'll see you later."

As I walked up the block I scanned around for anything that looked out of place, but I kept an eye out for a cable box that didn't fit. I passed by a number of narrow, two story houses, mostly to my left. To the right, past the bar and two more houses, was a large grassy field with a paved, arched parking lot. It looked like the site might have been a neighborhood gas station at one point, a long time ago. It was full up and I was willing to bet an order of Buffalo wings and beef on weck sandwiches, most of the drivers were up ahead of me at the intersection. Past a few more houses, on all four corners were men, women, and children out to show their Irish pride. Just then my cell vibrated again, this time it was Aldrich.

"Any luck, Jonathan?"

"No, how about on your end? Your sources dig up anything on what the bastard looks like?"

"Not really, but there was one thing though."

"What's that councilor?"

"At first the authorities believed Chulainn was killed in that blast that killed those officers, because they found a dead man near the blast point, but they realized it was a smokescreen, to give them time for a possible escape."

"Right."

"When they examined the remains of the farmhouse, they found a number of women's clothes and products, and believed these were items a possible female acquaintance left behind."

"Are you suggesting Chulainn's a woman?"

"You know better than most how dangerous the female of the species can be. It is not out of the realm of possibility, son."

"Anything else?"

"Yes, Chulainn always leaves his mark."

"What's that?"

"Somewhere at or near the site of each bombing is some image of a red, left hand and thumb, opened up. It is the symbol of the Red Hand Defenders."

"I'll keep my eyes open."

"Good, I contacted the New York State Police's Bomb Disposal Unit directly, informed them of the situation, and the seriousness of the threat. The cavalry is on the way, but I am not positive when they will arrive."

As we talked, I looked around for anything that looked out of place and knew I had a starting point, the cable box. I also knew those invisible fences had their limits and suspected Chulainn placed the device for the collar on a car or float in the parade. I didn't think the bastard could slip it into a Shriners's car without the driver noticing or in with a marching band. Which meant the bomb itself had to be along the parade route.

"Aldrich, I think the bomb is near the end of the route, you said it yourself; bloody and public and he goes for a maximum body count. Aldrich, there are a lot of families here."

"I understand. I will call my associate in the State Police right away and pass your theory onto him. I will make him understand how imperative it is they check the end of the route first. I suspect the regular, uniformed officers can check the rest of the route since we know a cable box is being used."

"Right, keep me up to date." I scanned around anywhere I could, which was tougher the closer I got to the intersection.

The four corners were jammed with folks and out in front were kids, toddlers, and babies in strollers, all to get the best seats in the house. I marched down Hamburg Street and finally I stopped when I got to a crowd of people standing in front of a pair of orange and white, workhorse traffic barricades. Over the crowd, I saw another pair of barricades to my left, blocking off O'Connell, giving the parade traffic one way to head, down Hamburg, then make a left at the intersection. It was just then that I ran out of time, coming down Hamburg were the lead marchers, carrying a street-wide banner. "Oh shit."

I had to think fast, hell I had to think like a mad bomber. If I wanted to kill as many folks as I could, with this sized crowd, I'd go for a corner shot. The size of the homemade claymore could easily kill anyone on the other three corners. It was a hunch, but it was all I had, so I began looking for a either a cable box and or a red hand symbol.

I went left and looked around, bumping into folks and apologizing. Some might have thought I sampled the Irish whiskey a wee bit early, considering I was looking around instead of at the approaching marching band. I got to the corner and didn't see anything, moved a bit and backed into someone, then heard, "You all right, lad?"

"Sorry, I'm…" I looked up and took step back because in front of me was a huge fella, who was older than me, and had to be six foot ten and three hundred pounds easy. He had dark red, thick hair, a Paul Bunyan like beard and was wearing a black, down vest, over a red and black flannel shirt, with faded blue jeans and work boots.

"Uh, sorry, I'm looking for something."

"No problem, lad," he said and offered his hand which I shook. "Patrick O'Malley, make it Pat."

"Uh, John Seraph."

"Excuse me, but you look like a man with something on your mind."

"Yeah, I do. I have."

"Comes from being a bartender. It's just second nature. What's your problem, lad?"

"Pat, you work around here by any chance?"

"That I do. Been tending bar just down the block for eight years now after I came over from Ireland."

"Have you seen anything peculiar or unusual up this way?"

"Like what?"

"Oh, maybe a new cable box hanging up around here somewhere or some graffiti, a left hand in red?"

"Funny you should say that." Pat pointed across the street at the telephone pole. "The boys from Time Warner boys must've put it up sometime this week."

"Oh, God." I ran behind the crowd as the parade got closer, and there was no sign of the bomb squad. I didn't realize Pat was right behind me, until I flew around the crowd and tried to shove my way through the line of people on the sidewalk. I looked for the box and there it was. Dull grey, plastic, zip tied to the telephone pole, with two black ties, and labeled with a triangular, yellow and black High Voltage sticker. Nice touch, no one would want to mess with it, and the cable and power companies wouldn't touch it since it didn't need maintenance.

As I moved closer I saw it, on the sidewalk, in spray paint was an open palmed red hand. It was well defined, with crisp lines. I suspected Chulainn used a template. "Excuse me, pardon me, coming through." I said all the right things but it was like going up K-2 in my boxers, then without warning a hand pulled me back and Pat demanded an answer.

"I see you're in a hurry, son, but ya' can't be shoving women and the little ones around like that."

"Jesus, Pat, Figlio di puttana! We don't have time for this shit." I only curse in Italian when I'm really angry or upset.

"Excuse me, John?" He seemed taken aback.

I grabbed the older, bigger man and pulled him away from the crowd, closer to the first house near us. "I need your help so don't panic and don't react. I can't get into it all right now, but I think there's a bomb in that cable box. If it goes off it'll kill most of these people."

"Holy Mother."

"Believe me, she and her boss already know."

"You're not joking are you, lad, I see it in your face. We need to get these people out of here. Come on." Pat began to run back towards the crowd, I stopped him.

"Pat, we can't cause a panic. Look at all the kids here. Besides, the terrorist, who's from Northern Ireland, may be watching, if he's watching he may have a remote detonator. So we gotta be careful."

"God damn his soul to hell."

We both looked up towards the intersection and the approaching marchers, followed by the first of the floats, which had kids on it. "Think fast, Angelo," I muttered to myself. I didn't have a knife, so I couldn't cut the zip ties. I could shoot them, which could get the bomb off of the telephone pole, but that might start a massive panic. Ten-to-one people would get hurt and then I had a flash. "Pat, I need you to follow my lead. You know how those electric dog collars and fences work?"

"Of course, lad, What are you thinking?"

"My source said the bomber is using one. I'm thinking he placed the collar portion on one of the parade vehicles, because the bomb is a homemade claymore, if it was on a float or car it'd kill those riding it ..."

"But not all the spectators—I see where you're headed. What do you need me to do?"

"I'm going to stop that parade. Once I do, you gotta check each car and float for what looks like one of those devices for dog collars."

"How you gonna stop the procession, lad?"

"Like this." I flashed him my gun. Pat gave me an anxious, worried look. I pulled it of my belt and said, "I don't want to use it, but I gotta stop the parade. You want out, I understand. I'll stop things until the bomb squad gets here."

"Pat paused for a moment then said, "All that is necessary for the triumph of evil is that good men do nothing."

"Edmund Burke." I opened the cylinder and dumped the rounds into my hand, pocketed them, then put my hand cannon back inside my belt. I wasn't going to take a chance of an accidental discharge and someone getting shot, so I had to bluff big time.

"You read the right books."

"Yeah, but my lips get tired." Pat smiled at that. "Ready?" He nodded, and I said, "Okay, Geronimo!"

Everything went out of my head as I charged up toward the intersection, then forced and pushed my way through the masses, yelling out I needed to get through and there was an emergency. I know folks looked at me and some began telling me to cool it and some pretty rude things, but eventually I was able to shove my way past everyone and through the barricade at the corner, just past the bomb and flew into the intersection.

I ran through the marchers, who'd been smiling and waving to the crowds. I had no idea what anyone was doing behind me as I ran up the middle of Hamburg Street, right at the parade vehicles coming at me. I think I moved faster than they were.

As I got close, I held up my arms to get the attention of the driver of a dark green, Cadillac convertible. It had white and light green streamers and carnations lining it, with a well-made up woman sitting on the back top, where the top reclines. She looked like some sort of prom queen. The driver began honking at me and waved me off and yelled at me, but I couldn't hear him over the marching band, the engine of the Caddy, the parade participants, and those there to enjoy the show. I was waving my arms, making an X, criss-crossing pattern. The driver kept honking and he slowed, but didn't stop. I charged towards the car and ran to the driver's side. "You gotta stop!"

"Get outta the road, you moron," he yelled back.

"Stop this car! There's a bomb up ahead!"

"Wha, bullshit!"

The woman behind him heard me and looked down. She got a scared look on her face. These days it pays to listen. "Are you serious?"

"Yes, I am!" I tried to keep pace with the car which wasn't easy. "There's a bomb that'll kill most of the people up ahead! Now stop! The bomb squad's coming!"

"Yeah, right," the driver said, dismissing me.

The girl said, "Toby, maybe we should listen."

"This is no game man," I said.

"Bullshit," he said back, then tried to speed up. We were on top of the intersection, I had to make my move now. I darted back in front of the car, pulled out my .44, took my stance, and aimed it right at the driver. Here's where I prayed I played enough poker and knew how to bluff well enough.

The car's breaks locked up and squealed tightly, then I heard people yelling out at me. Toby got a whole new appreciation for the situation. He just lifted his hands off the steering wheel. Just then, I saw Pat run up to the car and look it over. He looked around it, under both sides as best he could, then shook his head at me. Finally he ran to the huge float behind the car.

I shook my head as I mouthed "Don't Move!" to Toby, then I heard people on the sidewalks beginning to lose control, as others thought it was a show. I didn't take my eyes off Toby. I had to sell it, as if my Mateba was loaded. I hoped I could bluff well enough.

Just at that second a couple police officers came running up at me, with their weapons out and aimed at me. I could see their stances through my peripheral vision. From my left, I heard, "Drop the piece and lay down on the ground, arms spread!"

"I can't do that," I yelled back without taking my eyes off of Toby.

He repeated himself, "Drop the gun and lay down!"

"I can't. There is a bomb ahead of us. The triggering device is on one of these vehicles, if they go any further, seven pounds of C-4 will go off with enough shrapnel to kill everyone here! The state bomb squad's coming!" As a Scotsman once said, "The haggis just hit the fire." I could hear the masses around us begin to bounce the word bomb around like beachballs at a concert. *Here we go!*

"My name's John Seraph. In the telephone pole behind me, there's a fake cable box. Inside of it is C-4, with ball bearings, screws and rat poison. It's wired to go off if a singling device gets too close. Up ahead someone's looking for the device. Contact the state cops, but if the parade goes on people will die damnit! I'm not moving until the bomb squad gets here!"

From my right side I heard, "Jesus, what we do Larry!"

"We contact the Sergeant," the first unie said. I turned my head left and saw him, with his left hand he spoke into his shoulder mounted speaker walkie-talkie. I knew I was going to be in a lot of trouble for this stunt, but I also knew Aldrich could straighten it out, I hoped. After a garbled, burst of static, I heard the first officer say, "The bomb disposal unit's coming. We gotta clear this area now! But before anything else…"

"Thank God!" I handed my gun over to the first officer, who checked it and was surprised.

"It's not loaded?"

I shook my head. "I didn't want to hurt anyone."

Just then four blue and whites came screaming down O'Connell from Louisiana and stopped before the intersection. The officers cleared the civilians from the area and folks were scared, but the police kept order and got everyone out of the area without any major panic, then I surrendered to the first officer. Toby was told to put his car in neutral, then he and the lady were lead to safety. I placed my hands in front of me, ready to be handcuffed. "Sorry for the trouble, but I didn't know what else to do."

He cuffed me from behind, then asked, "Okay, so where's this bomb?"

I turned around and gestured towards the phone pole. "Over there, the cable box is a phony. The damn thing's a homemade claymore."

"You said someone's looking for the trigger?"

"Yeah, up ahead on the cars and floats. His name's Pat O' Malley. Big guy with a red beard, dressed in a red and black, flannel shirt."

Just then we saw the State Bomb Squad vehicles pull up behind the four squad cars and I silently thanked God. Two officers who just arrived, ran towards us with Pat keeping pace.

"John," Pat yelled to me. The arresting officer tried to stop him, but his escort cleared him. Pat was trying to catch his breath, "You were right lad. Back there on one of the cars is what looks like a small black box, zip tied to a car bumper in the rear."

The police led us up the block and the first officer asked, "Sir, you didn't touch it?"

Pat shook his head. "No, I'm not daft. Now do the sensible thing and release our friend. If he didn't stop the parade you'd be collecting body parts thanks to that damn maniac."

"Maybe so, but the way he did it …"

"I know, I know. But I'd like to see what you'd do if you were in my boots." Before anyone could say anything else another police car came screaming towards us. It was an unmarked, beige, detectives' unit, with a cherry on top of the roof. I felt a wave of relief when I saw Detective Hannah Chancellor get out. Like every other time I've seen her, she was dressed in her white rain coat, and looked more stylish than a homicide detective should. She always dressed well, but I never understood how she could afford her wardrobe on a detective's salary.

I gave her my biggest, warmest smile, of course it was for real, but it was one of my B.S. grins, too. "Hi Detective. So what brings you here? I'd shake but I'm a bit tied up right now."

As she approached us, she shook her short, platinum blonde haircut. "Officer, you can release him." She showed her ID to my new friend.

"Are you sure, Detective?"

"Mr. Seraph may get into some big messes and to many he's a pain in the ass, but he's also one of the good guys. Uncuff him."

After I was freed, I rubbed my wrists, "Thank. That was starting to pinch. How come you're here?"

"I have bomb disposal experience, in the Army I got E.O.D. training. Even though it's the state boys show, I'm here to supervise and lend any support. Now, John, what's the story?"

I gave her the complete rundown, made the proper introductions, pointed out the claymore and the Red Hand symbol, then Pat walked us back to where he found the triggering collar.

From a safe distance we watched as two officers set up a radio frequency signal jammer. Once that was done, they sent in a bomb disposal robot. While that was going on, two other boys from the bomb squad went to the car with the collar, wearing the E.O.D. suits, just in case. They examined the device and eventually determined it was safe to cut the zip ties, and deactivated it. Meanwhile, the robot did it's job, scanned the device, then the two officers in the suits went in, with a bomb containment chamber. It seemed to take forever, but eventually they clipped the zip ties, then, as if they were holding a newborn, tenderly placed the claymore into the chamber, and sealed it. It was decided it was best to detonate on site, which is just what they did, once everyone was at least a block back and under cover. Even that far away, I felt a ringing in my ears after detonation, which rocked the neighborhood.

Everything calmed down and the E.O.D. boys cleared the area, then the investigation began. The parade vehicles stayed where they were; the car that had the collar was gone over seven ways from Sunday by the CSIs and the E.O.D. personnel, and I pointed out to everyone the Red

Hand graffiti on the sidewalk.

Finally, Pat and I were released, and I got my gun back. The police weren't thrilled with my actions, as usual, but they said I saved lives. I was sitting on the hood of my car when I was approached by Chancellor. "John, we'll have more questions for later on. And we're going to want to speak to Mr. Kaufman, as well. What I don't understand is why you didn't just let us handle things?"

"A friend of mine was attending the parade. I wasn't sure where she was, and I wasn't going to take a chance. Besides, Aldrich called your people." I sat there with arms crossed, wondering.

"John, what is it?"

"Chulainn."

"What about him? Now that we stopped him the FBI and Interpol will be called in. We'll get him."

"You don't understand, Detective, Aldrich told me Chulainn was always there to watch, to make sure. He's here somewhere close, I can feel it."

"Where do you think he's at?"

"Well, you got more experience in this area than me, but he'd want to be close, but not too close. He'd want to be mobile, in case something hit the fan, I'm thinking."

"Right."

"Let's talk to Pat. He might have an idea." Chancellor let out a groan.

"I thought you had something there, John," she said as we crossed the street, went past the Old First Ward Brewing Company's brew house, which was crammed full of locals, and headed towards McCarthy's.

I shook my head. "I don't have a feakin' clue, Detective. I'm tired, frustrated, and hungry. Come on." Inside McCarthy's the celebration was in full swing. You'd think the Irish kicked the English off the Emerald Isle finally.

"Ay, there's the lad himself," Pat announced from behind the bar. "A round on me, in honor of our new friend, John Seraph, who may not be a son of Mother Ireland, but is a welcomed friend to us all." That got a round of cheers and applause from the huge crowd there. Suddenly, I was getting slaps on the back, handshakes, and offers for shots and drinks. I was appreciative and I didn't want to offend anyone, so I let Chancellor take charge.

She waved her badge and excused us as we made our way to the bar. After waving Pat over, we had to yell to let him know we needed to speak to him. He came around and we all went outside. "Sorry to pull you away, Mr. O'Malley, but we had a couple more questions for you."

"Ah sure, no problem, Officer. What else can I tell you all?"

"Pat," I said. "Have you seen any new faces around here in the past week or so? Any new barflys or folks hanging around the neighborhood?"

"Nah, lad." He shook his head. "It's just been our regulars, day in and day out. You don't suspect one of them, that'd be daft."

"Well, Mr. O'Malley, someone planted that bomb, now you tell us what's a bomber look like," Chancellor responded.

"You make good sense lass," he laughed. "You don't have a bit of Ireland in you somewhere, do ya?"

"Not a drop, half Finish, half German."

"Well, we won't be holding that against ya," he joked. "But to answer ya, the only new face around here's been Lizzy, but she's been working with us for about three and a half months now. So it couldn't be her."

I looked towards the bar, then saw Elizabeth through the huge front window of the Brew House. Chancellor said, "John, what is it?"

"Just something Aldrich and I discussed before." I went closer towards the window and watched as Elizabeth was serving customers. She'd ditched her sweater, maybe it was too warm to wear while working. I walked right up onto the frozen grass, next to the air conditioning unit, and stared right at her. She turned, laughed at something a customer told her and then I saw it. On her collar was a lapel pin, the symbol of the Red Hand Defenders. "It's her," I said under my breath.

Chancellor came up behind me, and asked again, "John, what is it?"

"Call for backup, it's her!" I pointed out her lapel pin. "She's Chulainn!" Without thinking I ran, jumped over the four foot gate, then down the cement walkway alongside the brew house. I found a door on the side and remember hearing Chancellor yell for me to stop.

Nyx must have seen me, because as I forced my way inside, I saw her bolting out the back fire door. I followed her, pushing and shoving customers out of my way and went after her. I lost sight of Chancellor and Pat, but when I came around the side of the beer house, I saw Nyx running and crossed the intersection of Hamburg and Republic. At the same time a freight train was approaching the intersection and as Nyx ran over the fork in the tracks, the train's horn blared out shaking the neighborhood and vibrating through my skull.

Pat and a couple unies came running down Hamburg towards us, and I heard Chancellor yelling behind me, and getting closer. I kept charging and saw Nyx reach into her pocket for something. "Put it down," Chancellor yelled out. I dodged in between a few cars and was within ten feet of her when Nyx pressed a small button. All I heard was an electronic chirp, then a helluva explosion went off in front of me. It erupted about eight feet in front of me, coming up from underground. The last thing I clearly remember was seeing a manhole cover being launched into the wild, blue yonder, seeing Nyx run to other side of the tracks and me being knocked on my ass. After that I was stunned and couldn't move.

Ten minutes later, I came out of the States of Null and Void. I had a major ringing in my ears and frontal lobe headache that was a bitch. The next thing I heard was a wailing of some kind, and for a second I thought it was the Banshees coming, but I know I had too much Irish on my mind. Especially when I saw it an approaching ambulance. Pat and the unies got caught up in the blast, but I took the lion's share.

Once all five of my senses came back and I did a limb count, I realized I was being helped into the ambulance. The paramedics began giving me a check over and I was all right for the most part, except for some bleeding out of my ears. At first, everyone thought my eardrums were shattered, but I lucked out.

They checked me for a concussion as Chancellor and I talked. "Is everyone else okay?" One of the EMT's flashed a light into my eyes.

"Good, eyes look clear."

"Yeah, except for the jackass who charged in like John Wayne," Chancellor said.

"You're such a comfort in my time of need, Detective. What about

110

Nyx, or Chulainn?"

Chancellor just shook her head, "She set up the blast as a distraction, just in case. Damned smart. She vanished after the train came through. Either she jumped on the train or vanished in the neighborhood on the other side of the tracks. Either way we've got people searching the area, also the FBI and Homeland Security is coming into the dance."

"Great, ten to one that bitch is in the wind already."

"You really think so?"

"Yeah, I'd bet my life on it."

* * * *

Well the EMTs said I was pretty lucky. I avoided any serious injuries, all I got was bruising, some sort of shockwave that hit me, and the biggest problem is my tailbone which is really sore from how I landed. I was released from the scene once my head cleared and stopped playing the Carol of the Belles.

Chancellor told me she and possibly a few federal agencies, and maybe an international agency might have questions for me, but that could all wait. By six o'clock I was back home, tired, hungry, and very, very sore.

I ordered a pizza from Jacobi's and made it my favorite; cheese, pepperoni, Italian sausage, green olives, ham, and pineapple. While I waited I checked my email and there was one with the Subject Title, CONGRATULATIONS & GOOD WORK.

I opened it and saw a video message had been sent to me. On the screen was a shadowy figure with a bright light behind 'him', if it was a him to begin with. "Good evening, Mr. Angelo, or perhaps I should call you Seraph. Please forgive me," he said. The voice was disguised by a voice distortion device. It was deep and had an electronic, heavy bass to it, and there was no way I could recognize the speaker.

"This is Hephaestus and I know this is rather unusual, I never communicate like this, but I felt it important to congratulate you on stopping Chulainn this afternoon. I understand she escaped and that the authorities have begun a manhunt for her. If she contacts me I will let Mr. Kaufman know and he can reach out to his contacts in the Buffalo law enforcement community. She may be a client, but there are certain things I cannot condone, and bombing a group of innocent children is unacceptable by any standards. If she crosses my path I promise you, I will take care of matters. You did excellent work today, you should be proud. I will be in touch."

This was a surprise to say the least. I saved the video to my laptop, not sure what my next step was going to be, but it looks I may gained both a new ally and a new enemy. God help me.

THE END

Easter:
It's Rabbit Season

After *Family Plots*

Here's to egg hunts, chocolate bunnies, and all of the Easter Bunny's helpers

April 18th

To say I've an interesting life is an understatement, I think the term FUBAR is now dead on. It stands for Fucked Up, Beyond All Recognition, which is a perfect description of my relations and my love life at various times. For example, I just dealt with a situation that could've been written by Janet Evanovich for one of her Stephanie Plum books, and I got into a fiasco which could have been Benny Hill sketch, thanks in part to my part-time girlfriend, Bobbie Bedell.

I met Bobbie at Cazenovia Park on Easter Sunday, our plans were she'd cover a charity Easter egg hunt and write up the story for the *Buffalo News*, then I was going to take her to brunch at the Hamburg Casino at the Buffalo Raceway. Scottish poet Robert Burns wrote, *The best laid schemes of mice and men Often go awry.* I think my life is a living example of that.

* * * *

Western New York Heroes is a non-profit, charity organization dedicated to making a major difference for veterans, servicemen and women, and their families. They offer financial assistance for disabled, returning and recovering soldiers, and multiple grant programs. Grants go to help veterans and their families with rent, mortgage, utilities, food, holiday meals, and medical bills. The Christmas toy drives, and School Backpack drives, are their biggest fund raisers, but this was their first Easter egg hunt. They had clowns, face painting, a magician, a petting zoo, raffle prizes, and of course the Easter Bunny himself was scheduled to be there for the egg hunt.

Now Bobbie normally covers the crime beat for the *Buffalo News*, but she agreed to help out and cover what some reporters might consider a lesser puff piece, on the cute and fuzzy beat, because about a third of the paper's staff was hammered with the flu that hit the city. I lucked out and didn't catch this newest strain, which I account to getting a flu shot in December and using hand sanitizer. Of course, carrying around a bottle of hand sanitizer with me once saved my life, but that's another story.

The kids and the WNY Heroes group lucked out, too, because the weather cooperated, as if it had been bribed. The last real wet day we had around here was Palm Sunday. The rest of Holy Week the sun was out, and temperatures rose from the mid-fifties to the low seventies, giving all the ground around here a chance to dry out. If not, there could have been mud puddles and saturated meadows all over the park and ruin the egg for the kids.

Taking up one hundred and eighty-six acres, affectionately known in South Buffalo simply as Caz, in nice weather, the park is always full of people, usually involved in some sort of sports activity. The park features a nine hole golf course, four baseball/softball diamonds, three soccer fields, four tennis courts, two basketball courts, and a swimming pool, and a ice rink that are both at the Tosh Collins Community Center. So it's not uncommon on evenings or weekends to find folks taking in a round of golf, a little league baseball or youth soccer game. And that's all on top of the splash pads spray jets and playground kids flock to in the spring, summer, and fall.

Cazenovia Park also boasts one of the more mature stands of trees in the city and recovered impressively after the Lake Storm "Aphid" a.k.a.

'the October Storm' that took place on Friday, October, 13th, 2006.

Cazenovia Park is less than seven minutes away from my apartment, so the drive over was short. I pulled off Abbott Road, onto the Warren Spahn Way, then parked in a small lot near the soccer fields where I found fifteen cars already there. Most of the parents were parked on either side of the road, just past the bridge over Cazenovia Creek in the heart of the park, and there were about thirty cars lining the road. I walked over the bridge and crossed the Way; once I cleared a huge hedge the playground came into clear view and I saw the setup.

There was a huge bounce castle in blue, yellow, and red next to the spray pad, which wasn't running, and there were some parents watching the action inside the rocking castle. By the playground were volunteers dressed as clowns, face painting kids, making them appear like rabbits, chicks, and turned some faces into dyed Easter eggs. In the center of the park is the Cazenovia Casino, where volunteers set up a stage and several chairs for Mario the Magnificent's magic show, several tables for raffle prizes, which included several smaller three inch chocolate bunnies of milk, white, dark, and orange varieties. There were also some boys and girls Easter baskets and candy sets from local chocolate makers Niagara Candy, but the main prize was a thirty-six inch, fifteen pound milk chocolate bunny, carrying a basket of candy Easter eggs on his back. As I scoped out the prizes, I thought it was a good thing the temperature was in the mid-upper sixties, any warmer and the term meltdown could take a whole new meaning for the bunnies.

Eventually, I found Bobbie and she looked amazing. She'd gotten her hair styled again since I last saw her. The girl could turn styling into an Olympic event. It was still her natural auburn, but now she was sporting a halo braid and trailing ponytail. She was wearing tan slacks, a white blouse, with the sleeves rolled up. Over her blouse she wore a black, western vest with a flowery pattern on it, and black loafers.

As I got closer I overheard her talking; she was in the middle of interviewing an older, white haired woman who dressed like she came right out central casting for the movie *Easter Parade*. The older woman was Ophelia Elden, a lead representative of WNY Heroes and in charge of the egg hunt. Elden explained where the proceeds would go to and who the money would help, and gave the real credit to her supporting staff and volunteers, and thanked the people of Buffalo and surrounding neighborhoods, like West Seneca and Lackawanna for their generosity. Besides Bobbie, there were some camera crews and reporters covering the story from Channels 2, 4, 7, and the Time Warner News Channel.

After the interview finished, and the camera crews went to get some shots of the activities going on, Bobbie made the introductions. "Thanks for the interview."

"My pleasure, Ms. Bedell." I took a step closer to Bobbie, who wrapped her arms around my right bicep after she put her digital recorder in away in her purse. "And who's this deliciously looking, handsome, young man?" Elden asked smiling deviously. The woman was obviously of good taste and impeccable breeding.

"Ah, Mrs. Ophelia Elden, this is Mr. John Seraph, a very special friend of mine. John meet, Mrs. Ophelia Elden, organizer of the Easter Egg hunt."

"A pleasure to meet you, ma'am," I extended my hand.

"Oh, this one has manners," Elden answered back. She shook my hand. "And he's awfully cute. My advice, dear, run away with him," she said with a flirting tone.

I smiled back. "Hmm Ophelia huh?"

"I know my mother was an English teacher. It's dreadful."

"Actually, John is studying to become a teacher himself," Bobbie told Elden.

"Well, really, that is something. Mother found it a reward career, she may not have gotten rich, but she always said it was fulfilling."

"I know what she meant," I said. "I tutor elementary students from time to time, as part of some of my requirements. Actually Ophelia's the name in one of my favorite Shakespearean plays. I always liked that girl."

"A gentleman and scholar I see. At least you read the right books. You two must excuse me. I need to circulate and make the rounds so please enjoy yourselves while you're here."

"Thank you," I said and we watched Elden begin to talk to parents and supporters. "I don't think she knows I only came by to meet you."

"Well, we'll keep that our little secret," Bobbie said.

"So her mother didn't make much teaching, huh."

"No." Bobbie shook her head. "Mrs. Elden made her fortune the old fashioned way, she married rich."

"Ahh, well, that also works. It did for my cousin."

We began to walk around the park watching the many events and I asked about her article. "So when's your piece due?"

"I need to post by eleven to make the morning edition. Now, can we still stop by your place before brunch?"

"Sure. You can use my laptop to email your story into the paper, and then we eat." We strolled back towards our cars, past all the activities when Bobbie dropped a bit of a surprise on me.

"Guess what?"

"What?" I asked as we passed under a large oak's shade.

"You're getting a roommate tonight."

"What?" I was stunned for a moment, felt myself stop and actually had to be dragged by Bobbie.

"You heard me, handsome, I'm sleeping over and we're going to spend the next two days together. It's been too long since we spent any time together and we're overdue." Before I could say anything we heard an eruption of crying. It was a little boy, then just as surprisingly a tan car screamed its way down the Warren Spahn, cut right and headed up towards Seneca Street.

Several volunteers, parents, and their children all looked to the little boy, and that included Bobbie and me. We ran over, which was a short jog. When we reached him his mother had him in her arms and did her best to console him. The little guy was dressed for the day, in a white, short sleeve shirt and blue dress shorts. His mother lifted him up in her arms saying "It's all right Jerry, shhh, we'll get you another basket."

People asked the typical questions: "What happened?", "Is he alright?", and "Did he get hurt?" Finally, the young and attractive mother, whose name I later learned was Sarah, said, "He's okay but some animal pulled up in his car and took Jerry's Easter basket."

Elden finally caught up to the small crowd and was brought up to speed. "I'm so sorry to hear that. I'm positive we can do something to help your son out." Elden took hold of Sarah's arm and told her Jerry would get another Easter basket. "There are still plenty of Easter eggs around the park. If you come with me I'll see to it that your son's all taken care of, my dear."

The crowd began to break up and the murmurings went from "that poor boy", to "it's super they're taking care of him", to a few wanting to find whoever stole Jerry's basket and performing a number things to him. The suggestions ran the gamut from beating the living shit out of him to being chained to car bumper and dragged all over South Buffalo. All right. I admit that one was mine. I've got a zero tolerance for anything done to kids.

"That's something," Bobbie said after the crowd scattered.

"Yeah, why would someone stop in the middle of the park and grab a kid's basket?" I asked rhetorically.

"No idea," Bobbie said as she resumed wrapping her arms around mine. "I somehow doubt this requires your talents or calling in anyone from your father's businesses."

"Yeah you're right," but I had a nagging feeling I couldn't explain away. We crossed the street and as I double checked for traffic something in the street caught my eye. "What the hell?" I said out loud.

"What's wrong, John?"

"Down there." We turned left, towards the tennis court and basketball courts, and I pointed towards them. "Look!"

On the grass, about fifteen yards from all the courts, was a light blue Easter basket. I began walking towards it with Bobbie in tow.

"John, what it is?"

As we got closer we could see it clearer. Inside the wicker basket, which still held plastic Easter grass, were a number of colorful, plastic Easter eggs. Nearby there were a couple laying on real, green grass. "John," Bobbie started to ask, almost hesitantly, "You don't think that's..."

I bent down to collect the spilled eggs and pick up the basket. "Yeah, Bobbie, I do. Before we head to my place let's find Sarah and Jerry."

A few minutes later we found mother and child hunting for plastic eggs, which were filled with candy and small toys. "Excuse me," I said as Bobbie and I came upon them. Sarah looked at us approaching. "By any chance is this Jerry's?"

Confused and surprised at the same time, Sarah was grateful. "Yes, it is," she answered as she reached out for it. "Where'd you find it?"

"Near the basketball courts."

"Well, thank you. I'm sorry I didn't get your names," she said as she kept an eye on Jerry.

"This is Bobbie Bedell. My name's John Seraph," I said as we extended our hands, which Sarah shook.

"Jerry, look at what these nice people have for you."

He came running over from the rock wall in the playground and once he saw his first basket he got excited and nearly tripped running to us.

"Easy, Little Man," I said as Bobbie stifled her laughter. "Here you go, Happy Easter."

"What do you say, Jerry?" Sarah said.

"Thank you," Jerry said as he tried to hold both his old blue basket and new green basket. Sarah took the green basket then transferred the five eggs from it into the blue basket, bringing his total to thirteen. As Jerry went back to his hunting, we all watched him as we talked.

"It doesn't make sense," Sarah said.

"What?" Bobbie asked.

"Why would someone snatch an Easter basket, then get rid of it seconds later? Nothing was missing." Sarah said.

"You're right," Bobbie said. I could see her putting on her thinking cap. "Any thoughts, John?" Bobbie then explained to Sarah how I was to a degree, a somewhat amateur detective. Sarah then gave me what I can only describe as a desirable, predatory look. I'd seen it before from cougars at some of the football players and other top athletes at Buffalo State College. It was a look that made me feel like a combination of Robert B. Parker's *Spenser* and a two-hundred and ten pound side of beef. Bobbie must've recognized it too, because she immediately re-wrapped her arms around mine, letting Sarah know I was hands off.

"The only thing I can think of is whoever snatched Jerry's basket was looking for something and didn't find it, unless he's pazzo, crazy in the head." I made a gesture with my right hand closed, carrying it to my right temple, then exploding it open.

That scared Sarah a bit. "You don't think he was after Jerry?" Then she looked at her son who was still hunting for eggs, unaware of his mother's concerns.

Immediately, I said, "No." The thought wasn't the most comfortable, but if Jerry was the target, the driver could've just grabbed him and taken off. I kept that to myself. "I doubt it, but I'd keep Jerry within line of sight just to make sure."

We talked for a few minutes longer, then all of the sudden we heard a man yell out, "Stop you son-of-a-bitch!"

Bobbie and I ran closer to the road so we could see further down into the park. Coming right towards us was a tan car. It sped past us, and flew over the small bridge above the Cazenovia Creek, then once on the other side of the bridge, it stopped. I ran ahead of Bobbie, and watched as the car stopped for a moment, then out of the passenger's window flew a pink Easter basket. The car then laid rubber on its way towards Abbott Road.

I ran up to the basket, collected the eggs, with Bobbie right behind me. "John, what the hell's going on?" she asked as she caught her breath.

"Pretty lady, I have no freaking' clue but, I plan on finding out." It was then I realized my size eleven inch fist balled up on its own, once I realized it I knew I wanted to swing it into the driver's jaw.

We walked back towards the center of the park, where most of WNY Heroes set up their gear. Again, we found an upset child, a furious parent, and understanding and supportive people surrounding them, offering empathy and a new Easter basket. And once more I handed over an Easter basket with plastic Easter eggs to a grateful parent.

"Thanks, man," the father said to me as he shook my hand. Walter Vail was bald, sporting a French cut goatee, and looked a bit like a biker. He pulled off a classy biker look with black jeans, boots, black pin stripe shirt, and black leather vest.

"No problem, brother, I just wish I'd gotten a look at the son of a buck, or his license plate," I said. "Did you get a look at him?" I asked.

Walter shook his head. "Nah, but once I saw him snatch Abby's basket I lost it."

"And went into a blind rage I take it?" Walter nodded. "Understandable."

Walter gave Abby her basket back and the five year was thrilled to death. The little blonde, who was sporting her hair in bunches, was wearing a white and pink trimmed top and blue jeans, like Jerry was beyond happy to get his basket back.

We'd talked near one of the prep tables the volunteers were using, by the circular turnaround in the center of the park and the Casino. There were trailers for the bounce castle and the petting zoo people, and Mario the Magnificent's van was also parked there as well. Besides me, Walter, and Bobbie, Mrs. Elden joined us with some of her people. Included were; Marina Doron, who co-chaired the egg hunt and Karmela Roosevelt, Ray Ogden, and Kendall Horst who were all volunteers from WNY Heroes, and finally Chevy Kerwin, boyfriend to Marina. Although he wasn't an official volunteer, Chevy was there to help his significant other, having been there myself in the past I knew what that meant.

Bobbie stayed quiet and I got the feeling she was mentally taking notes to get another feature article, like it or not she's a newswoman and this was news. Besides she's was likely to get an exclusive since it looked like the TV camera crews had split. "Tell me, has anything like this happened at any of your events?" I asked.

Elden began shaking her head, which really shook her turkey neck. "No, Mr. Seraph. What concerns me is the safety of the children. Do you think we should call the police? I know you've assisted them in the past."

That caught me off guard. "Really?"

"Oh, my yes, I recall Ms. Bedell's articles and your involvement with the former Senator Addar."

I admit hearing that gave a boost to my ego, but I stayed on track. "I don't think the kids are in any danger. I'm thinking the basket snatcher is looking for something. I mean, he grabs the baskets, runs away then he tosses the baskets and eggs away."

"Makes sense," Ogden said as he scratched underneath his chin. I'd bet even money it itched, because of the light facial foliage on it and he wasn't used to it. "But what's he looking for?"

I let out a brief chuckle. "That's anyone's guess. Tell me what's in these eggs?"

"Oh, all sorts of Easter goodies," Elden said. "I'm not positive of the complete list, ah Marina?"

Marina ran down the list "We have jelly beans, chocolate miniatures, Easter stickers, and small dime store toys. You know anything that would fit into standard, plastic eggs."

"And where'd you get the eggs and goodies?" I asked.

"We got everything at Party City and Toys R Us," Karmela said. "Ray, Ken and I got everything last week."

"And nothing funny happened before, during, or after your shopping spree?"

"Nah," Ray said, "Then again it's not like we were looking for anything weird." He took his glasses and cleaned them with a handkerchief.

"Right." I let out a sigh of frustration. "It might be worth calling the police, tell them what's going on. The problem is it's not an emergency situation, but maybe they can get a car to either cruise the park or have one on stand by."

"I'll call them now," Karmela said. She went by one of the trucks for a quieter spot, as she pulled out her cell and called the police.

"Where'd you put together the eggs and goodies?"

"We all took some eggs, candies, and toys to our homes and filled them there, then we brought them straight here this morning," Marina said.

"How long did you all take to assemble the eggs?" I asked not sure where I was going.

"Not long," Ken said. "Maybe ninety minutes, give or take."

"It only took us about an hour," Marina said. "Chevy helped me and we made popcorn and tried to make a game of it. See who could get more done in a certain time period."

"Who won?" I asked.

"I did," she boasted.

"Did the winner get a prize?" I joked.

"Yes, but nothing I'm going to admit publically," Marina joked back.

I liked her sense of humor. That got almost everyone laughing and Bobbie flashed me her best flirty smile. I knew what that meant, but there'd be time for that later.

"Mr. Seraph, could I impose on you?" Elden asked, then she walked a few steps away to give us some privacy. Bobbie and I followed her over and listened to her request. "I am unsure if the police will be able to assist us, so I was wondering if you'd be willing to stay with us for a little while longer and keep an eye on things for us that is if you can spare us some time."

"Ms. Elden, I'd like to, but I made a promise to someone and I'm planning on keeping it."

"Please, Mr. Seraph, this is important, I implore you. If necessary, I can pay you for your time. I didn't bring my checkbook but..."

"Now wait a second ..." I suddenly became strongly offended. "I gave someone very special my word, one hundred million dollars isn't enough for me to break my word."

"John," Bobbie quietly said as she placed her hand on my shoulder. "It's all right, the buffet will be going on all day and there's plenty of time to get my article in." She gave me a look of quiet understanding and in that moment without saying another word, Bobbie told me it was alright.

I let out a sigh of frustration and understanding. "Okay, deal me in. How long's the egg hunt on for?"

"We're here till three o'clock," Elden said and automatically I looked at my watch. *Three and half hours to go.* "Thank you, you don't know what this means. I did not mean to offend you."

Elden told her people I'd be around to keep an eye on things, after Karmela informed us the police would cruise the park, but they couldn't position someone there since they were short staffed due to the holiday.

As everyone got back to the festivities, Bobbie and I walked towards the road and Ken came by us and said he was glad I was sticking around. "Yeah, man, I read all about you and what you did. Glad to have the help, there's been too many odd things happening."

"What do you mean, Ken?" Bobbie asked.

"First we had a break in at our office up on Wehrle Drive in Williamsville. Then my freakin' costume vanishes, and now this nut's running around," he answered.

"What costume?" I asked.

Ken looked around to make sure he wasn't heard. "I was supposed to be the Easter Bunny. Somebody broke into the office and ripped it off, you believe it?"

"When did that happen?" Bobbie asked.

"Yesterday at some point."

"Was anything else taken?"

"Nah, and now that I think about it, there wasn't any damage to the office."

Bobbie asked, "Did you get a replacement costume? It'll be a shame for the kids if the Easter Bunny can't make it."

"A couple of us been calling around. We might be able to get something fast, but I don't know. I hate to think to tell the kids the Easter Bunny can't arrive."

"Yeah, I know what you mean," I said aloud, but not really to anyone because my wheels were spinning like they were qualifying for NASCAR.

When alone, Bobbie said, "Okay I know that look too well, what are you thinking?"

"Nothing really, but I don't buy the timing."

"What do you mean?" she asked as we passed by the petting zoo which included sheep, guinea pigs, goats, rabbits, miniature horses, camels, and miniature donkeys. They were in wire fenced areas, with plenty of sawdust laid out and they had a lot of visitors, both tall people and short ones alike. As cute as some of the animals were, the stench from something's droppings hit me like a knockout punch. We quickly walked out of breathing distance.

"Someone starts snatching the baskets, then ditches them almost as fast as he grabs them up," I said.

"And you already figured they're looking for something. Right. Makes sense," Bobbie said. "So what about the timing?"

"The Easter Bunny costume."

"You think they're connected?"

"I don't think the timing of the costume, the break in, or the basket snatcher are coincidence."

"So now what?" Bobbie asked as she took my arm again, which I grew to enjoy.

"I've an idea and hope it works, but we're going to need some things," I said.

"Like what?"

"First, let's find Ophelia, then, have you ever gone fishing?" From the look on her face I knew Bobbie was puzzled. "I've heard when you go fishing, live bait works best."

Thirty minutes later, Bobbie and I were staked out by the playground equipment, we stayed by the kid's rock wall. This was one time I wanted to see and not be seen. Bobbie was really excited. "Boy, this is thrilling."

"Patience, Grasshopper," I joked. "Trust me, Bobbie, this is a lot better than pissing off a murderer and priming him to try and kill me."

"Understandable."

She came closer to me and placed her hand on mine. I stopped watching Abby Vail, who was running around and collecting eggs, about thirty feet away from us. Her father, Walter, was about ten feet away, talking to Marina and Elden. "Actually, when you got involved with those murders I really got scared for you and…" Bobbie stopped talking. She looked up and across the street. I looked and coming towards us was the Easter Bunny. Okay, maybe it wasn't the real Easter Bunny, but it was decent copy of one.

There he was, with white fur, wearing a multi Spring colored vest, with a pocket watch, and carrying a cane, that was really just attached to his right hand. He had big black eyes and his right ear was bent, which looked like it was designed that way on purpose.

"Looks like Ken got that replacement costume," Bobbie said.

"Maybe." I felt myself go into predator mode and my eyes locked onto the bunny. My fist balled up again out of instinct and Bobbie knew something was up.

"John, what's wrong?" The bunny got closer to Abby, who had a nearly full basket. I heard his feet flip-flop on the blacktop walking path that acts as a circulatory system for the park.

I turned to Bobbie. "Be very quiet, I'm hunting wabbits. It's wabbit season." I smiled like a predator, and I felt it. Ah, if the old man could see me now. I turned back as the Easter Bunny approached Abby and a couple other kids who were nearby. My left foot took a step forward, as if I were in a track and field event and preparing to launch myself at the sound of a starter's gun.

The bunny got closer and the kids flocked towards him. He patted heads and shook hands, then it happened; the Easter Bunny grabbed the four baskets from the kids around him and bolted. As soon as he ran, I exploded out of the gate.

The bunny tried to run back uphill, the kids yelling at him and raising a fuss. Parents and volunteers ran over to see what the commotion was about. First at the scene were Walter and Marina, right behind Bobbie.

I was right on the bunny's trail, even though he had a head start, I could move faster since I wasn't stampeding around in an oversized fur suit. Some of the eggs bounced out of the baskets and I yelled out at him, "It's over, pal!" and that's when he made his mistake, he actually stopped before reaching the Warren Spahn Parkway, turned to see me charging right at him. He must've panicked, because he turned right and flip-flopped downhill towards Cazenovia Creek.

Not believing he was trying to negotiate going down a semi-steep hill in an oversized suit with floppy feet, I figured Ralph Nader had better odds at being elected President, than this fella had making it downhill without crashing and burning.

Now I'm not positive, but for a moment there I thought I heard Mr. Bunny screaming as I chased him and for some reason I felt like I stepped into an Adam Sandler movie. Mr. Bunny reached the bottom of the hill, but stopped himself by backpedalling his feet. I didn't stop. I came down at the angle full tilt and instead of stopping, I body-checked him right into the creek.

He flew about three feet into the water and his costume got soaked good. I was grateful there weren't any recent heavy snows with melting runoff or heavy rains, otherwise the banks would be covered in at least three or four feet of water.

I stood over Mr. Bunny who was on his belly, trying to stand up, but between the oversized feet and the muddy shoreline he didn't have a chance in hell of getting up, let alone getting away.

Walter came down right behind me and said, "It worked man?"

I nodded. "Yeah, I think so. Give me a hand?"

"Sure." We bent over and each grabbed an arm and pulled the Easter Bunny up. "Nice body shot you gave by the way," Walter said while smiling.

"Thanks, I played kick-off coverage in high school."

"Not bad," Walter said seemingly impressed. "You want the honors? I figure you earned it," he said as he shoved the Easter Bunny on his butt and pressed down hard on his shoulders.

I reached for the oversized, smiling head. At first the head flailed around like fish that landed in a boat. Walter kicked him in the side, hard. "Behave yourself. You caused enough trouble today."

I tugged at the head at first, then once I had a firm handhold I pulled hard, beginning to feel like I was in a *Scooby-Doo* cartoon. If whoever was under the mask called me "a meddling kid", I was going to duke the son of a bitch.

One good heave and off came the head, with a ripping Velcro sound, and before us sat Chevy Kerwin, Marina's boyfriend, looking like he was about to taken to the woodshed. From atop the small hill we heard "Oh, my God, Chevy, what the hell did you do now?"

Marina stood next to Bobbie, the kids and other adults. Walter and I both knew the tone Marina used. Chevy would have better off being swept down the creek and into Lake Erie than facing what was at the top of the hill.

After Walter and I dragged Chevy back uphill, we plopped him onto the ground. "If you even think about taking off again, Walter and I will turn you into the world's first human lawn dart, and repeatedly launch you off the bridge, over Cazenovia Creek in a distance contest. Walter had a definitive motive because Chevy messed with his daughter, I had motive since I missed breakfast and this whole fiasco made me late for brunch.

"Chevy, what the hell were you thinking?" Marina asked.

At first he stayed quiet then I encouraged him, "I have two detectives' phone numbers on my cell's speed dial."

"Okay, I was looking for something."

Elden asked, "What was so important you acted like a horse's ass?" By this point we were gathering a good sized crowd of parents and kids, who were asking who was dressed like the Easter Bunny and why I was chasing him. Mrs. Elden had a few volunteers give us some breathing room.

"Ah, it was something special," he said after he wiped the sweat from his face. I could see the man was ashamed and embarrassed and now it was time for it to all come out. "All right, honey, but in a way this is your fault."

Marina was shocked. "What? How in the hell is this my fault?"

"Remember the other day when we were putting the candy and toys in the eggs?"

"Yeah," Marina said, looking confused.

"I took one of the empty eggs and took it aside."

"What for?" I asked.

"Later on we're supposed to go out Mari's family for dinner, but I wanted to propose."

The realization hit everyone like a bomb just exploded underneath us all. "Oh, my God!" Marina said as she clutched at her athletic bosom.

"Yeah. I put your engagement ring in the egg, wrapped a ribbon around it and put it aside," Chevy said, then he looked right at his girlfriend, and added, "But yesterday morning I had it in the dining room, and when I came out of the shower it was gone."

Marina took over the story. "Because I saw it on the hutch, picked it up, and put it in with the others. I remember it."

"I got here as fast as I could, but by then a lot of eggs were hidden throughout the park. I first checked the containers with the leftover eggs and I didn't see my egg, then I couldn't think of anything else but snatch those baskets. I'm really sorry and want to make it up to everyone."

We let Chevy get up to his feet. "Can someone give me a hand getting out of this costume?" I took a look at the back and started to pull apart the Velcro pieces in the back.

"How'd you close the back up?" I asked.

"I put on the suit in my car, then backed up against a tree to close up the Velcro snaps. It looked like I was a bear scratching my back." As Chevy stepped out of the suit, he continued. "I really am sorry, I didn't mean to hurt anyone and I want to make it up to you and your daughter," Chevy said to Walter then he extended his hand as he apologized.

I could tell Chevy was truly sorry and never wanted to hurt anyone, but he was desperate. He promised to make things up to Walter and his daughter as well as Sarah and Jerry too. We all agreed the police didn't need to be called and Chevy would make amends with the families and WNY Heroes.

After everything got cleared up and the WNY Hero volunteers were told about the engagement ring situation they began running around to all the kids and checked the baskets for a blue plastic egg with golden ribbon wrapped around it. And Mrs. Elden was grateful. "Mr. Seraph, I want to thank you for your assistance. I know this was unlike the previous situations you have dealt with, but there was no telling what would happen, especially when it came to the children."

We shook hands. "Not a problem, Ma'am."

Bobbie asked her, "So what are you going to do with Mr. Kerwin?"

"I believe he'll be volunteering for our organization quite a bit, starting this afternoon with the cleanup. I think he'll start helping out with the petting zoo." We all laughed at that one.

"Well, to be honest I've known some really bad men, dangerous, too. Chevy doesn't come close to those fellas. I'm just glad we got this wrapped up."

"Ah, that's right, your promises to keep?" Elden asked.

"Yeah." I looked at Bobbie, who took my arm again. "And believe me I've miles to go before I sleep."

"You certainly read the right books Mr. Seraph," Elden said.

"Right back at you Ms. Elden."

* * * *

Ten minutes later, Bobbie and I were back at my place and she was using my laptop to email her story to the *Buffalo News*, which didn't take her long. I let her get right to work and kept quiet, I figured the sooner she finished, the sooner we could get to the buffet. Sitting on my loveseat, next to me was Bobbie's overnight case and, as I sat there, I just thumbed my fingers on top of it, wondering what Bobbie brought with her and had in mind for later.

Shortly after, Bobbie finished up and sent her story in. "And, done. Now we can eat." She got up, wrapped her arms around my shoulders and neck, and looked me square in the eyes. "So, you hungry?"

"You know I am," I answered as I led her to the door. "So what do you have in your bag?"

"You're just going to have to wait and see handsome," she said as she gave me her flirty smile again and went out the back door to my parking lot. After we got back from eating I found out what she brought, but that's for Bobbie and me to know and no one else to find out.

THE END

Independence Day:
No Child Left Behind

After *Family Education*

Here's to the children everywhere.
May they all be happy, peaceful, & safe, now & forever.

July 4th

Let me start off by saying I hate the summer. The heat, the humidity, and the hot winds all conspire to make me miserable, and want to pole vault over June, July, and August and land somewhere in the middle of autumn. When temperatures rise, so do people's tempers, and I figured out a long time ago it's easier to warm up with a cup of tea and a crackling fire, than to cool off with a cold soda and a fan.

Last week was the Fourth of July and I was forced to deal with something that left me thinking about the road not taken and the regrets of things lost. There was a child abduction I helped resolve and this was the closest I've come to committing a cold-blooded murder. I've killed before, more than once, but every time was a case of self-defense: that wouldn't have been the case this time, and I wouldn't have lost a minute of sleep. I know if I ever see the uno che va in culo a sua madre again I will kill him, because he kidnapped a five year old girl, who could have been my daughter.

Years ago, I believed my life was headed in one direction, but it wound up taking a different path completely. It may be argued I didn't get what I wanted, but I got what I needed.

C. G. Eberle

* * * *

Every summer a carnival is held in Buffalo's Cazenovia Park, on the Fourth of July weekend. Caz Park is in the heart of South Buffalo and is home to baseball fields, basketball courts, swimming pools, soccer fields, and a tennis court for local athletes. Other visitors enjoy the winding walkways, a playground, and a splash pool, which is a welcome relief during the summer to children and adults alike. The center of the park is home for the old casino building, which back in the early 1900's housed boats for the man-made lake that used to be part of the park.

The carnival was set up in the center of Caz Park, as the locals call it. At the center of the park, the Warren Sphan Parkway forks off, with the right branch going up to Seneca Street and to the left fork going past two baseball fields on the left, and the Cazenovia branch of the Buffalo Public Library, ends at the intersection of the Parkway and Cazenovia Street.

Once set up, the carnival blocks off traffic from the fork to the left and takes up a fair of amount of real estate with a Ferris wheel, merry-go-round, giant slide, a portable funhouse, numerous carnival games, and of course the food vendors. Parking along the nearby streets and in the available lot at the closed St. John the Evangelist Church can vanish faster than a virgin on prom night. It gets so out of control, locals will just walk over, which is always a smart play.

Normally I don't go to events like the carnival, but two weeks ago my neighbor, Dixie Baxter, began riding me like Secretariat about going. I'd been doing some part-time work for Dix and her husband, Charles. They run their convenience store around the block from my apartment and they live a half a block away. When I moved to South Buffalo, Dixie took on the role of surrogate mother and saw it as her motherly duty to 'take me in', since I cut most of my family out of my life. It may have been due to the empty-nest syndrome she got after her youngest went off to college and that Dixie saw me as a replacement.

It was nice to get some parenting from Dix and Charles from time to time, so when she strongly suggested I go to the carnival, it was hard to argue with the woman. Hell, fighting the Chinese Army would've been easier. "You're going and that's it baby!" There was no arguing with Dix when she got like this. I was at the store when Dixie felt compelled to point out the flyer announcing the carnival that was taped up in their front window, among other banners, announcements, and flyers.

"Ah…that's great Dix, but I hadn't planned on going."

"Well, I think you oughta, honey." When her Georgian accent came out I knew she was determined to get me to go. "Baby, you been spending too much time by yourself. You didn't come over for our Memorial Day barbeque and how many other times have we invited you over since Christmas? Now tell me, when's the last time you got together with your family, or either of those girlfriends of yours?"

"They're not my girlfriends," I said trying to correct her, but to be honest I wasn't sure of how to classify my relationships with Bobbie Bedell and Crystal Bell. "I'm sort of in a holding pattern with them and not sure where things are headed."

"That's my point. John. You need to get out and have some fun. You've been off from school for what, almost six weeks now, and all you've done is home and work. There's more to life than that and that crime solving you're always getting yourself wrapped into. Now listen …" I knew Dixie was serious, because she lifted her reading glasses from her face, to rest them on her head, so she could look me square in the eye. "If you don't go, have some fun, and meet some people, I swear by my Mama watching down from Heaven above I will make you regret not going every time you come into the store."

At that moment I knew I was sunk. Dix had nothing but good intentions for me, but she had an annoying way of helping me. Eventually I agreed to go and it's a good thing I did; if I hadn't gone a sexual predator would've forced a series of nightmares onto the daughter of my ex-fiancée.

* * * *

I drove to the parking lot at St. John's around five. The church closed in 2009 and the building had been up for sale for as long as I could remember. The carnival had been going on since ten a.m., but I figured it was best to go in the later afternoon when the heat of the day had started to die down. Although the lot was full, I was able to park on St. Johns Parkside Street. The park was full of folks looking for food, fun, and games.

I was glad I brought sixty bucks with me because once the appetizing aromas from the food vendors came downwind and invaded my nostrils, my appetite woke up and my stomach roared. There was plenty to choose from; pizza, hamburgers, hot dogs, tacos, and Chiavetta's chicken. It's a local brand of marinade that makes the chicken so juicy and tender, the meat practically falls off the bone. And of course, there were plenty of goodies for the sweet tooth; cotton candy, ice cream, fried dough, funnel cakes, and candied apples. Naturally the end result was a mess of cups, paper plates, and napkins scattered about despite the many trashcans around.

This is one carnival where the games are not rigged, city and county officials are on top of events like these, and if you want to play Balloon and Darts, the Water Gun game, or the Crossbow Target game you've got a fair chance. There's always the popular Bingo tent which affords folks a chance to play for prizes, while sitting down and relaxing, which seems to be a favorite of the senior citizens.

Okay, my plan was I'd tell Dixie I came over, got something to eat, played a few games, maybe I'd take a ride on the merry-go-round, or go on the Zipper Ride, and of course I'd go down the giant slide, but in the words of Robert Burns, "The best laid schemes of mice and men go often awry,"

I started simple and ordered myself a couple of Italian sausages, with a bit of mustard, a large side of curly fries, and a large Diet Pepsi. As I ate I watched the people and I felt like an outsider, which is something I'm used to. I saw the couples, those starting out and those who've lived their whole lives together. There were the groups of friends looking for a good time, families with parents who caved-in to their children to go on this ride, or play that game to win a prize, anything from a live goldfish in a bowl to huge stuffed animals, bigger than most of the kids. Then there was me.

To be honest, I wasn't opposed to coming over as much as I may have protested to Dixie, my problem was coming over by myself. Going out alone isn't a lot of fun, and when I see the couples and families together it just reminds of how cut off I really am. Dixie was right about how much time I spend by myself. I know I could have called up either Crystal or Bobbie and invited them out, but I'd been having problems with both girls. Of course, if I wasn't so damn bullheaded I'd just plow through our issues, put them behind me, and make things work again.

After eating I headed over to play some games and allowed myself a limit of twenty dollars, because I didn't want to lose too much, and who knows, maybe I'd actually win something.

I started with the crossbow shot game and actually surprised myself, and the pimple faced teenager running the game, by hitting a bull's-eye with my first shot. Then again, it's been speculated by friends and family that I'm one of those natural shots. The carnie, who was just out of his teens, was stunned and began using me as an example of how easy his game was by telling folks how I scored a bulls-eye, as I walked away with a huge, three foot, white teddy bear with a blue bow tied around his neck. I felt a little silly carrying him around, but what the hell.

I moved on and walked by the Duck Pond game and suddenly the pathway got crowded with scores of parents behind, or almost on top of, their kids, watching them pick up a duck for a smaller prize. I was forced to walk sideways, because to the right was the games, and on the left were the food vendors, and there were crowds in between. As I moved on, I bumped into people left and right and held my breath, nearly putting Mr. Bear in a chokehold since I don't like crowds and am a bit claustrophobic. The warmer temperatures didn't help and I did my best to keep my cool. Eventually I inched my way through and got to the end of the row of parents at the Duck Pond, when a fella, with long blonde hair, and a beard to match, who was so obese he looked like he needed his own zip code, bumped me into a lady at the game. "Sorry," I said as I turned to face her. She turned to face me and I literally felt the wind get knocked out of my gut.

"No problem ..." She froze as I did. Neither of us could believe this moment had come because, I was looking into the eyes of Kim Manchester, my ex-fiancé.

I couldn't speak, hell I couldn't think. I was looking into the face that I wanted to spend the rest of my life with and the memories swept over me like the tide coming in.

* * * *

Actually, Kim's real name is Katherine Iris Marie, Marie being her confirmation name. After we became friends and I learned her full name, I jokingly began to call her Kim for short, and it stuck, at least for me. We met when we were both attending Buffalo State College, and within weeks of meeting we became fast friends. We began to hang out, go to the movies, dinners, nothing serious. We'd spend hours on the phone talking about our problems, giving each other's point of view from the opposite sex. Over time we grew closer and it seemed we talked about everything, both lighthearted and serious.

After two years I realized I'd fallen in love with her, and I wanted to share my life with Kim, but the timing was never right. I was always afraid of ruining our friendship, so I settled for her to be my best friend, next to Katsuro Ryuu. As much as I loved her friendship, hearing about the guys she was seeing wasn't the easiest thing in the world. Hell, a proctologic exam from a rhino would've been easier.

Eventually I had to tell her how I felt and had no idea how she'd react. It took time and we talked things out, and eventually we spent more time together, until finally we were officially involved. I know it sounds old fashioned, but I'm an old fashioned guy.

I saved up as much as I could for a down payment on an engagement ring, and the night I was going to officially propose on one knee, with roses and champagne, that is until we had a discussion, which led to one of the biggest fights I ever had. Kim thought I should go back to my old man and join the family business. The blood oath I gave my mother that I would make something she could be proud of, led to our problems and eventual break-up. I believed Kim was the Queen of Hearts, but like a lot of other women I've dealt with, she was the Queen of Diamonds. Of course my actions afterward didn't help matters.

* * * *

"Oh, my God, Gio?" she asked, as she brushed her hair back over the left side of her face. *Some things never change.*

"Ah, yeah, it's good to see you Kim. You look amazing," was all I could squeak out. She still had that big, bright, zest for life in her eyes. Her shoulder length hair still looked like darkened hay, and she straightened it, having taken the waves out of it. She was dressed in some sort of lightweight, short sleeved, white blouse, jeans, and sneakers. Her cheeks looked like pale roses and even though it'd been almost eight years, Kim still had a great figure. In one brief moment, the world vanished, there was only her, me, and our memories, both the good and the bad.

"What are you doing here?" I asked sounding like a moron.

"We were in the area visiting family, heard about the carnival, and thought Josie would like to stop by."

"We?"

"Oh, yeah, my husband Victor."

Santo cazzo! "Kim, when did you…" *God, if you have any mercy, take me now!*

"Five and a half years ago, just after Josie was born." Kim turned back towards the duck pond and came back out with the sweetest face I've ever seen. Josie was a true heartbreaker, just like her mother, she had the same eyes and olive complexion. Her hair was jet black and done up in a ponytail and she was carrying a small Disney Princesses child's purse. "Gio, uh sorry, John this is Josie, Josie this is John Seraph, a friend of mommy's." As Kim said those last words she glanced at me. Since things were left like the wreckage after a plane crash, she thought she had to be careful about using the word friend in describing things. I couldn't blame her.

I bent over and smiled as warmly as I could. "Hi, Josie," I started and stuck my hand out. "I'm John and your mom's right, I'm her friend." I glanced back up at Kim. She smiled back and Josie eyed Mr. Bear, who I didn't know what I was going to do with yet. "Looks like you did well," Kim said eyeing my prize as well.

"Yeah, those marksman skills the old man taught me come in handy every so often." I noticed Josie wrapped herself around Kim's leg, I guess she was nervous with me there, which was totally understandable.

"I bet they have, I read about you in the news. Solving two murders and exposing a group of Neo-Nazis, that's amazing."

"Well, someone had to take out the garbage," I joked. Kim laughed in the same musical way I remembered. "Actually, from what I heard, the FBI and a few other agencies are looking at those boys, hard." With Josie in tow we walked off the main path, away from the swarms of fairgoers and began to catch up as we headed towards the fun house, behind a ticket booth, and more food vendors, by the Casino House.

It was quieter away from the mob and as we began talking we heard a voice yell out, "Kath!" A big man, about 6'4" with jet black hair and blue eyes was rushing after us. He was wearing a light blue polo, faded jeans, and sneakers. When he caught up Kim introduced us. "John, this is Victor Vajurovak, my husband. Honey, this is John Seraph. We used to go to school together. Back then he was known as Giovanni Angelo." Victor and I shook hands and immediately I knew he was sizing me up, just as I was to him. Then he smiled.

"Nice to meet you, John, or is it Giovanni?" he said with a big toothy grin then bent over to pick Josie up, who was laughing once she saw her daddy.

"John's fine," I said.

"I got the tickets, so any idea what she wants to go on first?"

"No," Kim said, shaking her head. "Josie, what ride do you want to go on?"

"That one with the horses," she said and pointed to the carousel.

"Okay kiddo, one big horse ride coming up. Since I got dad duty now, I'll let you two catch up." Then Victor put Josie down and took her hand. "John, if you're not busy and care to join us for a drink, I'd love to hear about some of Kim's wilder days back in college." I guess Josie was impatient and began tugging Victor's hand.

I laughed at seeing that. "I'm not going anywhere."

As Victor and Josie vanished through the crowd, Kim said, "Alright, I know this isn't easy for either of us."

"Listen, before you go any further, please know I'm sorry," I said. "Maybe it was naïve of me to think we could still be friends after everything we'd been through, and I know I pushed way too hard to get you back, as my best friend. All my texting and phone messages didn't help, but all I wanted was for us to still be friends, and I always wanted you to be happy."

"And the rest?" Kim asked as she brushed her hair over her left ear again.

"At one point in my life I was in love with you, I think in a way I always will be. I mean, you were the first, but now I know I love you, but I'm not in love with you. Understand?"

She nodded, "Of course I do." Kim looked like she'd grown some herself since we said goodbye. "Yes I know the difference."

We walked towards the merry-go-round and Kim asked me, "Why did you push so hard with the calls and texts? You really made me uncomfortable."

"I'm sorry, that was never my intent." I couldn't look at her as we talked. "The best I can figure is, next to Katsuro, you were my first real friend in such a long time, since Fred died. I'd have given anything to keep our friendship alive, then I go and do one of the dumbest things ever. I just hope you can forgive me someday."

For an uncomfortable moment the only sounds were the crowd, the music from the rides, and as we got in front of the merry-go-round we heard Josie as she yelled out to Kim. "Mommy look!" She was sitting up on top of a white and yellow horse that was going up and down. Behind Josie was Victor, holding onto a brass pole with his left hand, and Josie's back with his right.

Kim smiled with a broad grin I'd never seen before. It had to be from being a mother. As they came around again in the blur of faces, Kim waved and laughed out loud.

"She really is beautiful," I said.

"Yes, she is," Kim said without taking her eyes off her family, until they were out of sight.

"Tell me, are you happy?"

Kim looked at me. "Yes Vic makes me extremely happy, and Josie totally fulfills my life. I can't imagine life without either of them."

"Then I'm happy for you. You got what you wanted."

"Thank you, John, and what about you? I think back when we were involved, I was taken in too much by your family's wealth and power."

"It's a strong temptation, believe me, kid."

"I admit back then I wanted things, money, security, all the things you and your brothers and sisters had growing up." For a moment she looked a little ashamed and turned away from me. "Can you understand?"

I nodded, "Of course. You wouldn't be the first. I know my brother-in-law Beau and one of my sisters-in-law married into the family for the same reasons. But marrying in, you're making a deal with the devil. It's just, I'm the white sheep of the family."

"Now what about you, I mean do you have what you want?"

"I'm not sure what I want anymore."

"What's that mean?"

I gave her the *Reader's Digest* condensed version of my life and my problems with Crystal and Bobbie. She seemed to take the whole story with a surprising amount of quiet awe, then Josie came running up to Kim and grabbed onto her.

"Did you see me?"

Kim picked Josie up. "You bet I did, baby, you rode that horse really well."

"Mommy, he's not really a horse." Victor and I stifled our laughs because Josie tried to sound grown up. Josie put her hand and mouth to Kim's ear, a second later Kim explained that Josie needed a trip to little girls' room.

"Ah, does anyone know where the..." Kim started to ask while looking around.

"Yeah," I said while pointing past the funhouse. "Over that way, the facilities are in a small, brick building overlooking the baseball fields."

"Thanks, John. We'll be right back." They headed off which left Victor and me alone.

After an uncomfortable moment of silence, he said, "So this is awkward, huh? Nice bear by the way."

"Thanks, and yeah it is," was the only thing I could think to say. Finally, I said, "So Kim says you guys were visiting around here?"

"Yeah, my mom lives over on Indian Church. Being the holiday and all, we get the family over for dogs and burgers. You know the whole thing. Well, Mom told us about the carnival and with her resting, Kath and I figured we'd tire Josie out a bit."

"Smart idea, but I only know about child rearing from family and friends."

"Bachelor?"

"Practically confirmed. Hell, these days there are Holy Men who've got more action than I have." Victor laughed at that. We headed over to a vendor that was selling drinks and ordered four lemonades, then spent the next couple minutes talking and getting to know one another a little bit.

"Man, why do you call Kath, Kim all the time?"

"Let me tell you, Vic, it started as a joke to get her goat, and it just sort of stuck with me. Here's what happened ..."

After an uncomfortable beginning we found a common point of reference and shared a couple stories about Kim. About a minute later, Kim came rushing up to us.

"Is Josie here?" she asked without looking at us. Kim scanned all around for Josie, and the anxiety level went right to Defcon One.

"No," Victor said. "What happened?" he demanded to know, dropping his lemonade which splashed on the blacktop.

"We finished up in the restroom, I was washing my hands, and Josie said she was just going outside, I told her to wait but ..." her words trailed off and we all knew what Kim wanted to say.

I realized I was going to have a pair of panicked parents on my hands and I'd have to help keep them calm—trust me it's easier said than done. "What the hell were you thinking?" Vic yelled at Kim. His voice drowned out the sounds of the carnival.

"Easy, Vic. Josie has to be around here somewhere," I tried to defuse the situation, then I noticed neither had heard a word I said. "Guys, we'll find Josie. I think there are some police around here."

"Where are they?" Victor asked.

"Down that way, towards the center of the park." I pointed in the direction of the Casino building. "When I first got here I saw a police car and an ambulance, after I crossed the street."

"I'll get some help, you two start looking for Josie." He rushed towards the police, calling out Josie's name.

"Victor ..." Kim began to say, but he was already gone. It was here I saw the tears welling up in her eyes, because Victor seemed to be blaming Kim.

I put my hand on her shoulder. "It'll be alright, we'll find her. Come on."

The look Kim gave me was one I had never seen. She was scared and desperate, her fear was raised to a whole new level, one I never saw or couldn't even begin to imagine. She didn't know what she was going to do, and Kim then looked to me for council. I had to keep her from losing her mind.

We scanned the faces of the crowd, which seemed to have grown, or maybe it was my imagination. No one we spoke to had seen Josie, it was the same with the vendors, the barkers running the games and rides, and anyone we stopped along the way. Parents told us they'd keep an eye open for Josie, and if they found her they'd either get her to the police, one of the carnival's workers, and call my cell phone since I gave my number to everyone we met.

Kim was running on a raw nerve and I couldn't blame her or Victor. As much as I want to be a father, I doubt I could cope let alone stay in control if my child got lost, or worse. I admit when I first realized Josie was Kim's daughter, the idea that I could have been her father and the idea of the road not taken, and everything that it meant overtook my mind. It was no longer a matter of if, but when we would find her. I would not fail the Vajurovak family.

We reached the Warren Spahn Way, which had been closed to traffic for the carnival. I asked Kim, "Would Josie cross the street by herself?"

She shook her head. "No, I don't think so. She's very good about that sort of thing. But there are no cars here, so maybe."

Kim finally broke down and sobbed horribly. I stopped and grabbed her shoulders in my hands and looked into her eyes. "I give you my word, we'll find her."

"Alright," she said softly. "Now what?"

I scanned around and saw an attendant in the parking lot next to St. John's. "Come on."

"You don't think she made it up here do you?" Kim asked as she was a step behind me and hurried to keep up. It was here I realized I was walking at a hurried pace, just short of running.

"Anything's possible, but I doubt it. At least, if we confirm, we can eliminate it and we'll have the attendant to keep an eye open for Josie."

"Okay," was the only thing Kim seemed capable of saying.

Since we were right by my car, I tossed Mr. Bear inside, then we headed for the kid, directing cars and taking in lot fees. He looked to be nineteen or twenty and I knew from the kid's t-shirt and hanging badge, that he worked for one of the lot attendant companies here in Buffalo.

"Hey man, have you seen a five year old girl up here?"

He took his ball cap off and wiped his brow. "Ah, what does she look like?"

Kim fearfully said, "She has black hair, in a ponytail. She's wearing a white shirt with pink trim, pink jeans, and carrying a small Disney Princesses purse."

The kid looked horrified, "Uh, yeah, she was rushed into a car by some dude."

"Mary, Mother of God," was Kim's only reaction as the terror came over her face like a death shroud. "John …"

"I'm going to say this once. This is that girl's mother, whoever that man was has kidnapped her. Now tell us everything happened?"

"Oh man, uh …" the kid seemed to go totally blank.

"Calm down, breath and tell us."

"Uh right, well, he had his hand on the girl's shoulder and everything seemed okay, and walked her into his car."

Kim plummeted into a stupor and doubled over, gripping her knees, and closed her eyes in disbelief. I think she was a step or two from shutting down. "Did you get his license plate?"

"Ah, yeah," he said and dug into his pocketed waist apron. I saw money on one side and from the other he pulled out a booklet of parking tickets and receipts. "We gotta write down plate numbers when customers check in, so we know how long to charge them for the time." He began to flip through the receipt booklet scanning for the the right numbers. "I know it's here."

"Oh God, John," Kim said.

I turned to her. "Does Victor have a cell phone?" She just stood there looking like the spirit had been whipped out of her good. "Kim!" I grabbed her shoulders, almost ready to shake her back into reality.

"Uh yeah, but I don't have mine," she responded.

"Take mine." I pulled my cell from my jeans and put it in her hand. "Call him, see if he spoke to the cops yet, if not, call 911." While she made the call, I turned back to the kid. "Find that bastard's ticket?"

"Yeah, here it is man, XTJ-1785."

"Can you describe his car?"

"Uh yeah, it was a big dark red one, maybe a Lincoln or a Caddy, but it must have had some work done."

"Why's that?"

"The front fender had primer on it. It's going to need a paint job."

"Can you think of anything else?"

"Yeah, I think that he's from around here."

"Why do you say that?"

"He's been here the last couple of days," the kid answered. "When he pealed out of here, he flew out so fast, he cut across Seneca, without looking and almost T-boned a car across the street."

I could barely think straight. "You see where he went?"

"Yeah." The kid pointed across the street, "it was impossible not to notice the way he drove. "Over there. He hauled ass and went up Duerstein." I looked across Seneca and past the small grocery store. "I don't think he went too far."

"Why's that?"

"Like I said, he was really squealing his tires and his engine was revving fast, anyone around could hear his car racing down the street, but then almost as fast, he hit the brakes, they were just as loud."

"What did he look like?"

"Ah, let me think. He had on a white dress shirt, blue jeans, sneakers. Black hair, cut short, with gray in it, kinda salt and pepper, you know what I mean?" I nodded. "He had about three days' worth of five o'clock shadow on his face."

"Thanks for the help." I stuck out my hand. "The name's John Seraph, and we really appreciate your help."

"Sure, name's Ken." We shook hands. "If I'd known what was happening I'd have done something."

"It may be a good thing you didn't. If that guy was armed something bad could've happened to Josie or you. The cops will want to go over all of this with you too, so I'd keep that receipt book handy."

"Right," Ken said as he put it back in his apron.

"John," Kim said as she handed me back my phone. She was shaky. "I spoke to Victor. He's got in touch with the police in the park. They're calling for more help to search."

"We've got something here," I said then Ken and I told her what happened. As I finished, something caught my eye. "Ken, where was the car parked?"

"Right over there," he pointed. "It was in that corner spot, near the sidewalk and he cut out fast."

"Makes sense. He'd want to get out of here as fast as possible. Tell me, did he leave those tracks through the mud and dirt there?"

Kim and Ken looked to where I indicated. Between the sidewalk and lot was a stretch of muddy grass. It'd rained pretty good the past week and everything wasn't a hundred percent dried out. It looked like when the car pulled out of the lot, it tore over the patch of grass and mud, and left a trail onto Seneca that was still fresh.

"Kim, I'm going across the street and see if Ken's right, and to see what else I can find out."

"Not without me, John!" Finally, there was that spark I knew she still had inside her, even after all the years that had passed.

"I don't know, I mean …" I would've continued but Kim took off and began running towards Seneca.

I chased after her and knew I'd have to stay on top of this situation. If not, things could go from worse to nightmarish in a New York minute. I called back to Ken, "The cops should be over here any time now. When they get here tell them what you told us and where we went."

"Right and good luck!" he cried back.

I caught up to Kim and we jaywalked over to Duerstein as soon as traffic permitted. "Kim, listen to me. I …" I stopped for a second and realized I almost told her I knew how she felt. There's no way I could even begin to understand what she and Victor were going through. "I know this is a lot to work through, but you need to play it cool, if the car's over here. And I'll need you to do what I say when I say it."

"Some bastard has my daughter and you're telling me what to do?" she asked as we walked by the grocery store.

I stopped her by grabbing her shoulder and turning her towards me. "Yes I am! Look at me," he said and she finally did. "This situation has Hiroshima written all over it. If something goes wrong, only God knows what will happen. When we find this Arrogh'e merda we'll only have one shot and we can't afford to risk Josie. You said you read about me in the papers, well what you didn't read is how bad things happened and how lucky I got. Also, in both cases I was armed. We don't have time for me to run home and get my .44."

"What are you saying?"

"Just this. It's like golf, and we need to play it were it lays. First we find the car and the house, if he's here. Then we check things out. We can't afford to go running in like a horde of Vikings raiding a village, alright?"

"Okay." I saw the anger in her face, but I knew it wasn't towards me. I just happened to be there. Kim's wrath would come and rain down on whoever took Josie. I knew what she was capable of, and I didn't feel sorry for the bastard in the least.

We followed the muddy tracks down Duerstein, over the cracked and broken asphalt, and we looked down the street at each driveway. About four or five houses down the trail turned right into a driveway of a house. We didn't see any cars in front of the house or alongside it, but the mud path went to a garage in the backyard.

"Now what?" Kim asked.

"Now we play it frosty and make sure we got the right place." We crossed the street and in spite of neighbors around and kids being out, riding bikes and playing street hockey, we chanced it and headed towards the garage.

I scoped out the house on our way to the back. It was a two-story, pale yellow house, and all seemed peaceful and quiet. My gut told me it was neither peaceful or quiet, at least on the inside. The house fit into the neighborhood of two and three story homes. Most were two family structures with a lot of folks renting out the second floors. Some of the houses were large enough to hold three or four apartments, but I knew someone who would abduct children needed privacy and wouldn't want tenants or a nosy landlord around.

We didn't see or hear anything. No one was in any of the windows. We headed towards the garage and as we got closer we saw that mud trail went under the main door.

"Now we force our way in," Kim said more than asked.

"No, first we verify." I led the way to the backyard and the side of the garage. There was a side door and window. When we looked through the window we saw a dark red Buick.

"John ..." Kim started.

"Easy kiddo, we're going to check out that car," I said turning the door knob, which was locked.

"How can we get in now if it's locked?"

"Well, if Katsuro was here he'd get us in without a mark or a sound, the man's a ghost. As for me, ..." I kicked in the door, near the knob and it flew inwards, slamming into the inside wall. "I can't pick locks like Kats, but I've my ways." We stepped inside fast and I shut the door so we wouldn't attract attention.

"What if this isn't the right house?" Kim asked.

"I'll pay back the owner," I said as I went around the car. "But somehow I doubt that's going to be the case. Look here." Kim came around next to me and we found the front left fender with primer on it.

"Oh, John," Kim said as I scoped out the inside of the Buick. It was dim inside the garage and even darker in the car, but I thought I made something out and tried the door handles. Driver's door was locked, but the left passenger was unlocked.

I poked my head in and got a better look, inside and outside of the car. Then I reached in and pulled out something, and my stomach sank. "Kim?" I handed her Josie's Disney princesses purse.

She took it from me and clutched it with both hands. "Oh, God, John, where is she?"

Think fast stupid. "Okay, ah Kim? I want you to call Detectives Chancellor and Bishop," I said as I handed my cell back to her. "Their numbers are both in the speed dial. If you can't reach them call nine-one-one. I'm going into that house."

"How?" Kim asked as she took my phone.

I looked at the house and tried to come up with options. I could only see one. I dug into my wallet and pulled out a savings club card to one of the grocery stores I shop at. "Kats is teaching me to master lock-picking, but I'm not there yet, besides I don't have the proper tools with me, but he did teach me to use a card to open a door. I'm going to go inside and see what I can find out, call the police like I said, and call Victor, tell everyone where we are and what we found."

"John, you're not leaving me behind, she's my....."

"I know what you're going to say and as much as I agree with you, we need cool heads, not hot blood. Besides, if something goes wrong I'll

147

need you out here to let the cops know where I am. Trust me." The woman I once loved was going through hell and I didn't want to think about what Josie may be going through, but I sure did not want Kim to see what was going on and have to live with those images for the rest of her life.

"All right, John. I don't like it but I'll do it." If there ever was a time for her to trust me, I'm glad she picked now.

As I ran from the garage for the side of the house and began mentally reciting one of my favorite poems to boost my courage; *Cannon to right of them, Cannon to left of them, Cannon in front of them Volley'd and thunder'd; Storm'd at with shot and shell, Boldly they rode and well, Into the jaws of Death, Into the mouth of hell Rode the six hundred.*

I did a double take of the windows, both those belonging to the house and the next door neighbors. Now I've done plenty of stupid things in my life, some dangerous ones too, but for some reason breaking and entering made me edgier than when I squared off against those who tried to kill me.

I slid the card into the vertical crack between the door and the doorjamb, then I tilted it so the side closest to me almost touched the doorknob. Next, I bent the card the opposite way, which made the card slip under the angled end of the bolt, and forced it back into the door. I leaned against the door while doing this, wiggling and jiggling it a bit. Finally I maneuvered the card in and I was able to open the door. I let out a big sigh, *nothing to it but to do it* I thought.

Ahead of me was a small staircase of five steps and I let my hearing take over. At first I couldn't hear anything, so I grabbed the railing and pulled myself up the steps to be as quiet as I could. At the top of the stairs I peered into a small kitchen that was a dull yellow, white, and brown, and in need of a good cleaning. There was a dark wood table and chairs, on the countertop, next to the sink was a vanilla frosted birthday cake with candles sticking out of the top of it. For a second I thought I was about to barge into some kid's birthday party, then I heard, "Stop crying, damn you!" Then almost apologetically the man's voice said, "I'm sorry but we're going to have so much fun because it's a party for you and me." My stomach turned into a container full of battery acid, and I knew my hatred was going to erupt from a cellular level.

The voice was coming from the front of the house towards the kitchen's front door. There were two doorways, one to the rear, by the back hallway door, where I was and the door in the front that led into what I discovered was the dining area and around to the living room. It came around into the hallway that led to the rear and past the first kitchen door.

I heard the man's footsteps come into the kitchen, and I held my breath, trying to stay absolutely dead still. I flattened against the wall along the banister and stairs as best I could. I cocked my fist, ready to throw it if he if so much as stuck his chin into the hallway. I knew the last thing he'd expect was to have an eleven inch fist rammed into his face. It was one of the few things I was grateful that I inherited from my grandfather.

When I heard him go back into the front, I peeked around the corner and saw the cake had vanished. I carefully stepped into the kitchen and I could hear a child's crying. "I wanna go home, I want my mom and dad!" It was Josie and I thanked all the Saints and God in Heaven above she was all right, but I knew she wouldn't be unless I did something, fast.

Then I heard the host, "I told you back at the park, if you don't do what I say and have fun with me something really bad will happen to your mommy and daddy. They might even die. Now we're going to have a lot of fun. See, we got presents, cake, games, balloons. First we're going to sing Happy Birthday, and blow out the candles, then we will eat cake and play games." *Games yeah, you Testa di merda., Figlio di puttana.*

I heard the host begin to sing Happy Birthday and he tried to get Josie to sing along but she was too scared to sing right. All she could do was cry.

"NO! That isn't right, you're ruining our party! Now you sing right or I'll hurt your mommy and daddy!"

They started over again as I looked around the kitchen for anything I could use to my advantage. I stepped inside further and saw the stove, fridge, microwave, and all the normal kitchen wares one would expect. Then a flash went off in my head.

As they continued to sing, I looked for the silverware and found it in a pull out drawer, then grabbed a couple handfuls of knives, forks, and spoons, and jammed them all in the microwave. Next I went under the sink and pulled out a couple of aerosol cans, one was oven cleaner and the other bug killer. I threw them on top of the silverware, shut the door, and set the microwave for sixty seconds. I moved back into the hallway and down the stairs. I wasn't sure how big of a bang this would be, but I knew I didn't want to be on the other side of the same wall.

From my position I heard crackling sparks, pops, and sizzles. The party host must have too, because I heard him walk into the kitchen, and he said "What the hell's this?" Then the sudden panic of realization hit him because the next thing he said was "Oh my Go …" followed by one of the loudest bursting explosions I have ever experienced. I felt the wall shake behind me.

In the kitchen all I could hear was "Ahhh!" But I didn't give a shit. I ran up the stairs and into the living room, where Josie was sitting at a child's table, wearing a cone shaped party hat. I didn't have time to be subtle because I didn't know if that bastard was armed. If we were lucky the blast killed him. I already knew he was one fucked-up son-of-a-bitch, and I had just pissed him off majorly. I grabbed for Josie, who was scared stiff, and of course I understood why. "Your mom is outside, I'm going to take you to her." I picked Josie up in my arms, just as the man ran back into the living room.

"NO! What are you doing? You're ruining my birthday party!" He looked messed up and must have ducked or ran from the microwave because he seemed unharmed. I recognized the crazed look in his eyes. It was official. I'd pissed him off majorly, it's one of the things I excel at doing.

Kat's taught me a couple things about protection. When body guarding someone you never fight when the client is in the room, otherwise they could get hurt or worse, unless it's absolutely necessary. I didn't see a gun or knife, but I didn't know what this bastard was capable of, so I put Josie down behind me, keeping myself between her and the birthday boy.

I had to get Josie out of there as fast as possible. There was a wild look in this maniac's eyes. I'd seen it in rabid animals. He had planned a

150

world of hurt for Josie, and God knows how many other kids, and here's where it would end.

Without taking my eyes off the bastard I told Josie to get out of there. "Your mom's outside, honey. Go down the backstairs and out the backdoor. Josie you run and find her. When you're outside you yell out for her, now go honey!"

Like an Army Private Josie followed my orders and ran through the kitchen and out the way I had come.

As she ran, the asshole, who I finally got a good look at, yelled out "No, she can't leave!" He had short, sweaty hair, almost matted to his head, pot marked acne scars over his cheeks and yellow stained teeth. Otherwise, he was as Ken described. He began to head to the door that led to the kitchen, and I moved to block him. I charged at him hard like I did when I played kick-off coverage in high school, or as we called it 'the suicide squad'.

I grabbed him around the waist and drove him into the doorway's wooden frame. I started wailing on him like I was in my gym working over the heavy bag. "You're never going to hurt her or any kid again, that's my promise to God and Josie!" I yelled out as I drove him into the tan wall-to-wall carpeting.

"You bastard! You ruined everything! I just wanted to play with her," he screamed at me as he fought back. He got in some good body shots, but he couldn't do any real damage. I'm six foot two and two-hundred and ten pounds. He was five-ten, maybe and about one sixty-five. Guess who had the physical advantage.

I got the leverage I needed and forced his head down, then twisted and pulled his left arm backwards and up in a kind of chicken-wing when I crossed his left hand with his shoulder blades. He screamed out in pain. Now I just had to think of what to do next since I was making it up as I went.

As I considered how to break his neck, the back door opened up and heavy footsteps stampeded up but before either of us could say or do anything else we heard "Let him go!"

A uniformed police had his sidearm aimed at us. I immediately let the creep go, took two steps back away from him and kept my hands in the air.

"Oh, thank God you're here," the scumbag said as one officer helped him to his feet. Another searched me good for weapons. "This freaking maniac came in here and physically attacked me when I was just sitting here."

"You John Seraph?" the second officer asked.

"Yeah, ID's in my wallet."

"Get it, slowly," he ordered.

I turned slightly so he could see me reach into my right rear pocket and ease my wallet out. I pulled out my driver's license and handed it to the officer. "Arrest him, he broke in here!" the pedophile yelled as he was checked for weapons. I learned in situations like these to stay calm, treat the police with respect, do what they say, and keep my big, smart-ass mouth shut.

"The rest of the house is clear," one of the two remaining officers said as he came into the living room.

"Is Josie okay?" I asked.

"The little girl? Yeah, she's with her parents outside," the first officer said.

The jackal said, "Whatever she tells you, she's lying! She followed me from the park ..."

"The girl told her mother you told her you'd kill her parents if she didn't come with you back at the park," one of the officers said.

"And you believe her?"

"Well, I certainly do," I said. "Besides, there's a witness back at the St. John's parking lot, who saw you shove Josie into your car. And I also doubt you can explain how her mother and I found Josie's purse in your car."

He looked like someone walked over his grave and stood there with nothing to say. "Did Detective Chancellor or Bishop show yet?" I asked.

"No but Chancellor's on her way," one of the officers answered.

"Good, because the air's getting a bit thick in here for me," I answered back as the officers handcuffed the kidnapper and read his Miranda rights.

* * * *

Three hours later the Vajurovaks and I were in the South Park station; we gave our statements to Detective Chancellor, who was there as an observer, and two detectives from Buffalo's sex offender squad.

Everything we told them gelled, especially when the police took Ken's statement of what he saw happen. In private, Chancellor said, "John, you shouldn't have done what you did. It was dangerous, risky, and the girl could have been hurt. Now that the 'official reprimand' is out of the way, good work and you should be proud. Hell, your whole family should be proud of you." Before we left, Chancellor said, "Two things John—first, you sure can pick them."

"What do you mean?"

Chancellor read from some papers that came off the fax machine. "This just came in from the NCIC, the National Crime Information Center, from the FBI. It's a report on your friend back in the holding cell. His name's Levi Page, a.k.a. the Birthday Boy. He's a sexual predator who preys on girls like Josie." She looked at Kim, Victor, and Josie, who were all waiting in the outer office. I was grateful because I didn't think the family needed to hear this. Josie had fallen asleep in Kim's lap. "Anyways, Page is wanted in Washington, Oregon, and California for nine counts of child molestation and child pornography. I'll spare you the details, but he's also suspected in the rape and deaths of two more children in Santa Fe, and has been on the run for the last eight months."

"And somehow Scummy made his way to the Queen City," I added.

"Yeah, this is one bad guy who needed to be taken off the streets. Almost makes me wish New York still had the death penalty," Chancellor added.

"You and me both. So what's the second thing?"

"Page wants to speak to you, John," Chancellor said.

"What?" I couldn't believe it. "Are you shitting me?"

"No, he was quite serious. We can arrange it. He's in a holding cell for now. But in about an hour we'll be transporting him downtown to the Holding Center. Eventually the FBI is sending some folks from the Behavioral Analysis Unit to talk to him, they may take over the case."

"Do you know what he wants?"

"No, but he was quiet insistent about wanting to talk to you," she added.

I looked at Kim and Victor, then stared at Josie and again thought of how she could've been mine. Maybe in another world, in another life. "Oh hell, all right, I'll do it."

Further inside the station, Chancellor and a male officer escorted me to where local drunks were usually kept to sleep it off. These smaller cells were one man lockups, and Page would have to be segregated from here on out.

Chancellor and I walked to the cell, which was essentially a cage that was long enough for someone to lie down on the cot, next to a toilet. Page was sitting there looking deflated. We stepped up to his cell and he rose. The cell house was warm and there wasn't any airflow.

"Detective Chancellor said you wanted to see me," I said.

Page hung his right hand from the upper bars on the door. He stared at me coldly, then swallowed the corner of his lower lip. Finally, he spoke quietly, "You, you ruined my special day. We were going to have so much fun, I was going to make it her birthday today."

The way he said birthday made what was normally a special day of celebration sound reptilian and vile. I looked at Page, into his dead eyes. They appeared like a doll's eyes, cold, black, and lifeless. Even worse, they reminded me of a shark's eyes when a shark bites into its prey and its eyes almost seem to roll back in its head, in an orgasmic feeding frenzy. What Page had planned for Josie was no different.

"All I know is, you sick fucker madre, you had nothing but pain, agony, and pure hell planned for that little girl, just like those children out west. The only thing I'd change if it was to be done over again, is I'd have my .44 with me."

Page raised a single eyebrow inquisitively. "Are you saying you want to kill me? Not quite the brightest thing to do in front of a detective, wouldn't you say?"

I glanced at Chancellor using only my peripheral vision, then looked back at Page, and I smiled. "I never said a word about killing you, I mean if I shot you in both kneecaps and your nutsack you'd live."

"Ah, very good, you can play it cool." Page then began to pace back and forth, as much as he could. "You know, I could sue you for trespassing, breaking and entering, assault, even attempted arson. By the way, that was a nice touch, distracting me with the microwave." He

154

looked at me slyly. "How'd you come up with that?"

"Made it up as I went, seemed like a good idea at the time."

"Ahh, well it worked," he answered back.

"Detective, can we have a moment alone?" I asked. "I'll behave myself, hell I won't even come any closer to the monkey's cage." Then I took two steps back.

"I can't leave you alone with the suspect, you know that," Chancellor said.

"Oh, I don't mean for you or the officer to leave the area. I just want a private moment alone with our friend here."

"I guess that'll be okay." Chancellor went over to her fellow officer leaving me to tell Page what was really on my mind.

"I know you could try and sue me but I don't think that'll happen."

"Why not?"

"Because you're going to admit to everything and sign a full out confession you son-of-a-bitch."

"What makes you think I'm inclined to do anything like that?" Page asked as he slanted his head to the right.

I turned my volume down to a whisper so only Page heard me. After letting out a sigh I played my ace. "If you don't, I'll see to it that every inmate at the holding center will know you're there awaiting trial and what you've been accused of doing. Think of it, the blacks, the Latinos, the Aryans, the real hard cases, everyone will know who you are and what you've done. And you know what that means. You're the bottom rung on the criminal hierarchy ladder. Everyone's going to want a piece of you. You come across some inmate who's got a child in their life who was victimized by a piece of shit like you, and it's going to be Olly olly oxen free."

The somewhat cocky look vanished, and was replaced with a moderate look of concern. "You're bluffing."

"No, I'm not. I know people on both sides of the law. Hell, I'm related to the side you don't want to cross. I have no trouble spreading the word, sitting back, and letting nature take its course." Now I gave Page my coldest stare, and like I told him, I wasn't bluffing.

He began shaking his head. "No, no you won't do that."

"Yes, I will. It won't be hard to find a corrections officer who'd be willing to turn off a couple monitors, and leave a cell door or two opened giving someone the perfect opportunity to perform what a large number of the population would consider a public service," I told him.

"You can't do that, I have my rights."

"Guess what? I'm not a cop, too bad for you."

"It isn't fair; they're so pretty, and friendly, and look so nice, like they want to have fun at my parties." Page sounded like he was in total denial of his guilt.

"They are children, you're an adult. You may have some bad wiring in your head, but you know what you did was wrong. Confess what you did or take your chances inside. Even if nobody touches you at the holding center, how long do you think it'll be before someone, somewhere, somehow gets to you?" I left Page with a quote, "Writer Publilius Syrus said, "The fear of death is more to be dreaded than death itself.".' Confess your sins or get ready for some real fear. If you ever get out I will find you and I will kill you." I turned and left Page with his thoughts and the warning I had given him.

* * * *

It finally cooled down thanks to a drop in the temperatures and a chilling wind that was like a fresh air conditioner the city needed. By the time we finished, the stars were finally out and the air felt good. Above us fireworks of all colors and designs were screaming and exploding all above us. I briefly talked with Kim and Victor outside the police station, Josie was dead to the world and they wanted to get her home. Back on Duerstein, Josie was checked out by paramedics and she wasn't hurt in anyway. Hopefully, she'll recover emotionally. "John ..." Kim was speechless but the look she gave me said it all.

I took her hand in mine. "It's okay, kid. I know."

Victor extended his hand and we shook. "Listen, John, you saved my baby girl, if you ever need anything you call us."

"You're welcome, I just wish I could have stopped Page before he took off with Josie."

"Well, you got her back before anything could happen, that's what's important," he said.

"Does your family know what happened?"

"No," Victor said. "I didn't want to freak anyone out before everything was settled. First Kath called, then she called after I was talking to those cops in the park, and then we rushed over to join you guys, but had to take the long way around the park." I nodded. "Otherwise we'd have been there sooner." Then came the time to say goodbye. "Ah, I'll be in the car. Listen, John, if you need your car washed for three years, or a free moving van, let me know," Victor joked. "Seriously we'll have to have you out for dinner sometime. Thank you again." We shook again as he gripped my right shoulder.

"Sounds good, Vic. Give me a call sometime." I looked at Josie through the rear window. "Whenever you guys feel she's ready, I don't want to freak Josie out, and I might drum up bad memories. You guys let me know."

Victor went to their car leaving me and Kim alone again. "Well, uh …" I said.

"Yeah, umm we really should get going. We got to get Josie to bed, then tomorrow I know I'm going to have a lot of phone calls to make, to our relatives."

"Yeah, I know what you mean, once word gets out and my old man and our lawyer gets word I'll have a lot of questions myself."

I was nervous again, but it was a different type of nervousness. "Listen, while I was talking to that asshole, I let him know that if he somehow gets out I'll be waiting for him. And my family contacts might just visit him inside, no matter where he winds up. My old man, brothers, and their staff may be crooks and bad guys, but they don't tolerate shit like this. I spread the word, they may do me a favor." I gave Kim my best evil smile.

"John, I don't have the words, I will always be grateful. Before, when we were close it was one thing, then we fell apart. You'll always have a special place with us. I hope you know that." She leaned in and kissed me gently, placing her hand on my cheek.

"You and Vic just take care of that little girl of yours and we're even." I looked into her brown eyes and caressed her face. I turned to Victor who was watching us through the open car windows. "Hey Victor, you take care of our girls, you hear?" I smiled, and so did he, then he waved to me. I waved back, then kissed Kim goodbye. Before

157

she could anything, I turned and walked away, whistling *The High and the Mighty.* Something told me I'd never see Kim again.

THE END

New Year's Eve/Day:
Reflections

After *Family Education*

Here's to the future, the undiscovered country.

December 31st/ January 1st

They say New Year's is a time to sit back, reflect on the past and wipe the slate clean. It's a time for fresh starts and new beginnings. I'd like to believe all that, but there's a part of me that won't—no, scratch that—can't let things go as much as I'd like to. The problem with memories is once they start, they don't stop. They keep on flowing like an overrunning river, breaking it's banks, especially when you've got a memory as good as mine.

Now, I've never been much of a New Year's kind of a guy, besides I hadn't had much holiday spirit this year. To be honest, I've been in a pretty foul mood since May, after I was suspended from college, but I'll get into that in a minute.

Lately, it seems all that's been going through my mind is the song *I Dreamed a Dream* from *Les Misérables*. I've been looking back at my life, thinking about how the hell I got here, and wondering what changes I could have made that would have given me a brighter future. I admit, I've been feeling a lot like Hamlet for a long time.

All that said, this New Year's Eve I find myself sitting in a small conference room of the exclusive suites, of Gevira Associates Inc.

reflecting on my past and considering my future.

Gevira Associates is housed on the top two floors of the Huntington, a high class residency hotel that towers over the Allentown neighborhood in the Queen City, and is run by my friend Denise Gevira.

Denise runs a high-class escort agency in the Buffalo area. We've been friends for some time and I've been doing some part-time work for her since early June. Either I'm driving her girls to and from their appointments and making sure they're safe, or I'm sitting around the suites/offices waiting, like I am tonight. Most of the clients behave themselves, but on occasion someone gets out of hand and one of the girls needs help. When that happens I answer the call. I split my time with two other security men, Steve and Tony, usually on the weekends.

To be honest, it was quiet for a holiday weekend, most of Denise's girls were off and out celebrating, or getting ready to go out to party. We were short staffed, because a few had taken a Christmas break and were out of town for the holidays. There are four girls entertaining tonight. The clients were mainly well-behaved and New Year's here redefined the term 'ringing in the new'. But as the saying goes, boys will be boys, especially when one mixes in alcohol and Viagra. Because of that, someone had to stand watch. Both Tony and Steve wanted to go out and celebrate the New Year, so I told them I'd watch the store. This gave me plenty of time to think.

In our office there's a six person conference table, a rectangular desk, which houses eight security monitors. The cameras cover the elevators, the entrance, the hallways, and the main conference room, which is home to a bar, and is primarily used to get clients to relax and socialize a bit with the girls before retiring to the girls' private suites. Naturally, there are no cameras in the rooms, but if a girl needs help with a client who gets out of control they press an intercom button, and security comes in with an electronic pass key, then it becomes our deal.

Work starts at four p.m., so I got in around three-thirty. Both the hotel and offices were fully decorated in Christmas décor. A huge ten foot, spruce tree stood tall in the lobby and was fully trimmed in lights, garland, the old-fashioned glass ornaments, and tinsel. Upstairs the office/suites and Denise's suite were all decorated for the season, which the girls did during a decorating party, while the boys and I picked up and moved a nine-foot tree for them. It was a bitch of a job, but the ladies were all very grateful.

Tonight I came in and went right to the monitoring room, after making myself a small pot of tea in the kitchenette in the conference room. So this is how I celebrate New Year's, keeping an eye on TV monitors, as I reread Robert B. Parker's *Promised Land,* with a pot of blueberry and goji berry tea to keep me company.

I've read Parker several times and he's one of my favorite authors, but I couldn't get past the first chapter tonight. My mind kept on going back to this past May and what led to my suspension, and eventually to my decision not to return to Buffalo State College.

To be totally fair and a hundred percent accurate, things really started to change for me two years ago, at Halloween. I'd been attending Buff State for about a year and half, when in the fall semester, in late September, a headless motorcyclist began running around campus terrorizing students. I was working a Halloween party on campus and when the Rider, as the headless motorcyclist was called, made an attempt to kill a professor, I stopped it from happening. Little did I know this would be the start of things for me.

That Christmas I was working a seasonal job at a local, indie bookstore, when a co-worker was killed and I figured out who did it. The following spring, I made local headlines when I uncovered the truth behind the disappearance and murder of Dana Tillis. In the process I derailed the political hopes of many, including former Senator Kingsley Addar. On Black Friday, I cleared my sister of a murder charge she was being railroaded into, then just before last Christmas, I hunted down the people who killed my neighbor Rory Duffy. My only regret is that I couldn't kill them more than once.

On Valentine's Day I got a helluva scare when I received anonymous secret admirer valentine poems. At first I thought it was someone I had pissed off, which was growing to be quite a list, but my admirer turned out to be an eighth grade student I was tutoring.

St. Patrick's Day weekend I prevented a Northern Irish terrorist from killing a lot of innocent people here in Buffalo, but the lunatic got away. On Easter I dealt with what at first I thought was a madman, targeting children at an Easter egg hunt, but really he was just a guy looking for an engagement ring he lost. Then came May.

Just before the spring semester ended, a student was found shot to death at Buff State and it looked like his professor did it. Several people at the college wanted to close the case and make it vanish and didn't care if an innocent man was being framed. I dug around and exposed the truth. This was the beginning of the end for me and the start of the downward spiral which lasted throughout the summer and that I'm still dealing with.

I lost my job at the school library, and got suspended from school. I was told if I wanted, I could enroll for the upcoming spring semester, I decided against it. I had had my fill. I fought hard to clear an innocent man, it was a hard-hitting, rough road where I was assaulted several times by so-called friends and classmates, and almost got killed on campus. Then I got thrown under a moving train for protecting myself. Granted, I armed myself and carried my .44 Mateba on campus, but I do have a CCW, that's a Carry Concealed Weapon license. If that's how the administration and the student body were going to treat me, the Devil can have them all. After that all ended I was reminded of an Italian saying; Meglio un giorno da leone che cento de pecora. Translation, better one day as a lion than a hundred as a sheep.

The real gut kicker for me this year was on the Fourth of July. I ran into my ex-fiancée, her husband, and their daughter, who was kidnapped by a pedophile wanted by the FBI. I helped find and save the girl, then told the pezzo di merda if he somehow ever got out, I'd be waiting for him.

I was worn out from the attempts on my life, of dealing with my family, of Buffalo State College, and of the fiasco my love life has become. In the past eighteen months I'd been involved with two amazing women, but I needed a new definition for complicated around Saint Patrick's Day. Honestly, I can't blame anyone but myself. In one case, it had become a matter of trust and of my own bullheadedness; in the other, it was a matter of career goals over my feelings and privacy. I still love both Crystal and Bobbie, but I think I'm at the point where I need to let them both go. I'm reminded of a line from *Julius Caesar,* where Cassius says, 'the fault, dear Brutus, is not in our stars, But in ourselves, that we are underlings.'

So here I sit, sipping tea and thinking about the future, or as Shakespeare called it the undiscovered country, not knowing what lies ahead. I've been able to pay my bills thanks to Denise and some friends of mine, Charles and Dixie Baxter. They run a small Mom & Pop store around the block from my place, and I've been able to pick up a couple days a week with them cashiering, stocking, and cleaning the store, that sort of thing.

After four hours of sitting around, I got up to stretch my legs and double check everything. I knew our floors were secure, but I take my job seriously. Denise and her staff trust me, and I won't let them down. Steve told me it doesn't hurt to do a walk through every three or four hours. I found the place nearly deserted but I knew better.

I walked the beige hallways, decorated with some landscapes on the walls, and the occasional side table lining the halls. Passing by the girls' suites every so often I'd hear some sort of noise, nothing I hadn't heard before. I headed by the conference room and found Denise and her assistant, Autumn, who was tending bar. Denise was seated on one of the bar stools, as her feet dangled, barely touching the earth like us mere mortals. "John," Denise greeted me warmly. "Care for a drink?"

"Ah no thanks, I'm working."

Denise was wearing a dark teal, long sleeve blouse, with a V-neck cut, and dark slacks. Around her neck was a silver, antique choker, and she had a matching silver bracelet on her left wrist. Of course with her short, black haircut, and amazing makeup Denise could be wearing a grain sack and she'd still look like she was ready for a night on the town. "That's one of the reasons I love having you around, you're always watching out for us."

"You sure you don't want a belt, John?" Autumn asked. Tonight she kept it simple, a mushroom colored light sweater, a matching scarf, tan slacks, and light brown pumps. The first thing I noticed about Autumn, when we met, was how stately and regal she carried herself, despite the fact that she had an under-the-desk gun aimed at me. I found out later on that she had been a model in a previous life. I felt a special connection with her because back in May, she and another friend of mine, Charles Boudreaux, saved my life.

"Ah, no thanks red. So is Charles coming down here to ring in the new with you?"

"No, damn it, he's out of town on business." Charles and Autumn began seeing one another after they shot down one of my old man's capos, who tried to kill me. "But he promised to make things up for me in February."

"Nice." I tried to put on a happy face, but they both knew I'd been in a shitty mood for quite some time.

"Come with me," Denise said as she took my left arm in hers and walked me back out into the hallway. "Okay enough of this mopey attitude. This has been going on long enough, big man."

"Sorry didn't know being in the holiday spirit was required for bouncing out the drunks and asses, not that that happens a lot around here." Denise gave me her "Don't be a putz" look. "Sorry kid, it's just, I've been thinking about the past a lot, and what I'm going to do with my life. At one point, I was going to be a teacher, but now ..." I just trailed off.

"That's right, I forgot all about that. Aren't you eligible to re-enroll, right?"

I nodded. "Yeah, but I'm not going to."

"Why not? You're not that far from earning your teaching certification, right?"

We got back to the monitoring room. "Yeah, but I'll you, Denise, I think I lost my passion for it. What happened in May helped put it in perspective for me. I realized some folks can sit back and let bad things happen to innocent people and others can't, which is ironic considering my family's history." I pulled out a chair for Denise and we both sat, but I did at an angle, so that I could keep an eye on the monitors.

"I didn't want to say it, but..." She looked at me like she knew she had skated out onto the thin ice.

"It's okay. I've called my old man and brothers every name in the book, and right to their faces." I rocked a bit back and forth in my chair with the monitors to my right.

"So what are you going to do?"

I shook my head. "To be honest I've no freakin' clue. The only thing I'm positive of is that I've got to find a new path. But the one thing is, I've got to keep my word to my mother. You remember my car accident and Fred?" Denise nodded slowly. "Afterwards, Mama made me take a blood vow that I'd make something of my life, that I'd be a benefit to others."

Denise got a funny look in her eyes. "You know with that track record of yours, have you ever considered becoming a police officer?"

I couldn't help myself and laughed out loud. "That would really kill my old man and grandfather." Then I joked, "Hmmm maybe I should call the police academy next week." Denise began laughing, then suddenly the intercom buzzer went off.

We both looked at the monitors and the line of the intercom alarm. "Room 8."

"Oh, Christ, that's Rachel's room." We moved in unison. I grabbed the electronic key, and we charged into the hallway.

I asked, "Who's Rachel seeing?"

"One of our more high-level, confidential, and political clients."

"Wonderful." I knew what this meant, and it wouldn't be easy. I knocked on the wood door giving a two second heads up, then inserted the key-card. The lock beeped and Denise and I rushed in. "Security!" I announced as we marched in.

In front of the middle of a well furnished suite, with antique style décor, was Rachel, who resembled Rita Hayworth. She stood there tying her light blue and white silk bathrobe. Next to her was a potbellied man with curly, thinning, white hair. He was doubled over and from his stance I knew exactly where Rachel hit him. He was in his striped boxers, wife beater tee-shirt, and black socks. He'd been in such a hurry he hadn't taken off his wrist watch, or wedding ring, and believe me it was not the most flattering or pleasant view of former New York Lieutenant Governor, Henry Finch. This was more of the man than I ever wanted to see; he still makes the news from time to time and he wasn't the best looking fella, even with his clothes on. Seeing him like this didn't help matters or my stomach.

"Rachel, are you all right?" Denise asked going to her. In times like these she acted more like a mother.

"I'm fine, Denise, but he still doesn't get it."

"You bitch," Finch grunted out as he clutched at his nutsack. "I swear I'm gonna sue you, and your boss, and even this guy. Hell, by the time I'm done I'll own this building."

"Everyone calm down and tell me what happened, Rachel," I said.

She looked me square in the eye. "Finch is one of my regulars and I've told him the things I won't do. I've had to tell him more than once. Usually things are fine, we had a few drinks when he arrived but we got back here and he again tried to talk me into having anal sex, he knows it's something I won't do."

I had to give Rachel a lot of credit, throughout the entire situation she never lost her ladylike demeanor. I knew she, like all of Denise's girls, were professionals, in the sense they were trained to handle difficult and challenging customers.

"He then grabbed my arm and tried to convince me to change my mind. I told him no, then he forced me onto the couch, so I drove my knee into his nuts."

"You're paid to do what I want you to do, bitch!" Fitch yelled out.

"Calm down, bubba, you know there are rules here," I said. "What happened then, Rachel?"

"When are you gonna listen to me and stop listening to these whores?"

"You need a course in manners, but I promise you this, you call these ladies whores or anything more like that, you will be sore and bleeding before the night's over."

Fitch straightened himself up, "Are you threatening me, son?"

"Yes, I am. It's a promise you can bank on."

"You know who I am, you little shit?"

"Yes, I do, and I don't care. Take a good look in my eyes, see if I care? Now get dressed." I turned to Denise. "It's your call."

She kept a scornful eye on Fitch. "We've had this discussion before Lt. Governor and you have been warned. This time you touched one of my girls. You are banned. Now get out."

"You can't do that to me!" Fitch's swollen face turned red and he pointed his right thumb back at himself. "I am Henry Fitch, I am still a big man here in New York and I will run you all into the ground." Then he focused on Denise. He pointed his finger in her face. "I will make sure the only clients you ever see are when you're walking the streets. You're nothing more than a prostitute, you cu…"

"I think that's enough." I grabbed Fitch's fingers and twisted them upwards and hard. He screamed out loud and fell to his knees. "Denise how about you take Rachel for a drink? I'll escort Mr. Fitch out of here, once he collects himself."

"Good idea, John. Come on, Rach." The ladies went down to the bar, while I kept an eye on Fitch.

I found his clothes scattered on Rachel's loveseat, which was a pale rose and white number that looked like a replica out of the **Marie Antoinette** collection. I tossed Fitch his blue suit, white, pinstriped shirt, and a blue and white tie.

As he dressed I made sure the prick behaved himself but he kept on cursing out me, Denise, Rachel, Autumn, the rest of Denise's girls, the hotel staff, anyone he could. After he got his black pumps on, I tossed Fitch his suit's coat but hung onto his gray, winter topcoat. "Is that all of it? You have everything else?"

He gave me a dirty look. "You people are something, I'm…"

"I'll take that as a no. Now that's enough," I yelled back. "You were told the rules, you don't want to follow them, you're out it's that simple, bubba. You are leaving." I walked Fitch to the elevator and on the ride down he stayed quiet, sort of. He was muttering under his breath.

"Here." I handed him the top coat. Fitch put it on still cursing us out. I reached my line in the sand, flipped the emergency stop button and the elevator car jolted to a hard stop between the second and first floors. I pushed Fitch against the wall, grabbed the collars on his top coat, and got closer into his face than I normally would have liked, but I needed to make a point. "I'm going to say this once. You don't show yourself here again, ever. You bother those women again and I promise you, you Faccia di culo, Mangia merda, it'll be the mistake of your miserable lifetime. You don't have any real creditability left in the state, after that intern scandal. It may have been two years ago, but people remember when a politician winds up with a nineteen year old and twenty-one year old on the floor of the assembly chamber in Albany. Now how much ecstasy and Viagra was in your system? It must've been a real surprise when that security guard walked in on you three."

Fitch got very quiet and I saw the anger still seething in him, but he backed down. "Just remember, Denise and her employees are also protected by those who are seriously interested their welfare, and these are people who have no doubts or reservations about using violence to make their point clear. Here's what's going to happen. I am going to escort you through the lobby. You will behave yourself, if not, I will cross your shoulder blades with your right forearm and hand, then throw you into the street on your doughy ass. Do we understand each other?" Fitch finally comprehended how serious I was and nodded. I flipped the switch and we reached the lobby.

We crossed the lobby, passed the good sized crowd at the hotel's Irish bar, McDowell's. It was actually a really clever and well thought-out design. The wall of the bar was a building reproduction that looked like a white, two-story, Irish pub. The second story windows had flowerboxes, and wrought iron lamp posts with hanging plants lining an area of white, tile patio. The patio was separated from the rest of the lobby by a wrought iron fence that lined the right wall and came up to the outside patio door, and ended at the fence line. On the tile were ten patio tables with matching chairs for each.

Guests and diners could still get an outdoor feel, even indoors during the winter months, like tonight. So you had the option of eating on the patio or inside the Irish bar. McDowell's was hosting a New Year's celebration. It was still early and only a small crowd arrived, but it was sure to grow.

I lead Fitch to the main glass and brass doors and saw it was still lightly snowing. It was my favorite type of snow, a light coating of big goose feather like flakes. To me it was the most magical kind of snow and made me feel as if anything was possible and that the world was full of wonders.

Outside, I followed Fitch to his black town-car parked in front of the Huntington. "Also, Mr. Fitch, I'm going to inform the hotel's staff that if you're seen around here again, they should call the police for trespassing."

"You think you people have heard the last of me? I swear this isn't over."

"It's time to say good night, old man."

Just then Fitch's driver came out and opened the back door, then joined us. "Is there a problem, Mr. Fitch?"

Fitch looked at his driver, who was a foot taller than me, half a foot wider, and the man had to be a Zulu warrior in another life. He was dressed in a suit and black top coat, looking professional, and then he looked back at me. "Yeah, Charlie, there is." Fitch got a cocky look of confidence on his face. "This 'gentleman' says I can't go back inside. Have anything to say about that?" Fitch looked pretty smug, as if Charlie settled most of his problems for him.

"Is that so?" the huge black driver said. Charlie clenched his fists, flexing and balling them.

"Your boss knew the rules and he broke them. He didn't want to behave himself, so he gets bounced."

"I don't think so," Charlie said as he got into my face. "Mr. Fitch is going back inside whenever he wants."

"No, he's not. He shows his wrinkly ass here again and we'll call the police. And Charlie, I can see what you're thinking, now being a company man is normally a good thing, but it's not worth a beat down."

"Really?"

Fitch still looked like a smug prick used to getting his way.

"Yeah, and I'm sure you have better things to do tonight then wind up in the E.R."

"You that confident?"

I gave him a semi-nod. "Yeah, about ninety-percent sure."

"Not good enough." Then Charlie took a wild swing with his right. I'm betting he was used to handling folks who were intimidated by his size and didn't have any experience. I crouched, extending my right leg out and bending my left leg so I got at waist level with Charlie, then I drove my right fist into his balls as hard as I could. Instantaneously, Charlie let out a wail that could have been heard by residents at the Buffalo Zoo. He cupped his nuts and collapsed on his left side.

"Good night, gentlemen," was all I said as I headed back inside and out of the cold.

* * * *

After speaking to the hotel concierge, Jerome, and telling him Fitch was banned, and if he ever showed up it was time to call the police, I headed back upstairs.

I didn't see anyone around so I headed back to the monitoring room where I watched on the screens some of the girls heading into the pool area. The Huntington features an all-weather, enclosed, rooftop, heated pool. A minute later, Denise came in; she had changed into a red and black bandeau one-piece, under an opened black and silver beach robe.

I couldn't help myself and let out a wolf-whistle. Trust me, seeing Denise dressed like this would turn my male gay friends straight. "You sexist pig," she joked as she sat on the corner of the table just above me. "So is everything alright?"

"Fitch tried to sic his driver on me."

"Are you okay?" Her concern was immediate.

I nodded, "I'm fine, but Charlie's hitting the high notes in the Star Spangled Banner. Fitch has also been warned that if he shows up again he will be arrested. I also told Jerome, so his people downstairs will keep an eye open for Fitch. What's going on here?" I indicated towards her outfit.

"While you were downstairs throwing out the garbage," she joked, "our last three clients finished and since we don't have any more appointments, I'm closing up early. The girls wanted to party at the pool, and I liked the idea, so we're having some party platters delivered from downstairs and we're going to break out some champagne. Of course, John, you're welcome to join us."

"Thanks, but I didn't bring my trunks."

"I don't think the girls would mind considering what some have seen and dealt with." She thought that was funny.

Denise placed her hand on my shoulder. "Seriously, John, I was thinking about what you were saying before, and knowing you I know your becoming a police officer wouldn't fit. They have too many rules and regulations for your personality."

"True, if I brought in a guy who was smacking his wife and kids around as recreation, I know he'd have a serious accident on the way in."

"Agreed. That said, have you ever considered becoming a private investigator? Look at what you've done, the people you've helped and the killers you've help catch. And you'd still be keeping your promise to your mother."

"Sounds good, but it wouldn't work. See New York has certain

170

requirements for P.I.s having some background in law enforcement."

Denise moved her hand to mine. "There was one other idea I had, considering how you're wired and what you've done. Have you considered becoming a bodyguard?" A spark went off in my head, the idea sounded very appealing. "Didn't you tell me last year you were in Vegas with Katsuro and you helped him protect some gambler?"

"Yeah, his ex-girlfriend tried to kill him when he went back to his wife."

"And didn't Katsuro say you'd be a natural?"

"Something like that."

"Why not look into it? You've got the smarts and skills. I think with the right training you'd be great at protecting people." I admit the lady gave me a lot to consider. "Listen …" She got up, took my arm, and pulled me in tow. "As your boss, I see you need some fun, so we're officially closed, you're off the clock, and I'm ordering you to kick back with us and have some fun pool side. Besides, how many guys will be able to say they were the only man with a group of high-end, escorts, partying in a rooftop pool on New Years? Besides, we can see the fireworks when they go off at midnight and the show's worth it, believe me."

"All right, I'm in."

It was a good night, and like Denise said, how many guys can claim they hung out with scantily clad women, in a rooftop pool, with good food and drink, and the fireworks launched from the old Niagara Mohawk building.

The girls swam and drank and partied, and after the fireworks I stood near the greenhouse-like windows, thinking. As one year passed away, a new one was born, and I realized this was a time for new beginnings. I suddenly recalled what Friedrich Nietzsche wrote: "What does not kill me, makes me stronger."

I now see the past two years had been a baptism by fire, so to speak, and I was ready. Denise was right about me being a natural for protecting those who couldn't protect themselves. Then the irony hit me; the original purpose of the Sicilian Mafia was to protect those who could not protect themselves, like the rich nobility and land owners could thanks to their wealth. The law was seemingly always on their side and somewhere, at some point, the Mafioso lost their way. Ironically, after my actions, I could never join my father's organization, let alone lead like he hoped I would someday, and here I am about to embrace the original ideals of the Mafia. God had to be laughing in Heaven above us all at that. From here on I would protect those who needed safeguarding and God help those who crossed me.

"Hey, stranger," Denise said as she came up behind me. "Thinking hard or trying to count the stars," she joked. I turned and realized she'd just gotten out of the pool. Her hair slicked back and the swimsuit clung to her tanned and sculpted body. Denise had a white beach towel over her shoulders.

"Oh, I'm thinking about the future."

"Really, and what about the future, John?"

I leaned in and kissed Denise, which surprised her. Her eyes turned into cup saucers and her face became flushed. I heard some cat calling from Autumn and the girls, but ignored them. "Happy New Year's boss. I'm thinking this year's going to be a good one."

THE END

Glossary

Beef on weck is a sandwich found primarily in Western New York. It is made with roast beef on a kummelweck roll. The meat on the sandwich is traditionally served rare, thin cut, with the top bun getting a dip au jus. Accompaniments include horseradish, a dill pickle spear, and french fries.

About the Author

C.G. (Christopher) Eberle is a proud life long resident of Buffalo, New York. A writer since he was 5 years old, C.G. started with his homemade comic books and story books, and then seriously took to writing in high school. While in college, studying English Education, C.G. was published twice in 2004 & 2006, and then switched gears to one of his major passions, mysteries.

Besides writing C.G. is a amateur Old West Historian, an avid classic movie fan & collector, a lover of most styles of music, an avid reader, a student of cryptozoology, an amateur Ripperologist, and dabbles in the kitchen quite well. Currently he is finishing his follow up mysteries Family Friend, Seasons of Murder, & his three part serial thriller: The Father's Day Saga.

Other books by the author at Melange

Family Ties, A John Seraph Mystery
Family Plots, A John Seraph Mystery
All Hallow's Evil, A John Seraph Mystery

Reach the author at:
https://www.facebook.com/chris.eberle.353
http://cavillier1970.wix.com/theamateurdetective
https://twitter.com/cavillier1970

THE
FREEMAN

A NOVEL

BY
J.C. HARACH

The Freeman

© 2022 by J.C. Harach

Published by J.C. Harach, Calgary, Alberta

Edited by Ebook Launch

Cover Design by Bigpoints

Printed in Canada

ISBN: 978-1-7781855-0-2

ACKNOWLEDGMENT

I'd like to thank myself.

I know that's not what you're supposed to do. You're supposed to thank your wife, your kids, your parents, your friends, or a teacher who changed your life. You're supposed to thank them for their support, their guidance. You're supposed to say without them, none of this would have been possible and that you're so incredibly grateful for their help.

I'm not going to do any of that. I'm not going to do that because it's a lie. The truth is, I wrote this alone. No one talked to me about it. No one sat next to me at night when I worked on it. No one offered to read it or gave me a word of encouragement when I was feeling sad, frustrated, and doubted myself.

I did that myself.

For doing that, I'd like to thank myself.

PROLOGUE

I hook up with a girl I find on the internet. Eight months after that, I'm tying a pharmaceutical CEO to a chair and saying, "Whoever controls your sexuality controls you." I would have never done anything like this before though. I was just like everyone else.

With both hands, I give the rope a hard tug and say, "There are a lot of ways that we're controlled."

Mr. CEO wiggles a little, side to side, loosening the rope, so I slap him on the back of the head and say, "If you don't stop moving, I'll smash a hole in your head." He stops right away. Then he looks down at his feet. Spread out on the floor beneath him is a jug of bleach and a saw. He sobs.

"Oh, shut up," I say, rolling my eyes. "You know you deserve this."

Mr. CEO can't see what I'm doing. I'm standing behind him, reaching over to pick up a power drill off a desk. Scattered across this desk are pieces of paper, scribbled on and crumpled into balls that are falling onto the floor. I kick one to the side, cutting my toe on a nail sticking out of the floor.

This apartment of mine is going to be torn down soon, and all throughout it are rusted nails inching out of the floorboards to snag your foot. Stepping over another nail, I take a step closer to Mr. CEO. I bring the drill to the back of his head, pressing the trigger.

Mr. CEO shakes his head back and forth and screams, "No, no, please, no."

I smile.

Tonight has already worked out so well—better than I had hoped—and the feeling that I get is I'm one of those office accountant types. You wake up every morning. Piss. Get dressed. Drink coffee. Shit. Force-feed yourself. Drink more coffee. Then you fight your way through traffic to get to work and sit in a cube. To stare at a screen.

You've never thought about any of that; you just did as you were told.

"With your help," I say, fingering the drill's trigger, "that's going to change." I've got a plan.

The world won't be the same after tonight, and it's not going to be nice. It's going to be messy. It has to be, and that's okay, because things like this can only be accomplished by violence.

Leaning over to whisper in Mr. CEO's ear, I say, "We're all the victims of violence."

And no, I'm not crazy.

I giggle.

Oh, don't play dumb, Mr. CEO.

Don't pretend like you don't know.

I know.

I know about what you've done to your employees.

At this point, Mr. CEO lets out a pretty intense cry and says, "I have money. I'll pay you whatever you want."

I laugh.

"You don't understand," I say. "I don't want your money."

This is about so much more than just money.

Me, I'm standing behind Mr. CEO, watching a grown man whimper, sniffle, and sob, and for a super brief moment, I almost forget what this is about: the kidnapping, the anger, all that ignorance and soon-to-be-released social rage. It's not about helping those poor employees or teaching a CEO a lesson. It's about persuasion and control, and Nastasia.

I've got this whole psychological crisis thing going on. I hate my life. I don't like my wife. Then I find Nastasia on the internet, and she changes everything. Without her, I would still be nothing, and none of this would be happening.

By now, I've worked Mr. CEO into a pretty good scare, so I know he's almost ready to go. I press the drill tip into the soft spot on the back of his neck and ask if he's going to help me.

"Stop," he whimpers. "Please stop. I'll do whatever you want. I don't want to die."

I smile.

"Don't worry," I say. "You're not going to die, although what I'm going to do to you will make you wish you had. What happens tonight changes everything."

PART 1

1.

I'm going to a party. The wife told me I was going yesterday. Or maybe it was earlier in the week. I don't know for sure. She reminded me it was tonight just a moment ago. "It's going to be so much fun!"

The wife looks at me with clear eyes. The decision has been made, at any rate. No point thinking about it now. The wife has a list of things I need to do before we go. I need to buy a nice bottle of wine as a gift "Because," she says, "that's what you do when someone invites you to their place." And since I'm already heading out, I might as well as grab a few groceries as well.

I head to the supermarket, only five minutes away. I take the car, as usual, since I want to be quick and don't like walking. Outside, there's a hint of gray in the clouds. It feels like rain. I park near the store's entrance, so I can get in and out fast, only it doesn't take long before I run into trouble.

While I am standing in an aisle searching for a box of crackers, a pile of cans crashes to the floor behind me, and someone taps me on the shoulder. It's a woman. She's ugly and a bit on the heavy side. She looks at me with beady eyes. Then, she says I pushed her kid. I look behind her. Sure enough, there he is, pointing at me with a fat little finger. The mom says, "You should be ashamed of yourself."

Now, I don't know what type of expression she sees on my face, but she steps right in front of me and starts poking me in the chest with her finger. In no time at all, she creates a big stir. My head swivels from side to side. At the end of the aisle, I spot a teenager holding his phone. He's recording us.

Even though I just got to the grocery store and was not near the cans, I think the mom might be right. After all, she seems so sure of herself. Just in case she's right, I say, "I didn't mean to do anything." I even add, "It wasn't my fault."

She turns around quickly and walks away, but not before huffing hard. Then I think, *I shouldn't have said any of that.* After all, I didn't have anything to apologize for, and she's the one who should be doing better parenting.

I leave the store in a big rush. When I get home, the wife meets me at the door. She checks inside the grocery bag. As soon as she crosses her arms, I know I've done something wrong. Apparently, I bought the wrong type of cheese. The wife gives me this disapproving look. I'm about to tell her she didn't tell me what type to get. Instead, I check my watch and turn around without saying a word. I take the car again and go back to the store.

Outside the clouds are heavy. The store is busier this time. I go to the dairy aisle, then I head to a long line at the cashier. Two women, one in front of me and one behind me, have both found strawberries on sale and are talking very loudly because it's a good deal. They're going back and forth as if I'm not even there. I want them to stop. At one point, I turn to them and am about to say something, but they both look at me and I quickly change my mind. I fixate instead on the magazine rack

and the glossy covers of beautiful people. On one is the Hollywood action star The Rock. He looks very serious. His arms, muscles bulging, are crossed, and his eyes look very confident. Behind him is a dumbbell rack. The cover says he's one of America's one hundred most influential people.

Then, the cashier says something I don't quite catch. That's when I realize it's my turn. I hesitate for a moment before telling the cashier I'll be right back. I pick up the cheese and walk to the produce aisle. I wander around for a bit and get a little mad. Eventually, though, I find the strawberries. They're at the supermarket entrance and 35 percent off. I walk back to the cashier with the strawberries. The line is shorter this time. When I get to the front, I notice the cashier. She's a pretty, young blonde in a white, button-up dress shirt too big for her. What strikes me the most is how the top two buttons on her shirt are undone. For a moment, I swear she gives me a look; however, that might be a false impression.

As soon as I get home, I walk into the kitchen. My head hurts a little bit, probably from me getting dehydrated from all the back and forth. I drink two glasses of water, only I do it too fast and some spills down my chin. I wipe it off with my sleeve. Just as I finish, I realize the wife is upset. She's standing there staring at me with her arms folded. Of course, I hadn't cleaned the house yet. Because of all the rushing around, the mishap with the angry mom, and the two trips to the grocery store, I didn't manage my time well. I say that to the wife. Then I tell her about the strawberry sale. Right away, she picks the grocery bag off the floor, digs inside, and grabs a handful of strawberries. Without even bothering to wash them, she bites off the bottom half and hands me the stems.

"These are good!" she says, reaching back for more. Then she smiles and says, "Are you going to clean the house now?"

I say, "Yes."

I drink some coffee before cleaning because I'm tired. I like coffee, particularly when it's black. I don't like it as much if it has milk or sugar in it. As soon as I'm done, I start to clean. First, I vacuum. Then I move on to the bathrooms. After I'm done, I take a shower and get dressed for the party. While I'm changing, I notice the wife has put on a low-cut green dress that shows off her neckline, which is very slender and nice. She looks good. I tell her that, even saying she looks like a magazine cover model. She admires herself closely in the mirror, spinning from side to side.

I move toward her, but she quickly pushes me away. "Not now," she says. "If we don't hurry, we'll be late."

It's true. The party starts at eight o'clock, and it's seven thirty. We don't have much time. The two of us go outside to wait for the taxi. I glance at the sky. The clouds on the horizon are dark. The taxi arrives right away. It takes twenty minutes to get the party. The wife reads her phone the entire time. I look out the window at the clouds. As soon as we arrive, she walks right up to the door and rings the bell. I stand behind her. It's starting to rain a little. The host, a work friend of the wife, answers the door. He's bald, fat, and kind of pink.

"Hello," he says. Reaching over, he grabs my hand and shakes it so long I wonder if he'll ever let go. Then he exchanges words with the wife for a minute before turning back to me.

At that point, he says something I don't quite catch. I say, "What?"

He looks at the wife, and they both laugh. That's when he points to the sky and says, "Do you think it will rain long?"

I say, "I don't know." And he lets us inside after that.

The host's wife walks up to us. She takes the wife by the arm and leads her away. The host guides me down a narrow corridor into the living room. The entire room is very bright, whitewashed with a skylight on the roof. The furniture consists of cream-colored couches and some high-top metal chairs. In the middle, there's a large table. Spread out across it are bottles of wine and platters of meat, cheese, crackers, and nuts. I'm not hungry, but I make myself a nice-sized plate. Then I pour some wine. I have nothing else to do anyway. The host has sort of just dropped me off in the room before leaving to meet more guests.

I stand there for a bit and watch as people walk into the living room. They come in one at a time. It's a slow trickle, to start. Then everyone arrives at the same time. Some of the guests pass by me. One says "hello" and introduces himself to me. He even shakes my hand and asks who I came with. He stutters a little when he asks. I point to the wife across the room.

He only glances at her for a moment before asking, "Have you been married long?"

I say, "I think so," because I can't remember the exact number of years and don't want to be wrong. After that he's quiet, and I feel like I shouldn't have said that.

Throughout the night, the guests gather into little groups and talk. Almost all the men have bellies, and their shoulders, which draw back when they talk, make their stomachs stick out even more. Most of them talk

about work. Some mention the rain outside, which you can hear beating down against the skylight. The sound from all the conversations rises up throughout the night. It reminds me of the muffled jabber of barnyard animals.

At one point, as I'm walking to get more wine, I see a man waving his arms. He has his back to me. I can't see what he's doing, but he's very loud. He's drawn quite the crowd. I fill my glass with wine and head right over. He's talking about a small airplane that crashed in Africa, killing all but one of the passengers.

"If I didn't see it on the news," he says, "I wouldn't have believed it myself." The plane was descending to its destination when a crocodile someone snuck into the plane in their carry-on bag escaped. One person noticed the crocodile and ran to the front of the plane in a panic. Then every else did too, even though the crocodile was a baby and not much bigger than a can of soup. With all the passengers running to the front, the plane became off-balance and dove into the ground."

At that point, I interrupt him to ask, "Was the crocodile a pet?"

Immediately, the man blushes and apologizes. "You probably think I'm making this up," he says.

I step toward him, so he knows that I'm serious. "No, not all," I say. After all, I thought what he'd been saying was interesting and made sense.

I drink my share of wine for the rest of the night and help myself to more cheese and meat. I don't see much of the wife, which is fine by me since I see her all the time at the house anyway. Toward the end of the night, though, I come across her by accident. She's facing a woman in her late thirties or early forties, and they're

talking about a homemade hamburger recipe. The woman says the recipe has both Worchester sauce and French onion soup mix in it. I look at the other guests to see if they actually want her to go on. To my surprise, they're all smiling, but I can't tell if it's because they're interested or just being polite.

Just then a man comes up behind her. He must be her husband because he practically runs across the room to join her. He confirms for the group that it's a very good recipe. "We made it other weekend for some friends," he exclaims. "Everyone liked it."

Not long after that, the night comes to an end. The guests leave slowly. The wife finds me in the corner of the room. She says it's time to go. I nod. She leads the way to the door. On our way out, and much to my surprise, a few of the guests standing by the door who I haven't talked to all night shake my hand as if we've just taken part in an important conversation and, because of that, have now come to a common understanding.

The taxi ride home is quick. The rain is really coming down. I'm feeling a little bit lightheaded since I've had my fair share of wine. It's snuck up on me. As soon as we walk through the door, the wife turns on the lights. It immediately hurts my eyes. I notice the wife looks good. I reach for her, trying to place my hand on her hip. She moves away, and I fall forward. Then she gives me a kiss on the cheek, but it's not a very good one. She says she's tired, in no mood for that type of thing, and that I should go to bed. "We can tomorrow, if you want."

I say, "Okay." After that, I try to go to sleep, but I can't. It must be all the wine, because I keep thinking about the pretty young cashier from the grocery store. I

feel a sudden surge of blood racing through my body. I get out of bed and walk to the bathroom. Closing the door quietly, I set my phone on the counter. It only takes a moment before I find a super-hot video. She's a skinny college girl with pillowy lips. I get into it very quickly. It takes no time at all. Almost immediately after starting, I'm done. I crawl back into bed, closing my eyes. All I can hear is the wife's snoring, but I know I'll have a good sleep.

2.

I have a hard time getting up in the morning. My head hurts. I roll over, put a pillow over my head, and sleep until 11:00 a.m. After that, I lie there, sort of just collecting my thoughts until noon. That's when I remember it's Sunday. I don't like Sundays. Tomorrow will be Monday, which means five more days until the weekend. I don't like thinking about that, so I get out of bed. I make my way downstairs and into the kitchen, where I pour a cup of black coffee. From the next room, I can hear the wife laughing. I walk in to see what she's doing. She's lying on the couch, wrapped in a fleece blanket, watching TV. I try to sit to watch with her, but the show isn't very funny; mostly it's just dumb. It's about two guys who've found a briefcase of money and go on a spending spree.

The wife asks, "How much money do you think they found?"

"I don't know," I say.

"Do you think they'll get to keep it?" She just won't stop with the questions. It's as if I have to keep explaining things to her.

I get up and walk to the kitchen. I stand there for a moment. Then I look in the fridge and the cupboards. For

15

some reason, I don't know what I want to do. Even though I don't feel hungry, I decide to make something to eat. I yell loud enough for the wife to hear and ask if she wants anything. She says no. I make eggs, bacon, and toast. Just as I finish, I notice the wife is standing behind me with her hands on her hips. She's dressed in tiny jean shorts and a tank top. She asks, "What do you want to do today?"

I'm about to answer when she says we should go to the pool with her sister, her sister's husband, and their two small kids. "I think it would be fun. Know what I mean?" I don't understand why she's added that last bit. Of course, I know what she means.

Just to clear that up, I say, "I understand what the first part of your sentence means." She gives me a look, but I don't pay too much attention to her after that.

To be completely honest, though, I don't want to go to the pool. I'd rather go to the beach. I like the sand and the smell of the ocean. But the wife has said before, on several occasions, that the ocean isn't a good place for her sister's small kids because of the currents, so whenever she brings that up, I always act nice and pretend to agree.

Turning to face her, I say, "Okay." I set my breakfast on the table.

I walk up upstairs to the bedroom to get ready for the pool. I put on a pair of shorts and a T-shirt. On my way back downstairs, there's a knock on the door. It's the sister-in-law. She says hello. I say hello back.

I ask, "How are you?"

She says, "Good."

After that, I'm not sure what else needs to be said, so I yell—but not loud enough to be rude—for the wife. "Your sister is here."

She hollers back, "I'll be right there."

I stare at the sister-in-law. She's so skinny she almost looks sick. She fidgets a little under my gaze. Then she says, "What did you do last night?"

I say, "I went to a party."

She asks, "Who was there?"

Now, I'm not sure why she does that. She wouldn't know anyone there. But I list off all the names that I can remember. After that, I yawn, and I think she gets it. I peer over her shoulder to look outside. There are puddles of rain on the street left over from last night, but not a cloud in the sky. I'm thinking it will be nice day when the sister-in-law interrupts. She says her husband has only dropped her off to visit while he grabs a few things for the pool. He'll be back in a minute with the twins. "If you like," she says, "you can squeeze in with us."

I say, "Okay," but only because I feel drained and don't want to drive.

The wife comes up behind me. She reaches in, hugging her sister. "It's nice to see you," she says.

Right away, I turn around and walk into the kitchen. I don't notice until I finally sit down at the table to eat my breakfast, but all the bacon is gone. I stand up and walk back to the front entry to talk to the wife. I ask if she's eaten it. She says there's no time to argue about that now. Then she laughs and says, "If anything, you should know better than to not make enough for two people, and you best eat quickly because we're leaving in a few minutes."

The brother-in-law drives us to the pool. He's short and always wears T-shirts that are tight around his arms. He's grown a beard since I last saw him. I stare at it for a

moment until I finally realize what it reminds me of. He looks like a garden gnome. I sit at the very back of the van with the wife. The puddles on the street have gotten smaller, and I'm surprised by how fast the sun is rising in the sky. As usual, the parking lot is full. We drive around for a bit. Then the sister-in-law says, "There's one!" And the brother-in-law turns right into the parking space.

I help unpack the minivan. The brother-in-law keeps handing me things. He puts chairs in each of my hands and slings a cooler bag over my shoulder. We start walking to the entrance. The midday sun is starting to beat down. A few beads of sweat drip down from my forehead and onto my face.

The pool is busy. The brother-in-law picks a spot on a small hill. It has a good view and is between two pools. One is for little kids. It's shallow and has a giant plastic mushroom in the middle that shoots water into the air. The other pool is for adults. It's deeper and has a diving board. The wife and the sister-in-law take the twins to play under the mushroom. The brother-in-law and I sit in two chairs on the hill. I watch the twins play. They start playing a game with some other kids. Very quickly, they organize themselves into a little group and decide the rules together. At first, they play fine, but after a while, one of them must have disagreed and broken the rules because the rest of the kids gang up on him and make him leave. The sister-in-law jumps in after that, but it's already too late because the kid has walked to the far side of the pool and started to cry.

A little later, a group of twenty-year-old girls lay beach towels in front of us. There're about five girls in all, and they giggle while they talk. Almost all of them

are wearing bikinis, and the string at the top, which is tied tight around their chests, makes the sides of their breasts stick out even more. I watch them for a bit. Then they disappear into the pool, and I lose track of them.

For the rest of the afternoon, the brother-in-law and I drink beer. He keeps glancing over to check on me. If my beer is almost empty, he hands me another. The heat is really cranking down. The sun is shining directly overhead onto the grass. The brother-in-law sees the sweat pouring down my face. At that point, he motions to the sky and says, "Hot out."

I look at the sky and say, "Yes."

After a while, the wife returns with the sister-in-law and the twins. She stands in front me. I lift my head up. I'm surprised by how much energy it takes to look at her. For a moment, I'm overcome by a brief bout of dizziness, and I almost fall over in my chair.

"It's getting late," the wife says. "What should we do for supper?" There are a few ideas thrown out, but not any good ones.

Composing myself, I suggest the homemade hamburger recipe the woman from the party mentioned. The wife likes that idea. She gets on her phone, sending a text to get the recipe. After that, she says, "Should I invite my parents?"

I shrug and say, without looking at her, "If you want to we can. I'm not too fussed either way, but it might be easier if everyone just eats at our house." After that, we pack up and rush home. The mother-in-law makes the hamburgers. As expected, they're quite good. I have two big burgers with the works and devour my share of fries. During dinner, the wife and sister-in-law take turns

trying to get the twins to eat their food. The brother-in-law tells a story, blurting out bits and pieces of sentences through his ridiculous beard about when he was a very young kid and painted a racing stripe on his father's car with a can of paint. Everyone laughs, and I laugh too, even though we've all heard it before.

The father-in-law says, "That's literally the funniest thing I've ever heard." I stare down at my plate. I dip the only remaining fry on my plate into a puddle of ketchup and move it around, tracing out circles and squares.

I clean the kitchen after everyone leaves. The wife goes to the living room to watch TV. When I'm done, I join her. I sit next to her and put my hand on her leg, but she doesn't seem interested. I remind her she said we could. "You promised," I say.

"I know," she replies, "but I just started my show."

After that, I don't want to sit with her. I don't want to watch TV either, and since I just ate, I don't feel hungry, so I go to the basement. I lie on my side on the couch, pull my phone out of my pocket, and watch videos of girls. At one point, I accidently hit an ad at the side of the screen. It's for some sort of dating site. I figure there's no harm in looking. Besides, it might even be funny if I recognize someone, and I have nothing else to.

It only takes a few minutes to make a profile. The site is for young girls looking to spend time with older, well-off guys. It asks for my income. That immediately puts me off at first, but given the nature of the site, I understand why it makes sense. I decide to add a little on top, just to fit in and be safe. The hardest part of the whole thing is finding a good picture of my face, but I manage to find one from a few years ago with very good lighting that I put a filter on.

I message a few girls. It only takes ten minutes before some message me back. Most of them are college students, though I think some are professionals. It's interesting to talk to them, and they're all very friendly and appreciative, but mostly I just like the pictures and attention. I lose track of time.

Without even realizing it, two hours pass. I need to go to bed, or I'll have a hard time getting to work in the morning. I figure I'll check my messages one last time. There's just one anyway. It will only take a minute. It says, "I love your profile." I look to see who it's from. Her name is Nastasia.

3.

The wife shakes me by the shoulder, waking me up from my sleep. If not for her, I might have not gotten up at all, but she keeps at, relentlessly. "If you don't get out of bed," she says, "you'll be late for work."

I roll out of bed, go downstairs, and drink some coffee. I take a shit. I get into the shower. As I'm drying off, I hear my phone ping. I wonder who it is. No one texts me first thing in the morning. Then I remember I gave Nastasia my number before I went to bed. I think it must her. It is.

She says, "I had a great time talking to you last night." She'd like to meet me. "I'm sure we can come to an arrangement that works for both of us." I don't really understand, so I ask her to explain.

Just then, the wife yells that I better get going or I'll miss my train. "Hurry up," she says. I check the time. She's right. I put my phone in my pocket. I wave goodbye as I run out the door. It's already getting hot out, and the train station, which resembles a gray concrete pencil case on the horizon, is shimmering in the early morning heat.

The train pulls up to take people downtown to work. People are crowded into the seats and hanging from the handrails. Several of them are bent over their

phones, staring at them in silence as if they were nothing but piles of stones or dead trees. Suddenly, the train screeches to a stop. I hold on tight to my handrail. More people pack in. I turn to gaze out the window. I watch the houses and neighborhoods speed by. Then, we dip under the river through a tunnel. All I see is darkness broken up by the blur of white and yellow lights. We shoot out the other side and climb past a row of office towers wrapped in blue steel and black glass.

My phone pings from inside my pocket. With one hand still on the handrail, I read the message. Nastasia says it's best to come to an agreement on what we both want right way. "That way," she explains, "we can put the uncomfortable part behind us and have some fun." She wants a small monthly allowance. In return, we can do anything I want. "I'll officially be yours," she says.

I ask, "Anything?"

She says, "Yes." Then, very abruptly, but not in a pushy way, Nastasia asks, "Do you want to know how much?"

I do, but I hadn't thought to ask. Nastasia gives me a price. I don't know what to say after that. I know you're not supposed to pay for sex, but I'm not sure why. It feels silly to not do it and just blindly accept that it's bad when I don't even understand why it's wrong, particularly if both of us are okay with it. It's going to be expensive. But if I use my savings, I'll probably be fine.

Fortunately, I look up at that exact moment. It takes me a second to realize what's happened. I've been so immersed in thought that I missed my stop. I push my way to the door. I'm ten blocks from the office and almost late for work. I have to run. People are walking

up and down the sidewalk and crossing the street. I race past them, almost tripping a few times along the way. A truck rattles by me with the muffler coughing, and a hot wall of exhaust hits me in the face. Between the running and the fumes from the truck, I can hardly breathe, and by the time I get to the building, I've started to sweat. In the elevator, a few people holding coffee cups and donuts look at the wet stains under my arms and laugh. It's a Monday all right.

I work hard all morning. My neck is a little stiff from stooping forward in my chair, so after a while I lean back to stretch. That's when I check the time. It's lunch, which surprises me because the morning has gone by very fast. I figure I better get something to eat—not because I'm hungry, but rather because it's lunchtime. I take the elevator into the lobby and walk to the food court. None of the restaurants are that busy, but there's a long line at a taco stand. It winds all the way from the cashier into the middle of the food court. I walk to the end of the line, stopping in between a row of tables.

I've only been standing there a minute when I hear a dad arguing with a kid at a table. He's telling his kid, who's probably no older than six, to drink his milk. "Go ahead," he says. "You need to drink it to grow big and strong."

The kid says, "Nooo!" but the dad persists.

At that point, the mom jumps in to say, "If he doesn't want to, he doesn't need to."

Right then, the dad raises his voice, and a few people eating nearby turn to look. The dad is pale and yellow like a spoiled egg. He says, "I've never done anything in my life I've wanted to. Why should he be any different?"

The kid looks at the mom, and the mom looks back at the kid. "Drink your milk," she says.

At that point, the line moves forward, and I'm glad that it does. It's not long before I get my tacos. As soon as I see them, my mouth starts to water. I rush back to the office and eat them in my cubicle. It's beige and carpeted to muffle the sound. I'm leaning back in my chair, eating and swiping through pictures and videos on my phone, when I finally get the courage to text Nastasia back. I've been thinking about her all morning, but even more so now because of the uncomfortableness caused by the interaction with that dad from the cafeteria. The fact that he seemed unhappy—and that I sometimes feel unhappy too—is what really brought Nastasia's question to the front of my mind.

I'm a little embarrassed, and I'm not sure what to say, but I thumb back a text. "I'm not sure about paying," I say. "I haven't done that before. It feels weird."

Nastasia is nice about it. "That's normal," she says. To provide some context, she explains all her girlfriends do it to pay for college because school is expensive, and they also like having a little money to buy nice things. "This type of thing," she says, "is very common with my generation—sort of accepted but not really talked about—and when you think about it, men already pay for dinner and dates. Only this way, there's no pretending. It's all very upfront, and you get exactly what you want."

I haven't thought about it like that before. It's as if Nastasia is from a different world, which until a moment ago I didn't know existed. For a while, I don't know what to say. But I want to keep talking to her, and I impulsively text her that I'm married. Right away I feel ashamed, but

Nastasia texts back and says that's not a problem. "I've heard marriage is sort of boring anyway."

She's right, and I agree. After that, I decide there's no harm in meeting. The past few days have been so dull and repetitive, and I have nothing else to do. We make plans to meet on Saturday, even though Nastasia wants to meet on Friday. However, as soon as I put my phone in my pocket, I immediately beat myself up for not changing my plans to accommodate her. I text her back and say, "Friday is fine."

Nastasia says, "Great! I can't wait to meet you!" I put my phone back in my pocket and decide to do some work.

I have to design a new logo for a car dealership, and after that an ad for a billboard. At one point, the owner comes by. He started the ad agency. He's in his late sixties and gray. Generally speaking, he's very well liked. The word around the office is he's looking for a successor. He leans over to see what I'm designing. It's a logo in cornflower blue. He says, "You should make it Chanel red." Then, without sounding critical, he says, "It's important that it has a distinct and recognizable look, so it gets noticed. That way people will remember it."

I turn in my chair to face him. He has bright, lively eyes and a comforting, grandfatherly smile. He says that after the famous shoe designer Christian Louboutin made his first pair of high heels, he examined them closely and realized they didn't feel right. The shoes lacked liveliness. They didn't catch the eye and pop like they should. Frustrated, Louboutin looked around until he saw a woman wearing bright red Chanel nail polish. *That's perfect!* he thought. He decided to use that same color on

his shoes. Now all Louboutins have red-lacquered soles, making them unique and easy to recognize.

I turn away from the owner to look at the color palette on my computer screen. "That makes sense," I say. "I'll do it."

After that, I assume that we're done, but the owner doesn't leave. He stands in my cubicle for a moment before asking if I'll do him a favor. Without giving me time to answer, he says, "We have a new employee in sales who started today, and usually I like to make a good impression with new employees and have someone take them out. I can't do it. I'm double-booked, and no one else is available." He pauses for a moment, and it occurs to me that it's my turn to talk, but just as I open my mouth, the owner says, "I've got box seats to the game tonight. Would you mind going with the new employee? It would be great if you showed him a good time and answered any questions he has about the company."

Now, normally I don't like watching sports, but since the owner has asked and he's technically in a position of authority over me, I agree.

"Great!" the owner exclaims, patting me on the shoulder. "I won't forget this. I'll owe you one." Then he eyes me up and down. With a chuckle, he says, "You can't go wearing that." He disappears. When he comes back, he has a gold jersey in his hand. "You're lucky I've got an extra," he says. "Put it on. It can get pretty ugly at the game. It's best if you're on the right side."

I leave the office a little late, at 6:00 p.m., with the new guy from sales. He's an ex-athlete and a big sports fan. We take the elevator to the main floor and walk through the front door. We decide to take the train. The

stadium isn't very far away, but we'll get there faster that way. As we get closer, I make out the gold flags sticking out from poles on the roof of the stadium. The sales guy says, "It's a heated rivalry."

I watch the steady stream of gold and blue jerseys funneling into the stadium. I say, "I had no idea."

The sales guy draws himself up and starts to laugh. "At least you've got on the right jersey."

The sales guy leads the way to our seats. He has shoulders like a capital *T*, and despite being quite big, he moves quickly like a cat. We cross two levels and climb a big set of stairs that overlook the field. The stairs are covered in peanut shells and popcorn, and the concrete in-between the aisles is sticky from spilt drinks. As expected, the seats are quite good, and the stadium fills up very quickly. As we're watching people funnel in, the sales guy leans over to whisper in my ear. "It's an open bar," he says. "We best take advantage of that." I nod.

The game starts right away. The speakers blast music, and I find it a little disorientating with all the cheering and noise, but at the same time I'm swept up in it all. I even catch myself standing up and yelling at a few very bad plays. It's only then, way on the other side of the stadium, that I notice a man in a blue jersey taunting a group of fans wearing gold jerseys. At that point, the sales guy says something that I miss, and when I look back again, two fans in different colored jerseys have started going at it. The sales guy says, "I told you it was a heated rivalry." I nod and turn my gaze back to the field, keeping my eyes glued to the game.

As soon as the game is over, the sales guys says, "Follow me." He leads the way down a concrete set of

stairs into a big corridor. Hordes of fans are funneling in from every direction like cattle. The sales guy darts in between two people. I follow close behind. I try hard to keep up, but there are too many people. I grit my teeth and push ahead, fighting for space and bumping up against people along the way. Ahead of me, I see the exit— a dozen double doors—but only one is open, and everyone moves to that door. The crowd surges forward. From behind me, I hear hollering. From the noise, I can tell another fight has broken out. Then someone punches me hard in the back, and I fall forward. I'm only on the ground for a moment, and I'm about to cover my head when someone pulls me up. It's the sales guy. He's puffing out his chest.

"Poor winners," he yells. He's spitting while speaking and when looks around to find the person who punched me, there's no one to be seen. That person has disappeared into the crowd. That's when the sales guy turns to face the exit and yells, "Hey! Open the rest of the doors!"

Someone at the front looks back and gives him a nod. Then he opens a door. Everyone else nearby must have been watching because the rest of doors swing open after that, and it clears out very quickly. As soon as we're outside, the evening hits me like a slap in the face, probably because I'm a little drunk and drained from the weight of the crowd. The sales guy is beside me. He's still worked up about me being knocked to the ground. He wants to teach the blue-jersey fans a lesson. I think if I stick around, he'll do it for sure, just to put on a show. All I say is, "I want to go home." I thank him for the evening and shake his hand goodbye.

A little later, I get on the train. Through the window, I watch the black-tinted glass office towers go by. The train ducks into the tunnel under the river. I watch the blur of white and yellow lights go by. Inside the train, people are bent over staring at their phones in the same way they did this morning. My back feels stiff, probably from sitting in the stadium chair for so long and being hit in the back.

Before long, the train arrives at my stop. Outside, night has fallen, and darkness has gathered above the trees. I think about how the fans in the stadium hate each other so much, as if each has it right and the other has it wrong, but at the same time, I'm a little distracted by the sky. It's more blue than black. I stare into it as if I expect to see something, but the clouds block my view, and I'm already fatigued from the walk. Fortunately, I'm not far home. I get to my house and pause for a moment on the step to catch my breath. Through an open, upstairs window, I can hear the wife snoring. I stand there, still. With the key to the door in my hand, it occurs to me that another Monday is over. Tomorrow I'm going back to work, and for the first time in a very long time, I have something to look forward to. I can't wait to meet Nastasia.

4.

The next day, the owner is nice to me. He comes by to look at the logo. He says, "That looks great." I'm glad. I did just what he told me to do.

After that, he asks if I enjoyed the game. Even though I don't want to be rude, I figure it's best to be honest. "Not really," I say.

"I'm sorry to hear that," he says, pausing for a moment before asking why. He's wearing a freshly pressed gray suit with a bright sunflower tie.

Without giving it much thought, I say I liked the seats and the free beer, but I didn't like how the two teams disliked each other so much. "It was as if it was more than just a game," I say. "It was like they were really enemies."

The owner doesn't answer right away. Then, in a very measured voice, he says, "That makes sense." I look at him, and there's a short silence. Then he pulls up a chair and sits down. Facing me, he starts to explain. Thousands of years ago, he says, human beings evolved to listen to large groups of other people. This was helpful because of the survival benefits it offered. People who organized themselves and learned to work together and think in groups were more likely to survive the harsh environment they lived in. "Today," the owner says, "we

still act and think in groups. It's part of our biology and psychology. You see it in sports with heated rivalries, and you see it here at the ad agency." Pointing to the red logo on my computer screen, the owner says, "In a way, this logo works the same way. Once our client starts to use it, their customers will gradually begin to identify with it and feel like they're part of a group—just like how a sports fan identifies with their team or a fashionista identifies with Louboutins."

The owner asks me if that makes sense. I nod and smile. He grins back. Then he checks his watch and gets up. "I've got to go to a meeting," he says. Before leaving, he looks at me closely and says, "It's interesting you didn't like the game." After that, he turns around and leaves.

At one o'clock, I go to my only meeting of the day. It's in the boardroom. The sales guy is there, sitting at the front of the room. We're meeting a new potential client. The client isn't there yet, and it's very quiet in the room. Then someone makes a few jokes I don't understand. Everyone laughs, and I'm about to, too, when the owner comes in. He's with the client—two men with wavy Havana-brown hair, both in their thirties. They're opening a clothing store and want to attract a lot of customers. They've heard good things about the agency and want to see if we can help. One is wearing a Hawaiian shirt and the other has his hair tied up in a silly-looking bun.

The owner puts a hand on each of their backs. He offers them both a chair at the front of the room. He moves with such elegance I mistake him for a sort of vision. Now, normally the owner never attends meetings like this, he's always busy with bigger company things,

but when new staff come on board like the sales guy, he often takes an interest and likes to attend to help train them, particularly when it comes to landing new clients. In meetings like this, I'm not supposed to say anything. I'm only here so the client can meet the entire team or maybe answer the odd design question.

The owner starts the meeting by asking everyone to introduce themselves, say what they do, and then tell something interesting about themselves. When it comes to me, I say, "My name is Seth. I'm a graphic designer. I've been working at Acuscent Media Interactive for eight years, and I don't do anything interesting."

There's a silence that lasts for several seconds. Then someone bursts out laughing. For a moment, I feel like I'm being criticized, and I'm about to explain, but the owner interrupts. Looking at me sympathetically, he asks the next person to go. The introductions keep going after that.

The owner does all the talking once the meeting officially starts. He says very calmly he knows the two men are meeting with other ad agencies to potentially promote their clothing store, but Acuscent Media Interactive is a better choice because of the way we approach advertising. He pauses for a moment, holding the gaze of two men until they ask him to go on. "What separates us from others," he says, "is we leverage psychology and research to make advertising that works!"

To prove his point, the owner starts talking about a popular experiment that demonstrates why advertising is so effective. In it, a researcher paid a man to walk down a busy street in New York and then stop and look up at the sky. Most people walking by ignored the man and kept walking, but a few—about 4 percent—stopped and

looked up to see what he was looking at. Then, the researcher paid a larger group of people to stop and look up. When it was several people, more pedestrians stopped to look up—nearly 20 percent, or five times more than when it was just one person.

"This is how good advertising works," the owner says. "People take their signals on what to pay attention to and do from other people. If one person looks up, no one cares. But if ten people look up, there must be something important to see. That's where we come in with advertising: We get people to stop and look up."

At this point, both men are facing the owner. They're practically sitting on the edge of their seats. The owner dims the lights. He turns on the projection screen at the front of the room and says, "There are lots of ways we can help your clothing store get more attention and business." He plays a series of videos. In them, different items are cut in half by a black-bladed kitchen knife: a frozen egg, an old leather belt, even a small tree is hacked into pieces after only a few swipes. With the lights still dimmed, the owner says, "We called this ad campaign 'Cut it up.' It got a lot of attention. People liked watching unusual things like soda cans getting cut in two, and because it was unusual, people talked about it, they told their friends, and they shared the videos. The whole video campaign got 150 million views on YouTube. That got a lot of public attention. In the end, we helped our client, Samurai Super Knives, sell lots of knives because it showed how durable their knives are, and it made anyone who bought them feel like they were part of a special group that owned a very cool and cutting-edge product."

I find what the owner has been saying to be interesting. I want to keep listening. But at the same time,

I hear my phone ping in my pocket. I want to see who it is. Carefully, so as to not draw too much attention to myself, I glance quickly at my phone. It's Nastasia! She asks if we're meeting at someplace fancy on Friday for a drink. "I want to look good for you."

I feel my face start to flush. I haven't picked a place yet. Embarrassed, I text: "I'll have to get back to you on the place." For the rest of the meeting, I hunch forward in my chair, and with my phone hidden under the table, I text Nastasia. I ask her all sorts of questions, and she answers back right away. She's a law student in her last year of school who's in the city for the summer doing a work internship. "I don't know the city or anyone in it," she says. "I only got here a few days ago." Nastasia is renting an apartment on the southwest side of downtown. I know the area. It's full restaurants and bars.

"When I was younger, I used to go there," I say. "It's a good spot for you to stay for the summer." On more than one occasion, as I'm texting, I catch a few people glaring at me, which is understandable since my head is down and I'm looking at my phone. After that, I'm careful to only text when the owner is either talking or has his back turned to me. Eventually, I ask Nastasia why she's on the website. "Why don't you have a boyfriend your age?"

Nastasia responds, "I like older men." She says guys her age, whom I notice she calls "boys," are immature. "I'd rather spend my time with men who have experience," she says.

After the meeting, I go back to my desk. A little later, the owner sends for me. At first, I'm annoyed because I think he's going to criticize me for spending

too much time on my phone during the meeting. That isn't the case at all. As soon as I take a seat in the chair in front of his desk, he tells me he wants to talk to me about something. "It's just an idea at this point," he says, "but I'd like your opinion on the matter." Behind him are several big bay windows. The room is filled with beautiful late-afternoon sunlight. On one wall there's a shelf full of books and on the other are several photos of him shaking hands with famous people and lots of awards. The owner says he's thinking about bringing his son in to be a director and he wonders how that might be received by others in the agency. "He's just finished school with an MBA," he says. "He doesn't have any real work experience, so I don't want to be seen as doing him any favors, but it would be good to bring him into the family business."

The owner says I seem honest and not concerned with getting promoted, so he figures I'll give it to him straight and not just tell him what he wants to hear. Then he pauses and says, "I hope I haven't offended you."

He hasn't, and I tell him that. After that, I don't say anything because I'm not sure if it's my turn to talk. The owner looks at me. I never noticed until now how deep his eyes sink into his head. He says, "What do you think?"

All I say is, "I don't think people will like your son." But I can't give a reason why, and the owner is right to point out that I don't even know him yet.

At that point, I only catch a few fragments of what the owner is saying because I can feel my phone buzzing in my pocket, and I find it distracting. The owner tells me that thirty years ago when he started the agency, he

rented an entire floor of the Lewis-Walter building, even though he didn't have any employees or clients yet. "I've taken a lot of risks," he says, "but I've worked very hard, and a little discomfort is good—both in business and in life." The owner wants to know what I think. I don't have anything to add but that I agree. Then he asks me again if I think he should bring his son into the business or if it will create problems. It seems to me it would be bad. I open my mouth to say that, but the right words don't come out, and I fidget awkwardly for a moment until I mumble something about understanding him wanting to do what's best for his family.

After that, the owner stops talking. He says he's taken up too much of my time, but he appreciates me listening. He says the workday is almost over. Then he says, very quickly and with an embarrassed look, that he realizes that some people in the office think I'm odd, but he understands that people like me are always a little bit eccentric and that's part of my appeal. "If anything," he adds, "that's good, and you should let that come out more."

At that point, all I'm thinking is I hadn't realized people thought that about me, and I always figured I was well liked. For the first time since I started working at the ad agency, the owner offers me his hand. I feel the brittleness of his bones crack under his skin as I squeeze. He gives me a little grin, and as I walk through the door to leave, I think he's old, and I wonder what it will be like after he dies.

5.

The next day is slower in the office. Only a few ads come in that I have to design. The owner stops by to check in on me a few times. He gives me some advice on what to do to make them look good, and then he disappears.

After work, the wife and I meet her sister and brother-in-law for dinner. The two of them have left the twins with the mother- and father-in-law. They're eager to have an adult's night out. The brother-in-law has on a green short-sleeve shirt. Sticking out on his forearms are patches of thick, black hair. I find it a little repulsive. He orders a ribeye steak. I order one too. The brother-in-law starts smacking his lips as soon as it arrives.

The sister-in-law leans all the way over in her chair to see. Salivating, she says, "That looks delicious." As soon as I've taken a bite, she asks if I like mine. I say it's good. Then she smiles and says, "Just good?" I say yes.

After dinner, I head home with the wife. As soon as we walk through the door, she goes straight to the couch. She's streaming a new show on TV. "Sit down and join me," she says.

"Let's relax," I agree, and I'm glad that I do. Parts of the show are very good. I like how fast it moves. But I don't like how just when the most interesting thing happens, the

show ends. Fortunately, it only takes a few seconds before the next episode starts.

After a while, I check the time. Several hours have passed. I'm tired. I want to go to bed, but I want to see what happens next too. I tell the wife we should push through to see what happens. "Just one more episode," I say. But she won't have any of that.

"It's time to go to bed," she says. I follow her upstairs. As usual, she falls asleep right away and starts to snore. I put my pillow over my ears to block out the noise.

The next morning, I feel completely drained and have a slight headache. At work, I drink lots of black coffee. The secretary makes fun of me. She's good friends with the owner. She's old like him and has been with the agency from almost day one. She says I've got a zombie face on. At lunch, I go to the food court. I order a double cheeseburger, fries, and an extra-large milkshake. I feel sleepy after that. I think that's why the rest of the afternoon seems to drag on. I practically have to think of things to do.

For most of the afternoon, I slouch deep in my chair and think about women. I think not so much about a single woman, but rather all women—the ones I've seen in the videos on my phone and what it would be like to have one like that. I'm obsessed by that desire. In one sense, it kills the time. In another, it throws me off-balance and I start texting Nastasia.

She asks, "How long has it been since you've done it?"

It's been awhile, and I feel embarrassed to admit that. It has been at least two months. Maybe longer. The

last time I remember for certain is the night the wife lay on the bed with her socks on, still like a starfish, while we had sex.

Nastasia laughs and says, "Dead starfish sex is the worst." That gives me a bit of a stir, but I leave it at that. Nastasia says she started late. "My dad was strict," she says. "He didn't let me go on dates." As a result, Nastasia didn't get started until she moved out to go to college. "I was twenty," she says, adding, "I like sex a lot now."

The rest of the week goes by very fast. In no time at all, it's Friday. At work, there's a meeting with another potential client. This one is in a different boardroom. It's a large room, with glass walls and a large, distressed walnut-colored table. This meeting is a meet and greet with a guy and his girlfriend who want to open a pizza restaurant. I don't catch either of their names, but the guy is a gorilla of a man, with a head like a fire hydrant. His girlfriend is a real looker, and I can't help but think he's lucky to have her.

The owner is at the front of the room with the new sales guy. The two of them have been practically inseparable this week, and the owner's been helping him a lot, even with small, insignificant clients like this one. I can't see the owner very well because I'm sitting at the back of the room, but I can hear his voice. He's listing off a variety of things that can be done to get people to visit their restaurant. Once they land on one that works for them and their budget, he turns to the sales guy and says, "We can develop a plan to market your restaurant."

The owner says one of the easiest things they can do is get a local celebrity who people like and trust to endorse their restaurant. Right away, the gorilla man shudders.

The owner assures him this no joke. "It's based on science," he says. The owner gets out of his chair. Staring right at the gorilla man, he asks if he's heard of the Milgram experiment. The man shakes his head.

The owner paces back and forth at the front of the room. He says it's a famous psychology experiment that has been repeated more than a dozen times with the same results, so you know it's true. In it, an actor pretending to be a scientist was able to get college students to give other students taking a test little electrical shocks that increased in severity every time they got an answer wrong just because he was wearing a lab coat and holding a clipboard. Of course, the owner continues, some of the students didn't want to shock the other students, but they did it anyway after they were told to.

"All it took," he says, "was for the actor with the clipboard and lab coat to encourage them to do so!" In the end, he explains, what this experiment showed was that people will listen to other people they see as authority figures, even if they don't like the instruction. Then the owner chuckles and says, "That's why on TV you see actors in ads pretending to be doctors to sell drugs."

The gorilla man turtles his neck into his shoulders. He says they don't have a lot of money to spend on advertising, particularly a campaign that uses a local celebrity, but they want people know about their new restaurant, and he realizes there're lots of pizza places out there, so he's not sure what can be done that's inexpensive to help them stand out.

The owner steeples his fingers together. After a short pause, he says he has an idea. "How about you create a

new item on your menu for a fifty-dollar slice of pizza?" At that point, the girl fidgets and whispers something into her boyfriend's ear. The owner interrupts right away. "I know that's outrageous, and that's exactly the point! A fifty-dollar slice of pizza is something people will talk about. Even if people don't go to your restaurant to try it, they'll talk about it to their friends, and even more people will hear about your restaurant. That will cut through the noise. It will separate your restaurant from others."

The gorilla guy rests his elbows on the table and cups one hand over his mouth. Right then, the owner reveals the rest of his plan. He'll tell local media outlets about the fifty-dollar slice of pizza and the gourmet ingredients on it—like black truffle and ovoli mushrooms—that make it so expensive. He says, "The media writes about whatever is new, novel, or controversial because that's what gets people's attention. That's good business for them, so they'll cover it, and once that happens, other people will find out about your restaurant."

The gorilla guy asks a few questions. He and the owner discuss things I don't understand. I gather it's about pricing and the deal. After a short time, the gorilla guy turns to his girlfriend, who gives him a nod. He walks over to the owner. Extending his hand, he says, "This sounds good to us. You've got a deal."

I leave the office right after the meeting. As soon as I get home, I take a shower. I make sure to give my whole body a good scrub because I'm seeing Nastasia later tonight. I get dressed in a casual pair of pants and a button-down shirt. By then, the wife has gotten home from work. She looks at me dressed up. I tell her I'm going to meet a new friend from work. "He's in sales," I say.

She says, "Have fun."

I leave the house. While I'm driving, it occurs to me that Nastasia might want a ride home after. But my car is old, dirty, and not very nice. I can't have that. I immediately decide to park and tell her I've taken a taxi to meet her if she asks. I pull into a parking spot on the side of the street. With the car still running, I listen to a song on the radio. The sun has started its descent in the sky, and the clouds have taken on a soft reddish glow. Two guys in a black pickup truck pull up behind me on the street. They think that I'm leaving, but I haven't waved them in. I sit there a little longer, listening to the radio and staring at the sky. It's getting redder by the minute. The guys in the truck honk their horn. That startles me, and I drive off.

It takes me awhile to find a new spot to park. After that, I walk to the bar. There's hardly a breeze, and with the smog bearing down on the city, the walk to the bar feels inhuman and oppressive. It doesn't take long to get there. Inside, there are varnished wooden tables, brass poles, and a big floor-to-ceiling wine rack. I notice the bar is empty. There's only one person sitting at it—a woman on a black leather stool at the very end. Right away I recognize Nastasia from her picture. I walk up and say hi. "Have you been waiting long?"

She looks at me with big brown eyes and says, "No."

Nastasia has dark hair that's been curled and cute chipmunk cheeks. I've only sat down for a moment when the waitress comes up and asks for our order. I get a beer. Nastasia gets wine. We talk for a while about what I do for work and how she likes being in the city. She laughs the whole time. I think that's nice. At one point, she

presses her leg against mine, and because I don't do anything, she leaves it there. On more than one occasion, I catch myself staring at her. I can make out the shape of her breasts through the low-cut top of her tiny black dress.

I assumed I'd have to get her drunk first, but I've barely started my second beer when Nastasia asks calmly—as if it's no different than asking for a glass of water—if I'm going to take her back to her apartment. "Normally I wouldn't have someone over right away," she says, "but you just seem so nice and harmless."

At the same time, I see the look in her eye and say, "I'll get the bill."

After that, everything happens so fast. I help Nastasia into the taxi, and as I do, I brush against her breasts. Everything starts to reel. All of it—her beauty, her calmness—is making it hard for me to think or see straight. I can feel my face flush and the blood race to my cheeks. For some strange reason, I start thinking that Nastasia is very experienced, this isn't going to end well for me, and it might be bad for everyone else in the world too. But then I tell myself that's a stupid thing to think, that she's just a girl, and I should go on with it and have some fun.

Just then, the taxi goes over a pothole. It shakes both of us hard, and our bodies collide. I peer out through the car's front window. The sun has set below the buildings, and the entire sky looks intensely red to me. My hand begins to shake. Nastasia reaches over and grabs it. Her fingers begin to stroke mine. I feel the smoothness of her skin, and there in the taxi, under the weight of that oppressive red sky, I squeeze her hand back.

PART 2

1.

The moment I get to Nastasia's apartment, she grabs my hand, pulls me into her bedroom, and before I know what's happening, she's on her knees undoing my belt. "I want to suck your dick," she says, looking up at me.

With my mouth hanging open, I nod, stumbling with my words before I say, "Okay."

There's a full-length mirror leaning against the wall that catches my reflection, and in it I can see Nastasia kneeling in front of me from the side.

Her body is tight in the way that only a twenty-four-year-old body can be. For a moment, just from the view, I feel like I'm watching someone else, like a popular porn star, and I suddenly get very excited, not so much from being with Nastasia, but rather from the thought of being someone interesting and important who gets what he wants and who people want to see. Still fixating on Nastasia in the mirror, I watch as she undoes my zipper, slides down my boxers, and puts my dick in her mouth. She does this in a series of fast, fluid movements. Both the speed and eagerness in which she does this catches me by surprise. The wife never does this. With her, I always have to beg and plead, and when she finally does, she always looks very uncomfortable as if she's

completing a terrible chore. But with Nastasia there's no hesitation. Just a big smile on her face and an excited twinkle in her eye.

Looking down, I watch as Nastasia starts licking my dick in such a way that it feels like she's paying tribute. This type of attention is something I've never experienced, and for the first time in a very long time, I feel appreciated and pleased with myself as if I've listened to myself and am being rewarded for finally doing that.

Pulling back to grin at me, Nastasia wipes off a little bit of saliva that's dripping down her chin with the back of her hand. "So," she says, "are you ready to have some fun?"

I say, "Yes."

With her knees still on the ground, Nastasia bends down in front of me, and with her palms on the ground she starts crawling on all fours to the bed. She moves very slowly, and I watch in amazement as her butt sways back forth. When Nastasia reaches the bed, she pulls herself up slowly, draping her body over the edge. From where I am standing, a few feet away, I can see the back of her body. Her legs are tiny, and her butt is perfectly curved.

Nastasia starts twerking her butt, bobbing it up and down to invite me in. Looking over her shoulder at me, she says, "I like it rough so don't be afraid to slap my butt as hard as you like or pull my hair."

I take a step forward, placing my hands on Nastasia's hips. With both hands, I slide myself inside her. I start having sex with Nastasia, and all that I'm thinking is, *I'm doing it! I'm actually doing it!!*

My hands are running up and down Nastasia's hips pulling her in close. I'm driving myself in, but I'm too afraid to slap Nastasia's butt or pull her hair, even though

she said I could, because I'm afraid I'll scare her away. The intensity of my thrusting sends Nastasia forward and before I know it, she's crawled up onto the bed on all fours. Without thinking even about it, I follow her forward and get into a squat while still holding on to her hips. I'm giving it to her as good as I can, and almost immediately, I start to get tired and am about to rest by getting onto my knees when Nastasia says keep going.

"That's the spot," she says. "Don't stop! You're hitting the spot!!" My legs are burning and my hips hurt, but I don't want to give up. I want to listen and please Nastasia, so I squeeze my eyes tight to block out the pain. I'm fighting to keep at it, to get Nastasia off, when she finally yells, "That's it! I'm coming!!"

Collapsing to the bed, I look up at the ceiling and place a pillow underneath my head. Lying down next to me, Nastasia rolls over and looks at me in surprise. "Wow," she says. "That never happens . . . particularly the first time with a new guy." Nastasia pauses, looking at me with interest before adding, "We have good physical chemistry."

I couldn't be happier hearing that, and for a moment I'm not sure what to do. Even though I'm very pleased with myself and my accomplishment, all that I can think to say is, "Thank you."

Nastasia laughs and says, "You're cute. It's adorable how awkward and inexperienced you are."

At first, I'm not sure if that is meant to be an insult or just an observation, but after examining Nastasia's face, I decide she meant nothing by it. To be completely honest, I'm feeling too good about myself to care.

We lay on Nastasia's bed, and I examine her body while running my hands up and down her back. All that

I'm thinking about is Nastasia's reflection in the mirror and how good she looks. That's when I surprise myself by blurting out, "You give really good head."

Turning towards me, Nastasia says, "That was fun for me too." Then laughing at herself, she says. "I actually love sucking dick."

Nastasia gets out of bed and starts collecting her clothes off the floor. "Happy girls always suck dick," she says. "If your girl's not sucking your dick, she's just not that into you."

It's at that point that the expression on my face must have changed because Nastasia suddenly smiles sympathetically and leans over the bed to kiss me. After that, she starts getting dressed. She says she's hungry and that she's going to get something to eat.

"There's a KFC a block away that I'm going to go to so we can walk out of the apartment together," she says, placing my pants on the bed in front of me to put on. It occurs to me that this might be a line to get rid of me and that Nastasia isn't really hungry, but since I still feel pretty good about myself, I agree. Besides, I have no reason not to listen to Nastasia.

As I watch her slide on a pair of jogging pants and a baggy sweater, I say, "That sounds good."

2.

The next morning, I wander into the bathroom after waking up and stay in there for a very long time thinking about what I've done.

Closing my eyes, I lean forward against the sink, turn on the faucet, and splash water on my face. My head is a weird mix of emotions, and I'm still piecing things together from the other night. I turn off the tap and examine myself in the mirror. I notice my hair has receded more than I previously thought, and the hairs in my ears and nose are too long. Little by little, I've slowly let myself go over the years. I examine myself a little closer in the mirror and start to wonder why I let that happen and if I've neglected more than just my body. That's when the wife knocks on the door.

It startles me. She wants to know what I'm doing in there. I say, "Nothing."

"Hurry up," she says. "You need to take a shower."

By the time I get out of the shower, her sister and brother-in-law have arrived with the twins. As usual, they want to go to the pool. I don't want to do that. Speaking up, I say, "We should go to the ocean instead."

The wife and sister-in-law both look at me in surprise. Right away, the two of them put up a bit of a

fuss. They give me a look as if I've broken a terrible rule. Then they remind me, in a snide sort of way, that the beach isn't a good place for kids.

"It's always windy," says the wife.

"And," the sister-in-law adds, "it's hard for the kids to swim in the ocean because of the waves."

On one hand, they are right, and it makes perfect sense. On the other, it doesn't; lots of kids go to the beach and swim. At any rate, I can tell the idea makes them very uncomfortable. I think they are holding it against me just because I suggested an idea that is new and different than what they're used to. I feel the urge to explain. At the same time, that seems like a lot of work, and I realize it's always easier not to bother.

That's when the brother-in-law jumps in. He comes up behind me, and very politely, he says, "It's only one in the afternoon. If no one likes it after today, we don't need to go back." He gives me a little grin. For the first time, I don't mind his silly beard.

After a short silence, the sister-in-law agrees. That surprises me because she's completely changed her tune.

She says, very quickly and in a jubilant voice, "The kids can build sandcastles."

Shortly after that, we drive to the beach, which is only thirty minutes away. To get there, we take separate cars. The brother-in-law leads the way, and I follow close behind. We drive down a long plateau with yellowish rocks that overlook the sea and then drops steeply down to the beach. It's covered in the whitest sand set against a soft clear sky. The sand is packed hard in places, so we drive straight onto the beach and park near the sea.

It doesn't take long to unload the vehicles. We set up a row of chairs underneath two big umbrellas. The

brother-in-law brings out a small barbeque to cook some meat. After that, I head down to the water to get a closer look at the sea. I'm not thinking about anything because I'm still tired from the night before with Nastasia. She took a lot out of me. The water is pleasantly tepid, and my mouth smarts from the salt in the air. Now and then a little wave comes up higher than the others and runs across my feet. I fixate on the froth forming from each breaking wave. Over the sound of the ocean, I think I hear my name. Only I don't know for sure, so I look back to see. That's when the wife catches sight of me. She waves for me to come back. She twirls her arm around and around in a big windmill. I figure it must be important, so I rush back.

As I walk up to her, she asks if I packed the ketchup. I say, "Yes."

She asks, "Where?" and I point to the cooler.

After that, the brother-in-law says something I don't quite catch and snickers underneath his breath. I don't say or do anything. I just stay very still and dig my feet into the sand. The sister-in-law looks at both of us quickly. There's a brief silence, and I'm not sure what's happening. Then she takes the wife by the hand. They go to the ocean for a swim. The brother-in-law watches them walk away.

As soon as they've left, he motions to an empty chair. I sit down, and we lean back in our chairs. Way off on the horizon, we make out a series of tiny fishing boats moving almost invisibly across the sea. The brother-in-law hands me a beer, but I decline—mostly because the way I'm sitting slumped forward causes my belly to bulge out more than usual, and I'm feeling strangely self-conscious.

That's when I ask the brother-in-law for advice on how to lose weight, because even though he's short, he's thick and well-muscled. I say, "What should I do?"

He gives me a once-over with his eyes and, flexing his arm, says, "You need to go to the gym and lift heavy weights." Then, reaching over, he slaps my belly and says, "Just start off slow. We don't want to give you a heart attack."

Soon, I forget about all that. It's very hot out. I enjoy the heat and moving my feet through the sand. I'm immersed in the feeling that both are doing me a lot of good. As expected, the kids keep fighting. They're playing right in front of us, and we take turns teaching them to share. Their constant bickering keeps breaking the peace of the day. At one point, one of them throws sand in the other's face. I catch the brother-in-law staring at them intently. He's very upset. I realize then that all normal parents have, at one time or another, regretted having kids.

The wife and sister-in-law return from their swim. The sister-in-law separates the twins. She stands in between them, pushing them apart with her arms.

The brother-in-law says, "You arrived just in time," and everyone laughs. Then the sister-in-law disappears into the back of the van. She's only gone for a minute. When she comes back, she lays out a pitcher of fruit punch and a bowl of potato chips onto a blanket. That shuts the kids up.

For the rest of the afternoon, we sit in the chairs. The wife and sister-in-law discuss people and things I don't know about. At one point, I gather they're very worked up and don't approve of something someone has

done. They seem to both agree there is a better way. To me, however, it all seems like a ridiculous game, and to tell the truth, I find it hard to follow what they're saying—first because the kids are still annoying me a bit, but also because the heat radiating off the sand is bringing with it a kind of dizziness. It's getting hotter by the minute, and I'm starting to feel sleepy. The wife and sister-in-law keep fanning themselves in their chairs.

It goes on like for this for a while with the sun, the heat, and the blistering sand underneath my feet until the sister-in-law finally stands up. Very abruptly, she says the kids have had enough sun for the day. "It's time to pack up and go." The wife instantly agrees. After that, we pack up and leave.

Later that evening, I have supper with the wife. I cook some fish I bought from a seafood stand at the side of the highway, which I think she enjoys, even though she pokes her head into the kitchen while I'm frying it to chastise me.

"You shouldn't have bought tilapia," she says. "You know I like salmon better."

Apart from that tiny annoyance, it isn't a bad dinner. I only pick at my food because I'm not hungry; both the heat of the day and the brother-in-law's belly slap have left me with little appetite. After we finish eating, I clean up. The wife heads to the couch. I tell her I'm going for a walk.

She gives me a sideways look and asks, "Why don't you sit down and relax?"

All I say is, "I'll be back in a bit." After that, she waves her hand over her head to say goodbye. There are families outside strolling around, and little boys and

seniors walking dogs. It's nice out. The heat from the day still lingers, and the sun has started to drop in the sky.

Along the walk, from the sidewalk I can see people watching TV inside their homes, the blue light from their TVs flickering through their living room windows. It's getting dark quickly, and what few people are still left on the street are suddenly in a hurry. I make my way home.

As soon as I arrive, I walk into the living room. The wife has wrapped herself in that same fuzzy blanket. She asks, "Where have you been?"

I remind her, "I went for a walk."

Then she says, "Why did you do that?" But before I can answer, she rolls over to face the TV.

Right away she starts laughing at people running through an obstacle course. They keep getting hit by a giant swinging bag that knocks them into a pool of water. I stand next to the wife for a while before I realize she's forgotten that I'm there, which is fine by me because I don't have anything say and I only came into the living room to tell her I was back.

I go downstairs. I haven't talked to Nastasia since last night. All day, though, I've been thinking about her, but mostly I've been thinking about the adorable pout to her lower lip. I text her, and she texts right back. She says, "Last night was fun." Then she asks, "Did you do anything interesting today?"

I tell her we took a break from the pool and went to the ocean, which I think she misunderstands, because right away she asks, "You have a pool?"

I say no and explain that we often go to the public pool on the weekend. "It's sort of a routine," I say.

After that, Nastasia doesn't text anything for a while. I set my phone on my lap and fixate on it. Then I bring

it up to my face and reread her old text messages. That takes several minutes. After that, I ask text her, "How was your day?" She says it was good and that she spent most of it thinking about her student loans and shopping.

"I bought cute shoes," she says, admitting, by laughing at herself with a stuck-out-tongue emoji, that she spent more than she would have liked, but that was okay. "They were two thousand dollars," she says, adding, "Sometimes you need to treat yourself, even if it doesn't make sense."

We go back and forth like that for a bit, not talking about anything in particular. Then, without working up to it, Nastasia says, "We're lucky to have found each other because usually it takes a long time to find a good match."

Now, I don't know if that's true or not, because I don't have any experience with this type of thing, but I tell her I agree. "I liked spending time with you," I say. I immediately feel embarrassed for admitting that to Nastasia, but she seems satisfied with the response and doesn't press it any further.

"I understand," she responds. She adds, "We can spend the entire summer doing that, if you like."

After that, I feel a little nauseous, which make sense because I haven't eaten a lot. I think about letting Nastasia go and lying down to rest. At the same time, I want to keep talking to her, so I ask her about her previous arrangements. She says she's seen three other men like me. One was from Chicago, the others from Toronto and New York. "All of them have been fun," Nastasia says. "One was a doctor, the other a lawyer, and the last a businessman. I liked being around them because they were smart, and I learned things from

them." They'd fly Nastasia down to visit for a weekend and go to fancy restaurants or ballgames.

I ask, "Do you like baseball?"

Nastasia says, no, but she likes the food. "Of course," she says, laughing at herself again with an emoji, "We also had lots of sex."

I think that's all very interesting, and I ask if it was scary to meet them for the first time because they were strangers and it was something new. She says no. She explains that when she was young, she was a military brat, so her family moved a lot and she always had to make new friends. At first, she got teased because she was always the new kid, but with practice she learned what people liked, and after a while, the teasing stopped.

"Now," Nastasia says, "whenever I meet people, I know exactly what to do and how to act, and they always like me."

That makes sense to me. After all, Nastasia seems very likeable and confident. I try to imagine what it must have been like for her as a young girl traveling to a new city for the first time to meet a stranger. I'd be very nervous if I had to do something like that, and I think she must be very brave.

"I don't think most people could do that," I say.

Even though it's not meant to be a compliment— it's just an observation—Nastasia suddenly seems very pleased and thanks me enthusiastically. "I guess I'm just a woman who's not afraid to try new things and do whatever she likes."

From upstairs, I can hear the wife rumbling around. I realize then that it's late and time for bed. I tell Nastasia I've enjoyed our talk. "Good night," I say.

She replies, "Nite, nite."

I go upstairs and crawl under the covers. I try to sleep but can't. I lie there, restless. Even with my head resting on a super soft pillow, my mind won't stop spinning. I keep coming back to the same idea. I think Nastasia has a very interesting life. In a way, her life is one type of life and mine is another. Both are very different, and I can't help but wonder if one is right and better than the other.

3.

I don't enjoy taking the train to work in the morning. I feel sleepy and want to drink more coffee, but I only have time for one cup before leaving the house because I've slept in later than usual. To make matters worse, on the train to work the guy next to me is talking into his phone very loudly. I'm not sure why he needs to do that. The train is packed full, so I'm practically pressed right up against him. I realize I've landed in a very unfortunate spot because I can't get away. Most of the other passengers are stooped over reading their phones. Their subdued murmuring, coming from below me, forms a kind of background hum to the conversation happening in front of my face. I take all this in very quickly while glaring at the man on his phone. At one point, I ask him to stop talking so loudly but I speak too quietly, and my voice is drowned out by the other passengers' murmuring.

From the way he's talking, it's as if he wants everyone to hear him. His insistent chirping is making it hard for me to think. Finally, without thinking about it, I blurt out, "Put your phone away!"

He turns to me abruptly. Narrowing his eyes, he says, "Why don't you mind your own business?"

I clench my fists by my sides, and a few of the other passengers look at the man in disdain. The man glares at me, then he looks down at my hands trembling at my sides and up at the passengers by me. After that, he turns his back to me, putting his phone in his pocket. Even after that though, and despite my best efforts, I can't understand why he had to talk so loudly. The answer only comes to me as I'm leaving. It had to be some sort of performance, but I'm not sure why, and by then I am already stepping through the train's door and onto the sidewalk.

The unpleasantness only gets worse on the street. At the crosswalk, I have to listen to some guy standing beside me blabbering on to his friend. I only catch pieces of what he is saying. The company he works for has been taken over. He isn't happy because they cut his pension. I only look at him for a moment because that's all I can bear. He has an honest face. What strikes me the most though are his fingernails. They're painted bright purple. I think he must have a young daughter who painted them like that. It's the only explanation that comes to mind. Even though I don't stare too long, he catches me looking, and to my amazement, he doesn't get mad. He gives me a pleasant look, as if we're old friends. I turn away from him after that. The streetlight has changed color, and it's time to go.

As soon I get into the Lewis–Walter building, I go straight to the coffee room because I desperately need a second cup. Several people are already there. Most of them I recognize from the meeting the other week with the two men opening the clothing store. They're all standing in a little group in front of the coffee machine, and they laugh when they see me. One of them says, "So . . . did you do anything *interesting* on the weekend?"

At first, I'm not sure if I should take him too seriously. Then I say, "I cheated on my wife," and the room goes silent. It only takes a second before the secretary bursts out laughing. She's standing behind me, rummaging through the fridge.

Poking her head out, she looks at me with curiosity and says, "Honestly, Seth, that's so funny." Even though I'd prefer not to lie, I thank her for the observation. I walk to the coffee machine after that. The little group of people standing in front of it parts silently as I approach, but no one says anything to me, and I pour my cup of coffee in peace.

For the rest of the day, I take my time designing a brochure for a client. At the end of the day, I email it to a coworker who works in client services. It's her job, not mine, to send it to the client. I go home after that.

The next day, I get feedback on the brochure. I'm told by the coworker in client services that the client isn't happy. I read her email very carefully. It says the client wants it completely reworked. At first, it's hard not to take this as a personal attack, and I wonder if I've overlooked an important instruction. That's when I remember I designed this brochure after I was laughed at in the coffee room. That must have set me off in some subtle way.

Just as I'm pondering what to do, my phone pings. It's Nastasia. "How's work?"

While still rereading the email on my computer screen, I say, "It's not going well," and without trying to be too dramatic, I voice my frustrations. "A client is being difficult," I say. "I need to redo my work."

At that point, Nastasia takes a keen interest and says, "Have you ever designed anything I would've seen before?"

Just off the top of my head, I rattle off a few things that I've worked on in varying degrees over the years.

"Wow!" Nastasia says. "Those are big companies. You must be very important!" I'm so preoccupied with the brochure that I don't respond. "It sounds like you need a break," Nastasia says. "I know just what you need to clear your head."

As luck would have it, Nastasia happens to be in the area, close to my office. She's just finishing up at the courthouse, watching a trial, and says she has time to swing by my office to give me some encouragement.

"Can you meet me out front in fifteen minutes?" she says.

I say, "Yes."

By the time I get outside, Nastasia's already there. She's wearing a tan, double-breasted blazer, high-rise slacks, and the most incredible pair of heels. Catching me staring at her heels, Nastasia says, "Aren't they lovely?" Then, lifting a foot into the air, she adds, "They're Dior. All the women at work adore them." She bats her eyelashes. "They're two thousand dollars and way too expensive for me." She flutters her eyelashes a few more times.

I look at her, and then I look at the heels. And for some reason, Nastasia sighs. Then she reaches for my hand. "I'm parked nearby," she says. "Come with me." This makes me a little bit nervous, since as a married man I can't be seen being too chummy with a pretty young girl in public. I resist for a minute before finally pulling my hand away, and not a moment too soon because just as we're coming up to the garage where Nastasia has parked, I hear a familiar voice from behind me. "Seth, is that you?"

It's the brother-in-law. I start fumbling my words, and Nastasia steps in. She turns to the brother-in-law, extends her hand, and introduces herself as an intern at my company. "I just got here the other week," she says. Nastasia speaks very slowly, and I notice her tone is more pleasant and innocent than usual.

The brother-in-law gawks at her for a bit. Then he says, "What are you two up to?"

"We're grabbing a coffee," Nastasia says. "I can't drink the stuff in our office. I'm addicted to Starbucks." She laughs, and as soon as she does, the brother-in-law starts laughing too.

It's impressive to watch Nastasia in action, and as soon as the brother-in-law walks away, I say, "That was close."

"Yes," she says. "I figured from your reaction he knew you well." And we both have a good laugh.

With all the excitement, I don't even notice we've arrived at the parking garage. It's a five-story building, with cars pulled into spots partitioned by concrete pillars. Nastasia is parked in the far corner, with a few empty spots on either side. Opening the door, she says, "Get inside." I take a seat, and Nastasia comes round to the other side, taking her seat behind the wheel. As soon as the door closes, she leans over to kiss me and whispers, "You sounded so stressed before. I figured you needed a release." Then, reaching down, she undoes my belt. At first, I'm very nervous and look side to side, but Nastasia says, "Just stay still and relax."

I wiggle, then squirm. It's at this point that Nastasia pulls back, and with a little bit of drool dripping from her chin, looks up at me in such a way that I have to believe

she's really enjoying herself. Not long after that, Nastasia pulls a Kleenex out of the glove box and dabs her lips dry. "How do you feel now?" she says with a laugh.

"That was amazing," I say.

"Good," Nastasia says, sitting up in her seat to adjust her blazer. "We can do that more often if you like," she says. "We have the entire summer together, and its best to enjoy this, because time always moves very quickly, and before you know it, I'll be gone and you won't have anyone to give you parking lot BJs when you're having a bad day."

Both the bluntness and the casualness of Nastasia's words cause me to chuckle. "That sound great," I say.

"Of course," Nastasia says, licking her lips. "If you're good to me, I'll be good to you." Then, looking down at her heels, she says, "I like having nice things and want to look pretty for you, so every little bit on top of my allowance helps."

"Okay," I say, looking out the car window.

When I turn my head back, Nastasia's already leaning in and gives me a kiss. "Great!" she says. She gets out of the car after that. I follow her out of the parking garage. Outside on the street, I make sure not to touch her because I don't want to be seen acting suspiciously, but I thank her again and say goodbye.

"Text me later," I say.

"Of course!" she says. When I get back into the office, I can't help but wonder if everyone around me can tell by the look on my face what happened since I can't seem to wipe this silly smirk off my face. I realize then they likely don't have someone like Nastasia in their life. It's a convenience I can definitely get used to.

The rest of the week flies by. At the end the week, I go to another meeting with the same couple who agreed to sell the fifty-dollar slice of pizza. Waiting outside of the meeting room is the new sales guy. He quickly pulls me aside and confides in me. He says the owner is going to teach him how to upsell the client to purchase advertising. I nod as we walk into the room together. Midmorning sunlight is pouring from the sky and in through the windows. It spills into the room, bringing with it a kind of brilliance.

The owner shuts the blinds. He has on a dark suit, a wing collar shirt, and a bright tie with broad blue-and-gold stripes. He dims the lights. On a projection screen at the front of the room, he clicks through a series of slides pulled from news headlines over the last week. The expensive slice of pizza has generated a lot of attention. All the local newspapers, radio stations, and TV channels have published short pieces on this overpriced slice of pizza and the restaurant that sells it.

"What we created," the owner says, "is a conversation piece. It's so unusual that people can't help themselves. They have to talk about it. And it's gotten so much buzz, even a few local influencers, like the mayor and a couple of professional baseball players, have posted pictures of themselves on social media eating it. That's good news because they all have large followings, and when an influencer that people like or trust says something like that, it can have a big influence on what other people do."

Both the gorilla guy and his girlfriend are pleased. Business, they say, has been busier than they were expecting, and they're happy it has worked out. The owner ends the slide show. Walking over to the far corner

of the room, he turns on the lights. He moves with such confidence and conviction I barely notice his old, brittle body. "Yes, it's worked out," he says, "but it won't last long. This type of thing is only helpful for a momentary bump in attention, and interest in your restaurant will begin to wane unless we do something to keep up that momentum." Without working up to it, the owner says, "You need to advertise."

The gorilla guy leans over and puts his arm around his girlfriend. "We don't have a lot of money to spend on advertising," he says. The owner looks at both of them intently. I vaguely understand at that moment that in his mind he wants to make this sale, and the fact that the couple doesn't want to doesn't matter, because in the end, after he converts them to his line of thinking, it will work out better for them anyway.

The gorilla guy starts to speak, but the owner interrupts. Drawing himself up to his full height, he says, "In a few weeks, people will forget about your restaurant because you need lots of repetition to change a person's opinion or instill a new habit in them." To further convince the couple, the owner explains that in the 1960s, the Russian secret service did some interesting psychological experiments on this very thing. "What they discovered," he says, "is if you bombard people with messages nonstop, in two months or less, most of the people will believe those messages, and it will change how they think."

I feel an ominous chill in the air. From the looks on their faces, I can tell everyone in the room finds this fascinating, yet at the same time a little frightening, and I can't help but wonder how else this method is used.

There's a long silence in the room. The gorilla guy says nothing. He makes no gesture of any kind. He sits completely still in his chair.

The owner walks over and puts his hand on his shoulder. "Listen," he says, lowering his voice. "I've only mentioned this to give you an example of the type of research we put into our advertising campaigns and the duration that's most effective to make sure your restaurant becomes a permanent fixture in peoples' minds, but I know you don't want to buy ads, and that is fine. All that I ask is you give it some thought, and if you change your mind, think of us first."

After that, the owner gives the couple some space, and I'm not sure if the meeting is over. The owner walks all the way over to the far side of the room. The whole thing must have taken a lot of out of him because he suddenly seems very tired. His bony hands have started to shake. They remind me of two tiny, trembling animals. The owner stands by the window. First, he looks across to the other office towers, then down at the cars on the street.

Behind him, the couple have started to talk to each other. Despite it being very quiet in the room, they're managing to make themselves not heard by talking in low voices. After a few minutes, the gorilla guy speaks up. The owner turns away from the window to face him. For a moment, it looks as if he might fall over. He seems completely drained and is propping his entire body up against the window by leaning on his elbow. As soon as the gorilla guy begins to talk though, the owner perks up.

The gorilla guy says, "You haven't let us down so far, so we'll dip into our savings. We'll get some ads."

The owner is elated. With a sudden surge of vigor, he crosses the room and extends his hand. "Excellent," he says. "We'll get working on an advertising proposal that will keep up this attention."

4.

I rush straight to Nastasia's apartment after work because she says she has a surprise for me. I don't normally like surprises, but in this instance, probably due to the way Nastasia said *surprise*, I'm intrigued.

I notice the door to her apartment is ajar as soon as I arrive. This startles me, and I stand there for a minute wondering if I should knock or just walk right in. I finally decide to knock.

"It's open," Nastasia yells from inside the apartment. "Come in."

I walk in, and Nastasia's standing there in nothing but pink thigh-high stockings, her hair tied in two pigtails with a matching pair of ribbons. "This is for you," she says. "I hope you like it."

Suddenly, I realize how touched I am. The wife has never done anything like this for me. Closing the door, I take Nastasia by thehand and lead her across the apartment to the balcony window. I open the blinds overlooking the street. I put her hands on the window. With her palms pressed against the glass, I put my dick inside her. I do it just as I've seen a hundred times before in the movies I've watched. My only thought is pleasing Nastasia. But probably because the last thought in my

head was of the wife, my mind starts to drift. Instead of thinking about Nastasia, images roll through my head of all the people I've come to abhor: the ugly woman from the grocery store, the coworkers who laughed at me, that loud-mouthed guy on his phone in the subway, even the brother-in-law with his stupid belly slap. It's as if all these things have suddenly come together to set me off.

With Nastasia's hands still pressed against the window, I grab her hips and bury myself deeper into her. I look out the window at the pedestrians walking by on the street. All I see are their ashen, indistinguishable faces. A red fog rises inside me. I think they, like everyone else, have been holding me back, and I want to hurt them, to teach them lesson. Then, I don't know why, but something deep inside of me snaps. I yank Nastasia by the hair, and with each violent tug, Nastasia's head jerks back, and her body slams into mine. I'm pouring everything I have into Nastasia—my cries of anger, years of frustration, unhappiness, and pain—and Nastasia seems to enjoy it, to even encourage it."

Yes!" she says. "Harder. Don't hold back." And then she screams, "I want more!"

Once again, all I can feel is that anger rising up inside me. I move like a man possessed with a newfound sense of clarity and purpose. Yet, I don't say a word, and it's only after I've finished, slumping to a sweaty, puddled mess on the floor, that I finally speak.

"I'd like a glass of water," I say, smacking my lips.

Nastasia disappears into the kitchen. The fan on the ceiling is churning the thick summer air. I watch it, completely mesmerized by its spinning blades. I close my eyes and almost nod off.

When I open them again, Nastasia's standing in front of me. She hands me a glass of water and asks, "Did you like the stockings and ribbons?"

Nodding, I say, "Yes, they were great!"

"Good," she says. "I thought I'd do something nice for you since you were sweet enough to pay for my shoes." I look over at the new pair of Valentinos at the front door.

Even though the money transfer I sent Nastasia the previous week drained more of my saving than I would have liked, I say, "No problem."

Then, Nastasia lies down next to me on the floor. With her head resting on my shoulder, she traces shapes on my stomach with her finger. The entire time, the fan twirls overhead, the air cooling our sweat-soaked bodies. Nastasia begins talking about her internship and her classes at school. I'm not really thinking anything except that I feel very satisfied. Then I shuffle my body a bit, placing Nastasia's head squarely on top of my chest. Without really following too closely what Nastasia is saying, I process that she's starting to read a self-help book about the importance of surrounding yourself with smart people. She's talking in a very calm, confident voice. I can tell this is important to her, so I listen more intently.

"That's why I like this lifestyle so much," Nastasia says. "I get to meet older, successful men like yourself."

This rattles me since I don't where she's got that idea from. I certainly can't recall a time when I've mispresented myself, and all that I can come up with is that she must have misunderstood something I had said earlier and now thinks I earn enough money to afford a pool. But all I say is, "That sounds like an interesting book."

After a few minutes, Nastasia gets up and walks across the room. She picks up her phone from the countertop and checks her text messages. I'm struck by how beautiful she looks. I want to tell her that, but at the same time, I'm completely drained and feeling sleepy. I focus on the ceiling fan instead. Then I close my eyes. I must have fallen asleep, because I when open them again the sounds of the street are drifting in though the open window. The evening has come to an end.

I get up and put my pants on. Then I walk into Nastasia's bedroom. She's under the covers, reading her phone. "Sorry," she says. "I didn't want to wake you. You looked so peaceful. I thought I'd let you sleep." Putting her phone down, she asks, with a serious look on her face, "You're not going to get in trouble now, are you?"

I look at my watch. It's late, and it's only then that I realize I should check my messages. I pull my phone from my pocket. As expected, the wife's been texting me. There are at least eight texts from her that I quickly scroll through. "Where are you?" she asks in one. And in another, "When are you coming home?"

I say to Nastasia, "I've got to go home."

I walk out of her apartment. Outside, I step off the porch and onto the concrete paving stone pathway to the street. I stand there, motionless, underneath the cloudy night sky. All I can hear is the sound of leaves and tree branches rustling from the wind. Still holding my phone in my hand, I text the wife back. "I've just been out," I say. "I'm coming home."

5.

The next morning, I stroll into work as if I'm ten feet tall. Passing people on my way to the elevator, I hum, and when I get there, I hold open the sliding door, waiting for everyone else to get inside before stepping in. As soon as the door closes, a man starts talking about the weather. He says, "It's supposed to rain today."

"Oh, no," a woman says. "That's too bad. I don't like rain."

It's a conversation I've heard many times before, and I listen to it as I make my way to the back of the elevator, pressing my shoulders against the wall.

I notice both the man and the woman are staring at each other agreeably, but I only watch them for a few moments before the elevator comes to my stop. Just as I step out, the man says, "Have a good day."

Reaching back to hold the elevator door open, I say, "Don't tell me what type of day to have!" Pausing just for a second before softening my stare, I add, "I'll have whatever type of day I want to have!"

I let go of the elevator door after that and skip down the hallway. For the rest of the morning, I sit in my cubicle. With my design software up on my computer screen, I scroll through different color choices, clicking

from one to the next. At first, I feel great, better than I have felt before, but later in the day my mood quickly changes. Something Nastasia said the other night has started to bother me. And by midafternoon, it's left me with this stupid urge to cry.

I decide to talk to the owner. He's the smartest person I know, and he said before he'd do me a favor. I ask the secretary if he's free. "I'd like to talk to him about something important," I say.

She glances up from her computer. "He's busy all afternoon," she says, "but if you need to see him, knock on his door at the end of the day. That's the only way you'll catch him."

I show up at five o'clock. Even though his door is open, I knock. The owner motions for me to come in. He points to a chair. I sit there while he finishes up on a call. Behind him, the blinds are open. It's cloudy outside, and patches of sunlight spot the room. Spread out across the owner's desk are stacks of papers with his signature in red pen. The owner hangs up the phone. He examines me closely without betraying any definable emotion. I'm about to explain why I'm here, but before I can start, he says he's been watching me in the office and I seem less taciturn and withdrawn.

"Something has changed with you," he says. I say nothing back. I make no gestures of any kind, but it's the first time in my life that I've wanted to hug a man.

The owner asks, "Why are you here?"

I say I feel silly for bringing this up, but without mentioning Nastasia's name I mention I heard from a friend that we are the average of the handful of people we spend the most time with and that bothers me because

the people I spend the most time with aren't very interesting; in fact, they are all sort of boring and dumb. Of course, I'm thinking about the wife, her sister, the brother-in-law, and the mother and father-in-law. I'm thinking about all of them, but I know better than to say that. All I say is, "Is that true?"

The owner thinks about it. After a short silence, he says that's a good question, that I interest him, and that he will do what he can to help me. He stands up. The light from the window casts a soft silhouette around his slender frame. He walks over to the corner of his office and stands in front of his bookshelf, which he scans with a determined look on his face. Then he walks toward me. "I know what your friend is talking about," he says. "It's a popular idea. Because of it, a lot of people think they need to be friends with a savvy entrepreneur to be rich and successful."

It's true. Nastasia has said that before: All of her previous sugar daddies but me were important people and she liked being around them, sometimes adding that in order to be successful, you need to surround yourself with successful people.

"That's why I like older men so much," she often repeated. "Men my age," she once said, "are immature boys only interested in how much protein is in their protein shakes, but that gets old very quick, and I'd never choose a six pack over someone with six cars."

The owner agrees that we're influenced by the people around us. They affect how we think and behave. However, that influence, he says, doesn't stop at the four or five people you spend the most time with. It's more widespread than that. It even includes people you haven't

even met. After that, things get a little confusing, at least for me. The owner opens the book and reads a few statistics. He says two smart psychologists have drawn some surprising conclusions from the famous Framingham Heart Study. The owner explains it's one of the largest and longest-running health studies. "What the psychologists found by examining that data," he says, "is if a close friend of yours becomes obese, you are 45 percent more likely to gain weight, and if a friend of your friend becomes obese, your likelihood of gaining weight increases by 20 percent—even if you don't know that friend of a friend!" The owner closes the book. Sunlight streams in through the window.

"My point is this," he says. "You're not the average of the five people you surround yourself with. You're the average of all the people who surround you." Something stirs within me, and I realize then that I'm trapped. I look down at the tips of my shoes. Fumbling a little with my words and realizing how ridiculous I sound, I say, "I don't want to be fat and dumb anymore."

The owner starts to laugh and then stops himself. "You don't need to be," he says.

There's a long silence. Then the owner asks earnestly if I expected him to solve the problem. I say that would be nice, but I'm not expecting anything. I only wanted his opinion on this matter. "And," I add, "I'm not sure there is an answer."

The owner seems pleased. He agrees that it's hard to know what to do. He sits down in a chair across from me and crosses his legs. After that, he stares into space and his eyes start to water. I think he's not well, because he seems to have instantly drifted away. The focus of our

conversation quickly changes after that. When the owner next speaks, it appears as if he's forgotten my question, because he says thirty years ago when he started the ad agency, he rented an entire floor of the Lewis–Walter building even though he had no employees to work for him. "It was a big gamble," he says, adding. "Not everyone is bold enough to take a chance like that."

I only smile. I don't bother to tell him I've heard this story before. Clearing his throat, the owner says, "I wouldn't have done that if it hadn't been for a friend." There's a flicker in his eye, and I know he's going to say something good. The owner tells me he grew up with this friend. They had gone to school together and even kissed the same girls growing up. When they were younger, his friend had talked about becoming a mechanic because he liked cars.

"When we were young," the owner says, "we had lots of ambition, but as we got older, we quickly forgot about that."

According to the owner, his friend ended up working at a convenience store. He hadn't been happy with it at first, but after a while he'd pretty much got used to it, and he no longer regretted it because it was easy and it paid well enough to take care of his bills. Then one day his friend didn't feel well and went to the doctor. The doctor did a bunch of tests and discovered several tumors the size of grapes in his stomach. The doctor said he didn't have much time, so his friend booked one last vacation with his family. "The tragic thing," the owner says, "is he never got the chance to go. The cancer was so advanced he died before the vacation."

I say, "That's a sad story," and the owner agrees. To be completely honest though, I'm not sure the story has

anything to do with the owner's success. After finishing, the owner collapses into his chair and exhales loudly through his nose. At that point, I'm not sure what to do. My only thought is he's tired and I should go. I stand up quickly and thank him.

He says faintly, "I enjoyed our talk." Then, with a serious tone in his voice, he says if it weren't for what happened to his friend, he would have never had the courage to start Acuscent Media Interactive.

"Before that happened," he says, "I'd been working at another ad agency. It hadn't been very challenging work, and I often wonder what my life would have been like if he hadn't died."

At that point, the owner looks at me carefully and says he didn't have any experience running a business back then, but he read everything he could about marketing, advertising, and doing business. "That helped me," he says, "and it might help with your problem too."

I'm listening, but I don't really understand. Probably because I don't feel smart and have never bothered to read that much, but also because I feel like the owner is tired and I'm preoccupied with the idea that I should leave.

That's when the owner speaks up again. "Reading," he says, "is like having a conversation with someone with another perspective, and if you can't change your circumstance or friends, you can at least choose what you read."

For some reason, and I still don't know why, I tell the owner I'm glad it worked out for him and it's unfortunate about his friend. Right away though, I know I've made a mistake and have misinterpreted his intent, because I recognize the look on his face; it's disappointment.

He gets up from his chair and walks to his bookshelf. He hands me a few books. "These will get you started," he says.

6.

I can honestly say that the time I first met Nastasia to now has gone by very quickly. I can hardly believe we only have a few weeks left together.

For the entire summer, I've been sneaking away after work or in the evenings to see her, just for a couple hours at a time, but this week I've been fortunate enough to see her every other night. The wife's gone to a beach house to vacation with her sister, brother-in-law, and parents. I told her I couldn't go. "I have to work," I said.

The wife looked at me quizzically but said, "I understand."

Tonight, Nastasia and I have gone shopping and then out for dinner. Sitting across from her, I make out the fullness of her breasts and the adorable dimples on her cheeks. Nastasia asks about my day. Now, I always hate when people ask me that, and I never know what to say, but she seems very interested, so I give her an honest answer. "I don't know what I did," I say. "I breathed a lot. I probably got bored by someone talking about the weather and stared at them awkwardly . . . The list goes on."

Nastasia lets out a laugh right away. "Oh my God," she says. "You're hilarious."

After that, she orders a glass of wine that she drinks very quickly. The waiter must have been watching, because he comes by immediately and asks, "Would you like another?"

She says, "Yes." Then Nastasia takes a big gulp and starts talking about packing up her apartment and moving back to school. I don't know how much time goes by, but after a while, probably because I haven't asked many questions, Nastasia says, "You're such a good listener."

I answer, "You think so?" but it's mainly just to say something, and what I'm really thinking about is finishing dinner and heading back to her place.

Then quickly, and in an empathetic voice, Nastasia says, "Yes, most men only talk about themselves." She pauses for a moment before adding, "All the men in my life have been like that, even my dad." At that point, Nastasia starts speaking softly, because the room around us is quiet, and I take it she doesn't want to be overheard. Leaning in, slurring a little as she speaks, she says she doesn't like her dad that much and her parents had a bad marriage. "I feel sorry for my mom because my dad is very controlling," she says. "He's the jealous type, probably because my mom's always been a real head-turner. He's always had it in his head that my mom will leave him, so he doesn't like it when she goes out, meets new people, or visits with friends."

Nastasia shows me a picture on her phone and says, "See? I've got a hot mom."

I peer over to see. It's true. She's a very attractive woman. Now Nastasia doesn't want to ever be in the same situation as her mom.

"I don't think they ever had much sex," Nastasia says. Of course, she can't imagine ever living like that. "I just want to be free and well off enough to do whatever I please."

I don't say anything for a little while because I'm giving Nastasia's words some serious thought. Based on what she's said, it seems as if her dad forced his way of life onto her mom. That's when I point out to Nastasia that it's ironic because, when you think about it, rules are by their very nature a type of control, and when Nastasia becomes a lawyer, she will be enforcing those rules, just like her dad enforced his rules over her mom. "The law is no different," I say, "because it's an interpretation argued by two sides, so in a way, you're a lot like your dad, provided you end up being a good lawyer and are on the winning side."

Nastasia kicks me underneath the table and says, "Stop teasing me."

Anyway, I can see that Nastasia's conclusions have a certain type of casual consistency to them, and I understand why she doesn't like marriage. My experience hasn't been that different. Even the day I proposed to the wife seemed to only happen because I had been coerced to do so. That day, several years ago, I was at the wife's parents' house for Thanksgiving dinner. Several weeks before, I had made the mistake of admitting to my parents that I had been entertaining the idea of getting married because most of my friends had already and it seemed like the next thing to do, but I hadn't said more than that. And to be completely honest, I considered the matter closed—until my dad called me that afternoon while I was at the wife's parents' house getting ready for Thanksgiving dinner. He asked if I was

ready to do it. I didn't understand. He explained he had the entire family gathered at his house for Thanksgiving dinner too. Even the grandparents and cousins were there. "I've got the champagne ready to pop as soon as you break the news," he said.

After that, everything happened with such force it felt as if it was beyond my control. Maybe it was for that reason, but also because I wasn't familiar with all of the procedures, that I asked the wife to go for a walk, and five minutes into that walk, I got down on a knee and asked her if she thought we should get married.

I watch Nastasia closely across the restaurant table while these thoughts run through my head. She has a suntanned face and is wearing a printed floral dress. She looks very beautiful. I breathe in the smell of her cherry lip balm, and after a few whiffs, I forget all about what I'd just been thinking. None of that matters anyway. I fix my eyes on Nastasia. This entire week with her has gone so well—it has felt so natural, so effortless, and she has been so attentive—that I have the ridiculous feeling I've become a new type of man. The problem, I've come to believe, is I've never learned to live right. I have a body that is meant to be enjoyed. I see no point in letting anyone stifle that, or any other natural inclination, anymore. I want to experience it. To be engulfed by it. To sublimate it—if I can. I've come so far, yet each new experience leaves me wanting another, and by the end of the week, it's hard for me to believe I've ever enjoyed anything other than the special nights like those this week where Nastasia has led me into her bedroom, undressed, and said to me softly, "Don't forget. I'm not your wife. Do to me whatever you can't do with her."

The next morning, I wake up with Nastasia's arm around my body. With the two of us still lying in bed, Nastasia says, "In the middle of the night, I caught you hugging one of the pillows instead of me, so I took it from you and threw it to the floor." At first, I don't know if she's serious, and it takes some doing on my part to understand this is real.

"That's sweet," I say.

Nastasia smiles and squeezes my arm. Then she gets out of bed.

I follow her across the room with my eyes. I take in her dark, adorable eyes as she sits cross-legged on a blue pillow on the floor, putting on her makeup in front of a mirror. Shortly after that, we leave her apartment to go to work. On the street, we say our goodbyes because our offices are on opposite ends of downtown, and we're heading in different directions.

I'm kneeling down on the sidewalk, tying my running shoes for my thirty-minute walk, when Nastasia says, "If you don't step on it, you'll be late."

Then, probably due to the motherly tone in her voice, she laughs at herself in such a way that I stand up to kiss her. "Have a good day," I say.

"You too!" she says.

I start my walk. The streets are packed, and the sun is glaring. Despite the clouds, it's punching its way through in places and blotting its beams onto the sidewalk. My walk doesn't take as long as usual since I've been walking a little bit every day and have started to feel quite strong. In fact, by the time I reach the Lewis–Walker building, I'm in such an ecstatic state—with the warmness of the early morning sun, the briskness of the

walk, and that morning kiss from Nastasia—that I don't even notice the scaffolding I've walked underneath as I make my way to the building's revolving door. "This entrance is closed," a construction worker says, stepping in front of me to shove an open hand in my face. His tone seems needlessly aggressive. I'm about to say something when someone taps me on the shoulder. It's the secretary, who's come up behind me.

"There's an important company meeting in the boardroom," she says. She has on a new white blouse that stands out on her loose, blemished skin. I look at the construction worker. Then I turn toward the secretary. Without saying a word, I follow her into the building. Along the way, she confirms my suspicions. "The owner," she says, "is going to announce his successor." We take the elevator up to the auditorium floor. Then we walk down a narrow corridor before coming to the room where we can hear voices, shouts, and chairs being dragged across the floor.

I find an open seat in the middle of the room. It takes me a while to adjust to the noise. At the front of the room, sitting above the shapeless mass of spectators, I see a young man sitting next to the owner. The two of them are watching people file into the room one at a time. I realize then that they're related, and that the young man must be his son.

The meeting begins right away. The owner stands up and raises his hand. The room falls silent. He says he's going to start working less, and his son, who he's hired as a director, will be helping him while he eases into retirement. "It's my expectation that all of you will treat him well," he says. After that, he turns the meeting over

to his son, the new director, to say a few words. The son puts his hands on the edge of the podium, and you can tell he has something prepared. I know right away he's going to talk about his MBA, and at the same time, that irritates me. I get bored very quickly with the son's speech. Only random bits—a gesture or a single word in his long and repetitive monologue—catch my attention or arouse my interest. The point of what he is saying, if I understand him correctly, is that he has gone to a very prestigious business school and has lots of good ideas for the agency. I've never heard someone talk so much about the same thing in my life.

After a while, the meeting finally ends. Despite wanting to leave, I stay seated in my chair, not because I want to, but rather because I don't want to be stuck in a line with the other people. I watch everyone funnel out of the room, one at a time. In front of the only door exiting the room stands the new director, shaking peoples' hands as they leave. I watched him closely. I see a lanky man with deep blue eyes and lots of thick, wavy blond hair. He strikes me as being not as smart as the owner and overall a bit of a disappointment despite his obvious attempt to be friendly and dress well.

Eventually, after the line is almost gone, I get up to leave the room. I shake the new director's hand on my way out, but my congratulations aren't sincere because I'm tired from the meeting and no longer interested in what's going on.

For the rest of the day, I sit in my cubicle. I think about Nastasia. I don't want our time together to end. At times, the utter desperation of this realization seizes me by the throat and turns my stomach to knots. Even

though I know I need to move on, I can't stop rewinding things in my head. Sometimes I get to thinking about an outfit Nastasia wore for me, picturing every detail—every seductive piece of lingerie before moving on to her body: the look in her eye, the flushness in her face, her panting breath. I can spend hours doing that, renumerating in detail all the things we've done together. At the same time, it always gets me worked up, and the more worked up I get, the more I want her and the harder it is for me to accept that she's leaving. Due to these thoughts and the looming sense of finality, the workday drags on.

It doesn't help that I'm having dinner tonight with the wife and her family. They got back from their vacation today, and this will be the first time I've seen them since they left a week ago. The dinner is at my place. When I get home from work, they're already there. I say hello to the wife as soon I arrive. She looks at me with a perplexed expression. I shaved my head right after she left to hide my retreating hairline and to look better for Nastasia.

"Wow," the wife says. "That's different." I don't say a thing. Then she says, "It looks good," but it's not until the sister-in-law says it too that I know it is true.

The wife turns around and walks into the kitchen. "I need to make supper," she says, pausing for a moment before adding, "After a week of holidays, I don't feel like cooking."

Turning to face the mother- and father-in-law, she asks, "How does everyone feel about takeout?"

The mother-in-law says, "That's fine." The father-in-law agrees, and for a moment, just from the stupid

look on his face, I half expect him to say we should order something from a really good restaurant. After that, the three of them discuss the options very loudly before finally settling on Mexican. Supper doesn't take long to arrive. While we eat, everyone takes turns talking about the week. The father-in-law is glad he found such a beautiful beach house to rent and says, on more than one occasion, he negotiated a very good weekly rate.

"That's why we got to stay at such a nice place," he says. "You should have seen it. It was a real mansion . . . like a place from the movies."

The rest of the family also had a great time. The brother-in-law golfed every day. His golf swing has never been better, and the sister-in-law is pleased the twins have improved their swimming, saying, "They can tread water in the waves and do the backstroke!"

I gather all this is important. It's not bragging— more of a way to feel important and get noticed—but that doesn't prevent it from giving me a headache. At times, I try to steer the conversation to other topics such as things I've learned from the books the owner gave me or about other things I've recently read, but none of that takes. Maybe it's for that reason, and because it's hot inside and I'm getting bored, that I stand up and open a window. It's cooling off very quickly outside, and a gust of damp air drifts into the kitchen.

Every now and then, the brother-in-law glances over in my direction. He's drinking another beer and still wearing a golf shirt from his round earlier in the day. Eventually, during a rare break in the conversation, he asks, "What did you do during the week?"

I answer right away that I did nothing but work. "I've been very busy," I say.

His glassy eyes start to gleam, and I feel like he's going to interrogate me. "Oh, really," he says, slobbering a bit as he speaks. "What are you doing at work that's keeping you so busy?"

The room suddenly gets quieter, and the wife looks at me dejectedly. I can hear my own breathing. I look back at her, but I feel nothing. I'm too busy thinking about the brother-in-law's question. I know better than to answer right away, and I remember how easily Nastasia handled him at the beginning of the summer. I think about it very carefully. In the past, whenever I want to get rid of someone who is bothering me, I've always found it helpful to act as if I agree and as if what they are saying is interesting, so I turn to the father-in-law, since I've always found him to be the slowest of the bunch.

"It sounds like everyone had a great vacation," I say, adding that he must have excellent business acumen and that if he hadn't negotiated that rate, none of them would have been able to enjoy such a nice house for the week. Turning to the brother- and sister-in-law, I say, "You wouldn't have improved your golf swing, and the twins wouldn't have become better swimmers." Then, looking back at the father-in-law, I say, "Everyone owes that to you."

At that point, the father-in-law jumps in, agreeing triumphantly. "Yes," he says. "They definitely do!"

The noise in the room gradually picks up again. The brother-in-law opens another beer and starts discussing spending another week at the beach house and splitting costs with the father-in-law. The sister-in-law talks to the wife about the twins. Another breath of air wafts in through the open window, and I lean back and listen silently from my chair.

7.

As soon I get to work in the morning, the secretary rushes up to me. She's talking in an agitated, urgent voice. She says the owner had a heart attack over the weekend. "He's not doing well."

She's almost in tears when I say, "I'm sure he'll be okay."

She says, "Really? Do you think so?"

I think about it again. Then I realize I'm wrong. His life is likely coming to a standstill, and I instantly reproach myself for suggesting to her otherwise. I turn away from her, wondering if I should tell her the truth, but when our eyes meet again, I see the look in her eyes and stare at my hands.

In no time at all, the owner is dead. He dies during his sleep in a hospital on the outskirts of the city. At his funeral, the entire office is there, and everyone takes turns saying nice things about him. I sit near a relative that has too much makeup on. She mutters a few words about being his cousin. I'm about to tell her to be quiet out of respect, and so I can listen to the official program when she moves closer to me. She's wearing a lot of perfume and has a determined look on her face. Apparently, she visited the owner before he died.

"He wasn't the same," she says. For instance, he was forgetful and had a hard time remembering his own name. "During most of our visit," she says, "he sat upright in his bed facing a window that overlooked a big tree waiting for a squirrel to show up and play on its branches." The cousin adds that's too bad, though I don't know why. Then she says, "Did you know him well?"

At that moment, I spot a few people behind us crying, and I take a better look around. All around us in the church are maybe forty men and sixty women, all of them clinging together in pairs. Some of them are leaning forward, heads pressed together, crying. The cousin repeats her question, this time lowering her voice. "I take it you two were close?"

"I don't know," I say. "Maybe."

The next few days, it's very quiet in the office. There's a lot of standing around with people just looking at one another but not saying a thing. The owner's son, now the new director, is in the office to run things, but he isn't much help, probably because he's new to the job and still in mourning. At one point, the secretary comes by to check on me. I'm not really doing anything but sitting in my cubicle and staring into space. As soon as I see the look on her face, a shudder goes through me.

"I know this is hard," she says. "I'm sad too."

It might be because my thoughts are a muddled, murky mess in my head that I say, "It's not like that."

She stands very still and doesn't say a thing. Then she gives me a sad little smile. "I understand," she says. After that, she leaves, and I fall back into my chair. It's not hard for me to understand her perspective.

His death has been hard on everyone, but the last few days have been hard on me too. I haven't heard from

Nastasia in several days. She hasn't returned my texts, and she's driving back to school in a day. I don't know if I'll see her again. I'm very worried. That might be what is the hardest for me.

Sitting in my cubicle, I spend the rest of the day thinking about a lot of things. I think about the owner being dead, about Nastasia leaving to go back to law school, and a murder trial I've been following in the news for the past week. An accountant got into a fight with a man. During the fight, the accountant pushed the man, who tripped and hit the back of his head on the ground. That, according to the pathologist quoted in one of the news stories I had read, is what killed him.

What interested me the most about the whole thing wasn't the murder. It was the trial. It was hard to tell from the news stories whether the accountant's crime or life was on trial because the prosecutor kept focusing on very personal details. For instance, the accountant's parents had both died in a car crash a few days prior to the murder. During the funeral, the accountant had almost fallen asleep and not bothered to cry. Then, later that same day, he met a girl while having a drink at a bar, and the very next night they went to out for dinner and after that they had sex. The prosecutor took that as evidence of the accountant's callous, malicious nature and said in one of the stories, "The day of his parents' funeral, our suspect didn't shed a tear, and the very next day he was already out on the prowl, having a sexual liaison!"

In today's news story, the jury announced a guilty verdict, and the accountant's been sentenced to death. At first, it seems to me as if justice has been served, but after thinking about it more, I'm not sure, and I start to

wonder whether the jury would have come to a different conclusion if the accountant had cried profusely at his parents' funeral. At any rate, this is a very interesting legal issue, and I could have used Nastasia's perspective on it since, as a law student, she'd have a better understanding of it than me. In the end, what bothers me the most isn't that the accountant is going to die. It's that he didn't speak up or defend himself during the trial. He seemed content to simply observe and let things play out. It was as if his fate had been decided without his participation. You should never let that happen, so because of that, I feel like he got what he deserved.

At the end of the day, just as I'm getting ready to leave work, I finally get a text from Nastasia. She's been busy the past few days packing and lost her phone. "Sorry for not getting back to you sooner," she says. "I lost it underneath a box. It was stuck on vibrate so I couldn't hear it. I had to unpack a bunch of boxes to find it."

As soon as I read Nastasia's text, I laugh, probably because I picture her digging through boxes frantically like a silly cartoon character trying to find it. "That sounds terrible," I say.

"It was!" Nastasia says. "It was a total pain!"

Nastasia could use my help moving a heavy bag into her car. She says it would be a good way to say our goodbyes, and we can do it before or after—she doesn't care—so long as I help with the bag.

"I can do that," I say.

"I knew I could count on you," she says.

I head straight to Nastasia's apartment. The traffic is terrible, and there's construction everywhere. To make matters worse, not only does it take a long time to get

there, but when I do arrive, there's no parking so I need to circle the block several times before finally catching sight of someone leaving. I pull in right away and park. Then I rush to her door. It's shut, so I knock. I hear Nastasia fiddling with the lock from the other side. The door opens, and I walk inside. The entire place is empty and smells like bleach. Nastasia gives me a quick hug before stepping back behind the kitchen island. That makes it difficult for me to reach her. Pointing to an extra-large duffle bag on the floor, she says, "I'm so glad you're here. I've been able to pack everything into my car, but I can't lift that. It's too heavy for me. Can you help me?"

I look around Nastasia's apartment. Her entire life has been packed into boxes and carried away. The duffle bag is the last of it. "I'm happy to help," I say, lifting the bag. I carry it out of the apartment, down the hallway, and into the elevator. At that point, the strap slips out of my hand and the bag drops to the elevator floor.

Nastasia asks, "Is it too heavy for you?"

I say, "No."

I grab the bag with both hands, this time jerking it up high to rest on the top of my shoulder. I watch the circular elevator buttons count down to the underground parking garage. After a few moments, the elevator stops. The door opens, and Nastasia holds her arm out to keep it open as I squeeze by. Then she runs ahead of me to unlock the trunk of her car, and I follow her across the parking lot. The strap digs into my shoulder. All I can think of is the weight of the bag and the trunk of the car. I step forward, taking quick, short steps until I get to her car. With my fingers, I push the strap off my shoulder.

The bag falls into the trunk with a thud. Delighted, Nastasia reaches over and touches my shoulder. Then she shuts the trunk.

It's only after the trunk closes that I start to get mad. The bag contains the last of Nastasia's life, and I've just carried it—and her—out of my life. I feel that I've been tricked, and that I will be tricked again, just as I have been my entire life. Nastasia never intended to sleep with me one last time. She only wanted me to carry her bag. That same recalcitrance rumbles inside me, and for the first time I realize the obliviousness I've experienced but ignored my entire life. I've been on the receiving end of what other people want my entire life. At last, I know what to do. It's only the inkling of an idea, yet it's one I want to pursue. For this to end, for me to be free, I have to stop letting myself be controlled. I need to start pushing back. All that manipulation needs to be returned back to the world, and if I can do that in a spectacular way that other people take notice, I might be help a few people like me along the way.

Noticing the look on my face, Nastasia says, "Ah, cute. You caught a feeling." Closing the distance between us, she gives me a hug. "Don't worry," she says. "I'm not going to disappear. We can still text and be friends." With her arms wrapped around me, Nastasia squeezes a little tighter. I stand still, my arms loose by my sides, and she finally lets go. Pausing for a moment, she says, "I've got a long drive head of me. I guess I should go."

Part 3

1.

Since Nastasia left to go back to law school everything in the world around me has gone flat.

It's like trying to listen to a conversation after a gunshot has gone off.

One my way to work the next day, I walk underneath some construction scaffolding to get inside of the building, and this construction worker yells at me, "That entrance is closed! Use the other entrance."

I turn to look at him. He takes one look at the empty expression on my face and says, "What the fuck is wrong with you?" but it might as well as be white noise.

At work, later in the day, the secretary says, "What's wrong? You're not like yourself."

I agree.

The way my face looks like sunken, old fruit, you'd swear I was the walking dead. I miss Nastasia. Despite what's happened, I want her back. I want to hear her laugh, or to watch her sit cross-legged on that blue pillow on her apartment floor, putting makeup on before going to work in the morning. I imagine a scenario in the future when Nastasia finishes law school, and we can pick things up again.

The secretary tells me I look stressed and to get more exercise. "You should run," she says. "Maybe try a marathon."

I don't want to run.

I'm tired of running.

I hate everything in my life that's held me to it.

The secretary says, "You need to address whatever's eating you up before it ruins you."

She is right.

So I decide to leave the wife.

That afternoon I leave work early, go home, and pack two suitcases. I leave everything else of mine behind.

That evening, I spend the night in a hotel, reading apartment rental ads on my phone.

The next morning, my dad calls to tell me I've made a big mistake. "What's gotten into you?" he says. "You need to go back to her." This from the same man who tricked me into marrying the wife, just to pop champagne during a family dinner.

I don't want to talk to him.

All I want was Nastasia.

Oh, Nastasia.

Save me.

Make me feel less alone.

My dad says I can't do any better than the wife and to wise up. "Listen to me," he says, and then he raises his voice. Here I am, so close to freedom and I have never felt more alone.

Oh, Nastasia.

Free me.

Help me to be strong.

My dad says he is ashamed of me, that I'm weak and an embarrassment.

"I know that," I say.
He says I need help.
He's right. I do need help. We all need help.
And I hang up the phone.

2.

The construction worker outside my office building has been tearing people down for too long. Now, he's pushing his finger into my chest and has a fist ready to punch a hole in my head. Even with him being like this, no one has done a thing. You have to think though: If someone puts him in his place—gives it right back to him—it would change things. For the longest time, though, I would have never done something like this.

With this finger poking into my chest, the construction worker says, "You shouldn't be here. You need to leave."

I just look at him blankly.

The construction worker steps toward me. His hands are like a car wreck you can't help but look at: pitted and puckered, with a blood-crusted BAND-AID on his finger. It's impossible not to notice. When you look down and see a god-awful mess of a finger poking a hole in your chest, you've got no choice but to wonder what you're doing still standing here.

The other day, when I walked up to the Lewis–Walter building, this same construction worker was standing here, arms crossed, blocking the front door. "This entrance isn't being used," he said, pointing to a

sign propped up in front of the blue-tinted revolving glass door. "You have to use the designated detour and walk to the other side of the building while construction crews repair the building. This is to protect you from falling debris. Just listen and turn around."

This morning, I walk up to the Lewis–Walter building and, without even thinking about it, I step through the building's revolving glass door into the enormous sandstone lobby. I'm barely two steps in when the construction worker comes up behind me. You can tell he's mad by the line on his forehead. He steps in front of me. Already, my eyes are soaking in every cratered scar on his face. Every wrinkle and grizzled hair.

He says, "You weren't supposed to come through that entrance. There's danger from falling debris and building materials."

"Oh, yeah," I say, studying his potholed face. "I've already come through, and as you can see, I'm just fine."

The construction worker shakes his head. Stepping toward me, he says, "No. No. No." His nose is a spiderweb of broken blue blood vessels. "You'll have to go back through the door and enter through the designated entrance. There's a reroute sign."

From the corner of my eye, I can see all these people—all these clerical worker consultant types—have slowed down their walk to work to watch. This is better than real life. It's something you don't see every day: two men chest to chest, careening toward each other like two cars about to crash.

"Let me get this straight," I say. "In order to protect me from falling debris, you want me to walk back under falling building materials. Or am I missing something here?"

There's a long silence. The construction worker just looks at me. Time slows down. It's stopping . . . stopped . . . frozen.

Finally, he says, "I need your employee number." Then he puts that god-awful finger into my chest.

Tap.

Tap. Tap. Tap.

"Your employee number, I need it. Give it to me! I need it now!"

TAP. TAP. TAP. TAP.

These aren't light, friendly taps. There's going to be a bruise.

This is about power. It's about control. It isn't talked about. It goes unnoticed. And this construction worker will keep on doing this, treating people like this again and again.

Stand there and take it. Be better than that. Be good. Be nice.

To think this is how we're supposed to act.

I look at the construction worker's finger, at that blood-crusted BAND-AID, and picture breaking that fucking thing. I imagine grabbing it fast, before he has time to react, and feeling it snap in my hand like a dry twig.

People always say things like life is too short to be mean.

I think it's too short to let people get away with the same shit.

I slap the construction worker's finger away, swinging my arm in a roundhouse like in any action movie you've ever seen. My hand hits his wrist hard, catching him by surprise. He stumbles back.

I motion to the door with my head and say, "Go ahead. Move me through the door. Save me from the falling debris."

Please, please, please, please save me.

He just looks at me blankly.

And I smile.

I hold my arms out like I'm holding a baby and ask, "Will you carry me out to safety to protect me?"

This jackass grin on my face is sending the construction worker from zero to one hundred. Already, I can see him redlining. Blood is racing to his temples. His snarled-up hands are twitching at his side. Fists are forming. He's going to punch a hole in my head.

Will it hurt? As if I care. This whole thing is not even about him and me.

From the corner of my eye, I can see all those suits still staring at me as they walk by.

This audience is a good thing. A very good thing.

Take a deep breath.

Exhale.

I'm lighter than air, and the construction worker can't do shit with all these eyes on us. Even he knows this.

Relief.

This only lasts a moment because then there's . . . MUTTERING.

Mumble, grumble, grumble . . . and fuck it. "I'm done with you." The construction worker's sputtering word salad under his breath, and he turns to walk away.

One, two, three steps. And just like that, he's gone.

Where's he going? Maybe he's going to talk to his foreman about improving the worksite safety, or maybe he's thinking about how he will never act like that again. Standing in the lobby, I beam.

3.

I slip in between the elevator doors as they close and take a spot against the back wall. My heart is racing, and my thoughts are a tornado in my head.

You're a graphic designer for an ad agency and you're bored and angry, but mostly you're just angry, so one day you have enough of listening to others, and you say to yourself, *Not like this, not anymore*, and doing that feels good, as if it's something you should have done sooner.

Even now, standing in the elevator, my heartrate slowing, coming off that high, I feel alive. I had no real sense of life before because I had nothing to compare it to. I went to work. I came home. I watched videos of girls on my phone.

I did everything I was told to do.

I was stuck in a little hole of a life I thought was my own.

Just then, the elevator opens, and more people pack in. The secretary squeezes in against my shoulder. She's wearing a pearl necklace, and her jacket is tight and tailored to pinch around her waist. "Soooo," she whispers, raising an eyebrow. "What's new?"

Already, just from the way she asked, I know: She saw what happened with the construction worker.

I shrug my shoulders, staring at the plastic elevator buttons lighting up one at a time.

With a grin, the secretary presses even closer, looks up, and asks, "Are you sure nothing is new?" The pearls on her necklace sparkle when she speaks. I shrug, rolling my head back and forth over my shoulders.

The elevator stops at my floor. Stepping out, I glance back at the secretary, her face still lit up all wide and bright. "You know what?" I say, reaching back to hold the door open for her. "You're right. Something is new after all."

4.

I step out of the elevator and into the hallway. The secretary follows right behind me, still smiling with her eyes.

The secretary says, "Geez, Seth. That whole thing in the lobby was so incredibly awkward to watch. It was amazing."

Oh.

Right, the construction worker. "That was nothing," I say.

Just me being silly me.

Ha.

Ha.

Still, from what the secretary says, I know how today is going to go. All the talk in the office—all that water cooler chitchat—will be about what happened this morning with the construction worker.

One morning, you ask a crater-faced construction worker to carry you to safety through a revolving glass door like a baby and everyone in the office starts talking about you.

Oh, wow . . . He did that? No way. What I did, no one acts like that—ever. That's the point. I did something unusual, something unique, and because it's out of the ordinary, news of it will spread.

"That was fun," I say. "I think I'll do it again."

"No way. What's wrong with you?"

"Oh, nothing," I say. "I just feel like sometimes you need to correct people's behavior through the proper application of force."

The secretary's head jerks back. Her eyes go car-crash big. She says, "There's something seriously wrong with you."

I say there's nothing wrong with me.

Running my finger over the spot where my wedding ring used to be, I say, "Everyone wishes they had the guts to do what I did. You know I'm right."

Standing in front of the closed elevator door, I say the construction worker is a bully and he pushed me around. "I never asked him to press his finger into my chest, and if that type of behavior, that type of violence, is the only language he speaks in, it's the only language he'll understand."

And I smile.

I give her a dark, penetrating smile.

Then I turn and walk away quickly before she can do a thing. And she follows me. Right behind me, step by step. Through the key-carded security door, down a carpeted corridor, in-between an aisle of cubicles. The entire office is like a filing cabinet for workers. Everything is floor-to-chest-high upholstered plywood. Everything is industrial, low-pile beige carpet. Everything is ergonomic raising desks, dual monitors, and noise-canceling headphones.

Workers plugged into PCs. PCs plugged into the network. People put into a maze of boxed-in carpeted cubicles.

Mmmmrrrrrrrm.

A vacuum cleaner softly hums somewhere.

Once, in a haze, I got off the elevator onto the wrong floor and walked to my desk. Only it wasn't my desk. It was someone else's, and everyone looked at me like I was crazy.

Catching up to me, the secretary says, "I've never seen anyone do that."

"I know," I say. "No one has. That's the point."

I say that guy has been enforcing a ridiculous rule just to feel important for weeks now, and it drives me crazy when someone acts like that.

"I'm tired of people like the construction worker telling me what to do," I add. "If there was a safety problem, they should block the entrance so no one walks through it instead of having a chowderhead standing in front patrolling it."

"Chowderhead?" The secretary wants to know what that is.

I say that's what he is. If you took a can opener, put it on the top of his head, and spun it around, once you popped off the top and peeked inside, all you'd find where the brain is supposed to be is a big bowl of chowder. No brain. No synapses firing. Just some brackish-looking water and a few chunks of salty gray meat.

The secretary looks at me like I'm crazy. Still, she's loving this.

A blonde, twiggy woman gets up from her cubicle and walks toward us. She says, "What are you talking about?"

The secretary fills her in. Tilting her head to me and pointing her nose like a finger, she says, "He told some

construction worker in the lobby to pick him up like a baby and begged to be carried through the entrance to safety." The secretary does this cradle-in-the-air gesture with her arms and speaks in a googly-goo-goo baby voice.

With that baby-voice bit, the blonde, twiggy woman loses it. "Seriously?" she says. Turning to me, she asks, "Why'd you do that?"

Now just to have some fun, I crouch in close and ask, "Would you like to know the terrible truth?"

Nod.

Nod.

I say, "I'm here to apply a formula. It's part of a plan. It's a simple calculation that can be used almost anywhere."

> *You take the amount of force applied by one person to another (A) and multiple it by the individuals on the receiving end of that force (B).*
> *A times B equals C.*
> *C is the maximum amount of force that can be administered back.*

I crouch in even closer and say if that construction worker yelled at eighteen people for just ten seconds, that's three minutes of the same he's got coming back to him. I talked to him for less than a minute, so I could have given him a lot more, but I didn't because he didn't need it, that wouldn't be right, and I'm a good person.

My voice is monotone. The delivery is deadpan.

I don't say a thing. My lips are a hard, expressionless line. I just stand there, still. And wait . . .

The secretary says, "I don't understand."

The twiggy woman turns to the secretary and says, "Is this a joke?"

Lurching back, I toss my head behind my shoulders and say, "*Muhahahaha!*" My laugh is pure evil genius, like in any spy movie you've ever seen where the monologuing villain has just revealed his plan.

Shaking her head, the secretary says, "You're such a weirdo. I love it."

5.

Before I moved into my apartment, the landlord told me it was the cheapest building in the city.

I nodded while looking at the building from the lawn. In front of me stood a sort of halfway house for people either on their way to or coming back from rehab or prison. Everywhere were windows either boarded up with plywood or covered in Budweiser labels or pot leaf flags.

The landlord said, "We're waiting for the paperwork from the city to be processed, and after that happens, they'll bulldoze the apartment. That's why it's so cheap."

Stepping off the front step, the landlord asked if I'd like to go inside to see the unit. "No," I said. "I don't need to see it. I'll take it."

The landlord gave me a sideways look and said, "Suit yourself." Clearing his throat, he added, "I'll need your first and last month's rent in advance."

"That's fine," I said.

"Follow me." The landlord turned to go inside. "I'll need you to sign some papers, and I'll get you a set of keys.

"You're getting a great deal," he added. "At this price, you're practically staying here for free."

"That's what I want," I said, following him into the apartment.

With his back to me, the landlord said I didn't seem like the typical person who lived here. "Why are you renting here anyway?"

Running my tongue over my teeth, I said, "I recently spent most of my savings and will be spending a lot more money right away. So, this place is perfect."

6.

At lunch today, I go to a print shop near my office, and the woman working the till asks if she can help me.

"Yes," I say. "I'm looking for printing costs for a large print run."

She asks what I'm printing.

"Flyers," I say.

Lots of flyers.

Thousands and thousands of flyers.

"Well," she says, "the cost depends both on the quantity you're printing, the paper stock, and whether it will be black-and-white or color." She reaches for a piece of paper from a shelf and sets it on the counter. "So," she says, pointing to a list of prices with a pen. "What will it be?"

"The flyers will be glossy and mostly just one color," I say. "They'll all be Chanel red."

"That's a nice color," she says.

"Yes," I say.

After that, I dig into my pocket and pull out my wallet.

I pay her.

I walk away.

When I get back into the office, I head straight into the coffee room. The coffee machine is broken, and the

cup that I pour for myself is cold, but I drink it anyway. Placing the cup in the sink, I turn to walk away.

"Those don't go in there," a woman says, motioning to the dishwasher. "They go in there. We all share this office. We need to put our dirty dishes away."

She gives me this look, that same look you'd see from a parent scolding a child. Then she opens the dishwasher and points. "Look," she says. "There's a spot right there."

Until recently, it didn't piss me off when someone told me to do something.

Now I like getting right up and hostile in everyone's stupid little face.

I set my dirty coffee mug on the counter. I look at her, all ginger-haired, all freckle-faced, her hair pulled back so tight and perfect not a single strand is out of place. Then I smirk, just the way that I do now, and take a filthy, food-crusted plate out of the dishwasher and lay it on the counter.

Her face.

The shocked look on her face.

It looks as if she just realized she had to take a crap while driving on the highway and now has to pull over to use a truck stop restroom.

I say the cleaners are paid to clean the kitchen. They do it every day at 3:00 p.m. It's 1:00 p.m. That means it will get done in a few hours, and it might even get it done sooner, because sometimes they come earlier.

Pointing to the sink full of dirty dishes, I say, "No one else wants to clean the kitchen either."

Reaching over, I take the coffee cup out of her hand and put it on the countertop. Leaning down into the dishwasher, I pull out a plate. Bits of tuna casserole are

caked on concrete hard. I put it on the countertop also. I pull out a dirty glass. A dirty dish. A dirty fork. A spoon. I do this—again and again. I make a pile. A big filthy mess.

Then I give this dish woman my best fuck-you smile.

And her mouth drops open, and her face turns to ghost.

Stepping toward her, I say, "Stop wasting my time with dirty dishes and dumb rules. It's time to start thinking for yourself."

Everywhere you look you see people like this dish woman; the plain and predictable wear down the unique time and time again because they're greater in number. So there in the kitchen, with no one around to see, I give this dish woman the one thing that she needs: a nudge.

Then I reach into the dishwasher and hand her a plate.

"Take this," I say, pushing it into her hand. On her face is that same ridiculous look. She thinks I'm crazy, but she'll come around and see things my way, just like everyone else.

7.

After I moved into my apartment, I met the woman next door. She was standing in the hallway wearing torn fishnets and a jacket made of shiny gold sequins. Her skirt, a fake orange suede, barely covered her bum as she walked past me in the hallway.

This neighbor woman caught me fiddling with my key in the door after I got home from work and asked if I was doing anything *fun* tonight.

I said, "I'm going to Toastmasters."

She asked, "What's that?"

I said it's a place you go to get better at public speaking.

She asked, "Why'd you want to do that?"

Turning to face her, I said, "I want to be a better speaker and charming, so I can be with lots of women."

She laughed. "Honey," she said, "if you want women, what you need is lots of money and a good dick game." Then she looked at the hallway carpet—its piling pulled out, torn in spots, and blotted with patches of dirt and decades-old dog pee. "If you're living here, you probably don't have money, so I'd focus on making that pussy sing. What you need to do," she explained, "is give it butterflies. And maybe buy better clothes."

The next day, I took her advice. I had bought some nice clothes and gotten better in bed, thanks to Nastasia, but I wanted more, so I went shopping and then to a pharmacy in the neighborhood. Looking at me from behind a shield of bulletproof glass, the pharmacist said, "Can I help you?"

I had been doing some research and had prepared a list. I told him I wanted to be able to fuck for hours. What I needed was 100-mg tablets of Viagra. I also needed capsules of the Chinese herb *Epimedium brevicornum* and *Cordyceps sinensis* to increase my stamina and prevent myself from finishing too soon. I added I needed anything else he had like that.

From behind his glasses, the pharmacist said, "Why?"

"I want to be really good in bed," I said. "I want to last forever."

"Do you have a prescription?"

"No," I said, and I handed him a hundred-dollar bill.

The pharmacist disappeared into a series of white shelves behind the counter. When he came back, he gave me a brown paper bag. Holding it in the air right in front of my hand, he said, "This isn't going to fix anything for you." Then he handed me the bag.

I said, "Thanks. This is just what I need," and I ran back home.

The next week, I passed the same neighbor woman in the stairwell, and she asked what I was doing tonight.

I told her I was reading.

She asked, "Why do you want to do that?"

I said I heard from a friend who is dead now that it makes you smarter, and I was lonely.

119

"Reading," I said, "is like listening to another person talk. It makes me feel less alone."

The neighbor woman laughed. "If you're lonely," she said, "I can help. I guarantee you'll have fun."

I looked at her ring finger and shook my head. "Thanks," I said, "but I'm not interested. I have a different type."

"Oh, yeah?" she said. "What's that?"

I said, "I like married women."

8.

Coming up the street is a woman walking a Chihuahua, and the little dog's head is low, sniffing the ground from side to side. As the two of them get closer, I take a good look at her the same way you'd inspect a car on a dealership's showroom floor. Her eyebrows are plucked perfectly, and her sugar-cookie-colored hair is puffy, like a cloud in the air. Slung across her shoulder is a white leather purse on a long gold chain. She stops for a moment while her dog sniffs a red flyer stuck to the concrete, the dog's tiny, pink tongue licking away.

The newspaper said thousands of these flyers showed up the other week throughout the city—left on buses, under windshield wipers, in food courts and subway car seats, taped to buildings and parking meters.

No one knows why they're here or what they mean.

Stepping over the flyer, this woman looks up from watching her dog and down the street. I lean against the lamppost and take a deep breath.

"Nice looking dog," I say, bending over to pet it.

She says, "Thanks."

"What's its name?" I rub the pup gently behind the ears.

"It's Charlie." The dog licks my hand. She yells, "*Charlie!*"

"It's okay," I say, placing one hand on the ground and the other on top of its head. "It's okay, right, little guy? You don't mind."

I look up at her. "Nice day for a walk."

"I guess . . ." she says, adding, "I don't usually have to do this."

"Who walks your dog?"

"My husband," she says.

"So," I say, "why isn't *he* doing it then?" I laugh.

She laughs back.

"He's out of the city." She pauses, then adds, "Though if he was here, he probably wouldn't walk him anyway."

I stand up, straightening my back. "That doesn't seem right."

It's hot outside, and the dog is panting from the heat, his little pink tongue hanging out.

I look her up and down, making sure she sees me do it, and say, "I hate to ask this . . . Oh, never mind, it's not important." I turn around and begin to walk away, but she stops me after a few steps.

"No, it's okay. Please, go ahead. What's your question?"

"Well," I say. "This is going to sound *so* silly, but I feel like I know you. You seem very familiar. Have we met before?"

She says, "No, I don't think so."

I ask, "Are you sure?"

"Yes, I'm sure."

"That's too bad," I say. "We should change that."

The woman raises an eyebrow. "I'm just starting my walk. If you like, you can join us."

"Sure," I say, "but only if you tell me your name."

"It's Cynthia Drake. What's yours?"

"Seth."

Shuffling up alongside her, I say, "Let's go."

Cynthia Drake and I head down the street, and after a while she says she's got three kids and works as a nurse.

"That's really great," I say, looking at the sun.

There's not a cloud in the sky. I wipe my forehead, and Cynthia Drake looks at me. "Too hot for you?" she says. I say yes. "Would you like to go to my place for a glass of water?" she asks. "I'm only a few minutes away."

"Lead the way," I say.

We walk up to her place, which is two stories and covered in Silverado stucco, and just as we get to the door, Cynthia Drake, digging around in her purse for the key, says how the worst thing about being home alone when her husband is gone with the kids is how every little noise sets her off.

Here she is worried about noise, and she's letting someone like me into her place.

She fiddles getting the key into the lock and says, "This door is always such a pain."

"Let me try," I say, taking the key out of her hand.

I unlock the door and step inside after her.

As soon as the door shuts, I reach over, placing my hands on her hips. Cynthia Drake is the second woman this week.

It's still early in the week, though.

It's only Tuesday.

9.

"I can't believe that happened."

This is what Cynthia Drake says as we lie on the sofa. Her face is resting on my chest, the skin from our still-wet bodies sticking to the leather couch.

Her words stick my head. I can't think of anything else. Nothing else matters. Not that I just fucked a married woman. Not that I have no plans to stop. None of that matters. All that matters are Cynthia Drake's words and the opportunity I have.

"Oh," I say softly. "Was that your first time?" There's warmth in my tone, an appropriateness to my emotion.

"Yes. It was my first time," Cynthia Drake says. "I've never done that before. I've never strayed before . . ." Her voice trails off.

"It's okay," I say. "Don't let that bother you. Don't think about that now. Did you at least have fun?"

Cynthia Drake lifts her head off my chest. "Yes," she says, blushing. "I did."

I tell Cynthia Drake I know what she's going through. I cheated before too. "The hardest part," I say, "is realizing you don't need to feel guilty."

"You're the victim here," I say.

Cynthia Drake says thanks, and that it's a lot to process.

"It's okay," I say. "Take your time." I rub her hair, counting all the way down from thirty in my head before asking, "Do you and your husband do it often?"

"No," Cynthia Drake says. "We don't. Not like that." She rests her head on my chest and sighs heavily.

"That's too bad," I say. "Why not?"

Me, I'm asking all the right questions. Meanwhile, I'm running a finger along Cynthia Drake's back, tracing tiny little circles.

"I'm not sure . . ." Cynthia Drake trails off. "He doesn't like doing it, I guess. Maybe it's stress. Maybe it's the kids. Maybe it's me. Maybe it's something else. I don't know. Even when it does happen, it's not like that."

"I understand," I say. "My life used to be like that too."

After that, I sit up, slowly inching my back up the arm of the cream-colored couch. My back peels away from the leather cushion like sticky tape. For the next fifteen minutes, I run my fingers through Cynthia Drake's hair. I say all types of useful things like the people in your life should set your soul on fire. "The prerequisite for any person to spend time with you is they should nourish and inspire you. They should make you want to live and experience life.

"Life," I say, "is about growth and new experiences, yet so much of it is bogged down by repetition and familiarity, which deaden perception and diminish experience."

Cynthia Drake says, "You sound smart. I like hearing you talk."

125

I don't say anything. There's a long, uncomfortable silence. I let it be. I'm still running my hand through Cynthia Drake's hair when she finally asks if I'm married.

I say, "I had a wife." Then, "I left her."

"Why is that?"

"It wasn't working for me. I didn't like it."

"Why not?"

I say marriage is a ridiculous idea that makes no sense. "Just think about it. The idea that two people can meet at a point in time, hit it off, and then continue to follow each other like two parallel lines—in their interests, their growth, development, and regression."

Zig.

Zag.

I draw two parallel lines in the air with my fingers. Then I move my fingers slowly apart and the lines diverge.

"Eventually things will change," I say. "Eventually people will drift apart, or maybe they'll realize they never matched up at all."

Here I am, spouting out all types of useful information, and I'm filling Cynthia Drake's mind like a jelly donut. By now, her head is resting on my chest again, and she's running her finger along my stomach. She's even tracing tiny circles.

"Half of marriages fail," I say, "but if half of all parachutes failed, they'd design better parachutes."

Cynthia Drake chuckles. "I've never thought of it like that," she says. "Did you try fixing it?"

"No, I didn't. I didn't because . . ."

Yap-yap-yap!

Yap-yap-yap-yap-yap!!

I'm interrupted by the dog's barking—a high-pitched shrill. I locked the dog in the pantry after we started. Doing it, doing it, doing it. The dog kept licking my leg. Distracting me from my task. From my mission and my plan. Now, from across the hall, I can hear it yapping, trying to dig through the pantry door with its tiny paws.

"Just ignore it," Cynthia Drake says. "Keep going. I like hearing you talk. It's interesting. It's different."

I ask, "What's the question?" Then, without giving her time to answer, I say, "Would you like to know why I left the wife?"

Nod.

I say I didn't like the idea of a life of mandatory date nights or being denied a quintessential part of the human experience. "I didn't want a life sentence where the conjugal visits were few and far between, or worse, having to spend a life cheating and feeling guilty about it."

Me, I know there's lots of Cynthia Drakes out there. These are the super smart people who only now are starting to figure out that a white picket fence isn't the answer. Neither is a better job, bigger checks, or longer vacations. You get one life. In the end, no matter what you do, you end up in the same place: in a care home, looking out a window waiting to watch a squirrel climb a tree, and in between that and trying to remember your name, you rest your eyes and die.

By now, though, I'm starting to feel my dick get hard again, so I know I've talked too much. I grab the back of Cynthia Drake's head and move her face to mine.

With our cheeks pressing, I whisper in her ear. "You're so great," I say. "So special. You feel so good."

And Cynthia Drake must like what she hears, because she closes her eyes and grins from ear to ear.

10.

This is one of the reasons why I like married women so much. It's the doubt. After you stir that up, you can really get someone thinking and convince them of just about anything.

After filling Cynthia Drake's head full of all sorts of nonsense, I slip out the front door and wave to the neighbor, who's watering his rock garden with a green garden hose. "Evening," he says, looking at my still-unbuttoned shirt and just-fucked hair. "Nice night."

"Yes," I say. "It is."

It's still light outside, and I feel invigorated, so I go for a walk, crisscrossing through the streets, making my way downtown. The air is bathwater warm. As I'm walking, I pass by a homeless guy putting a red leaflet under a windshield wiper. He hands me one that says:

IT IS COMING
CHANGE IS COMING.

Tossing it in a trash can, I pass alongside an open apartment window. In the background, I can hear a basketball game playing on a TV and a baby crying. After I started this plan to change myself and the world, I told

myself I didn't care if people got hurt. That wasn't the point. The point was to teach each and every single person a lesson.

You are stupid.

All you do is listen and follow.

Your tiny life. Your useless job. All that wasted time. You never, ever thought about any of this before, and the most convincing argument for any action is "everyone else is doing it."

My only wish is for this to work and to wake a few people up along the way.

A lime-green scooter rushes by me, the hum from its electric motor fading as it gets to the end of the block. I watch it disappear and see two guys walking toward me on the street. One guy is big, but not scary big. He's shaped like a loaf of white bread, and the simple look on his face reminds me of a gentle giant.

Just then, from behind the two guys, I see a car coming up fast with a guy in a flat-brimmed hat hanging out the window. There's a bottle in his hand that's lobbed into the air, racing toward the gentle giant in a fast arch. The bottle bounces off the back of his head, sending him crashing to the pavement. His head hits the concrete like a watermelon dropped from a ladder.

His friend yells at the car. Then he falls to his knees and starts crying—big, watery tears. He's holding the gentle giant's head in two hands, and he wants to know, "Why? Why'd you do that?"

As the car screeches to a stop, the car doors swing open and two guys get out. A beer bottle falls from the car, breaking against the ground. The two guys stumble up to the teary-eyed guy draped over the gentle giant's body.

"He looks hurt," one guy says. "Is your friend hurt?"

Giggling, the other one says, "Your friend's got a headache." Circling around, they let loose a parade of profanity.

One guy's laughing so hard he loses his balance and falls to the pavement. Seriously, he does. Who's taught him this? No worries, no repercussions, no fucking clue.

To make matters worse, both guys' arms have big muscles bulging out of their T-shirts, because being a man these days means having a stomach that resembles a ribbed condom packed full of rocks. Because you are stupid and all you do is listen and follow.

Meanwhile, this guy lying on the pavement, head cracked open, has a concussion. It might be worse. His life may never be the same, and wherever I go, I see the same sort of thing.

> *You take the amount of force applied by one person*
> *to another without their awareness or consent (A)*
> *and multiple it by the long-term impact (B).*
> *A times B equals C.*
> *C is the maximum amount of force that can be*
> *administered back.*

I walk up behind the guy sitting on the concrete, holding his sides, still roaring with laughter. With his back to me, I plant a soccer kick to his neck in that soft spot where the spine meets the skull, folding him over into the pavement. Then I reach down and pick his beer bottle up off the pavement. His friend is just standing there with this empty look on his face. Squatting on the ground, all coiled up, I turn to him, curling my lips to

show both rows of teeth. I break the bottle on the concrete. Then I lunge at him, stabbing the shattered stem into his face, only he moves back, tripping to the pavement, so I scramble on top of him, driving it down past his crossed arms until it breaks through and starts splicing his face.

In all, it's less than a minute before I take a step back to admire my work. The gentle giant sits up. Without saying a word, he looks at the blood spilt across the concrete. Some of it is his. Some of it's not. He's holding a meat paw of a hand on his head, and all you can hear in the background are hospital triage-worthy groans.

Pulling the gentle giant to his feet, I say, "Are you okay?" He nods, staring at the mess on the concrete with a pained look in his eyes.

Turning to face the gentle giant, I say, "Don't worry, neither of them will act like that again, but other people still will. In the end, what happened here won't make a difference. Because no one is here to see it but us."

11.

I'm meeting Nastasia today for lunch at Mercatos, the new Italian restaurant downtown. I ran for sixty minutes this morning and even did a full-body movement calisthenics routine. Even after that, I'm nervous. I've only heard from Nastasia once since she went back to law school. She texted me several months ago after she arrived at her college apartment to say she was busy unpacking, but she'd talk to me soon. I asked, "When?" She didn't text back.

Last night, though, Nastasia texted me. "I'll be in the city visiting," she said. "Would you like to catch up?"

Now, that can mean only one thing: Nastasia still likes me, she misses me, and because she's asking to meet me, what she really wants to do is fuck me again.

This morning, just so we wouldn't run out of things to talk about over lunch, I read the news. The story everyone is talking about is this video two college kids posted last night outside of a bar.

By noon, the video is trending all over social media. It's brief, not more than thirty seconds, and shot from twenty feet away, so it's grainy at first, with only a few lampposts for light, but it gets better as they get closer. It starts with this suit stumbling along the sidewalk, his

head covered in a pillowcase, arms out, trying to find his way. He's yelling for help, stumbling back and forth down the street, until he walks into a lamppost and crashes to the ground.

Ohhhhhh, shit!

Bahaha!!

Geez, man, are you okay?

Brahahahaha!!

The two college kids' laughter shakes the phone. The video pans to the pavement, to the sky, then back to the pavement. Finally, it steadies as the kid holding the phone walks up to the suit pancaked out on the pavement. The phone hovers above the suit. The pillowcase is duct-taped around his neck, so even with his hands clawing at it, he can't get it off. The phone moves from the pillowcase to the suit's chest. Then the laughter stops.

What . . .

What is that?

There's a note taped to the suit's chest. Just the same as all those red leaflets scattered throughout the city. It says:

> HE IS THE FIRST
> HE WON'T BE THE LAST.
> EVERYTHING WILL CHANGE.

I'm standing in the lobby of the Rimrock Resort Hotel when the elevator doors open and Nastasia walks out. She's wearing a silk, sleeveless dress. It's green with petunias on it, and it orbits around her waistline. Nastasia looks stunning. Everything is murky. I'm on edge.

"Hi," she says. "It's lovely to see you."

I say hello. I put my arms around her. Hug. Nastasia feels thinner than before. She still feels good. Feverish, romantic notions race through my head. I remember all those nights with her.

Take a deep breath in.

Exhale.

What is that smell? Lavender? Crap, she smells good.

I pull away and tell her I got us a reservation at Mercatos. "It's only a four-minute walk," I say.

Nastasia smiles, tipping her head to the lobby door. "Lead the way."

Nastasia does all the talking while we walk. She tells me about school. About her law classes.

Yeah and yeah, Nastasia talks and talks. I'm listening to every word, smiling and nodding.

Oh, this is great. It's just like before.

Listening to Nastasia, my anger and pain—it all sort of just peters out. I think maybe I should be nice to people. Maybe I should relax, let things be and be like I was before, and then, at that most excellent moment, Nastasia turns to me and says, "I've got a man."

I press my lips tightly together, and Nastasia keeps talking. She can't believe it either. "It's all so sudden," she says. "It's been, like, only two months. It's happened so fast."

Nastasia licks her lips, making them wet and shiny.

I ask, "Is he a real boyfriend or is he's paying you?"

"It's real," Nastasia says. "If this works out, I won't need to do any more sugaring."

"That makes sense," I say. I shouldn't ask, but I have to know. "What's he like?"

Nastasia says he's nice. He has a way with people. "He's unlike anyone I've ever met before. It might be serious."

I feel helpless. Like nothing.

Nastasia stops talking and looks at me, holding my gaze with those deep, chipmunk-brown eyes. I need to say something, so I ask, "What do you like about him?"

"I don't know," Nastasia says, "A lot." She pauses, rolling her eyes. "He knows how to handle me."

What?

What the fuck does that mean?!

A bus goes by, kicking up dust. A hot cloud of exhaust hits us. Nastasia coughs. Stepping back, she stumbles. I put my arm out to catch her. She grabs it, and her free hand goes to my waist. I flex so she can feel I've been working out. Nastasia smiles. She really is cute. We keep walking. I see a TV playing the news in a storefront window. After that, Nastasia turns to look at the image on the TV: a freeze-framed image of that pillowcase-headed suit laid out on the concrete. Splattered like a bug on a windshield.

Nastasia asks, "What's that about?"

I tell her about the leaflets. About the red note on the suit's chest.

"That's terrible," she says. "Who would do such a thing?"

"No one knows," I say. "One guess is as good as the next. Anonymous, Black Lives Matter, the Me Too Movement gone rogue—no one has taken credit. Not the hacktivists. Not the social activists.

"For all we know," I say, "this is being done by a deeply disenfranchised individual who recently evolved

past our pitiful, psychological default setting and now, having attained enlightenment, is trying to educate others through a series of carefully curated publicity stunts."

Nastasia slaps my arm. "I forgot how funny you are."

Just then, her phone beeps. Looking down, she reads a text and taps a response.

I ask, "Is that important?"

"No," Nastasia says. "Not really." Her phone lights up again and she reads it.

We get to the restaurant. It's small and intimate, a hidden nook in the middle of the city. The decor is authentic Italian: wooden, handcrafted chairs and tables with Sicilian tablecloths, wildflowers in little copper vases.

We walk to our seats. Sit down. I can't help but notice that the couple at the next table—both the guy and the girl—are watching Nastasia closely. I'm not crazy. She's that good-looking.

I flip through the menu, but I can't read. I can't focus. I'm too distracted. Nastasia with a "man." I can't believe it.

"This guy you met," I say. "Tell me about him."

Nastasia says he's in his forties. Divorced. Two kids. He never sees them. He works a lot and is a partner in a consulting firm. "Agile team performance, or something like that," she says. Bringing up her phone, she shows me a picture.

Relief.

He's fat and bald, with a bum chin and big panda circles under his eyes.

Right away, Nastasia knows what I'm thinking because she says, "I wouldn't be with him if I didn't find him attractive."

"Don't worry," she adds. "I'm not in love with him." It's hard to imagine Nastasia in love.

What Nastasia likes about him is he enjoys bringing her out and showing her off. He takes her on trips almost every other weekend. The Sundance Film Festival. San Francisco. New York. The other weekend they partied all night in Philadelphia at the same club as the Philadelphia Flyers. "He has all types of connections," she says. "And he loves to party."

"He must have a lot of money," I say.

"It's unreal," Nastasia says. "He'll drop five thousand dollars like it's buying a sandwich."

Laughing at herself, Nastasia says, "I really like his money."

God, her laugh. It's so innocent, so carefree. She could say anything and make it okay.

The truth is Nastasia always liked money. Besides, it's what she's always wanted. You know, a bougie lifestyle so comfortable and free of financial constraints you'd swear it was the caption reel of an Instagram model—only with better food, bigger yachts, and a bottomless make-it-rain bankroll.

No kidding, and Nastasia doesn't want her man to know she likes his money, but she wouldn't be with him if he didn't have it, and blah-blah-blah-blah she finds him attractive.

"Great," I say. "Good for you."

The room suddenly seems cramped and sweltering, and even though the air-conditioning is on full blast, the air seems hot and recycled.

I ask, "What else is new?"

Nastasia isn't sure. It's so hard to pick one thing. So much has changed. Travel. Food. Parties. Sex. "I had a threesome," she says.

Of course, you did. Before I can ask her to elaborate, the waiter comes up. "Are you ready to order?"

He catches me by surprise. I fumble with my words and nearly drop the menu. Nastasia gets the spaghetti alla chitarra with seared amberjack and green tomatoes. The waiter flushes nervously while writing down her order, avoiding eye contact by hiding behind the frames of his thick-rimmed glasses. I get something called tagliatelle with hand-chopped ragu. Nastasia looks at me but doesn't say anything. As soon as the waiter leaves, I ask if the threesome was with her man and how it happened.

"It wasn't planned," Nastasia says. "We were meeting for a drink, and he asked if it was okay if he brought a friend. He has all these girls. All these side pieces. It was right after we first met, so it's not like I could say no. I had no choice."

"Right," I say.

"It was fun. Don't get me wrong . . ." Nastasia says, trailing off. "Though it was a lot of work, getting into position and thinking about what to do next."

By now, I don't feel like talking anymore. I'm just listening and nodding while Nastasia talks.

Nastasia tells me it's best to be the guest in those situations. That way, when it's done you can just get up and leave.

Nastasia tells me that school is expensive, and her scholarship only covers so much, so she's thinking about buying a blonde wig and working as a stripper in a city an hour away. "That way," she says, "there's no way I'd ever run into anyone I know."

139

The food arrives. I watch as Nastasia devours everything on her plate. How does she stay so thin? I move mine around, picking at it. I have no appetite. I try to taste it, but there's no discernable flavor.

Nastasia keeps talking.

She'd rather be lonely in a big house than happy in a small one. Her gorgeous friend from law school has a rich Chinese sugar daddy who doesn't really speak English, but he likes blondes like her friend, so before he fucked her, he took her out for supper with all his friends—both guys and girls—and they all looked at her, pointed, and laughed.

Hearing all this is exhausting and, suddenly, very, very boring.

Just for something to say, I ask, "Where else have you been?"

"Las Vegas."

Yeah, Nastasia's man's got a condo in Las Vegas. They go there all the time to party, but a few weeks ago they went to Miami. "Funny story," she says. "I got stopped by the security agents at the airport. They kept me for questioning. They even searched my bags."

"Why?"

"They wanted to know how a student with no job or money can travel every weekend."

"What did you tell them?"

"Nothing," Nastasia says. "I'm a baby lawyer in training, remember? So you're never supposed to tell them anything. They can't do anything to you if you don't tell them anything."

"That makes sense," I say.

"What was I supposed to tell them?" Nastasia says. "That my boyfriend pays for everything and that I'll suck his dick as soon as I arrive?"

I look down at my plate. I feel light-headed for some reason. "Why are you here?" I ask.

Nastasia says the law firms in the city are interviewing for first year associates. "I'm trying to line up a job for after I graduate in a few months," she says. "I've got two interviews tomorrow. If I get a job, we'll be moving here."

"We?"

"Yes," she says. "We . . . Does that bother you?"

I swallow hard.

"No," I say. "That's great."

12.

"You're mean."

That's the message I get from the woman who made the big deal about the dishes. I've been back from lunch with Nastasia for fifteen minutes when I get asked to a meeting in the boardroom. Only this isn't a meeting. It's an ambush.

Just a moment ago, the secretary stood in the entrance to my cubicle and said, "You better go into the boardroom. Hurry up." With her hands on her waist, she said, "Go fast."

I get up from my desk without saying a thing. I walk to the boardroom, right past the director standing by the photocopier, face tanned liked a barbecue potato chip.

Last week, he showed me a picture on his phone of a BMW he wanted to buy. "I'd like to treat myself," he said. "Since I'm running a company now, I should drive a nice car."

I walk right by him.

In the boardroom, I find that dish woman waiting for me with steak-knife-sharp eyes.

Until recently, I didn't realize it's good to be mad. Anger is just the feeling that something is not right and can be better.

At work these days, I'm doing this whole advice thing. When I see people in the hallway, I say things like: "Your life is your responsibility." "You're a product of your past, but you don't need to be a prisoner to it."

The pink-gummed smile doesn't leave my face. I'm walking around like a happy horror movie clown. Still, I'm totally honest and helpful like a pinpricked condom.

Me, I always knew the dish woman and I would have this talk. Last week, I saw her in the lunchroom picking at a goat cheese salad. I asked her if she was hungry. She said, "No."

I said, "Did you know 90 percent of people eat because it's lunchtime and the other 10 percent because they're hungry?

"Don't think of it as a meal," I said. "Think of it as relearning how to think."

Now the dish woman is in the boardroom, and the dish woman says I'm mean and I hurt her feelings. "This is workplace harassment," she says. Her normally pulled-back red hair has come undone. "I'm going to file a complaint with human resources."

I say, "Yeah, yeah, yeah, yeah." Without bothering to look at her, I say that was the point. "I'm glad you're mad. That had to happen."

What's new is always evil, and for change to happen, you need someone like me.

Stepping toward the dish woman, I say, "Would you like to know why I'm such a terrible person?"

She nods.

I say, "I'm tired of listening to people who want to live in a plain and predictable world. Without pain, people get too comfortable and lose their ability to do great things.

"Comfort is a drug. A life-killing drug. Once you get used to it, it becomes addicting. Give yourself good food, a mindless routine, and endless hours of idle entertainment and you might as well throw all your potential away, because that's the place where progress goes to die."

I breathe out smoke.

At work these days, people ask me why I'm like this. What happened to me? Why'd I change? I say a blah-zillion years ago we evolved to listen to other people rather than ourselves. This was helpful back at the very beginning of time because people who herded together to hunt and fight off wooly mammoths were less likely to die.

Today, I say, we still think in little groups and listen to others. We listen to others who tell us to go to school to get a job so we can have a career to be financially comfortable and secure so we can rest on the weekend, vacation a few weeks a year, and retire one day—having never bothered to live life along the way.

It was that evening in the parking garage with Nastasia that I started to see all this. That I began to realize what to do.

Now, I want to blast people free from history. To destroy everything that is *true*. Grab a feminist by the hair. Punch a woke liberal in the face. I want to drop a Wonder Bread-white conservative off in a Detroit slum and watch him work his way up from abject poverty.

Yeah, I want to do a lot of things. The world is too complex to be lived through the lens of a single explanatory framework. I want the dish woman to get that. I want to explain when I broke that kid's face with the flat-brimmed hat—when his face hit the ground, and his teeth split though his cheek, and he spat out all that

black jam—I knew it wasn't my violence. It was *his* violence, finally being returned back to him.

I want the dish woman to get all that. I want to tell her that most things are not only achieved by violence, but held in place and perpetuated by violence, but I know I can't tell the dish woman any of that.

Instead, to warm her up, to ease her into it, I say, "Have you ever heard of the Asch conformity experiments?"

Still looking at me with those steak-knife eyes, the dish woman says, "No."

"It's an interesting psychological experiment," I say, "that was conducted in the 1950s." And for some ridiculous reason, at this exact moment, I think of the owner. "In these experiments," I say, "a group of people were asked to a look at a vertical line on big card set up on a stand at the front of a room and then look at another card next to it with three other lines of different heights. Each person was then asked to say out loud, so everyone else in the group could hear, which of the three lines on the one card matched up with the single line on the other card."

Turning away from the dish woman, I start walking around the boardroom table. I run my finger along the top of the boardroom table as I say, "The only thing with this experiment was most of the people in the group were paid actors who had been told to give the wrong answer and announce to everyone else they thought two lines were the same height that clearly were not."

The dish woman's watching me, lips pressed tightly together.

With me on one side of the boardroom table and her on the other side, I say, "What ended up happening

was when everyone else gave the wrong answer and it finally got to a person's turn who wasn't an actor to say out loud what two lines they thought matched up, they also gave the wrong answer."

Leaning forward, I press both palms onto the table and say, "More than 30 percent of people went along and conformed with the group despite it being obvious the two lines did not match up.

"They did it just to fit in," I say.

From across the room, the dish woman's eyes start to soften. I watch her ease into a slouch after standing ramrod straight.

Maybe we'll be friends.

Maybe she'll understand.

Turning away from her, I walk to the floor-to-ceiling glass window and look down to the molten shag rug of cars crawling along, one right next to the other. One bumper to the next. Going somewhere. To do something. All in one big hurry.

Coming up from behind me, the dish woman's gaze goes down to the street. "I'm not sure I understand," she says.

"Don't worry," I say. "I'll teach you."

13.

On Tuesday afternoon, I fall asleep at work. When I wake up, my face is on my arms, which are folded over on my desk, and the dish woman is shaking me. The dish woman touches my shoulder and asks, "Are you okay?"

"I'm fine," I say. "I'm tired, that's all. I was up late last night working on something. I need a coffee. Would you like to join me?"

"Sure," she says.

We walk through a maze of cubicles covered in beige carpet and past the director, who's standing in a corridor showing the secretary a picture of the BMW he bought. The rumor around the office is he's planning something big. He is either looking to cut costs and will be letting people go or wants to sell the agency.

In the hallway, I tell the dish woman I owe her an apology. "I didn't mean to be a dick to you before," I say. "The opportunity I had . . . this is just something I have to do."

"That's fine," she says. Then she asks, "Why'd you do that, anyway?"

I say, "I needed to get your attention. I needed to get you angry. Anger drives people to action. Whereas if you're happy and content, you don't particularly feel like doing anything and stay the same."

This is something I know firsthand. If I hadn't been sexually frustrated, I would have never cheated on the wife with Nastasia. That was the first time I did anything like that, the first time I stood up for myself and broke a rule. Leaving Nastasia's apartment that night, I felt more alive than I had ever felt before.

That's when I began to understand what happens when you keep quiet in the world: Everything repeats and stays the same.

Nastasia helped me see all that. She was the first person to not care. Because I was paying, Nastasia had no expectations and said, "You can do anything you want to me. Be anyone you want to be with me."

That's why I love Nastasia.

In the coffee room, the dish woman says most people don't act like me and I need to be careful. I put my coffee mug into the vending machine and press the button for a black coffee. The machine starts to hum, and then it shakes. "I know I was rude," I say, "but if I had put my coffee cup away, if I had cleaned the kitchen like you asked, we wouldn't be here right now."

I take a sip of my coffee.

The director comes into the room. He puts a coffee cup into the vending machine. The machine starts to hum, and then it wobbles side to side. Turning to face us, the director says he bought a new car. "It's a BMW 8 Series that can do zero to sixty miles per hour in 2.8 seconds."

"We were talking," I say. "Now you're interrupting us."

The director keeps talking and asks if we've ever driven a car that fast. "It takes the wind right out of your chest."

I look at the dish woman, and then I look at the director.

In my head, I play it all back.

I think of Nastasia.

I say, "Do you know who the largest purchasers of BMWs are?"

The director says no.

I say it's young lawyers or MBA graduates who have just got a bonus or their first good paying job. The luxury car is a status symbol; it's a type of signaling behavior that tells others that you've made it.

"But let me guess," I say. "You're different than the rest of all those BMW buyers and didn't buy it to fit in."

The director, with his Ivy League education and sandy, beach boy hair, just stares at me, and after that he takes a sip of his coffee and leaves.

As soon as he's gone, the dish woman says, "You need to watch it. That's the type of comment that will get you fired."

"Trust me," I say, "if I get fired, it will be for something better than that."

14.

The secretary stands too close to my desk with her curious smile, her lips dry and wide open and her chest at my elbows. I look up from my computer screen at her. She's wearing a desert-brown paisley blouse. In her hand, the secretary's got her phone. She wants to show me something, but she peers down first to see what I'm writing and asks, "What's that?"

It's a commercial agreement. The kind you get a company to sign to make sure they pay you every month. These things always read the same:

> **Payment Agreement Contract**
> By this contract, (**Insert Company Name**) agrees to make payments to Acuscent Media Interactive, by the following schedule in exchange for (**marketing/ advertising services rendered**). This payment schedule is enforceable by law, and the methods described below will be used in the case of delinquent payments.

Last week, the director said I needed to help process the agency's contracts. You know, administrative stuff. The director is restructuring the agency, he tells me. His

dad running things created a lot of waste. The director learned all about this in college. He wrote a white paper on it. He needs me to do this. Processing this payment stuff is easy, he tells me. Write in a client's name, write in the agency's name, and send it to accounts payable. They'll send it to the bank. Even I can do that, right?

After hearing that, it's hard not to get riled up, if you know what I mean. Still, I had to ask the director why he didn't just get an accountant to do it. Right sizing, the director said. Synergies. Cost savings. "It's the right thing to do," he explained. "It's easier this way."

That happened last week, and today I'm making a few modifications. The secretary looks at the contract on my computer screen and then she looks back at me. "What are you doing to that?"

"I'm just having some fun," I say, closing the window on my computer before she can see.

The secretary straightens up, stretching her arms behind her back.

I say, "I like your blouse. Where'd you get it?"

The secretary says she saw it the other week on the cover of *People* magazine while waiting in line at the grocery store. The movie star Scarlett Johansson wore the same look in that movie she was just in. Now everyone is copying it. "Isn't it cute?" she says.

"Yeah," I say. "Cute."

The secretary shuffles around my desk in her desert-brown paisley blouse. Holding her phone out for me to see, she asks if I've heard.

"Heard what?" I say.

Jerking her head back in surprise, the secretary asks if I'm for real. "It's all over social media!" she says. "The

other week a pharmaceutical CEO was kidnapped, and then he was just let go after a few hours without a ransom. Two drunk kids found him right after he was released from a car that sped away." The secretary pushes her phone to my face. "This video just came out about the kidnapping." She turns up the volume and presses play. The video starts, showing an old, bald, buzzard-faced man.

This is Caspian Yates.

He's the CEO of Pharmakon.

Pharmakon makes and sells drugs.

Last year, Pharmakon made $47 billion in profits.

Last year, Pharmakon took over a company called Bayder.

After the takeover, Pharmakon began restructuring Bayder.

They cut employee benefit packages. Saving plans. Pensions.

The image on the screen changes. Caspian Yates's face disappears. What you see next is an aerial image of Pharmakon's corporate headquarters—all sixty-five stories in tinted, storm-glass blue with people coming and going like a line of army ants in time-lapsed, freeze-framed fast motion. Then the screen changes. You see another face.

This is Doug.

Doug used to work for Bayder.

Doug now works for Pharmakon.

Before Pharmakon took over, Doug had a good pension.

Doug decided how many kids to have based on that pension.

He thought that pension would be there for him to use someday.

The Pharmakon restructuring changed that.

Doug can't retire like he planned.

Doug doesn't have money.

Doug is struggling.

Next is a rolling photo montage of faces: employees, families, a parent looking into an empty wallet, an empty fridge.

There are 650 employees just like Doug.

All of these employees are struggling.

Does that seem fair?

Is that right?

The video ends, and the screen turns red.

Pulling her phone away from my face, the secretary says, "Isn't that crazy? Can you believe all those people?"

"That's terrible," I say.

Already, in my head, I'm picturing the secretary doing the rounds in the Lewis–Walter building in her desert-brown blouse, showing the video to accountants in the coffee room, the cleaning lady vacuuming the cubicles. On a dozen floors, in a dozen different cities, people will watch that video and think the same thing: Those poor employees. And what a terrible company.

"I bet he did it to teach that awful CEO a lesson by exposing him to the world," she says.

Of course, what the whole world wants to know is who is this mysterious person who kidnapped and released Caspian Yates? This doesn't happen in real life. The police have no leads on who this kidnapper might be. Perhaps it's a former disgruntled employee or an anti-pharmaceutical activist? But there are no suspects. No persons of interest.

153

At any rate, the secretary says Caspian Yates got what was coming to him. "I'm glad he was kidnapped and this is all coming out. At least now people will know what he did."

The secretary wants to know what I think.

I don't know what I think. I mean, I think a lot of things. I think all progress comes from people who are less bound, less ethically sure, and wherever progress begins, I think you'll find a totally sick and twisted degenerative fuck like me.

The secretary asks a lot more questions, and I start to wonder if she'll ever shut up. That's when I finally tell her Caspian Yates isn't the problem. "It's bigger than that," I say. The secretary thinks about it for a while. Then she agrees and nods her head.

"To fix a problem like that," I say, "you'd need a lot more videos. You'd need to see and hear it everywhere. That's how good advertising works."

15.

It's in the news today how another Caspian Yates video came out, and in it he says all sorts of terrible things.

People are stupid.

His employees are stupid.

Yes, that's right—they're stupid, and because they're stupid they got what they deserved.

The Caspian Yates hate parade is heading into its second week.

This morning, I leaked to the media another video of the Caspian Yates kidnapping, anonymously submitted from a fake email account using a public computer at the library. In the video, Caspian Yates looks at the camera and says, "We buy companies. We take what has value. We sell the rest. That is what we do. That's what every company does. We don't care for our employees. No company does. If you can't see that, you're stupid and got what you deserved."

This morning, Caspian Yates can't be reached for comment. He isn't responding to media requests. He's in Pharmakon's corporate head office working, doing CEO stuff, and outside every entrance to the building is a news van, satellite dish extended, waiting to see if they can catch Caspian Yates leaving the building for a comment.

Later in morning, the company's legal and public relations department issues a public statement to the media.

BREAKING NEWS.

Pharmaceutical giant responds: "It's not our fault."

You read the statement. It says Caspian Yates and Pharmakon are cooperating fully with the police investigation, but they can't comment publicly on Caspian Yates's recent kidnapping or the content of the video because this a police matter, and they don't want to compromise an ongoing police investigation.

But Pharmakon holds itself to the highest ethical standards. *And* the Bayder acquisition was part of their strategic plan to grow the company through bolt-on asset acquisitions. *So*, they identified opportunities to create structural synergies and advance unactualized cost savings.

The truth.

The truth is these days you see an entire way of thinking and acting that obscures reality, that hides the truth. Today, a company doesn't cut employee pensions. They actualize cost savings. They don't fire employees. They curtail human resource redundancies. The truth is people delude and self-sooth each other in so many ways to protect themselves from reality, to hide from the truth, but if you can't see the truth, you can't progress, and in order to grow, you need to face the uncomfortable and offensive.

No kidding, and Pharmakon's stock is in a free fall—a 20 percent market capitalization depreciation in the last week alone. *The Washington Post* said Pharmakon spent more money last year on advertising than researching new drugs, but none of that advertising is

helping them now. The panel of pundits on *Fox News* said Caspian Yates was probably forced to say what he did in those videos. People will do and say anything to stay alive and not die. They said Caspian Yates is a nice guy. He helps in the community—real soup-kitchen humanitarian-type shit—and Doug from that video isn't even a real Pharmakon employee. Their investigative team did some digging. He's just a picture of some guy taken from a stock photography website. Still, no one cares, not one bit, and it's not going well for Pharmakon.

This morning, it's Caspian Yates yelling at the camera, telling every blue- and white-collar worker they're stupid.

This afternoon, it's a fleet of homeless guys descending onto Pharmakon's head office with paperboy sacks, handing out flyers to all those Pharmakon employees leaving the building. On the front of the flyer is Caspian Yates's angry eagle Muppet face, frothing white-ocean foam at the camera. On the back of the flyer is a glossy, red background with the philosophical musings of an evolved and highly enlightened psychopath.

The office tower security guard told the homeless paperboys to go away. Beat it. Get lost. Get some help.

This is private property. You got to leave. They left, eventually. But not before talking to the media still parked outside of the building.

Oh, the media is loving this. Their ratings are breaking all sorts of records. Two major news developments in the same day. What incredible luck. Apparently, some guy approached the paperboys outside a safe drug injection site. He asked if they wanted to make some money. What they spent it on after? Well, that was up to them.

That bottle-blonde-haired anchor woman from *ABC News* interviewed one of the paperboys on the six o'clock news just before security escorted him off the property.

ABC NEWS EXCLUSIVE!

"Hello, sir. It's Amy Farrow here with ABC News. Can you tell me where you got those flyers?"

"Some guy gave them to me. "

"Do you know who he was?"

"No. He gave me a hundred dollars and a newspaper bag. He said hand out flyers."

"What did he look like?"

"Mmm, he had brown hair. Or it might have been black. I don't know. He was wearing a hat. It was hard to tell. He had sunglasses on. He was tanned, I think. Actually . . . now that I think of it, I don't know."

"Did he tell you why he wanted you to do this?"

"No."

"Did he tell you anything at all?"

"Yes. He said this is just the start. It's going to get worse. There will be more."

16.

Every Thursday, I see Cynthia Drake.

Today is Tuesday, and I'm already bugging out of my mind, so I settle for whoever I can get to meet me; I found this one the other week squeezing a melon in the produce aisle of the supermarket. I walked up to her and said hi. Twenty minutes later in the parking lot, I'm helping this melon woman put groceries into the back of her minivan. I ask for her number. She hesitates.

"I don't know," she says, showing me her hand. "I'm married."

"That's fine," I say. "I don't mind."

Seriously.

I don't.

She eventually gives me her number. I say, "Thank you. I'll call you." Then I leave.

Now I've got this melon woman back at my apartment on a Tuesday evening while her husband sits on the couch at home eating buffalo wings and watching baseball. With my hand in between her legs, I'm hitting it hard with three fingers, and her legs are moving like a shaking demon being exorcised from a body.

A few days ago, Nastasia texted me. She was coming into town for another job interview. She wanted to know if I would mind getting her a hotel to stay in for a night.

Nastasia can't ask her man to pay for it. "I'm a broke student," she said. "If I ask, it might scare him away."

Nastasia said if I did that for her, she'd do *something* for me.

Today, this melon woman—Kerry is her name, or maybe it's Kate, it starts with a *K*—this k-k-k-k-named melon woman's holes are taking a beating. I'm reaching back and putting a finger in her bum, double thrusting with the TV playing loud in the background to hide her screams.

Yeah, so I after I got Nastasia's text, I ended up getting her that hotel room, and last night I showed up to that room. I knocked on the door. We hugged her. We sat on edge of the bed. We talked. I inched in closer. And I tried to kiss her, and Nastasia said no.

No.

NO.

Turning away, Nastasia told me she couldn't. Closing both eyes tight, Nastasia said she wanted to, she thought she could, but, no, no, no, she can't. Nastasia likes her new man too much, but would it be okay, by the way, if she doesn't pay me back?

Now this melon woman has her mouth open, head hanging over the edge of the bed doing the flipped-over starfish, and I'm driving it down deep into the back of her throat. With the melon woman's throat gurgling, I'm wondering why. Why am I so weak? Why am I so gullible?

I'm fucking this melon woman's face at a regular clip, and I'm tired of being controlled. I'm not burying dick. Nastasia always knew. I'm burying feelings.

There's a puddled mess of drool on the floor, and there's a drowning in my head. There's gasping for air. I

slow down but I don't stop. I keep at it—slurp, gurgle, choke—even though my stomach's dropping off a cliff.

Nastasia.

I'm not in love with you. I don't care. This doesn't hurt.

Nastasia.

N-a-s-t-a-s-i-a.

What have you done to me? What have I become?

Rewind to that summer I spent with Nastasia; I should have known then.

I'm in Nastasia's apartment a month after we met, and Nastasia's running to the bathroom after we start going at it to get my condoms, the ones I left there last time under the sink. She comes back with an entire wicker basket full of all types: Ribbed large. Glow in the dark. Extra-large. Extra-extra XL. Big enough to fit a baby's arm holding a muffin.

Oh, thanks, these are great, but they won't fit. They aren't mine.

Rewind.

I'm in Nastasia' s apartment after she came back from visiting her mom in Arizona. I'm watching her hide, sitting at the opposite end of the couch, downing two quick glasses of wine, telling me she wants to talk, she wants to catch up, but she had such a busy weekend, she's tired, and she's pushing me away with her feet before moving on to glass three. After finishing it, she finally lets me get close, and not long after that I'm looking down at a three-day-old razor burn between her legs, shaved just before she left.

This is exhausting, and suddenly it no longer matters.

I used to believe what I was told.

I used to think you could find that one special thing, sit in the center of that, and it could work for you forever. What I'm learning now is living like this . . . whatever you do, whatever you choose, eventually you'll end up at odds with it and probably even yourself.

17.

It's Thursday, and I'm finally seeing Cynthia Drake.

Cynthia Drake comes to my apartment, and Cynthia Drake means role play. Dirty Disney princess. Slutty superhero captured and tied up. These are the things she can't do with her husband, and Cynthia Drake sneaks the costumes out of her house in a gym bag so he won't see.

Cynthia Drake strolls into my living room. She's only four steps in when she notices the coil of rope wrapped around the chair. Next to it on a mahogany-brown desk is an open book with diagrams of different knots. Single column. Butterfly. With a thud, Cynthia Drake drops her gym bag to the floor and, lowering her eyes, asks, "Are you into bondage now?"

I say no.

Cynthia Drake rolls her eyes and says, "I don't even want to know."

Taking a seat in the armchair, I watch while Cynthia Drake rummages through her bag until she finds what she's looking for. Naughty nurse. She tries on the outfit with her tiny legs pressed together, bent over, her butt and her back to me. Then we get right to it. For the next forty-three minutes, I tell Cynthia Drake she's sexy. She's

beautiful. "This," I make sure to tell her, "is so much fun." And after doing it in thirteen different positions, we lie on the couch to catch our second wind. Holding her in my arms, heart thumping, I tell her about all the things I've read.

I say there's good scientific evidence that if you put yourself in a new situation, something difficult that makes you uncomfortable, the stress will unlock new parts of you. "This," I add, "is scalable. The bigger the challenge, the more impossible the goal, the more this phenomenon gets turned on, and who knows how much there is locked away inside of you."

"What are you talking about?" Cynthia Drake says, pushing my arm off her. She gets up from the couch. She's still wearing the tiny white nurse skirt decorated with a first-aid cross with red trim on the edges. On her legs are white stockings running up to her thighs with that same-colored trim. Her eyes dart around my apartment, to the running shoes in the corner of the room, to the teetering bookshelves stacked full. "You're not giving me a line from some stupid self-help book, are you?" I shake my head. "Good," she says. "I don't want help. I'm just here for fun."

Cynthia Drake makes her way to the bookshelf, stepping over a few loose floorboards. "Have you actually read all these?"

"Yes," I say. She reaches up, pulling a book from the top shelf, and her skirt lifts up her leg revealing the start of her ass. She flips through the pages of the book.

What Cynthia Drake finds annoying, she says, is that reading isn't as simulating as a movie or TV.

I stare at her ass while she keeps talking.

Cynthia Drake says at the end of a hard day, all she wants to do is decompress. "Reading's just too much effort."

I'm still waiting to fully recover when Cynthia Drake makes her way back and sits next to me on the couch. Eyeing me up and down, she inches toward me. Wetting her lips, she leans in and reaches down. "What's wrong?" she says, feeling in between my legs.

"Nothing," I say. "Just give it a minute."

"Oh, don't worry," she says. "I can help with that." Kneeling down, Cynthia Drake looks up at me. And with big puppy dog eyes, she licks her lips and says, "You think too much."

I lean back and close my eyes.

I start to get hard.

It feels really good.

I'm trying to hold it together, to prevent myself from going off, and what I'm wanting to do is tell Cynthia Drake that behind all great individuals is a type of selfishness that drives humanity forward. After a while, all you hear is what other people tell you to be and you lose connection with what makes you unique. But who you are, your source of uniqueness, is your source of power, and the further you deviate from that, the more you become like everyone else, the weaker you become.

Sitting in an armchair with Cynthia Drake's head buried in my lap, I let loose an entire mouthful of mojo, and my head starts to clear.

Cynthia Drake stands up, wraps herself in a blanket, and spreads out across the couch. Lying down next to her, I wrap my arm around her waist and pull her in close.

With our bodies pressing together, I say an attack on uniqueness is an attack on the very roots of life.

"There are so many things that hold us back," I say. "Family. Friends."

Cynthia Drake furrows her brow and asks if I'm talking about her husband.

"No," I say. Then, "Maybe."

I'm sure he's part of the problem.

Cynthia Drake slaps me on the shoulder and tells me to stop talking about her marriage. Stop lecturing her and talking about her lame-ass life. It's not her fault. There's nothing she can do. What was she supposed to do?

"Stop," she says, "just stop."

I stop.

With my hand on her waist, I pull her body even closer to mine. Outside, it's starting to rain, and I can hear it beating down. When it rains like this, the water trickles down through the roof and everything wooden inside my apartment starts to swell. We lie on the couch for a little longer before Cynthia Drake finally sits up.

She walks over to the gym bag lying next to a puddle on the floor. Leaning down, she digs through the bag before finally pulling out an outfit. Playboy bunny.

"This is a classic," Cynthia Drake says, turning to face me. "It's something I've always wanted to try."

It's raining hard outside, and I force a waning smile.

"I'm sure it will look great on you," I say.

18.

The tears were really coming now. Down, down, all the way down that long buzzard face.

Oh, Caspian Yates.

Mr. CEO, Mr. Big Time Pharmaceutical CEO, you aren't so important now, are you, tied to a chair.

You looked down. You saw the shower curtain under your feet. The saw in front of you. The jug of bleach. The hammer. You closed your eyes. I said, "This is for you. Don't close your eyes." But you kept them tightly shut.

Sob.

Sniffle.

Tear.

You said, between cries, "I'm sorry. Please, please, I don't want to die. I have money. I'll pay you whatever you want. Please just let me go."

Oh, Caspian Yates, you don't get it. I don't care about you or your money.

You, my friend, my very special friend, you're going to give so much more than money.

Tonight, everything had already gone so well, and I had wondered how you might do. But never—no, never ever—had I imagined you'd be such a great help. I had

been watching you for months. Ever since I overheard that dad at the crosswalk—the one with the painted purple fingernails—say he worked for a pharmaceutical company that cut his pension. So I googled you. Yeah, it was that easy. And wouldn't you know things like this always have a ridiculous beginning. They're born on a street corner or a parking garage floor.

Yes, Caspian Yates, I know all about you and your company. Even before I met you, I knew you'd be perfect. But you work so hard, so very hard, and you shouldn't walk alone to your car while leaving the office late at night.

I waited for you that night. I knew the parking lot would be empty that late. I said, "Nice night" while you put your keys into the car door, and you looked up at me.

An hour later, when you woke up, you must have thought this was a dream, a terrible, terrible, dream.

Caspian Yates, this is not a dream. This is your life, and I promise you: It won't be the same after tonight.

You tried to move, but your hands were bound behind your back, your legs tied tight to the chair. I said, "Don't move. Don't struggle. Don't try to get free. If you don't do what I say, you will die."

You couldn't see me. You could only look ahead, but you could hear me fiddling with something behind your back.

VRRRRRMMM.

With a power drill spinning by your ear, I had your full attention, and you started to choke on your words. "In my wallet, there's money in my wallet."

I slapped you on the head. "I don't want your money." I tossed your wallet on the floor. It opened, and your family

pictures fell across the floor. "You've got a nice-looking family," I said. "Your son, he looks like you, and wouldn't it be terrible if something happened to him."

VRRRRRRRRRRMMMMM.

Oh, Caspian Yates, this can't be easy for you. One minute, you're the CEO of a ginormous company; the next minute, you're a person with a hole about to be drilled into his head, and can you imagine the sound it will make as the drill burrows into your brain?

You worked up a pretty intense cry at that point, so I pressed the drill into the soft spot of your neck and said life isn't fair, but most things aren't fair. A lion killing a gazelle isn't fair. The gazelle does not want to die. The gazelle doesn't want its life changed. The gazelle has the right to fight back, using the only language the lion understands: violence.

Sniffle, sob, sob.

Oh, what, you don't like animals?

Or being a freeman—being able to recognize and resist the influence of others, placing no constraints on yourself but your own.

Your new employees, I said. They were living their lives fine until you came along and changed that.

> *You take the amount of force applied by one person (A) and multiply it by the individual or group of individuals on the receiving end of that force (B).*
> *A times B equals C.*
> *C is the maximum amount of force that can be administered back.*

I said, "Let's play a game. Fill in the blank: If you have seven hundred and fifty employees, how many holes do I need to drill in your head before things become fair?"

One hole, two holes, three holes, four.

VRRRRRRRRRRMMMMM.

"Home, you said, sniffle, sniffle. You just wanted to go home.

"No shit," I said. "I bet those seven hundred and fifty employees think of their homes."

You said, "I have a family."

"They have families too."

You said, "I didn't mean to hurt anyone. It was only business. We needed to cut costs. I'll fix this. I'll make it right."

"I don't care about that," I said. "I just need someone who did something that will get people angry enough to hold their attention.

"Now," I added, turning his head to face a cue card on a stand in the room, "I want you to read something."

19.

The director waves a sheet of paper in front of my face and slams his hand down on my desk with a thud. He wants to know why I've done this. "This is the contract you've been processing with new clients," he yells, pointing to a part circled in red pen.

With furrowed eyebrows, the director starts to read. I don't need to listen to this. After all, I wrote it. Still, I go along and look at him blankly, my mouth a flat, indecipherable line.

Holding the paper with two clenched fists, the director takes his time, loudly enunciating each word.

+image+

In that blank space, I've been putting in other organizations' names. I pick and choose. Stomp Out Bullying. The LQBTQ Equality Task Force. The Slut Walk. One charitable cause is as good as the next, and now each will get a little something extra.

"Why? W-H-Y?!"

That's all the director can say, his voice crackling with each W, H, and Y.

This is one of those moments where you're supposed to say something, provide a reason, an explanation. Release the tension. Provide a resolution. I know that's

what you're supposed to do. Only I'm not going to do any of that. I'm having too much fun. Instead, I take a big breath in through my nose and let out a big sigh. Then I look up at the ceiling.

Me, I've got all sorts of time. In front of me is the director, bottom lip quivering, while I'm casually looking up at the roof, counting speckled ceiling tiles. I'm a total rock in a sea during a storm, and even violent waves crashing against a rock eventually break and become calm.

The director doesn't know it yet, but this is me helping him come out of the delusion that's been set in his head.

Just like Caspian Yates is helping. His latest weekly video is getting a lot of attention. It starts like the rest. A blank screen in eye-catching red. Then the red fades. What you see next is Caspian Yates's long Roman face, unforgettable and iconic. Staring at the camera, Caspian Yates starts talking.

> *"We live in a world of emotionally weak people who live a life of lies. We need to reveal the lies. To show the truth. It's easy to do. It's like watching a man attack a tank with a hammer: The truth exists in the gap between his intention and the reality he's in. He can't win. He will lose, yet the lie that he tells himself is he has a chance. There are all types of lies like this that we tell ourselves, and the degree to which they exist—from the smallest and almost imperceptible to the largest and most complex—is always in direct proportion to the two terms being compared. The bigger the gap, the bigger the lie, so look for that gap and expose it!"*

The director shakes his head. According to him, I need serious psychiatric help. People aren't supposed to act like this. I know that, and I don't care. I like the new me.

Besides, I have no hard feelings or personal quarrel with the director. The truth is I don't even blame the guy. After all, it's not like he knows any better. He's only doing what he was taught do.

The director looks at me and says, "Why did you do that? Tell me why."

I let my eyes sharpen slowly. Then I look at him with an intense, piercing gaze.

Why'd I do that?

Why not?

"I do what I want now," I say. "I'm a higher human, and in order to create, you need to first destroy."

The director just stares at me.

I say, "You've been at this job for what, eight or nine months, and you're already looking to cut costs and sell the business? Why do you need to do that? Because you learned that in school.

"I'd be worried if I were you," I say. "There are all types of rumors going around the office that could be very bad for your reputation. All I'm saying is we live in a very messed up world. There's a lot of angry people out there. There's no telling what one of them might do. I'd be scared about word getting out on social media or the news of an MBA student who got dropped into a senior position at his father's company right after graduating."

The director shakes his head. He thought I was a nice guy. What happened to me? Why did I change? The least I can do is give him an explanation.

"You'll have to excuse me if I don't answer you right away. I've been busy, staying up late, reading and researching. Figuring this whole thing out. You know, it's not easy changing the world or disrupting a life's worth of being told how to live, and did you know if you can get 5 percent of a crowd to head in another direction, the other 95 percent will start to follow? They use this to control crowds in stadiums to clear things out quickly and prevent people from being trampled, but I'm sure there are other uses."

The director is shaking the contract under my nose. "Is this funny to you?"

I gently pull the contract out of his hand as if my two fingers are tweezers. "This isn't about you," I say. I take a step in front of the director's face. "It's never been about you."

The director looks at me. He's got these soft, baby-blue, ocean eyes, and I slowly crumple the contract into a ball and open my hand, letting it drop to the floor as if it were a feather.

I say, "You want to know why? The truth is I don't have an answer. Pick a reason. One is as good as the next, and maybe I'm tired of listening to others, or bored. I don't know. I could have done it because you're a spoiled brat in a job you only got because your dad—the owner of this company, Don—was a good guy, and then he died."

The director's mouth drops open. "What you did is illegal," he says. His head goes side to side. "You're crazy. You need to fix this!"

"Don't get mad at me," I say. "I'm just trying to help you rebuild your workplace reputation. And you can't stop those corporate donations. The contracts have already been signed.

"I've already let a few news agencies know about your donations. They'll be here any minute. I promised them an interview. They're very excited to talk to you, so you've got two choices: one, you tell them how Acuscent Media Interactive is going to help others and these donations are just a start, or two, you tell them you're an unqualified, spoiled shit whose daddy got you a job."

The color drains from the director's face.

In his head, he's doing this whole looking up from the bottom thing, and he's getting to feel for the first time what it's like to be on the other side.

In a minute, I'll tell the director he needs to do things differently, and, no, I don't have the answer, and, no, I'm not going to tell him what to do, but I'm sure he'll figure it out.

20.

When I get to the restaurant, Nastasia is already in the foyer waiting, and she tells me that she got a job as a lawyer working at a firm in the city. Now she's back in the city with her man for a few days looking for a house, but she feels a bit blah because they were up all night partying.

Moving in together is a big deal, Nastasia says, while walking to our table. She's never lived with an older man before. She has so much fear and anxiety about it, but he's paying for it all, so it's not like she can say no.

I just look at her.

Nastasia's wearing jeans with a destressed black leather jacket, and her hair is pulled back in a dirty ponytail. Nastasia never wears jeans. Even from across the restaurant table, I can see Nastasia's face looks gaunt. Her eyes look more sunken than before. She's not wearing makeup.

Jeans. No makeup. It's hard to believe this is Nastasia.

Lunch is at a Japanese steakhouse. Nastasia orders something called Wagyu beef. She likes meeting guys like me that she's friends with. If her man can smell their cologne on her after, it makes him paranoid and want her more.

"After lunch," she says, "we need to hug to transfer your scent."

Nastasia is full of good advice, especially when it comes to keeping a man. If you're not sucking his dick when you're transitioning between positions, she says, you're not having good sex.

This is what I'm learning inside the restaurant.

Outside the restaurant, the entire world is falling apart, and someone, somewhere, gave it a name: red tagging. That's what it's being called now. People are finding videos online and posting them on social media.

Of course, I started this. Then I gave it a nudge. You know, by finding a video or two online and putting a red filter on it before pushing it out on social media. After that, though, I didn't have do anything. I just sat back and watched, and this whole thing took on a life of its own.

Yeah, it's crazy what you can find on the internet. There are all types of videos of people pushing their views onto other people, pointing out their faults while being blind to their own. And if you look hard enough, you might find a video of a Greenpeace climate-change activist putting his picketing sign—"The climate is changing: Why aren't we?"—into the back of his gas-run sporty Subaru Outback after the protest. Then there's that video of those two snowflakes with beards, arm sleeves, and toques sitting at a Starbucks talking about the evils of capitalism while sipping vanilla coconut milk cappuccinos with a $3,500 aluminum-plated MacBook Pro on the table.

Nastasia liked that video. I showed it to her on my phone as we waited for lunch. She licked her lips. Her

favorite coffee is a chocolate chip Frappuccino with no chips. "You should try one," she said. "They're really good."

That's absurd.

I'm not answering Nastasia now. She can do all the talking.

Nastasia has no idea what type of place her man will buy. She's acting like she doesn't care, but she really hopes it's close to downtown and big with walk-in closets. "He's got more clothes than me," she says.

I don't want to tell her where I've been living.

The image in my head is Nastasia living in a luxury penthouse with coffered ceilings, floor-to-ceiling windows, and marble slab countertops. That image is interrupted by Nastasia telling me about her new job in the city. She can't believe she got it. Most of the students in her law class didn't get jobs.

Not like her.

Not right after graduating.

After that, Nastasia looks at me and waits. This is the part where I'm supposed to say something nice, something congratulatory.

Oh, that's great!

You worked so hard!! I'm not surprised. I always knew you'd do it!!

This is what I'm supposed to say, only I can't do that, I can't be bothered, and even the thought of doing the bare minimum you're expected to do in these situations is exhausting to me.

What Nastasia wants right now is a medal, a trophy, and a high-five parade. What Nastasia gets is silence.

Nastasia moves on. She found out her man fucked a few randoms in Los Vegas without her, but it was before

they were super serious so she can't act like she cares. "He felt bad after," she says. "He was even crying and bought me a lot of gifts."

Seeing him cry was gross, and Nastasia didn't like that.

Nastasia holds up her phone. Turning it toward me, she shows me pictures of her gifts. I see boxes of Jimmy Choos. Louis Vuitton bags. Gucci handbags.

"Those look great," I say, rolling my eyes.

I change the subject.

I ask if she saw that story in the news from earlier in the week where some guy in a souped-up Hummer, bigger than any vehicle needs to be, got beat over the head with a plastic milk jug for parking his Hummer over the yellow line separating two parking stalls in a grocery store parking lot.

"Apparently," I say, "some good Samaritan thought he'd teach him a lesson in proper parking lot etiquette."

Lessons like this are important. A little trauma can change you.

The police are concerned. In two dozen cities, people are posting and sharing videos like this. The police say red tagging is bad. It celebrates violence and encourages vigilante justice. It needs to stop.

The infographic on the nightly news made it look like a virus. One dot on a city. Ground zero. Then a dot pops up in another city. Over time, it spreads like a bacterial stain in a petri dish, starting with that video of Caspian Yates being released from his kidnaping, then on to dear old Doug losing his pension. The homeless, drugged-up paperboys. The videos. The red tagging. The violence and more . . .

Now, they're spreading out, the stains infecting anyone who's ever been put down—even a bit—but never bothered to do anything about it, until now.

Lunch arrives.

The waiter sets a steak the size of a deck of cards in front of Nastasia. She sets her fork on top of it and presses down. A piece of steak slides off to the side like melted butter.

Through a mouthful of finely marbled steak, Nastasia says the people at her law firm were talking about the guy who got beat up in the parking lot. "Even if it was an asshole park job," she says, "people need to be careful. If more people start taking the law into their own hands and living by their own rules, they'll need a good lawyer."

Even if Nastasia is right, she's looking at this in the wrong way.

Before I started this, I hadn't thought about any of these things, but if you can see that rules are by their very nature constraining, you know that a man isn't born, he's made, and the fusing of a population into its useless flaccid form can only be done by repetition and the belief that everyone else has got it right.

Nastasia stops chewing and asks, "Why are you so quiet?"

"No reason," I say.

I don't bother to tell her that earlier today Pharmakon fired Caspian Yates as its CEO. In a TV interview, Caspian Yates said it's fine. He'll move on. He didn't want to be the figurehead of a weird social movement. He was forced to say what he did. He didn't mean any of it. He sat there for hours tied up in that

180

apartment. He thought he was going to die. He doesn't know who his kidnapper was. They stood behind him and wore a disguise, but like he told the police, he thinks he was by a brothel or a maybe massage parlor, because through walls, all that he heard was banging, panting, and moans.

Lunch is done.

But Nastasia wants dessert. Something chocolate. Maybe a brownie or baked fudge, but she doesn't want to eat the whole thing, just a bite. So, would it be okay if we shared it?

I say, "No."

I don't want to do that.

I wave to the waiter across the room to bring us the bill.

Nastasia looks at me.

I don't bother to look at her.

The waiter sets the bill on the table, and I push it toward Nastasia.

"You can get this one," I say.

21.

In the food court, the dish woman and I are sitting by a fountain filled with fish when we overhear a guy on his phone. He's talking about the latest red tagging video, and in this one someone spray-painted "herd animal" in red onto the hood of every Ferrari, Rolls-Royce, and Lamborghini parked on Rodeo Drive.

All around us in the food court are people in suits: single-breasted, black, charcoal, gray. They're just sitting there and eating, chewing their food.

The other week the dish woman said to call her Amy. "It's actually Amelia," she said, "but all my friends call Amy."

So, Amy and I are in the food court. And in front of us a line snakes out from a Panda Express restaurant into the seating area, while the space in front of the two restaurants next to it, a Baskin–Robbin and Chick-fil-A, is empty.

Amy asks, "What do you think of that?"

"I think people are dumb and do as they're told," I say, taking a bite of my sandwich.

Turning my head to the line, I say, "They think the longer the line to the restaurant, the better the food."

"No, no," Amy laughs. "I'm not talking about that. I'm talking about the video."

Taking another bite, I say, "What do you mean?"

Amy's gaze goes to the guy talking about the video on his phone and says, "What do you think about that whole video thing?"

A group of teenagers in gold jerseys run by us, chanting and yelling. It's game day, and a few people in the food court raise their hands and cheer. I wait for them to pass, for the noise to fade, before I say, "I think it's good. What we think is independent thought is actually imposed by society. It's an exploitation of evolutionary psychology."

Taking the last bite of my sandwich, I add, "I never wanted to get married. I only did it because everyone else was, because I was told to, and if I hadn't left the wife, I probably would have had kids because that's what she wanted. Because that's what her parents wanted. Because that's what everyone does, and after a while, all that wears you down and you start to believe that it's true. That it's the right thing to do, even if it's not the right thing for you."

Amy stops eating and her mouth is open, still full of food.

"This *whole* thing," I say, "at least it's exposing that. It's showing that for every right way, there's another way—something hiding in plain sight that's been held down like a foot pressed on a neck, waiting to be free."

"You're so dramatic," Amy says.

Amy swallows her food and takes the last sip of her drink. I stand up to leave, grabbing her garbage and packing it onto a food tray with mine, when the calendar on my phone pings. It's a meeting invite for an off-site meeting later in the week with the director to discuss my

work. He's going to get rid of me. With these things, they always do it off-site. That way, when they fire you, you don't make a big scene and spook the other employees. This is a totally reasonable thing to do, particularly if you're dealing with an angry libertarian anarchist bent on breaking society.

I pass my phone over to Amy. She reads the meeting invite. "Ouch," she says. "Are you okay?"

"I'm fine."

"Are you sure?" She puts her hand on my shoulder.

"Yes," I say. "I had to try."

22.

You wait in the elevator, watching the TV screen in the corner playing a real estate commercial with the news and the weather scrolling along the bottom of the screen.

Florida. Sunny with a 30% chance of showers.

The Chiefs rally to beat the 49ers.

It used to be you'd ride it up and down every day for work, and when people started talking, a little part of you died. If only the cable would snap.

Dropping in three, two, one.

Death.

Oh, wouldn't you know. In the elevator, what you hear is always the same. You'll never hear someone say they're not doing well. No, everyone is always doing good. Yet, it's just deluding and self-soothing. It's hiding a deep-seated psychological discontent, so everyone can smile cheerfully at each other while reciting the script that's been set in their head.

This afternoon, after coming back from lunch with Amy, I'm looking around the elevator. I see all these faces. All these middle-management consultant types. In the elevator with me is Amy, and I couldn't be happier with how far this has come. It used to be enough when someone asked you how you were, you'd say *good*. If they asked you what was new, you'd say *nothing*.

Because nothing was ever new...

Because you've spent your entire life doing and saying the same thing.

The elevator door opens, and more people shuffle in. I glance over at Amy. She tilts her head, pointing to some guy holding an oversized coffee cup and a double-glazed donut. This guy has the complexion of a soft-boiled egg, and his eyes, beady and deeply set, are pinched together next to his nose. On his shirt is a coffee stain the size of Russia. He catches me looking and says, "Good afternoon. I heard it's supposed to be warm later today."

I stare a hole into his head.

It's one sad fuck to see a guy like our egg man in elevator. Guys like this, they never say no. They never go dark or get angry. What you've got here is an entire generation raised by consensus to be the worst version of themselves. There's no difficulty here. Nothing that forces you to look into yourself and away from everything that's mild, mediocre, and good-natured.

Our egg man asks, "How's your day going?"

I turn around.

Amy can take it from here.

She points to the coffee stain on our egg man's chest and asks, "Rough day?"

Our egg man looks down at the stain and laughs. Someone bumped into him on the escalator coming back from lunch. "What a way to start the afternoon," he says. "It feels like a Monday!"

Amy screws up her face and says, "I understand."

Every day is a Monday.

"Just remember," she says. Her red hair is frizzled and flows wildly like electricity in the air. "Life is like an

arrow. It can only go forward by first being pulled backward, so when life sets you back with difficulties, what it's really trying to do is send you forward to kill something. Now go out there and *kill* it today."

The elevator opens.

Our egg man steps out. As the door closes, he looks back at Amy. His mouth hangs open, and his teeth are stained the same brown as the coffee spilt on his shirt. The elevator door closes. After today, he'll never forget her, and no one else in the elevator will either. Today Amy is someone interesting. Someone different and unique.

Oh, this is her start, and I'm such a proud teacher.

The other day, Amy asked me why I'm such an asshole to people. Only she didn't say it like that. She's nice, so she said, "Why do you have to make things so difficult for everyone?"

I said conversation is a game we play. Babies show happiness once they figure out they can cause a predictable outcome in the world, even if it doesn't matter. You bang a spoon against a table or spill a bowl of Cheerios on the floor, and you get the fun from being in control and knowing what will happen in the world around you.

"Conversation is like that," I said. "We say and do the same things to get the same outcome, and this is our fun, like what a baby gets from banging a spoon on the table."

For me, that sums up my whole old life. I never— no, never—told anyone this before, but before I met Nastasia, I almost tried one of those expand-your-chest routines and went on a high-protein diet. Now I laugh every time I think about how I used to live.

Long before Amy and I became friends, I realized I couldn't go to war without allies: Caspian Yates, the director, Cynthia Drake, all those married women. I'm not blowing my seed; one splatter of pancake batter at a time, spread out over a belly, a bedspread. I'm setting the stage, poking holes into one world at a time. And maybe they're not friends you'd go for a beer with or call to build a deck, but in a war like this, the enemies are everywhere, invisible and coming from all sides, so you take all the help that you can get.

And I could really use a friend.

23.

Fast forward a few days, and my entire world is falling apart. The director fires me, and if that weren't bad enough, I can't get it up.

Tonight, Cynthia Drake shows up to my apartment dressed as Tinker Bell. We start kissing. Cynthia Drake reaches down into my pants, and my dick's soft as a sponge.

"That's not like you," she says. "What's wrong?"

"I don't know," I say. "Give me forty minutes."

I run to the bathroom, shallowing a handful of Viagra as if they were Tic Tacs. After that, I stall for time. I ask Cynthia Drake about her day. I ask her what's new. I rub her feet on the couch. I'm looking at my watch, and I'm counting down the clock, waiting for my face to feel flush, for my heart to race, for my dick to get hard, but nothing happens.

"What up with you?" Cynthia Drake says. "You don't find me hot? You're not going to start preaching to me again, are you? You know, I put a lot of work into getting this outfit out of my house. The least you can do is show me some appreciation."

"I do find you hot!" I say. "Honestly, I do. It's just. It's just . . ."

189

Cynthia Drake walks to the door. "You're such a flake," she says. Her eyes dart around the apartment—to the yellow water stains on the ceiling, to the air vent packed full of crud. "This place is disgusting, and you're a freak," she says, slamming the door.

I watch from my window as Cynthia Drake drives away in her car. After that, I run to the pharmacist. According to him, a stronger dose won't get me hard. It won't make me better in bed. "There's nothing wrong with the meds," he says.

"What do you mean?" I say.

"It's psychological," he says. "The problem is you."

"What are you trying to say?"

Shrugging his shoulder, the pharmacist says, "I don't know. You tell me."

I look at him, wondering if he might be right. After all, all this sex started with me being a little horny and wanting more. In a different way, yet the same way, I'm stuck, just like I was stuck before.

I run back home.

It's dark outside, and in the moonlight, I tell myself the first thing I'll do in the morning is call everyone I'm sleeping with. I'll say I can't see you anymore. It's been fun, but it's over. I need this to end.

24.

Not a day goes by where I don't get to see a new male visitor led into the building by the woman next door who rents herself out by the hour. Her uniform is usually the same: beat-up black heels, torn fishnets, ripped jean shorts with a bikini top dotted in leopard spots, side boob showing.

In the morning, the smell of marijuana comes in through the two-finger-width crack underneath my front door. The neighbors across the hall light up to mellow out before the day starts. None of them work, and if you looked inside their apartment, you'd see bottles of Coke, empty cases of beer, and a crusted-up pot of macaroni noodles left on the stove.

The other day, the woman next door came over. Nice enough, I know, only she didn't come to say hi. In her pajamas on a Wednesday afternoon, she wanted to know if I had a lighter, and maybe if I'd like to come over to "hang out." "We can do whatever you want," she said. "My boyfriend doesn't care. He'll stay in the next room, watch TV, play video games, lie on the couch— whatever, but if you toss in a few bucks, he'll join in too."

Pushing her head in around the door, this neighbor woman peeks inside my apartment. Her eyes go to

191

bookshelves filled with marketing books. Psychology texts. To the desk covered in piles of crumpled-up pieces of paper falling onto the floor. To my work. You'd expect to see a wall covered in cut-up newspaper clippings, with strands of yarn pinned to the clippings, piecing it all together. "You some type of professor?" she said, peering in through the door.

"No," I said, shoving her face with my hand back through the door.

It's hard to believe that inside an apartment held together by red bricks and skeeze is where this work began. After I moved in, I brought in a desk sitting by a dumpster in the back alley—this antique, mahogany-brown desk, eaten away by termites and covered in white-ring water stains. For years, I lived in a world filled with furniture I didn't choose. The wife picked everything. I had become a stranger in my own home. Just for once, I wanted something of my own, so I dragged the desk in from the alley and worked at it every night. It wasn't easy. When you come home at the end of the day, it's difficult to stay focused and not give into weakness and temptation. Seriously, life is hard, so it's easy to sit back. Turn on the TV. Have a drink. Having to think every decision through from beginning to end is exhausting, so why bother? Just relax.

Of course, it's easy to stay motivated when you've got two tissue-paper-thin pieces of drywall separating you and the latest visitor next door rotating in by the hour. Tonight, through those walls, I hear a TV blaring from the apartment next door to hide the porn-performance howls. I can make out the late-night news playing. Without even listening, I know what's on.

By now, an entire line of police chiefs and politicians have come together, hand in hand, telling everyone all statesmen-like this has to stop. It isn't lawful. It isn't right. It's inciting panic. Making people mad. Only it's too late to put a fire blanket on this now, because deep down, everyone knows something is wrong, that things shouldn't be so fucked up, that someone, or something, has to be responsible. If you're able to tell people what that is and show them what they already want to know, you can get them to do just about anything.

25.

Nastasia texts me first thing in the morning and asks if I'd like to meet for a drink.

"Hey! It's been too long. We should meet! I've got so much to tell you."

It's been a month since I last saw Nastasia.

I don't want to meet her, but because it's Nastasia, I say yes.

I go to Nastasia's office after work. I wait in the lobby. I watch her come down the escalator, all scarecrow thin and ghostly sallow. In a Dolce and Gabbana pencil skirt and Gianvito Rossi pumps, Nastasia comes up to me and gives me a big hug.

I look at her after we separate. I can't help but notice her face looks sunken. Her eyes are more muted than I remember, and she's so thin. She must either be rich or almost dead.

"It's good to see you again," she says. "Where would you like to go?"

"I'd like a water," I say.

No wine. No fancy cocktail or champagne bar.

Just a glass of water.

Nastasia nods and says, "We can go wherever you want." Her brown eyes fix on me for what seems like

forever, and then she says, "It's really good to see you again."

"Yeah . . ." I say, trailing off. "You too."

Over three raspberry daiquiris, Nastasia goes on and on about how her life isn't that great. Living with her man is hard. He snores. She needs to wear earplugs while he sleeps, and he gets so loaded all time, so incredibly wrecked, he can't fuck her anymore and what's she supposed to do about that?

I take a sip of my water.

I set it down.

"I don't know," I say.

Nastasia tells me about work. Her office is great. The women in her firm are so pretty. They dress so nicely, and she'd like to get her boobs done, but they'd need to be big, because if other people can't notice, there's really no point.

I take another sip of my water.

Nastasia looks at my empty glass. Her glass is empty too, and she asks, "Would you like to go back to my place?" Her man is out of town. He travels a lot for work. She says that's convenient and adds, "I don't think he'd like it if I had another guy over. And this is probably the only way we'd be able to do this."

Nastasia's place is only a few blocks away, so we step outside and start to walk. In front of us a car is parked on the street with a red bumper sticker that reads: "If you aren't prepared to stop and fight me, don't honk your horn at me." Nastasia buries a heel in a crack in the pavement and trips. She grabs my arm to catch herself. Then she squeezes.

Looking up at me, she says, "Are you seeing anyone?"

Speculation.

Why is she asking me that?

I say sort of.

What I had been doing, I say, is seeing married women. The more married, the better. "It's been a wife, wife, wife buffet until I didn't want any more, so I guess you could say I had been seeing a few people somewhat regularly."

"That's terrible." Nastasia giggles. "Is that even right?"

"I don't know if it's right," I say, "but it used to be fun."

26.

The inside of Nastasia's place is what you'd expect a luxury Soho penthouse to look like. Everything is floor-to-ceiling glass. Big picture windows. High ceilings. All white and clean. "Isn't it wonderful?" Nastasia says, spinning around as we walk through the door.

I throw my jacket on a chair and take a seat on the couch. Nastasia disappears into the bedroom. From the next room, she yells, "Help yourself to anything in the fridge. I'm going to get more comfortable." When Nastasia comes back out, she's wearing kid-sized boxer shorts and a tiny crop top that shows off her belly. Her hair is loose by her shoulders. In her hand is a tiny plastic bag. She sets it on the table and says, "You don't mind, do you?"

"Go head," I say.

Even though it's none of my business, I want to know. "How long have you been doing this? How much do you do? It's a workday, I mean. So I'm curious. Will it be hard to get to sleep or go to work tomorrow?"

Nastasia gives me an annoyed look and kneels over the table.

S-n-i-f-f. S-n-i—i-i-f-f-f.

"I've got it under control," Nastasia says. "When I need to sleep, I smoke some pot. That always levels me out."

Nastasia tells me about her life.

For the next hour, Nastasia speed-talks her way through two dozen topics. Her tongue does the windshield wiper across her teeth, and her attention span is a clock-tick long. This, she tells me, is how she got to know her man so well. "When you stay up until morning doing lines with someone, you really get to know them."

Nastasia needs to talk to me about something important.

Her man.

That's why I'm here.

Nastasia's been going through his stuff like a crazy ex-girlfriend and found a bank slip for $70,000. Now she's wondering if he has more money. What if he doesn't have other bank accounts? Or if it's worse than that. What if he's all debt, like one of those guys who maxes out his credit cards. This, she says, is a very serious problem. He's got to have other accounts.

"Normally, I wouldn't care," Nastasia says, "but the other day he said I was his retirement plan, so I was obviously like, what the fuck does that mean?"

I'm listening to Nastasia talk, and I'm not hearing what she thinks. What I'm hearing is a way to think. Her money, her clothes, her trips . . . all that five-star food.

You could replace her with someone else who thinks the same way, and that means she might as well not even be here right now.

It's not good.

It's not good that I know what she's about to say and where she stands on things before she even says it.

Nothing about her is original or unique.

What does a guy do with that? What can you say, I mean?

In this one moment, Nastasia's life reflects my old life and new life, and all that I can see are life-stifling lies. But beyond the edges of all that, the truth.

Nastasia was never what I thought.

And I fooled myself.

I created a fantasy that had little to do with the person, and I fell in love with my creation.

Oh, Nastasia.

Look at you now, nose buried in a tiny plastic bag, sniff, sniff, sniffing away. All skim-milk thin, looking like a skeleton dipped in wax. While something horribly good is growing outside, something I started, I look at Nastasia and see it all.

Oh, Nastasia.

A man isn't a poverty-reduction device, and success isn't a sexually transmitted disease.

And fuck it.

Nastasia's gone.

That beautiful girl is gone.

And why else would she tell me her man snores, put on boxers and that crop top if she didn't want me to make a move. There's no other reason to bring me here.

I move in.

And Nastasia pushes me away.

What happens next happens so fast. Nastasia tells me it's time to go, and she rushes me out the door, down the hall, and shoves me into the elevator. Before I know what's happening, I'm on the front step.

The door shuts.

That is it. That is our goodbye.

I should be sad, feel a loss, regret, or have some profound insight, but it's not like that anymore.

I walk down the sidewalk.

I don't look back.

The streetlights aren't on, and it's black outside like a bottomless pit. I've been here so many times before that it's starting to feel like home. With a thick bank of clouds overhead, I walk down the street in between two rows of trees that touch at the top. My eyes struggle to adjust to the night. In darkness like this, your eyes play tricks on you, and you can see almost anything.

Straining my eyes, I look down the street—into the abyss, comforting and complete.

It finally stares back.

27.

At my trial, I explain it all.

Of course, I eventually got caught.

I don't know who it was. The neighbor woman from across the hall, the director, a homeless drugged-out paperboy, or an angry ex-housewife. Take your pick.

I lived a life where everyone told me what to do, with me thinking sex was the answer and Nastasia thinking money was the answer, with everyone thinking there is an answer, with everyone clinging to something, yet nothing at all—I became a hero.

My lawyer says my arrest has gotten a lot of public attention, and my trial will last two, maybe three days. Everything will be fine, he says, if I stick to the script we practiced.

"Just don't do anything dumb or you'll end up in jail," he says.

I laugh at him and say, "Sure."

The day of my trial, people are yelling and chanting outside when I arrive. Two police officers usher me out of the police car and lead me into the courtroom. Inside, it seems as if every major news outlet is here.

I take the stand.

The prosecutor asks for my name. "It's Seth Freeman," I say.

After that, he asks what I used to do for work. I say I worked in an advertising and marketing agency. I sat in meetings. I listened and learned. I learned how people listen to other people in positions of authority. About how people listen to other people in large groups. This is hardwired into our brains. It's our psychological default setting. A mayor and a few popular baseball players say to buy a fifty-dollar slice of pizza and people listen. A bunch of red tagging videos go viral, and a social movement starts to soar.

Pointing to the press gallery, I say, "These people will report anything out of the ordinary or controversial just to sell papers. And you people," I say, turning to the jury, "will believe anything you hear."

I look at my lawyer, who's shaking his head.

The judge says just stick to answering the questions; otherwise, I'll be in contempt of court. "Consider this is a warning."

I don't listen. I keep going.

I tell the prosecutor it's all just one big game of follow-the-leader. Birds fly in flocks. Fish swim in schools. People are hierarchical animals, I say. They think in herds.

Someone in the jury snickers at me.

I look at my lawyer, holding his head in his hands.

I don't stop.

I tell the prosecutor this is basic biology. It's a glitch in our evolutionary psychology. It's something that needs to be acknowledged and identified before it can be stopped.

The prosecutor wants to know if I'm okay. If I'm crazy.

My lawyer doesn't object.

I say all new ideas are crazy.

He asks if I felt guilty for all the violence.

I say no.

Violence, I say, is a part of life. It's the thing that no one notices or talks about. To live, you need to kill plants and animals without their consent. Entire cities are built that destroy the environment. Even intellectually, I continue, when a new idea emerges and becomes accepted, it displaces the old one, casting it to the side like a corpse. The car killed the horse and carriage. Email killed the letter.

"Basically, what I'm trying to say," I say, "is for anything to progress, something needs to be replaced. It needs to die."

The prosecutor has one last question: Why'd I start this?

"Because," I say, "I'm tired of being tricked. I don't like being controlled. There are other people like me who are starting to see this, and if you don't make your own path, you'll end up following someone else's. And guess what they've got planned for you: not much."

28.

In jail, I see my psychiatrist every day. She says to keep a journal and write things down. It's good therapy. Let it all out. Besides, she says, if you ever get better, you can tell your story. You're very popular outside, and there's an appeal coming up, so you never know; a lot of people have done that.

Of course, she is right.

Martin Luther King, Nelson Mandela, even the Marquis de Sade and Hitler—they all wrote books while locked away.

I listen to my psychiatrist. I thank her for her help. Every day I write.

Now, when I see my psychiatrist, I say, "I think it's working. I'm feeling better. I'm starting to understand. Before, I was bad, but I'm better now."

I say, "Can you tell the review panel about my progress? Let them know that it will be okay? I've learned my lesson. I won't bother anyone anymore. If they let me out, I'll be good. I promise. You can totally trust me. Just let me out and you'll see. All that I'll do is be free."

AFTERWORD

Thank you for reading my book.

If you enjoyed it, I'd like to know. Please leave a review on Amazon.

Your honest feedback is appreciated.

ABOUT THE AUTHOR

J. C. Harach is a media strategist for one of the largest pipeline companies in North America. In this role, he develops strategies to create public support for controversial fossil fuel projects and responds to crisis situations such as oil spills, natural gas explosions, and environmental protests. His work and media interviews have appeared in media outlets such as *Bloomberg*, *Reuters,* the *Wall Street Journal*, and *S&P Global Platts*. Prior to that, he worked in the publishing industry as a writer and editor. During that time, his work received half a dozen acknowledgments and awards, including a Western and National magazine award. He has master's degrees in both political theory and journalism. He lives in the foothills of the Canadian Rockies.